MW00460774

Dragons of the Great D
(Book 2 of The Cretaceous Chronicles)

It's one year after egg-laden meteorites struck the Continental Divide in Montana and Idaho, hatching out hundreds of Cretaceous dinosaurs, as recounted in *Cretaceous Stones*, Book 1 in the series. Now it's a new summer, and Dromaeosaurus, Tyrannosaurus Rex, and Triceratops are on the loose once again.

Cast of Characters:

Paleontologists/authors **Hayden Fowler** and **Nora Lemoyne** are involved in a torrid romantic relationship. They are fresh off the bestselling success of their first co-authored book, detailing their close encounters with the Cretaceous beasts. On the hunt for material for their second book, the couple experiences a few harrowing encounters in their travels.

Helicopter pilot **Peter Lacroix** resigns from the Montana Forest Service to become Hayden and Nora's personal pilot. It's big money, but the risks are even bigger. Peter's pregnant wife **Brin Lacroix** suffers high anxiety as he flies out each day, worrying whether he will return.

Jackson Lattimer is a celebrity wildlife videographer with a reckless reputation for getting closeup shots of dangerous animals. Due to his daring ways, the media has dubbed him "America's Gonzo Shutterbug." He befriends Hayden Fowler, joining him on several perilous outings.

Bryan and Loretta Gilliam, parents of three children, own Gilliam's Guidepost ranch, home of last summer's famed dinosaur habitats. The ranch serves as the heliport and home base for the dinosaur tracking teams.

Kelton Rendaya is an equine veterinarian moonlighting as an illicit animal trafficker who specializes in venomous reptiles and dangerous wildlife. His life implodes when he jumps headlong into the dinosaur trade.

Also, Indigenous women are disappearing off the Blackfeet

Indian reservation. The authorities are indifferent, claiming the Native women are being taken by hungry Tyrannosaurs. One of the women is Kanti Lyttle, the wife of Apisi, a longtime Gilliam ranch hand. Bryan Gilliam gets involved and his search leads to a startling discovery. Is it possible that animal traffickers have also moved into the human trafficking business?

Finally, a helicopter flight into Idaho's River of No Return Wilderness preserve in search of Tyrannosaurs turns deadly. The team of six learns a harsh lesson—the dragons of the Continental Divide are ruthlessly unforgiving.

Dragons of the Great Divide is fictional science at its best. But it's much more than a sci-fi thriller featuring the return of the dinosaurs to the contemporary American West. At its heart is a story that explores the human condition in all its multifaceted complexity. It's about the human spirit rising up in the face of extreme adversity. It's about families and romantic relationships. It's about unbridled greed and the blinding quest for fame and fortune. It's about life and loss, love and lust, and the human need for friendship. But most of all, it's a rip-roaring entertaining tale you won't soon forget.

DRAGONS
OF THE
GREAT DIVIDE

Jeff Dennis

Nightbird Publishing

By Jeff Dennis:

Standalone Fiction:
   The Wisdom of Loons (2009)
   Daydreams and Night Screams (2013)
   To Touch Infinity (2015)

Hobo Duology:
   King of the Hobos (2012)
   Hobo Jingo (2017)

Cretaceous Chronicles:
   Cretaceous Stones (2022)
   Dragons of the Great Divide (2024)

DRAGONS OF THE GREAT DIVIDE

Book 2 of the Cretaceous Chronicles

JEFF DENNIS

DRAGONS OF THE GREAT DIVIDE

FIRST EDITION

Print: 978-0-9911871-8-8
eBook: 979-8-2248787-3-4

Nightbird Publishing
Loganville, Georgia

jeffdennisauthor.com
jeff@jeffdennisauthor.com

First Printing: February 2024

10 9 8 7 6 5 4 3 2 1

Dragons of the Great Divide is dedicated to the memory of Virginia Rogers (1967–2023), a gifted graphic designer and kind soul, the visionary artist who created this striking wrap-around book cover. She was taken from us far too soon.

Predator and prey move in silent gestures,
on the seductive dance of death, in the silent
shadows cast by the vultures of the night.

—Luis Marques —

The Gonzo Shutterbug

June 2: River of No Return Wilderness Area
Central Idaho
One year after the meteorites came down . . .

THRILL JUNKIE.

Adrenaline Addict.

Reckless Renegade.

Those were just some of the names the press had hung on him. *People Magazine* had dubbed him the Digital Cowboy for his iconic videography work. The *Entertainment Tonight* interviewer called him the Wildlife Wild Man. *Rolling Stone* had done a feature article on him with the title: **Jackson Lattimer: America's Gonzo Shutterbug**. His cover photo showed him in full profile. A safari bush hat shadowed his weathered, sunburned face. A leopardskin hunting vest adorned his broad chest. He cradled an automatic rifle under his left arm. In his right hand he clutched a zoom-scoped Sony Cyber-shot camera. A smaller videocam hung from his neck. Behind him a pride of lions looked ready to pounce.

Gonzo Shutterbug.

Thrill Junkie.

Jackson Lattimer loved the attention. Reveled in it, in fact. He wore the labels proudly. The rogue hunter-with-a-camera reputation was good for business.

He mused on his public persona as he led his film crew along the uneven deer trail, alert for potential trouble. A bright full moon and a million shimmering stars illuminated the nightscape, casting a silvery sheen over towering western white pines and rocky gorges. The Salmon River whispered and gurgled in the distance. His team—Sam Beeson and Milton Haynes—huffed and puffed behind him, their LED miner headlamps casting wavy shadows along the path. Three pairs of hiking boots crunched out a rhythmic cadence as they ambled through the canyon.

Jackson Lattimer's risk-taking fearlessness is what made him one of the world's preeminent nature documentary filmmakers. His pet slogans were: "Anything to get the money shot," and "No predator too dangerous." He'd lost count of the number of times he'd narrowly escaped death to capture images of aggressive wildlife.

This excursion, however, presented the ultimate challenge. This trip was unlike any they had ever attempted—tromping through miles of remote Idaho backcountry under cover of night in search of Tyrannosaurus Rex.

The Tyrant Lizard.

Jackson couldn't wrap his head around it completely—going after prehistoric beasts.

Dinosaurs! It boggled the mind.

He had missed out on all the fun last summer when a cluster of meteorites had struck this part of the country. Meteorites that hatched out hundreds of Cretaceous Period dinosaurs. It had been the news story of the century—more accurately the biggest story since the beginning of recorded news—and he had missed out.

For much of last summer, Jackson had been on assignment in sub-Saharan Africa, filming a National Geographic special about hippos in Zambia, Mozambique, and Zimbabwe. As much as he had wanted to return to the U.S. to get in on the dinosaur renaissance, he couldn't. Especially not after the tragedy. One of his crew had been killed in a hippo stampede while filming underwater scenes in the Luangwa River. The dreadful ordeal was still fresh—a half dozen two-ton hippos, protecting their territory and young calves, charged the film crew in a churning, earthshaking wave of river water and massive bodies, their stout legs like the pillars of huge buildings stomping the river bottom. All but one of the crew got out of the water in time. The loss of Manny Mulenga, a Zambian contract guide Jackson had used on several previous Africa trips, hit everyone hard. Especially Jackson, who would never forget the tears shed when he informed Mulenga's family.

Jackson had done everything he could to educate his team on the dangers of hippos, stressing their aggressiveness and unpredictability. Most people thought the beast Africans called *river horse* to be fat, slow, and lazy. They couldn't be more wrong. The hippopotamus was the deadliest land mammal on the planet, able to move quickly through deep water and run at speeds up to twenty miles per hour on land. Hippos killed more than 500 people a year in Africa. He had drummed that into his crew. But even though he had prepared them, they'd still suffered a tragic loss. Accidents could happen so quickly in the wild. They had captured some remarkable footage of the giant aquatic beasts, but Manny's death cast a dark pall on the shoot.

Jackson wasn't about to be denied filming the Cretaceous creatures again this summer. He wanted—*needed*—to see a Tyrannosaurus Rex up close. It had been a desire burning deep within him all through the fall and winter as he worked a couple of other projects—photo documenting the decline of polar bears in Manitoba, Canada, and traveling to the South Australian Neptune Islands to film great white sharks and their migratory habits.

He had done a great deal of research before deciding on this vast nature preserve in central Idaho. He had watched a lot of what he considered to be amateur quality video of Dromaeosaurus and Tyrannosaurus Rex hatchlings and juveniles. He'd read numerous scientific reports pertaining to The Great Dinosaur Hatchout. He'd studied maps and read the Hayden Fowler-Nora Lemoyne book published to great acclaim in April, *Cretaceous Stones: The Return of Prehistoric Life to Earth*, where Fowler surmised this Frank Church River of No Return Wilderness had potentially the largest concentration of T-Rexes. It was also where that crash survivor helicopter pilot, Russell Cavanaugh, had evaded a pack of Tyrannosaurs for a week or more. Hayden Fowler contended that this remote area—with its extensive cave systems and scant human population—was a good possibility for where T-Rexes might hole up and hibernate during the harsh winter. And most paleozoologists agreed that Tyrannosaurus Rex was a nocturnal animal. With the spring thaw well underway, and a full moon to illuminate their night work, Jackson felt certain this was the time and place to spot one of the prehistoric beasts that he understood were now larger and much more deadly than grizzly bears. He wanted to be the first this summer to photograph one in the wild. He *had* to be first!

His reputation depended on it.

His self-respect demanded it.

He knew this was an entirely different level of danger from filming hippos. In addition to the risk of encountering flesh-eating dinosaurs, this area was known to be inhabited by bears and mountain lions and rattlesnakes. So far they had been lucky to avoid trouble. No snakes or mountain lions or attacking grizzlies. The three of them had been out here three days now, and they had not seen much wildlife. Just a family of black bears foraging huckle-berries on the opposite side of the Salmon River. A few mule deer and elk. A small herd of bighorn sheep tight-roping ridges up along the cliffs. Last night they explored a cave network just above Cave Creek, packed full of active brown bats. Lots of bat guano there but no sign of dinosaurs. No prints or tracks. No piles of scat. No dino-saur prey carcasses.

The search for Tyrannosaurus Rex continued in this two-and-a-half-million acres of unspoiled nature. This was Jackson's first trip to this part of Idaho. The area brought to mind a deserted planet. They had not seen another human being or a single dwelling on their three-day trek. Just a natural wonderland on the verge of breaking out in full summer glory. It was gorgeous, but he did have to admit, the isolation of the place spooked him at times.

They hiked on, headed for another cave system, this one larger than the one on Cave Creek, according to his research. The trail took an upward swing, the three of them breathing heavier with the increase in elevation. The rifle felt heavy in Jackson's gloved hands. His bulky backpack—stuffed with camera equipment, camping gear, make-ready meals, and drinking water—weighed him down. He felt the miles they had slogged in his legs and feet, the lack of sleep dogging him.

He heard Sam Beeson behind him. "How much further, Jack?"

"We're almost there, I do believe." Jackson stopped and pulled his inReach satellite communicator from his pack. "Let's take a short break, fellas, while I get our bearings."

"My feet thank you, my friend, as does my ass," Milt Haynes muttered, his words rolling out on puffs of tiny steam clouds in the chilly night air.

The three men lessened their backpack loads and propped their rifles against large stones that lined the path.

Jackson looked up from his GPS device, pointed up the trail with his chin. "Our destination is up over that ridge. Another half mile, give or take."

Beeson munched on a protein bar, drank Gatorade from a water bottle. He wiped his mouth with the back of his arm and said, "I hope we run across one of those dinos soon. The boredom's about to kill me."

Jackson smirked at him in the dim light. "You see a few of those Rexes coming at ya, you'll wish you were still bored. I hope you brought several changes of clean underwear, Sammy."

"Ha-ha. You're frickin' hilarious, Jack. They're just big dumb lizards."

"So you think," Milt Haynes said, lighting up a smoke. "I've seen enough of those videos from last summer to convince me we need to be on our toes. Those polar bears we tracked on Hudson Bay are child's play compared to these Tyrannosaurs."

"Yeah, *right*."

Jackson said to Beeson, "He speaks the truth, Sammy. We'd best treat Mr. T-Rex with utmost respect," he said, recalling the hippopotamus catastrophe in Zambia. Haynes and Beeson had not been with him on that trip. They had never experienced a situation like that. Jackson Lattimer knew just how quickly one of these wildlife shoots could spiral out of control.

Sam Beeson waved him off. "Maybe so, but I refuse to fear a dumb animal. If things go south, I'll just shoot the sonofabitch."

"Not if he eats you first," Milt said with a malicious grin.

Jackson shook his head. "Listen, guys, the only shooting we're going to do is photographic." He lifted the rifle from his lap. "These are last resort only. Self-defense, and only if it's life or death. Understood?"

Both men mumbled their acceptance.

After a 15-minute break to rest and rehydrate, they were back on the trail. Forty-five minutes later they stood at the gaping mouth of a huge cave, marked as Moose Valley Cave on the topography survey map.

"So here we are, guys. Time to strap on," he said, referring to their night vision goggles.

Jackson watched as Beeson and Haynes removed their head-lamps and pulled on the EyeClops infrared stealth goggles. He did the same. His view brightened to a ghostly green glow.

"It's showtime," he said, hooking his rifle over his shoulder and grabbing a handheld spotlight from his pack. "You guys know the drill. Keep your cameras ready and your guns close. No telling what we might find inside."

Jackson entered the cave. *Wide enough to drive three Mack trucks through.* His adrenaline ratcheted up.

This is what it's all about.

The risk.

The danger.

The mortal gamble.

The fear . . . my lifeblood.

The darkness enveloped him as he moved further into the interior. Beeson and Haynes followed close, glancing left and right, attentive, vigilant, the moonlit entrance disappearing behind them.

Jackson heard Milt Haynes exclaim, "Awesome! Shine your spot over this way, Jack."

Jackson turned and directed the powerful beam toward the far wall. Long columns of limestone stalactites drooped from the vast ceiling. Through the goggles they looked like giant emerald icicles. "Awesome is right, Milt. Grab a few frames."

"Got it covered," Sam Beeson said, snapping off a series of stills of the stalactite grouping, his Nikon shutter emitting faint *click-wheeze* noises with each shot.

They moved on. Jackson waved the spotlight side to side,

looking for evidence of life. They rounded a sharp bend and paced down a long straightaway. He heard water dripping in the distance. The air was damp and smelled of mildew and dust, a hint of sulfur.

They had trekked another forty yards when he spied a pile of brush bunched at the foot of a large boulder. The vegetation looked odd in a cave that had been all rock and dust to this point. He led Beeson and Haynes to the tangle, his curiosity mounting. Took a knee and inspected what looked like a snarl of tumbleweed and sagebrush.

"Hmmm, what have we here?" he said, reaching out to dig into the twist of foliage.

"Careful, Jack," Beeson said. "Could be snakes in there. Looks like some nasty thorns, too. Better glove up."

"Here, take this, Sammy," he said to Beeson, handing him the spotlight.

Jackson put his gloves back on that he'd removed when they entered the cave. Gloves made it difficult to operate his cameras. His hands protected, he reached into the brush and pulled the top layer back. What he saw nestled in the center sucked the breath from his lungs.

Eggs.

Six *very large* eggs. Elliptical, elongated. Like a half-dozen colorful rugby balls laid out in two symmetrical rows. The shells were marked with distinctive swirling patterns, appearing as though they had been dyed with paisley designs.

They didn't look anything like terrestrial eggs. At least none that Jackson had ever seen.

He pushed the goggle headset up on his forehead. The eggshell swirls glowed bright blue and green under the spotlight.

He touched one of the eggs. Tough and leathery.

Could it be?

Jackson's voice carried a tenor of reverence. "Gentlemen, I believe we have found our dinosaurs."

"Jesus H!" Milt Haynes said in a spellbound whisper. He lifted one of the eggs from the nest, needing both hands to extract it. "These things are damned heavy. Must weigh close to ten pounds.

And the shells are tough. Feels like thick canvas."

Jackson nodded. "I know. Can you believe it?" he said, his tone one of awe.

"I wonder how close they are to hatching out," Beeson said.

Jackson stood, a foreboding uneasiness coming over him. He stared into the darkness ahead. "I'm wondering something else," he said, looking back at the colorful egg in Milt's hands. "I'm wondering how close Mama Rex is."

A tremor in Sam Beeson's voice. "You really think these are Tyrannosaurus Rex eggs, Jack?"

"Well, they certainly aren't chicken eggs. Look at the size of 'em—the weird patterns. The thick shells. Gotta be dinosaurs. Big bastards like Rex. Shine that light up ahead, Sammy."

Beeson swung the spot away from the nest and down the tunnel. The powerful lamp lit up the path ahead. Nothing but limestone and granite all the way to where the walls curved out of sight.

Then, as if on cue, they heard a long, caterwauling cry from behind them, coming from the entrance.

Loud. Unsettling.

A reverberating warning.

The three of them turned in unison. Beeson jerked the spot around, throwing light on the cave walls back to the bend.

A slow anxiety began to rise in Jackson. "I believe mama bitch is here, fellas."

"And she doesn't sound happy," Sam Beeson intoned with a nervous tic.

The lone cry was joined by others.

Strident trumpeting sounds, like the cries of imperiled elephants.

More than one animal?

The three photographers stood rigid, gazing into the void, questioning, incredulous.

Jackson realized they were trapped with no way out. He should have known to keep close watch on their rear flank. Carnivorous dinosaurs like T-Rex were night hunters, and the hunt would be the only thing to take them away from their nest. Faint vibrations flowed through the soles of his boots as the creatures advanced. Apparently they were returning from their nightly feed. *How many of them are there?* he wondered.

He chastised himself for his lack of foresight.

And just then, three massive animals came around the bend. Blinded by the powerful spotlight, they stopped in their tracks, seemingly confused and irritated by the bright light. Jackson looked on in stunned disbelief. *Magnificent creatures*, he thought, transfixed by the sight. *They've gotta be nine feet tall and weigh six hundred pounds! Definitely Tyrannosaurus Rex. Much bigger than the ones filmed last summer.*

Standing on two heavily muscled hind legs, they were alien. Prehistoric predators. Bigger than mature grizzlies with oversized heads and wide shovel mouths. Rows of wicked teeth. Scaled hides that gleamed in the light. The one in the lead clutched a bloody deer in its deep mouth, a big buck. Flopping it around like it was nothing more than a lightweight rag doll. The two in back brayed like distressed donkeys. The three beasts glared at them through blood-red eyes in a malevolent stare down.

Jackson's all-consuming professional drive to get the impossible footage overpowered his survival instincts. He grabbed his videocam and began filming.

"What the hell're you doing, Jack?" Sam Beeson shouted, trying to keep the light steady on the beasts.

"Doin' what we came to do. Keep the spot on 'em, Sammy. It's holding 'em back."

"They aren't gonna stay put much longer," Beeson croaked, his nerves evident. "They look mighty pissed off. I say we run."

Jackson continued recording, eye fixed to the viewfinder. "Keep that goddamned light in their eyes, Sammy! You hear me?"

"This is insanity," Milt Haynes called out. He glanced down, surprised to see the egg still cradled in his hands. He tossed it back into the nest where it bounced but didn't break. "I'm not gonna die here with you, Jack. No way!" He brought his rifle up against his shoulder.

Jackson turned away from the videocam, watched Haynes

assume a shooter's stance and take aim. "Don't do it, Milt. They haven't made a move yet."

The unnerving braying and trumpeting increased in volume, but the creatures remained frozen in the light.

"They're . . . they're all . . . jacked up," Haynes yelled over the din, his finger firm on the trigger. "I ain't waitin' until they charge us."

"I'm telling you, Milt, don't do it," Jackson warned. "We're okay. The light has 'em stalled."

"So *you* say. This is nutso, Jack," Haynes boomed. "Time to take care of business."

The videocam whirred in Jackson's steady hands. He was capturing incredible footage and wanted to keep it going. But Haynes was freaking out. He was going to ruin the shoot.

"Jesus, Milt, get a grip!" Jackson snarled. "Stow the gun and get a frame on 'em. Do it now goddamnit!"

Milt Haynes ignored him, firing off a round, the rapid-fire blasts deafening. The first few shots sailed high and wide. Subsequent shots struck the lead animal in the throat and shoulder, making it drop the deer carcass, the buck's rack clacking against the rocky floor. The Rex let out an indignant growl, followed by a sorrowful cry, then began stumbling toward Haynes, who fired again. Three more blasts found the mark in the Tyrannosaur's chest and belly, the force knocking it backward. The beast let out an angry grumble before it went down on its back. The huge animal lay sprawled out beside the buck, blood pooling around its wounds, thick hind legs twitching spasmodically. It bellowed a loud death knell before finally eking out a weak sigh and going still.

Jackson felt a flush of anger as he watched Haynes trying to reload, fumbling the new cartridge and dropping it.

"Holy shit!" Beeson shouted as he backpedaled. The spotlight zigzagged across the two standing behemoths, both of which trumpeted their anger.

Jackson barked at Beeson. "Hold that goddamned light steady, Sammy."

"No way! Time to move, Jack."

The two remaining Tyrannosaurs came out of their trance and charged, pouncing on Haynes so unbelievably quick Milt couldn't get off another shot. Milt Haynes' scream was snuffed out as his rifle and headgear clattered to the floor under the onslaught. Beeson dropped the handheld spot and sprinted for a nearby rock outcropping while the animals tore into Haynes's lifeless body.

Jackson Lattimer was stunned and devastated. He thought he would lose it. He fought to maintain his composure as he continued filming, backing away swiftly from the T-Rex feeding frenzy. Through the night vision lens he witnessed the violent death of his longtime friend and employee, Milton Haynes. The Tyrannosaurs made quick, gruesome work of Haynes's corpse. But some twisted sense of professional duty made Jackson keep videotaping. *Have to get the money shots, no matter how painful,* he thought, feeling some shame at his photojournalist's creed.

In the viewfinder, he saw one of the beasts rise up from the feeding and turn its attention to him, blood and drool and stringy intestines dripping from its mouth. Jackson knew the time had arrived to cut bait and run.

Quickly, he shut off the recorder and jammed it into his pack, then turned and bolted to the rock pile where Beeson had fled. His heart racing triple time, he heard the Rex snorting and shrieking behind him as he reached the grouping of large boulders.

Beeson, peering out from a narrow gap, shouted, "Climb up top, Jack! There's an opening big enough to squeeze through."

Jackson hit the rocks at full speed and leaped just as the Rex made a lunge at him, trying to take him down from behind, clipping his boot heel and knocking him off balance. Breathlessly, he regained his footing and crab walked to the top of the rock formation, his lungs burning with each gasp. Found the entry point. His hands shook as he removed his bulky backpack and stuffed it through the narrow crevice, keeping his eye on the Tyrannosaur below, the animal repeatedly sliding off the smooth boulders in desperate attempts to climb up after him. Jackson bent and slid through the opening, dropping down into a dark claustrophobic enclosure and joining Sam Beeson.

Both men were silent, in shock, struggling to recapture their wind. Hearts pounding, they observed the pair of Tyrannosaurs through the narrow, floor level fissure, the animals snorting, drooling, and braying, trying without success to get at them. The opening was just wide enough to give them a limited window on the cave. Jackson realized their vantage point was too narrow to get a rifle barrel through.

Sam Beeson's voice was loud in their tight granite cubicle. "I wonder how long we'll have to stay in this coffin."

"However long it is, we're better off than Milt, God rest his soul."

Jackson reached for his backpack and rummaged through it for his satellite phone. He pressed the red power button. The small display panel lit up the tight space. He was immediately crushed.

Beeson noticed his downcast expression. "We're doomed, aren't we?"

Jackson nodded. "Plenty of power but no service. Too much rock surrounding us."

The two of them remained silent for a long while, watching as one of the Tyrannosaurs huffed and grunted and sniffed just outside the enclosure, frustrated at not being able to get at them. The space filled with a foul wild animal odor. Jackson shivered and scooted back as the big beast lowered its head and peeked through the narrow opening, its flame-red eyes searching for the human prey it could smell.

He heard Beeson say, "You're insane, you know that, Jack?"

"Well, yeah. Tell me somethin' I don't know. But I will say this. It should have been me, not Milton," he said, shaking his head, feeling the loss deep in his chest. "Poor bastard. Jesus."

Beeson said, "Why do you think they went after Milt and not us? I mean, we were out there in the open with him."

"Just guessing, but Milton was who they saw fondling one of their eggs. He's the one who shot at them. He was a natural target." Jackson glanced at the predatory crimson eyes peering in at them through the crack, listened to the Rex making high-pitched squeals like a startled horse. "You still think they're just big dumb animals,

Sammy?"

"Big, yes. Dumb? Absolutely not."

More long quiet minutes in the stultifying dark. Jackson thought about what they'd just been through. He'd lost his second crew member in less than a year. Both in horrifying fashion. Milton Haynes had been a good man. A family man with a loving wife and two young children. One of the best young nature photographers in the business.

He felt tears pooling in his eyes. His emotions teetered on the edge. He tried to hold back a sniffle. Couldn't.

"Are you crying, Jack?"

In answer, he let it go, erupting into a full-scale weeping jag. The gonzo shutterbug thrill junkie bawled like a newborn baby.

He was too devastated to be embarrassed.

Sam Beeson reached out and rubbed his shoulder. "It'll be okay, my friend. Everything will be fine."

Jackson Lattimer wanted so badly to believe him.

Gemstones in the Forest

June 4: Southwest Montana

THE COCKPIT RUMBLED AS THEY FLEW south toward their destination: the Custer Gallatin National Forest just north of the Wyoming border. Peter Lacroix sat in the navigator seat, observing the young pilot working the chopper's pitch sticks and tail rotor pedals. As much as he hated to admit it, baby-faced Robert Winkle was pretty accomplished, considering he looked about sixteen. But Peter shouldn't be surprised by the kid's self-assurance in the pilot's seat. The U.S. Forest Service hired only the best helicopter pilot candidates.

Winkle's résumé showed he was a twenty-three year old recent graduate of the acclaimed Northern Skies Aviation flight school in Laurel, Montana. Peter knew the program there to be demanding. Winkle had logged 500 hours of pilot-in-command flight time, 200 hours of mountain terrain flying, and 50 hours of low altitude instruction. Only the most determined and dedicated pilots made it through the Northern Skies training curriculum.

Peter had worked with the other newbie pilots, but this was his first flight with Winkle. The kid was so skilled Peter felt unneeded.

This assignment called for them to inspect extinguished wildfire sites for possible new flareups. Peter knew this was nothing but misdirection. Management could call this excursion anything they wanted, but he knew it was just a thinly disguised rookie pilot training session. Fresh outbreaks were rare after a burn area had been contained, doused, and terminated. This flight really wasn't about tracking burn sites. They were grooming Peter to be a flight instructor, and he didn't like it.

Since late March, he had seen his hours in the pilot's seat cut drastically. The Missoula brass—in response to budget cutbacks imposed by the USDA—hired Rob Winkle and three other young, inexperienced helicopter pilots. Peter knew the new aviators were making half his salary. The writing was on the wall: he was training the less expensive pilots who would eventually replace him and the other veterans.

Peter Lacroix—38 years young—had put in eight good years as a pilot for the Montana Forest Service. Management saw him as an ideal teacher for younger pilots, due to his ace flying proficiency, exemplary flight history, and excellent communication skills. At least that's how his boss, Gary Ralston, had phrased it. Ralston told him Flight Instructor was a promotion, a bump up from First Officer, the org chart job title for GS-12 FAA-certified helicopter pilots.

Peter wasn't interested. Even if it brought him a pay increase. He wanted to *fly* helicopters, not teach others how to do it.

The Peter Principle at work, he mused dejectedly. *Literally.*

As they flew to their first burn site, he watched Winkle coordinate the collective and cyclic pitch sticks with the tail rotor yaw pedals, the kid's hands and feet working in precise, synchronized tandem. They passed over the capital city of Helena, nestled in the foothills of the Big Belt Mountains, the mighty Missouri River winding through impressive rock formations and feeding the Canyon Ferry Lake Reservoir. They increased altitude, flying over snow-capped Sacagawea Peak in the Rockies. A herd of mountain goats cavorted along steep mountain trails. Then they were over Bozeman, the Gallatin River and its multi-fingered tributaries snaking through and around the city. Peter could see fly fishermen dotting the shores, looking like tiny stick figures casting their lines. He never tired of the remote beauty of Montana's stunning, panoramic landscape.

He checked the altimeter and lowered his headset mic, speaking over the raucous cockpit clatter. "You're doing great, Rob. Nice smooth climb."

He heard Winkle's voice in his headphones. "Thanks, boss."

"I'm not your boss. Gary Ralston is."

"But you're my instructor. That makes you my boss while we're in flight."

Instructor. There was that tag again. He hated it.

"I'm *not* your instructor," he said, more flippantly than he intended. "I'm a pilot colleague who's co-piloting a mission with you."

Winkle glanced at him. "You're calling me your colleague?"

"Yes. That's what you are, Robert."

"I'm honored," Winkle said, as if addressing royalty.

Peter shook his head, amused. He checked the instrument panel and reeled off flight information in a weary monotone. "Wind velocity eight knots, groundspeed at one-twenty knots. Rotor speed three-seventy-five RPM and holding steady. Altitude at fifty-five-hundred feet. Okay, we need to push east for fifty miles. Hit the stick ninety degrees east, toward Livingston."

Winkle reached down with his right hand and gripped the cyclic stick, pulled it slowly toward him and stepped on the left yaw pedal as he checked the gyroscopic compass for the pitch and roll attitudes of the craft. The chopper banked in a slow, level turn to the left.

"Good work, Rob," Peter said, admiring the rookie pilot's deft touch. He studied the dash GPS, checking their positioning, waiting for the craft to line up with their waypoint. Finally he said, "Okay now straighten her out. We're locked in to our destination. Livingston here we come."

As they flew due east over interstate 90, Peter deliberated on his reduced flying time. After last summer's tragedy at Camels Hump, where one of the infamous dinosaur meteorites demolished the fire watchtower and nearly killed the lookout, Fire Prevention management made the decision to close down the remaining towers, decommissioning eighteen fire watchtowers throughout western Montana. To replace the towers, the Forest Service invested in Unmanned Aerial Systems (UAS), better known as drones, to handle fire lookout surveillance. The drones also reduced the need for helicopter and fixed wing pilots as drones could fly in all weather conditions and get into spaces large aircraft could not. Management's official statement? "The switch to technology-based fire observation ensures employee safety." But Peter knew the move was nothing more than a cost-cutting measure. They would no longer have to staff those eighteen lookout towers. But he knew the chances of another meteorite hitting a tower, or any other natural disaster wiping out a lookout post, was negligible at best.

What's next? Decommissioning the Forest Service's air fleet?

Is my employment in jeopardy?

To rub salt in the wound, management was now requiring that Peter attend UAS training exercises one day a week. The other veteran pilots were required to do the same. They trained on the small robotic flying machines for use in this summer's controlled burn wildfire prevention program. Wildfire prevention is the process of thinning out overly thick forest areas by setting closely monitored fires to prevent future, out of control wildfires. These intentional fires cleared out brush and low vegetation that acted as fuel and flammable kindling. For years these intentional fires were generated from helicopters in a process known as aerial ignition, which were dangerous undertakings. Peter had flown a dozen or more aerial ignitions in his eight years with the Forest Service and knew firsthand of the risks involved.

Even still, he would prefer to fly them himself.

Beginning in April, every Tuesday, Peter went to a cavernous warehouse outside Missoula and worked with Quadcopter drones, operating a sophisticated OpenPilot flight controller board. Classroom sessions taught the concepts of drone flight, payload orientation, maintenance and cleaning, firing basics, and burn patterns. Tuesday afternoons were spent outdoors in a nearby field practicing dumping aerial ignition payloads onto targeted areas. The payload consisted of plastic spheres known as dragon eggs that were filled with potassium permanganate. The spheres ignited ten seconds after they were injected with glycol, so timing and accuracy were critical. Peter found the Tuesday experience to be interesting and challenging, but he still would much rather be flying.

It pained him. This wasn't at all what he signed up for.

I didn't spend all that time and money training to be a pilot to stand on the ground operating a remote control toy helicopter.

Drones threatened his livelihood. They threatened his *soul*.

Not since a serious knee injury ended his pro hockey career in Toronto had Peter been forced to think hard about his future. He had a newly pregnant wife—Brinshou—at home in Missoula with their two-and-a-half-year-old daughter. Brin was doing fairly well with her jewelry business, but rent on her downtown store had just gone up and she had a lot tied up in expensive inventory. And when he and Brin discovered she was pregnant in April, they started looking for a bigger house; their starter home where they had lived for four years was too cramped for his growing family. They desperately needed his full income for the road ahead. The new baby on the way made his salary imperative.

Peter had done a few job searches in the private sector on the sly (he didn't want Brin or the Forest Service to know he was looking). The poor economy didn't help his cause. Amazon Air, FedEx, and UPS were hiring only fixed wing pilots. Helinet Aviation—which flew helicopter charters for DHL and other big shipping companies—was not hiring. Nor were any of the emergency medical services that maintained helicopter fleets. He had been in demand eight years ago when the Forest Service hired him. But corporate America and the government sector seemed to be in cutback mode.

Rob Winkle's voice in his ear cut into his thoughts. "Livingston is ahead, boss. Straight up at twelve o'clock."

A shiver ran through Peter as he realized they were close to the site of last July's Roundup Rodeo massacre, where a pack of Tyrannosaurs had attacked and killed two dozen people and seriously injured a dozen more. "Bring it down, Rob. Reduce altitude to one thousand feet." He keyed Park County Fairgrounds into the GPS, feeling a bit disgusted with himself for wanting to take a peek at where the horrific slaughter had occurred.

Am I an evil voyeur?

They flew over the fairgrounds, but there wasn't much to see. Just a few cowboys leaning against a corral fence and a trio of horses pacing the enclosure.

Winkle asked if this was the location of the dinosaur assault.

"Yeah, it is."

Winkle frowned. "I can't imagine the horror those people went through."

"Me either. A couple of folks Brin and I know were here the night it happened. The two famous paleontologists, Hayden Fowler and Nora Lemoyne."

"The two who wrote that book everyone's talking about?"

Peter nodded.

"You know them?"

"Sure do. They came to our house for dinner once. Brin served them her delicious, go-to Kootenai meal—bitterroot-fireberry salad, baked camas, and grilled pheasant. Nora loved it, but I don't think Hayden cared much for it."

"Wow, you actually *know* them? You're famous, boss."

"*They're* famous. I'm not. And knock it off with the boss thing."

"Okay, sorry. How about captain?"

"I'm not a captain either."

What should I call you, then? Teach?"

Peter made a face. Exasperated, he recalled that old saying about teaching: "Those who can do it, do it; those who can't, teach it." He was a *pilot*, damnit! He could do it with the best of them.

He said, "How about my real name? Peter works for me." He glanced at the GPS display. "We need to push south again. Hit the stick forty-five degrees southeast."

Winkle pitched the craft into a wide veer to the right. Soon they were flying over the Beartooth Mountains and Custer Gallatin National Forest. Thick stands of towering Engelmann spruce covered the lower elevations in fluffy green blankets. Twenty minutes later they changed course, flying directly east, along the Wyoming border and the northern perimeter of Yellowstone National Park. Peter checked the GPS longitude-latitude coordinates he had entered when filing the flight plan. They were fifteen minutes from their first burn inspection site.

The wildfire that had destroyed the area had raged for a month before finally being contained and smothered two weeks ago. The result of a lightning storm, the Gallup Canyon Fire had devastated two thousand acres of woodland. Smokejumpers had fought the fire on the ground while fixed wing planes flew over spraying Phos-Chek fire retardant across the site.

They flew over a ravine and crossed a high ridgeline. The canyon spread out before them: a blackened valley of burnt stumps and ashy deadwood that seemed to go on forever. Set against the surrounding greenery of lodgepole pine and spruce firs, the scorched valley presented a startling contrast.

"Circle the site, Rob," Peter said, reaching below his seat for binoculars. He glassed the burned-out gulch, seeing a large mound of earth stretching across the bottom of the gradient, the result of mudslides from dispersed liquids and erosion. Fortunately there was no lingering smoke.

No new fires.

He was about to radio Missoula with an all-clear message when he noticed something odd along the top of the far ridge. Something large and dark jammed in behind the dense rows of lodgepole pine. The low hanging branches obstructed his view. As they flew closer, he could see the outlines of huge ebony boulders, sunk deep in the earth behind a curtain of trees.

They had to be the size of large pickup trucks.

Three of them.

Black as a moonless, starless night.

Quite different from the pale gray Madison limestone and white sandstone of the area.

"Take us up along the ridgeline, Rob," he said, continuing to scan the ridge.

"Why? What's up there? Whaddaya looking at?"

"Just do it, please. We need to give Missoula a thorough report."

Peter thought he detected a huff from the junior pilot, but Robert Winkle followed orders and increased altitude so they were flying along the ridgeline, parallel to where the seared earth met the trees. When they got to the boulders, he instructed the kid to hover in place. From here, Peter could see a glittery sparkle on the visible surfaces of the rocks.

A tingle of excitement touched his throat. He was convinced

he'd seen rocks like these before. Last spring. When he flew the Camels Hump medevac flight, rescuing badly injured fire looker George Dantley after a meteorite collapsed his tower. Peter had looked down the side of the cliff where the meteorite had struck and broken apart. These obsidian boulders had a marked similarity to the meteorite at Camels Hump. He'd also seen rocks like these when he worked the U.S. Air Force Operation Hot Rocks meteorite pickup program last summer, retrieving segments of the meteorites and flying them to a base in Idaho.

Meteorites.

Meteorites that had weirdly and inexplicably hatched out dinosaurs.

A thrilling jolt coursed through him. Peter pulled his iPad from the side pocket and logged on, checked the American Astronomical Society coordinates for the cluster of meteorite strikes from last May. He knew from his meteorite retrieval work with the Air Force that fifteen meteorites had come down and only nine of the stones had been recovered.

"Well, well, well, would you look at that," he said, staring down at his iPad. Two of the unrecovered meteorites had come down in this area—one ten miles south of Livingston and the other here, within four miles of their current lat-long GPS location.

"What? What is it?" Winkle prodded, keeping the craft in a steady hover.

"Let's find a level landing spot," Peter said, double checking the meteorite data.

"Um . . . this is supposed to be a flyover inspection. That's what the flight plan calls for. Our skids aren't supposed to touch the ground here."

Peter looked over at the rookie. "This isn't flight school, Rob. It's the real world. There's something up on that ridge we need to take a closer look at."

"I don't know, Peter. I don't wanna piss off the brass."

"The only way they'll ever know is if you tell them."

Winkle kept the hovering craft steady, thinking. Finally he said, "How're you gonna get up there?"

"By parking the bird and hiking up. And you're joining me."

"Say *what*?" Robert Winkle gazed out over the charred expanse of incinerated stumps and ash-covered surface, viewed the long steep incline leading up to the ridge. "No way," he said, casting a doubtful glance at Peter.

"Look, I've got fifteen years on you and a gimpy knee. If I can do it, you surely can. You passed a strenuous physical to get this job. So enough of the bitchin'. Let's land this bird and get up there."

"Where're we gonna land? It's a hillside of black daggers down there. The skids could get caught up and we'd be in a world of hurt."

"If you can't handle setting down in difficult terrain, I'll do it. I don't think that'll look too good on your evaluation, Rob."

"But we're not supposed to touch down here."

"Jesus! Enough already! We're losing valuable time and fuel sitting here arguing. I'm taking over."

Peter heard the kid sigh as he engaged the rheostat marked CO-PILOT on the control panel, placed his hands on the pitch sticks, and settled his feet on the pedals. The co-pilot instrument panel lit up, indicating he had flight control. He took the craft out of hover mode and made a looping turn out over the devastated valley. Robert Winkle sulked while Peter located a safe landing zone where firefighters had dug a shallow fire suppression trench line. It was a tight fit, but he brought the chopper down slowly, assuredly, until the skids settled into the soft soil.

He shut off the engine, the rotors slowing, winding down, then stopping. The silence was overwhelming after hours of rotor racket.

Peter looked over at Winkle and said, "Look, don't worry yourself over it, Rob. You did a great job hovering up there along the ridge. That was an impressive bit of flying. I'll give you props in your evaluation. In fact you've done quite a fine job getting us here."

The rookie pilot seemed placated by the compliments. But only momentarily.

Peter said, "C'mon, let's get on up to that ridge."

"Why do I have to go with you? One of us needs to stay with the aircraft."

Peter laughed. "What, you think somebody's gonna come along and hijack our chopper? There's nobody within fifty miles of this place. Don't be ridiculous."

Winkle stewed for a bit, then said, "What's up there that's so important?"

Peter stared at him for a long moment, trying to decide how much to tell the kid. Finally he said, "Okay, you've put up with my crotchety old self this trip so I'll level with you. You deserve that much. You remember that meteorite cluster that hit Idaho and Montana last year?"

"You mean the meteorites that brought back the dinosaurs?"

Peter nodded. "The very ones, yes."

"Of course I do."

Peter pointed up the hill to the ridgeline. "Well I'm pretty sure that's what those boulders are up there."

Winkle looked amused. "You're shittin' me, right? This is some kinda rookie pilot hazing ritual, isn't it?"

"The U.S. Forest Service isn't a college fraternity, Rob. It doesn't mess around with hazing nonsense. I'm being serious here."

Robert Winkle's amused expression disappeared, replaced with a look of stunned disbelief. "You mean there might be dinosaurs up there?"

"Doubtful. If those really are dinosaur meteorites, the creatures are long gone. It's been more than a year, after all. C'mon, let's secure the chopper and hike up there. See what's what."

Peter opened his cockpit door to step out, but Winkle hesitated, saying "There could be snakes out there, grizzlies up in the forest."

Peter turned, frustration evident in his tone. "The fire that torched this area chased most of the wildlife far from here." He stared at Winkle thoughtfully. "Just so you know, one of the things I'm supposed to evaluate you on is your courage and poise in stressful situations. You don't come with me, I'll be forced to give you a failing mark. I don't wanna do that, Rob. Get your shit together and let's make tracks."

He jumped down from the cockpit and walked around to the side of the chopper, a cool breeze blowing in his ears. Peter opened the rear cargo bay door and rummaged through the toolkit, grabbing a chisel, a hatchet, and a hammer. He heard the pilot-side door squeak open and Winkle step out.

The young pilot appeared from around the tail section, pointed at the tools. "Why're you bringing those?"

"To get some rock samples."

"Shouldn't we bring the rifle?"

Peter hated guns. The Montana Forest Service equipped their helicopters with .375 Ruger rifles for protection against bears and moose, but fortunately he'd never had to use one. "Bring it if it makes you feel better, but I'm telling you we won't need it."

They trudged up the steep grade to the lip of the ridge, Winkle with the Ruger strapped over his shoulder, Peter with tools in hand. It was an arduous climb, but they were aided by the pleasantly cool, dry, mid-sixties weather. They traversed the ash covered ground, sidestepping jagged, blackened tree stumps. The scent of damp smoke and dusty air made both men sneeze a few times.

Twenty minutes later they arrived at the top. Peter's knee ached and he was winded, but he bubbled with anticipation as they worked their way along the ridgeline to the boulders. The big black stones were wedged in tight, with thick lodgepole pine limbs wrapping the boulders in a verdant cocoon. He chopped out a few of the thickest limbs with the hatchet and Winkle helped him rip away some of the smaller limbs. Peter noticed several of the surrounding pine trunks were badly splintered. He glanced up and saw a wide gap in the overhead forest canopy. Some of the higher up pine branches looked scorched.

The wildfire didn't make it this far.

He looked back up at the gap in the overhead cover, at the charred branches around the perimeter of the opening. A flutter of excitement tickled his gut.

That opening has to be the entry point! These rocks are meteorite wedges! Much bigger than the ones I saw last year.

He squeezed in behind the largest of the rocks, saw a pair of long cracks running top to bottom, a shiny glaze coating the surface around the fissures. He did his best to kneel in the tight space and brush away ground cover at the base of the cracks.

The ground was littered with eggshell fragments. He picked up a couple of shards. Felt like hard leather. Faded bluish-green markings.

He crawled between woody trunks, sweeping away fuzzy green moss and pinecones, the act of which exposed dozens of small, three-toed tracks set in hardened mud, leading deeper into the woods.

He nearly fainted.

"What are you seein' back there," Winkle shouted from the other side of the rock.

Peter had a difficult time finding his voice.

"Are you okay in there, Peter?"

"I—I don't know. I, um . . . I believe we've just stumbled on a Tyrannosaurus Rex nest."

"*WHAT?*"

"Yeah, a dinosaur hatchout site," Peter said, looking deep into the forest interior, a fearful tingling beginning in his chest. "Come on back and check it out."

"I, uh . . . I don't believe I wanna do that."

Peter didn't blame him. This discovery was overwhelming.

He stood and quickly went to work, chiseling out small chunks of the dark, sparkly rock. The pounding clank of hammer against chisel echoed through the forest.

As he worked, he thought, *I've got to get in touch with Bryan Gilliam. Maybe even Hayden and Nora. The world needs to know about this.*

"Are you through yet?" he heard Winkle say between hammer clanks.

"Almost."

"Please hurry it up, Peter. This place is weirding me out."

You're not the only one, rookie.

Flicka, Monster Vids, and Intriguing Black Rocks

June 5: Gilliam's Guidepost
Heart Butte, Montana

"I LOVE THIS MOVIE SO MUCH!" Eight-year-old Lianne Gilliam squirmed between her parents on the den sofa. They were nearing the end of *Flicka*. The scent of buttered popcorn and creamed coffee hung in the air. Another family movie night at the Gilliam ranch.

"I know you do, Lee," Loretta said, pulling her daughter close and hugging her. "It's your favorite isn't it?"

"Yeah. I love how Katy changes Flicka's bad attitude. That horse was so wild, but Katy tamed Flicka and turned her into a nice horse. I'm glad my sweet Beau was never wild like Flicka," she said, referring to her own horse, Beauregard, one of a half dozen quarter horses stabled at Gilliam's Guidepost. "I wanna be like Katy when I'm a teenager, Mama. She's strong and pretty."

"You're well on your way, sweetcakes," Bryan Gilliam said, fluffing her hair. Their daughter was every bit as rebellious and willful as the 16-year-old heroine in the *Flicka* movies.

Lianne continued rambling with much of the same monologue she came out with after every viewing of *Flicka*. "I hated that mean old mountain lion that attacked Flicka. And the dad is mean, too. At least he was until Katy changed him. And Flicka changed him, too." She pulled out of her mother's grasp and hugged Bryan. "I'm glad you're not mean, Daddy. I wouldn't like it if you were mean like Katy's father."

An oft repeated refrain from his daughter, but Bryan never tired of it. He kissed the top of her head, said, "Your mother and I love you, Lee-lee."

"I love you, too, Daddy." She turned back to Loretta. "I love you just as much, Mama."

Bryan exchanged smiles with Loretta, smiles that said: *We sure are good parents, aren't we?*

Truth be told, Bryan was sick of watching *Flicka* and its seemingly endless number of saccharine sweet sequels. He loved the cinematography that captured the gorgeous Wyoming country-side, but he'd sat through so many viewings of the *Flicka* movies he could recite the unsophisticated dialogue in his sleep. But he continued watching Lianne's favorite flicks, knowing Wednesday family movie night was a beneficial form of therapy for their only daughter.

Last summer, shortly after the meteorite struck the Guidepost east meadow bearing the eggs of ancient creatures, Lianne experi-enced two terrifying close encounters with dinosaurs. The first occurred in the horse stables, when she was bitten on the leg by a Dromaeosaur hatchling. Two weeks later, in a wheat field at her aunt and uncle's farm in Shelby, she and her cousin Marnie had come face-to-face with a Triceratops, the animal getting close enough that Lianne could feel its warm breath against her thighs. A few nights after the second incident, Lianne's screaming nightmares began, keeping Bryan and Loretta up half the night. They'd sought help through a family psychologist in Browning. One of Dr. Helen Krickstad's first recommendations was weekly family movie view-ing. Appropriate movies for Lianne's impressionable young mind, the good doctor had told them. "Let your daughter select the movies," she'd said. Therefore Wednesday family movie night revolved around Lianne's greatest passion: horses. Lianne became obsessed with Flicka, the temperamental mustang mare that head-strong teen Katy McLaughlin tames and rides to glory, with a few bumps along the way.

Coupled with Lianne's twice weekly therapy sessions, it worked. Her nightmares ended. And the Gilliam popcorn fest was still going strong to this day. Bryan recognized it as good family bonding time, even though their two sons—Paul, seventeen and Ethan, nearly fifteen—had bowed out months ago when they couldn't watch their favorite gory horror flicks and violent action adventure thrillers. Bryan lamented the fact that he and Loretta were losing their boys to teenage independence, especially Paul, who was out tonight playing a gig with his increasingly popular rock band, Moonrise. Ethan was also out with his high school buddies on this first night of summer vacation. *All the more reason to keep Lianne close,* he thought. *It won't be long before she joins her brothers in wanting nothing to do with her stodgy old parents.*

But Gilliam family movie night had not been a continuous thing. The popcorn-fueled film night came to an abrupt halt last August 8, when Bryan lay in a hospital bed recovering from near fatal gunshot wounds. The entire Gilliam clan would be forever scarred by the tragedy that took place here nearly a year ago. Disturbing memories of that horrible day—the day of the ill-fated barbecue party he and Loretta had thrown for dozens of their friends—still haunted him. Terrorists from the Animal Emancipation Faction (AEF) had stormed the property, burning their farmhouse and outbuildings to the ground and setting free the ten dinosaurs being kept in Bryan's prehistoric zoo. He recalled the excruciating pain of being gunned down off the zoo's observation tower and tumbling into the Dromaeosaur enclosure. Twenty-three people died that day, Bryan coming close to joining them. Several of his Blackfoot friends and a wildlife biologist had been devoured by voracious carnivores on the loose. Bryan had seen his late brother-in-law Jimmy Enright—Loretta's older brother—dragged into the woods by a Tyrannosaurus Rex. Besides Bryan, seven others were seriously injured, requiring long hospital stays. He himself had remained in St. Patrick Hospital for a month, going through two grueling surgeries. Three months of punishing physical therapy followed. And Loretta and oldest son Paul had been hurt when their pickup crashed and rolled as they tried to flee an aggressive Dromaeosaur on the hunt. There had been no more Gilliam family movie nights until January of this year.

Yes, August 8 last year had certainly been a dark day of fire and smoke and the *pop-pop-pop* of automatic gunfire. The groan of industrial bulldozers on the move flattening zoo habitat fences and chilling animal howls and human screams still rang in his ears like a demented tinnitus. His two tours in Afghanistan had shown him some hellish, soul crushing shit, but that day of the barbecue was much worse because it was so intimately personal.

Loretta and the kids spent months in therapy with Dr. Helen Krickstad, with Bryan joining them after he recovered enough to attend. He recalled being heavily buzzed on painkillers during those sessions, his head and emotions drowned in a pharmaceutical stew. Life on the Guidepost—their 1,285-acre ranch on the southern edge of the Blackfeet Indian reservation—changed drastically. The family moved into The Cellar, the luxurious underground shelter that Bryan and Jimmy Enright had built after they returned from Afghanistan. The Cellar was the only structure not destroyed in the fire, and the Gilliams lived there until two months ago, when construction on their new farmhouse and barns was complete. It was a difficult time for all of them. All brought about by the fateful (fatalistic?) egg-bearing meteorite that struck the east pasture.

"Are you okay, Daddy?" he heard Lianne say. "You look sick."

Bryan looked up at the movie credits scrolling, embarrassed. He'd been lost in his gloomy thoughts again.

"I'm fine, Lee-lee," he said, caressing her hand and giving her a tight smile. "Just tired is all."

His kids worried about him, which he thought was sweet. But it also made him self-conscious, more aware of his current frailty.

You're fine now, right? he thought, not convincing himself. His battles with residual pain and inability to walk without his cane told him otherwise.

Only forty-three and feeling seventy-three on the bad days.

He snatched the remote off the coffee table and switched over to the TV from the DVD player. A news report was in progress A male reporter in his late thirties with slicked-back, pomaded hair and a fake tan sat behind a studio desk and spoke, his voice stern but carrying a lilt of hope:

". . . the photojournalist who went missing three days ago

was rescued earlier today in the outback of Idaho's Frank Church River of No Return Wilderness. As we reported in yesterday's broadcast, Jackson Lattimer, popularly known as America's Gonzo Shutterbug, is famed for his daring wildlife photoshoots. When he announced he was planning a quest to find Tyrannosaurus Rex in hazardous and untamed Idaho backcountry, many of his critics scoffed and predicted it would end badly. They were right. The expedition ended with the death of one of his crew. Milton Haynes, thirty-three and eight-year employee of Jackson Lattimer Images, was killed by a marauding T-Rex shortly after entering Moose Valley Cave. The San Francisco native is survived by his wife Connie and their two young children. We here at Boise KTVB Channel 7 News send our most sincere condolences and prayers to the Haynes family for their loss. Jackson Lattimer has also paid his respects to the family, saying his colleague was one of the best handheld nature videographers in the business and a dear friend whom he will miss dearly.

"Even though the loss of life is tragic, today we can be thankful for the rescue of Lattimer and his film crew colleague, Samuel Beeson. Both men were certain they were doomed to follow Haynes's plight. Lattimer will talk more about that in my exclusive interview with him. Lattimer succeeded in locating the mighty Cretaceous carnivore when so many have tried and failed. His finding is consequential. Many thought the Cretaceous creatures were finally gone. But no. The beasts are back! After a long absence during the frigid winter, these prehistoric invaders are coming out of hibernation and making a return appearance. And according to the astonishing video we are about to see, they are bigger than ever. Believe me, the footage is extraordinary. It's wildlife filmmaking at its finest . . ."

"Oh my god, here we go again," Loretta uttered as they watched.

Bryan shook his head. "You didn't really think they were gone for good, did you Lor?"

"I prayed those nasty animals were gone forever."

"Hayden and Nora said they were only shutting down for the winter. Look at the bright side. At least they're in Idaho and not on our property."

Lianne spoke up, her voice a frightened whisper. "Does this mean more of those meeteeyites have landed, Daddy?"

He peered down at her, gave her a gentle smile and touched her arm. "No, baby. No new meteorites. The man is talking about dinosaurs that hatched out of last summer's rocks."

"Oh. They killed that man. Just like what happened at our picnic last year."

"Okay, Lee," Loretta said, standing and grabbing her coffee mug. "It's time for us to go to bed, darlin'. We don't need to be watching any more of this."

"But it's still early, Mama. The man said they have video. I wanna see the dinosaurs!"

Loretta grabbed Lianne by the hand, pulled her up from the sofa. "No, Lee. C'mon, it's off to bed we go."

"No!" Lianne pulled her hand away and crossed her arms, planting herself on the sofa. "I'm staying to watch."

Bryan helped Loretta pry their recalcitrant daughter from the couch, his shoulder aching as he pulled at her. "C'mon, go with your mother, Lee. There's nothing you need to see here."

"No, I don't wanna go to bed. It's summer! It's too early."

Bryan said, "We watched your favorite movie and ate lots of delicious popcorn. So let's go . . . up with you," he said, pulling her up to a standing position, grimacing as his back cramped up on him. "Be sure to brush your teeth and wash your face. I'll be up shortly to tuck you in and kiss you goodnight."

He watched Loretta tug their complaining daughter up the stairs, listening to Lianne's grumbles of "It's not fair!" and "I'm not a child anymore."

After they disappeared, he returned his attention to the news-cast. They had just come back from a short commercial break and the reporter announced they would now show the "fascinating and frightening" video footage shot by Lattimer in the Moose Valley Cave, with a warning that some of the content could be disturbing for children.

Bryan watched as the first of the footage rolled. The lighting inside the cave was shaky, but Bryan could plainly see Lattimer's video framing a ragged clump of brush. He could clearly hear the three men trading ideas about what the pile of vegetation might be. He watched Lattimer putting on gloves and digging into the snarl. Heard the team's surprise at finding a nest of six brightly colored eggs, then saw one of the men pluck an egg out of the nest.

They're twice the size of the Dromaeosaur eggs we retrieved from our meteorite, Bryan thought. *Those blue and green swirling patterns are the same.*

The edited video quickly switched to a more stunning scene. He watched transfixed as big lumbering creatures appeared to be blind-ed by the bright spotlight shining in their scarlet eyes. Three of them stopped dead in their tracks, looking confused, their skimpy fore-limbs attempting to swat away the offensive light. They had to be eleven or twelve feet tall with broad breastbones. Enormous gaping mouths with jagged daggerlike teeth. The lead Rex clutched a bloody deer carcass in its mouth. Bryan could hear Lattimer's comments as he filmed: "Magnificent!" and "Splendid animals!"

They're much bigger and beefier than the pair of Tyrannosaurs we had in our zoo last year, he thought, shuddering.

And then the beasts were trudging forward. Some shouts about holding fire and standing down followed by explosive gunshots echoing off the cave walls. Shrieks from the creatures, one of them going down hard, hitting the rock floor with a sickening thump. The other two beasts charged the shooter—Milton Haynes—and made quick work of him. Lattimer recorded the other crewmember run-ning, then swung the camera back to the pair of T-Rexes feasting on Haynes before he took off sprinting himself, recording the action behind him as he ran. Then, thankfully, the screen went dark.

Bryan took a deep breath and tried to calm his nerves. The scene had evoked dreadful memories of last summer's barbecue in the east meadow.

The reporter was now interviewing Jackson Lattimer in front of St. Luke's Boise Medical Center, where the famous photographer had been treated and released at noon today. The gonzo shutterbug appeared to be late forties, maybe early fifties. He was lean and wiry with a ruddy complexion and strikingly blue eyes. Strong, square cleft chin. Hawk nose. Thick strands of dark shaggy hair draped his shoulders. His searching expression and excited, quick-tongued speech pegged him as an aging hippie adventurer.

"I'm happy you are alive and well, Mr. Lattimer. Please tell our viewers how you survived those Tyrannosaurs in the cave."

"Thank you. Yeah, so we really lucked out by having that cluster of boulders nearby. Sammy and I hid there, um, well, after my dear friend Milt went down. It's gonna take me a long while to get over that. But yeah, we ran there and slipped down inside where the beasts couldn't get at us. They tried, oh, man did they try. It was like a small cave. Really claustrophobic in there, I'm tellin' ya. Sammy called it a granite tomb and he wasn't exaggerating. Anyway, we could smell their fetid breaths as they snorted and huffed and sniffed and drooled, poking their big snouts into crevices, trying to get a piece of us. We were safe in there, but couldn't get any connectivity with my satellite phone. We knew we wouldn't be able to escape until they left the cave, which they didn't for nearly a full day. One of them always stayed put to guard their nest. It was close to eighteen hours before we were able to get out and radio for help. It was a terrifying ordeal as you can imagine . . ."

A faint humming noise drew Bryan's attention away from the TV. He sat up, cocked his head to the side, listened. Grabbed the remote and muted the audio.

The pulsating noise came from outside the house, the droning increasing in volume.

What the hell?

He stood, using his cane for support, his lower back and hips aching with the effort. He ambled down the hallway, going through the living room to the front door. Hand on the doorknob, he stopped, listened. Strong *wop-wop-wop* clatters cut through the hum.

A helicopter?

He opened the door and stepped out on the porch, the cool evening air making him shiver. He looked west, the snow-capped peaks of the Rockies lining the horizon. The navigation lights of an approaching helicopter lit up the dusky twilight sky. The chopper flew low, heading straight for Gilliam's Guidepost.

What is going on? he wondered, gazing at the approaching copter. The thumping rotor blades thudded in his ears, louder and louder, Bryan doing his best to fight off a headache.

The big chopper slowed as it came in over the house, the strong downdraft ruffling his sweatshirt. He spied the green and yellow **U.S. Forest Service—Department of Agriculture** crest on the fuselage as it flew over.

Is that Peter Lacroix?

Lacroix hadn't been to the Guidepost since the ill-fated barbecue last August.

Bryan watched the aircraft disappear over the roofline and descend behind the house, settling down in the quadrangle yard near the utility barn. He shuffled back inside, leaning heavily on his cane, bumping into a questioning Loretta in the hallway.

"What's going on, Bry? Is that a helicopter I'm hearing?"

"Yeah. I think it's Peter."

"Peter Lacroix?"

"Yeah," he said, moving past her.

"Are Brinshou and Kimi with him?" Loretta had befriended Peter's wife and their toddler daughter when they stayed here last summer while Brin worked for Bryan designing Cretaceous meteorite jewelry and trinkets. Loretta had fallen in love with sweet little

Kimi.

Bryan moved out into the sunroom, the helicopter landing lights reflecting off the glass. Loretta followed close behind.

"I don't know what's going on," he said over his shoulder. "Let's find out."

He hobbled out into the quad as the chopper powered down to a low idle, the noise level dropping a few decibels.

The cockpit door opened and Peter Lacroix stepped down, clutching a large canvas bag. "Fantastic! I'm glad I caught you at home, Bryan."

"Your odds were good. We don't get out much anymore."

"I hope I'm not dropping in too late."

Bryan checked his watch. "It's only a little past nine. We're not old geezers yet," he said with a laugh. "It's great to see you, Pete, but this is quite a surprise. What gives?"

Peter approached and set the bag down, gave Bryan a half-embrace man hug, then hugged Loretta. "You're both looking good," he said, Bryan thinking it was a goodhearted lie. "I wouldn't normally just drop in unannounced like this. I called you several times the past few days, Bryan, but I kept getting your voicemail. Did you get any of my messages?"

Bryan shook his head. "I keep my cell phone off most of the time. Not much need for it these days. Sorry about that." He looked down at the bag. "Whaddaya got there?"

Peter's eyes brightened. "Something I think you're gonna like a whole lot." He kneeled and yanked the drawstrings, opening the top. Pulled out a fist-sized obsidian rock.

"What is it?" Loretta asked.

"You don't recognize it?" Peter said to her.

"No."

"Well *I* do," Bryan said, a flutter of excitement rippling through his chest. He turned to Loretta. "It's Cretaceous meteorite rock, Lor. Where'd you get it, Pete?"

"Three-hundred miles south of here, in the Custer Gallatin National Forest. Just north of Yellowstone. We were inspecting a wildfire burn site when I spotted the meteorite, broken into thirds."

Peter emptied the contents of the bag. The half dozen black stones dusted with tiny sparkles spilled across the ground. "I couldn't believe it. There they were, perched high atop a bluff, looking like a charcoal Stonehenge. They're huge, too. Boulders really. Much bigger than the ones I picked up flying that Air Force operation last year."

Bryan leaned on his cane and bent over to pick up one of the stones. Flipped it over in his hand, examining it. "This is phenomenal, Pete. Looks like the real thing. But how can we be sure this is authentic Cretaceous stone?"

"Easy," Peter said, getting to his feet and reaching into his aviator bomber jacket pocket, pulling out his cell phone. "There are three-toed dino tracks leading away from hatchout crevices in the rocks," he said, swiping on his phone. "I took some pics. Here." He handed Bryan the phone. "Take a look."

Bryan scrolled through the photos, seeing shot after shot of dinosaur tracks around three huge wedges of black meteorite rock. "Pete, these tracks confirm it," he said, showing them to Loretta. "And those rocks? Holy shit! They dwarf the meteorite that hit our meadow last summer."

Peter reached inside his jacket and pulled out a couple of small, flat objects, held them out in front of him. "And these will confirm it beyond a doubt."

Bryan squinted, the dimming dusk light making it difficult to make out what the pilot held in his hands. "What are they?" he asked.

"Pieces of eggshells. *Dinosaur* eggs. I found a few of them scattered around the base of the rocks, at the bottom of the cracks where they hatched out."

Bryan handed Peter's phone back to him and moved in for a closer look. The egg shards were colored with bluish-green swirls. Greatly faded and diminished, but noticeable. A slow dizziness washed over him. He had just seen these same color-patterned eggs on tonight's news report. In video shot by that gonzo wildlife filmmaker.

"Um, I believe these are Tyrannosaurus Rex eggs, Pete."

"Huh? Why do you say that?"

"Because I just saw this very same egg on a news report not fifteen minutes ago. Some crazy ass photojournalist shot footage of T-Rexes in a cave in Idaho. He and his team found their nest. Their eggs look exactly like what you're holding."

"Wow! Really?" Peter said, staring at the shell fragments.

"Yep. The dinos are back, Pete."

Loretta spoke up. "What say we move this discussion inside, gentlemen. It's cold out here."

"Unfortunately I can't stay," Peter said. "We're overdue back at the base and I have a pilot trainee waiting on me in the bird."

"One last question before you fly off," Bryan said. "Why has nobody found this meteorite the past year?"

Peter leaned over and began stuffing the meteorite stones in the bag. "Because those rocks were well concealed in thick forestland until a wildfire exposed them."

"Well, why didn't firefighters see them?"

"Because they didn't know what to look for. The Air Force trained me to find dinosaur meteorites."

Bryan felt a thrill rise up in him. "Those rocks are a treasure, Pete," he said, referring to the public's insatiable demand for the Gilliam Cretaceous Stone line of jewelry and charms last summer. Bryan and Loretta had made a small fortune off the dinosaur meteorite that had crashed in their outlying pasture, with Bryan hiring his Blackfoot neighbors to churn out the merchandise to meet the demand. Anyone who was anyone (and who had the money) just had to have a piece of the famous prehistoric rock.

"Yeah, I'm aware of that," Peter said evenly. "I know those rocks are potentially worth a king's ransom." He held the canvas bag out to Bryan, urging him to take it.

"You're giving them to me?" Bryan said, surprised.

Peter nodded. "Consider this my partial payback for the meteorite rock I stole from you," he said, with regard to last summer, when he first visited Gilliam's Guidepost to pick up the Gilliam's meteorite per federal government orders. Peter had been flying for the Air Force in a failed meteorite recovery operation known as Operation Hot Rocks.

Bryan clasped the heavy bag against his chest. "You didn't steal from me, Pete. The U.S. government did."

"Even so, I was a player in that fiasco. Hence, my payback. That'll get you started making more of that beautiful jewelry."

"Well, thanks," Bryan said with a grin. He glanced at Loretta, who remained impassive, then turned back to the pilot. "Listen, is there any way of getting the rest of that rock back here to our ranch?"

"No easy way. It would be extremely difficult. That area is as wild as the Amazon jungle. Completely inaccessible. There are no roads in. And hiking in is impossible as trails are few and far between. I'm sure those rocks weigh in at a ton or more each and they're entrenched deep in hardened marl and limestone. The only way to yank them out and transport them is with a heavy-lift chopper. We have one of those in our Missoula fleet—a Sikorsky Skycrane—but my superiors would never sign off on it. Or if they did, they would turn all the rock over to the appropriate federal agency. My employer is by-the-book big government all the way."

Bryan nodded, thinking, finally saying, "What if we went in with a regular helicopter and took them out in smaller chunks? You know, bring the meteorite back here in pieces?"

Peter stared at him for a long moment and Bryan wondered what was going through the pilot's mind. Finally Peter said, "It could be done, yes. But it still requires a chopper and the Montana Forest Service would never go for it."

"So, let's get us our own chopper then."

Peter laughed loudly. "Do you have any idea how much a helicopter costs?"

"Not really, no."

"Even a small ultralight eggbeater starts at thirty-five grand. And they're not safe. To get a decent, airworthy craft to do what you want? We're talking, minimum, hundreds of thousands. More realistically, seven figures."

"What about rentals?"

"They're around three- to four-hundred an hour."

"Now you're talkin'."

"But you'd still need a pilot, Bryan."

"Well, you're a pilot, Pete. And a damned good one at that. And you know right where the goodies are."

"*Bryan!*" Loretta warned, taking his hand in hers. "I think we should let Pete get back to Missoula. It's late and I'm sure Brin wants her husband home with her and Kimi."

Peter turned and walked back to the chopper. Opened the cockpit door and stepped up, plopped into his seat.

Bryan yelled out, "I'll call you in the next couple of days, Pete. I've got some ideas I'd like to run by you."

"Okay, I look forward to it," Peter said, pulling the door shut.

Bryan watched the main rotor rev. The engine whine escalated into a roar. The helicopter lifted, rising above the quad and disappeared over the roof.

Loretta pulled him back into the sunroom. A hard, angry tug.

She faced him. Twin fires flamed in her eyes. "Now you listen to me, Bryan Richard Gilliam. I will *NOT* go through this with you again this year! I saw those entrepreneurial wheels turning in your head out there. Last year you dragged our entire family into your stupid dinosaur zoo scheme. You saw how well that worked out for us, didn't you? Now you're talkin' crazy smack, trying to recruit Pete Lacroix to fly some ridiculous meteorite missions. It's fucking insane, Bry! You're in no condition to be flying out into the wilderness to retrieve a bunch of rocks. Didn't you learn anything last summer? Jesus! Don Quixote has nothing on you!"

Bryan pulled away. "You misunderstood, Lor. I wouldn't be flying out with Pete. I'd hire him and a small team to do the work."

"With what money? The kids' college funds?" she said, glaring at him, her breaths coming hard and fast.

"Oh don't try to pin that on me, Loretta. You know I would never touch their college money. I'm talkin' about the insurance money."

"Most of that went to rebuilding the Guidepost. And to grieving Blackfoot families."

"Your accounting methods are suspect, oh dear wife of mine.

Last I checked we still have a substantial amount in savings. And Atlee assures me that—"

"Oh, Atlee Pinnaker can kiss my ass, Bryan! Our so-called blue-chip attorney's been promising us a multimillion-dollar settlement from the AEF for nine months now. I'm beginning to think we'll never see a penny from that shyster!"

"I just spoke with Atlee yesterday. The lawsuit is finally being presented next week," Bryan said calmly, trying to get the conversation on an even keel. "He guarantees a quick and generous settlement."

"Well goody-goody hot shit for Atlee!" Loretta shook her head in dismay. "Haven't you heard the old proverb about counting your chickens before they hatch?"

Bryan sighed, tired of his wife's lecture. "Of *course* I have, but—"

"But *what*, Bryan?" she huffed, glaring at him. "You're looking at spending tens of thousands—shit, *hundreds* of thousands—of dollars chasing another of your goddamned idiotic pipe dreams. It's money we don't have. So I say fuck you, Bryan! I'm sick of your pointless fanciful dreams. I won't be a part of another one."

They both noticed Lianne standing in the doorway, dressed in her horse-patterned pajamas, staring at them with a look of wounded fragility.

How long has she been watching us? Bryan wondered. *Did she hear everything?*

"Are you okay, Mama?"

Loretta flushed, embarrassed, then recovered. "Mommy's fine, Lee-lee," she said, pulling the girl into her arms. "C'mon, let's you and I go to bed, sweetheart."

Bryan watched his wife and daughter leave the sunroom, Lianne weepy and teary-eyed. He felt hollowed out and defeated, emasculated. A mere shell of the man he was just an hour ago.

Loretta used to tell him she was his dreamcatcher.

Apparently she had given up catching his dreams.

What's Love
Got To Do with It?

June 7: Eden Prairie, Minnesota

SHE WRAPPED HER ARMS AROUND HIM under the tangle of damp sheets. Tried to catch her breath in a bedroom smelling of perspiration and sex. Once again, Hayden had sent her to the moon and back with his skillful lovemaking. Nora had climaxed so hard she was still trembling.

"Wow, my man sure knows how to please a lady," she sighed, running her fingers through his thick beard.

"Your G spot *est mon ami.*" He smiled through labored breaths.

"My G spot is your friend? Really, Hayden?"

"*Et tu te plains?*"

"You're going to have to translate that one for me, dearest."

"I said, 'And you complain?' "

She laughed. Since they had returned from their Paris trip a month ago, Hayden had taken to rattling off clips of French. Nora got a kick out of the way he mangled all the romance out of the language. He had also become fond of wearing a red beret, rakishly tilted to one side. His new French schtick persona was ridiculous but somehow endearing.

He continued. "I'm well versed in the Gräfenberg spot, better known as the excitable G spot. I've studied it almost as much as I've studied Cretaceous creatures."

She gave him a mocking smile. "Should I thank all those young trophy sluts you've slept with over the years for your expertise?"

"There's some truth to that. And to think, when we first met you reprimanded me for my playboy lifestyle. *Tu m'as apprivoisé,* Nora."

"Translation please?"

"It means you tamed me. You've tamed the wild stallion in me."

"Impossible. There's no taming Hayden Fowler."

"Well *you* have. How about taming me some more," he said, slinking beneath the sheets. His voice was muffled. "Let's see if I can make your G spot sing again."

"God, Hayden," she said, feeling him between her legs, his beard tickling her thighs. "You've got to be the horniest forty-eight-year-old man on the planet."

"*Et tu te plains?*"

She smiled widely and closed her eyes as he sent her rocketing to the moon again.

Nora Lemoyne met Hayden Fowler last year. She had come to this very house in the Minneapolis suburbs to recruit the well-known author/paleontologist for the Smithsonian Paleo Expedition team that she was heading up At a beefy six-foot-four with wild mountain man hair and untamed beard, he was physically imposing to a petite woman like Nora. She remembered her apprehension about meeting the man she had idolized since her college days as a Paleontology and Evolutionary Biology grad student at the University of Michigan. His bestselling books, *Ancient Life, Final Strife* and *Interpreting Cretaceous Fossils,* had a huge influence on her. She had referenced those texts liberally in her graduate dissertation, and recalled her stupid fangirl crush on the man the scientific community called The Boy Wonder of Paleontology. She would gaze at his dust jacket photo like a schoolgirl in hormonal heat, which was completely absurd with him being just three years her senior. But last summer, twenty years later, the boy wonder was known for his drinking and womanizing more than his dinosaur knowledge. She'd had major concerns over how he might behave around several beautiful young college interns she had hired on for the Montana excursion. Then again, he was a preeminent paleontological scholar who specialized in the Late Cretaceous. Having Hayden Fowler on her team would give the expedition major credibility. She remembered his excited look when she asked him to join her dig team, with a warning that she would not stand for any funny business on the two month expedition. He had eagerly accepted her offer and agreed to behave himself.

The first week out in Choteau, Hayden went back on his word, getting rip-roaring drunk on the job. Nora read him the riot act, threatening to send him back to Minnesota if he misbehaved again. Her extreme dressing down of him in her trailer that early June night was a turning point in their relationship. He walked the straight and narrow after that. He quit drinking and didn't bother the young girls on the expedition. He started looking at Nora with a newfound respect, acting more gentlemanly around her. Gradually his arrogance softened, though he still maintained an unfiltered directness. Surprisingly, his no-beating-around-the-bush approach and naughty charm turned her on. Increasingly she found herself enjoying being with him.

It was all innocent coworker infatuation at first. But then things escalated. Shocking as it was to her at the time, their relationship exploded into incendiary red-hot couplings when the Smithsonian moved them off the paleontology dig and reassigned them to duties as dinosaur trackers. They were joined at the hip pursuing Dromaeosaurs and T-Rexes and Triceratops through northwestern Montana, shooting video footage and compiling data on the creatures. They even captured a few animals, transporting them to the Gilliam ranch in Heart Butte, which had become dinosaur central, where the creatures were kept in natural habitat pens and studied by teams of wildlife scientists.

Hayden made a few bold passes at her before she gave in. They started sleeping together in hotel rooms, Hayden saying they needed to share a room (and a bed) to cut down on travel expenses. They both knew the Smithsonian was paying for their accommodations. Nora had laughed, but went along. After that first night they'd slept together, "cutting down on road expenses" became a running joke between them.

And then fate took them to the tragic July 4th Livingston Roundup Rodeo, where a pack of Tyrannosaurs invaded the fairgrounds as the fireworks show concluded, slaughtering dozens of rodeo fans. She and Hayden had witnessed the grisly feeding frenzy from the top rows of the spectator stands. And the fickle finger of fate also took them to the horrific AEF terrorist attack on Gilliam's Guidepost. August 8 was a day she would never forget: hard-charging gunmen and powerful bulldozers, escaped dinosaurs, torched buildings, Gilliam partygoers running for their lives. Nora and Hayden had viewed the mayhem from a helicopter, with gunmen shooting at them from the ground.

Yes, it had been a crazy, insane year. She had experienced many highs and lows—days of whimsical, dreamlike fantasy punctuated with shocking nightmarish events. Strange scientific phenomena. Egg-bearing meteorites. A return of the dinosaurs. Lots of mind-blowing sex. Human tragedy on a ultraviolent scale. Highest of highs and lowest of lows. As fate would decree, she and Hayden had been there from the very beginning (the Gilliam meteorite) witnessing one of the most earthshattering happenings in modern history.

She still didn't understand how it came to be that they were the chosen ones. Them and the Gilliams.

All of it led to Nora selling her house in Wisconsin and moving to Minnesota to live in Eden Prairie with Hayden.

The highpoint of her past year had been the lucrative book deal she and Hayden had signed with Penguin-Random House to write of their dino tracking experiences. Their book, *Cretaceous Stones: The Return of Prehistoric Life to Earth,* published in mid-March, was still number one on all the important bestseller lists (*New York Times, USA Today, Publishers Weekly, Booklist, Amazon*). Nora recalled with fondness all the eager fans they had met on their three-week, whirlwind book tour, even though Hayden seemed put off by all the attention. The book's generous advance had made them both a lot of money, more money than Nora had ever seen during her globetrotting paleontology career. And there was more wealth headed their way. Hayden's old literary agent, Henry Wycliff, told them that with sales booming the way they were, they would start seeing very large royalty checks soon.

The popularity of *Cretaceous Stones* earned them a second co-authored book, which Nora was having difficulty getting a jump on. She and Hayden had poured all of their dinosaur experiences into the first book and there wasn't much material left over. They needed new experiences to write about, which was difficult since the creatures had been dormant and out of sight over the long winter and uncommonly cold spring. All she had managed to come up with to this point was a working title: *Dragons of the Great Divide: Running with the Cretaceous Beasts.* The Great Divide was a popular name for the Continental Divide, the long stretch along the Rockies running through Idaho and Montana where the dinosaur meteorites had struck and unleashed their invasive cargo. Hayden didn't like her title and they had argued over it a few weeks ago:

"I like the Great Divide. But *Dragons*? Come on, Nora, our dinos are not mythical fire breathing beasts. They're real zoological animals."

"It's metaphorical, Hayden," she'd said, feeling the need to defend her title.

"No. It sounds too much like a medieval fantasy novel." He laughed. "Even worse, *Dragons of the Great Divide* could be a book about our dysfunctional U.S. Congress."

She laughed with him. "You're quick, Hayden. I'll give you that. But I like that title and until you come up with something better, I'm keeping it."

And so far he hadn't suggested anything to change her mind.

As to new content for the second book, Nora was becoming more optimistic. The Jackson Lattimer video shoot in Idaho was all over the news the past few days, showing spectacular footage of the three Tyrannosaurs he and his team encountered deep in a cave. Hayden had called Lattimer's company Wednesday, interested in joining the gonzo photojournalist on a return trip to the River of No Return Wilderness area. Lattimer had been unavailable and Hayden didn't want to go into details without speaking with him directly. The young woman answering the phone told him Mr. Lattimer was very busy after his rescue and that she personally had taken more than forty calls the past two days. And there had been a few sightings. Hunters had reported seeing Dromaeosaurs in Lolo National Forest and farmers had scared off Triceratops rooting through their wheat fields east of Great Falls. The dinosaurs were entering their post-winter phase as the weather warmed, just the way Hayden predicted.

She looked over at him, asleep now, mouth wide open, emitting a rumbling snore every third breath. Without her glasses, Hayden's form was a blur, looking like a big brown bear that had buried itself under the covers. This man who had been a big part of her life the past year excited her. He stimulated her intellectually and made life interesting. He challenged her and was generally a lot of fun to be around. There was no denying any of that.

But do I love him?

Or is this another in my long line of bad relationship decisions?

At age forty-five, Nora's romantic résumé was littered with failures. Two marriages leading to two acrimonious divorces. Another long-term love affair gone bad after a few years. A therapist once told her she had intimacy issues. She didn't agree. She could be plenty intimate with the male of the species. She took great pleasure in pleasing her man. Nora *liked* men. She just didn't know if she could ever fully *love* a man. She had told Hayden she loved him. But was it true? Was she lying to him? To herself? She had long thought the concept of love to be a mental disease, an act of temporary insanity. They called it *falling* in love, not *rising up* in love. Falling, as though descending into a deep, dark abyss. Perhaps her pessimistic view of love derived from some deep-seated emotional flaw. Maybe her twisted perception of love was a form of quiet selfishness. Regardless, Nora didn't care to examine it too closely for fear of hating herself. Hayden Fowler certainly loved her. He made that abundantly clear on a daily basis. He'd even asked for her hand in marriage twice before she convinced him that marriage was definitely not in her future. Even if she had been interested, Nora knew Hayden's three divorces made him a terrible spousal candidate.

So nobody was more shocked than her when she pulled up stakes in Whitefish Bay, Wisconsin, to move to Eden Prairie and cohabitate with Hayden. Never in her life had she done anything so impulsive.

But as confused as she was about Hayden, their week together in Paris rekindled some of the heat from the early days of their relationship. Hayden had presented the European vacation to her at the end of their book tour as a celebration of their publishing success. He organized the trip, making all the reservations. Paid for everything. She remembered the glint in his eyes as he flashed her the plane tickets. Her heart had swelled. As much traveling as Nora had done during her career, she had never been to The City of Lights, or as Hayden had whispered in his uncooperative French tongue: *La Ville Lumiér*.

They stayed in a deluxe suite in the gorgeous Hôtel San Régis in the Golden Triangle of the Champs Elysées district. Nora was enchanted with its luxurious Egyptian cotton bedsheets and richly textured silk spreads, Louis XVI period furniture, Italian marble bathroom, and porcelain and crystal objects of art. They had done the touristy things—Eiffel Tower, the Arc de Triomphe, Montmartre, the Louvre, Jim Morrison's tomb (Hayden's request). They took a *bateaux-mouche* (flea boat) cruise down the Seine. They drank fine wines in Parisian bistros and dined like a king and queen in prestigious Left Bank restaurants. They picnicked along the river at Pont des Arts in the 6th arrondissement and walked hand-in-hand along the Seine at midnight. And they screwed like rabbits in heat the entire week. The romantic Parisian air and bright nightlife worked on Nora like a strong aphrodisiac.

By the end of the week, she thought she might actually be in love with Hayden Fowler.

Whatever love was.

Hayden's cell phone blared from the night table, the crunching chords of Metallica's "Enter Sandman" startling her.

He came awake, bleary-eyed, confused. Grabbed the phone, checked the display. "Unknown caller," he said to her. "Hello?"

Call of the Wild

June 7: Eden Prairie, Minnesota

"IS THIS HAYDEN FOWLER, THE PALEONTOLOGIST? The famous bestselling author?"

The voice was gruff, unfamiliar to him. "If you are a politician calling for a campaign donation or the IRS, it's not me. Anybody else, then yes it's me," he said, glancing at the wall clock, wondering who would be calling him this late. He saw Nora grinning.

The caller laughed. "Jackson Lattimer here, returning your call."

"Oh, yes, hi, Mr. Lattimer."

"It's *Jack*, please. Sorry for my delay in getting back to you, but I've been quite busy, as I'm sure you can imagine."

"Yes, I can. That's quite an ordeal you went through in Idaho. I've seen your video and watched you on TV doing interviews."

"Yeah, the goddamned newshounds won't leave me alone for a New York minute. They're hardcore stalkers, every last one of 'em."

"Oh, I know that all too well, Jack. Sorry to learn about the loss of your crewmember."

"Thanks. Milty had been with me many years. I miss him dearly. So tragic, Hayden. May I call you Hayden?"

"I've been called much worse."

"Haven't we all? The press still refers to me as America's Gonzo Shutterbug fer Chrissakes. Anything to sell magazines or boost ratings."

"So true."

"So what can I do for you, Hayden?"

Hayden thought about how to word it so he wouldn't come off

sounding like a stalker. Decided to just go for it. "I was hoping we could connect and hit the caves where you filmed those Tyrannosaurs. There's so much more research I want to do on those Rexes and there hasn't been any sign of them for eight months until now. I'm climbing the walls here at home, itching to get back in the game. You seem to have found a Tyrannosaurus Rex breeding ground."

"Yeah. We struck gold finding that nest. I knew those eggs were not of this world."

"You're right. I saw your photos of them. They were twice the size of the Dromaeosaur eggs we hatched out in a chicken incubator at the Gilliam ranch. That was quite a find, Jack. Tells me we're in for a lot more T-Rex hatchlings this summer."

"Yeah, we are. They're quite impressive animals, Hayden. And that area is crawling with them. We saw at least a half dozen more of the big bastards when we were airlifted out of there. None of that footage made this week's newscasts. I'm holding it back for the TV special I'm planning."

"Your video showed them to be much larger than the two we studied in captivity last year. I'm curious as to what they've been eating over the long winter."

"I don't know, but there's something in those caves that attracts them. Maybe they see caves as protective enclosures? A fortress so to speak. Or possibly they've found a subterranean food source we don't know about? All I know for sure is your book pointed me in the right direction. You were spot on about winter hibernation."

"You read my book?" he said, seeing Nora frowning at him. "*Our* book, I mean."

"Of course I did, Who hasn't?"

"Well, it's mostly Nora's book," Hayden said, winking at Nora. "It's her prose that made it a bestseller." She smiled at him.

"I enjoyed reading about your dinosaur chasing adventures. I learned a lot, too. You and Ms. Lemoyne have certainly earned your stellar reputations in the scientific community. Especially now that you are official Smithsonian dinosaur trackers. Am I to understand you're writing a followup book?"

"Yeah, but we're off to a sluggish start. Nothing much new to report. That's why I want to take a trek with you out to Rex country. I want to monitor their mating habits, their diets in the wild, check out those cave habitats. Much of what we covered in *Cretaceous Stones* was observation of them in captivity where they lived on processed meat byproducts. I'm surprised they ate that shit, to be honest. At any rate, it's not an authentic take on wild animals. Especially prehistoric creatures."

"Believe it or not, Hayden, I was planning on contacting you about this very thing."

"What? You mean about me accompanying you in Idaho?"

"Yes. I could use someone with your dinosaur expertise in the field. And, no offense intended, but you could use a professional videographer. I checked out some of your footage on YouTube. It's cool but a little shaky."

The comment rankled Hayden a bit, but he said, "Well, I'll never have your steady hand under fire. But trust me, I have a much steadier hand and accurate aim shooting tranquilizer darts."

"That'll come in handy," Jackson responded. "I plan to make another trip to Idaho in three weeks. I've got another project contracted I have to do first—a trip to Northern Australia to photograph saltwater crocodiles. Up close and personal. The Adelaide River is teeming with twenty-foot sea crocs. I'm excited about it, but I'm also eager to get back to filming Mr. Rex. As you've pointed out, there are many unanswered questions."

"So, is it a go? You and me to Idaho?"

"Yes, absolutely, Hayden. But I must warn you, things can get pretty dicey in those caves."

"So I saw. I faced some intense situations last year. I can handle it."

"I believe you can. Ordinarily I balk at taking on outsiders, but you have major field cred. After reading your book I feel we'd make a good team. But there's one thing that might make you reconsider."

"Oh? What's that?"

"Those caves are in some of the most isolated areas of the U.S. It's a minimum three-day hike in. And that's moving at a rapid pace. Very grueling and dangerous. Snakes and bears and the occasional mountain lion. Not to mention carnivorous dinosaurs."

Hayden thought a minute before answering. He wasn't keen on hiking miles through unforgiving wilderness and risking his life needlessly. "I might have a solution to that, Jack."

"Hit me with it."

"I'm good friends with a Montana forestry helicopter pilot. Maybe he'd be willing to take us in close and set us down near the caves."

"Are you familiar with the Frank Church River of No Return Wilderness Area, Hayden?"

"Only what I've seen on a map. It's pretty big."

"That's a massive understatement. It's two-and-a-half million acres of the most rugged terrain you can imagine. Every acre of it is federally protected, and as such, there are rigid restrictions about aircraft flying over, and into, that expanse. Aircraft of any type must land at, and take off from, FAA designated airstrips, which are far and few between. The closest one to our T-Rex caves is the Mahoney Airstrip, a USDA Forest Service base. It's thirty-three miles away. Hence the need for our long hike to those cave networks. There are severe penalties for touching down in non-designated areas, so unless your helicopter friend wants to risk losing his pilot license by breaking federal aerial laws, he won't be of much use to us."

"My friend has been known to be a renegade. He might be willing to get us closer."

"Is that the same pilot you wrote about in your book?"

"Yeah, Peter Lacroix."

"And you said he flies for the U.S. Forest Service?"

"Yeah."

"Where does he fly out of?

"Missoula."

"Well then, I doubt his employer would authorize him flying into Idaho unless there was a wildfire or rescue that Boise couldn't handle. Plus he'd be a fool to jeopardize his job with a crazy stunt."

"No disrespect, Jack, but I thought you were the king of crazy stunts."

"That's just puffery the media slings. I follow all laws and regulations. I pay my taxes on time. My crazy extends only to filming dangerous wildlife. That's my jam."

Hayden pulled at his beard, thinking.

Jackson said, "Look, that hike is a really tough slog. I'm guessing we're both about the same age. How is your fitness level?"

"I don't know. I guess I'm in decent shape for someone fast approaching fifty."

"You guess? Not good enough, Hayden. When I'm not on assignment I follow a regimented workout routine. I demand all of my employees do the same. My work requires physical strength and endurance, and I don't want any weaklings along who can't handle the stress."

"I am *not* a weakling."

"I'm not saying you are. But I do think you'd be better prepared if you came out to my ranch in Jackson Hole and worked with my trainer for a week."

"Oh, I don't know about that, Jack. Nora and I have a lot of work to do on the new book. Is the training a prerequisite?"

"In your case, no. I'd be willing to accept knowledge and experience over conditioning. You've already faced these beasts head on."

"I have at that. Okay, let me think it over and talk with my pilot friend. I'll get back to you in a few."

"Sure thing. I'd love to have you on my crew. Your knowledge of Tyrannosaurus Rex might keep us out of trouble. Good talkin' with you."

Hayden disconnected and set his phone aside.

"What's the deal?" Nora asked from her side of the bed. "What's this about not being a weakling?"

"Apparently there's a long-ass hike to and from the caves. There'd be a week of camping in remote areas getting in and out. Jack suggested I spend a week at his Wyoming ranch going through physical training exercises."

"Hmmm. What was that about Peter Lacroix being a renegade?"

He told her about the firm restrictions landing aircraft in that area. "None of the designated airstrips are close to where we need to go. I told Jackson that Lacroix might . . . well, you heard what I said. If I know Pete, he enjoys a good challenge. He might not even know about those laws."

"I'm sure he does. After all, he flies for the U.S. Forest Service. But if he doesn't know about them, you'd have to tell him."

"We'll see. I'm going to call him tomorrow, discuss it with him."

"You haven't spoken with him since we had dinner with him and Brin at their home. That's been what? Three months?"

"More like four. We were in Missoula the beginning of February."

"And you actually think the Forest Service will let him take a chopper out on a mission like that? Chasing after man-eating T-Rexes in the wild?"

"No I don't."

She regarded him warily. "You mean this Jackson Lattimer character wants to return to the place where his colleague was killed? Where *he* came close to dying?"

"Yeah, Jack is hot to trot. But he's got an Australia trip first."

She shook her head, looking at him doubtfully. "Jackson sounds like a jack*ass*! The man is cray-cray gonzo for sure."

He smiled at her. "People have said the same about us, Nora. He's just obsessed with his work. It's what makes him so good."

"You're not going, Hayden. It's a risk you don't need to take. Besides, I'm quite sure the Smithsonian would never approve of it. In case you've forgotten, we still work for them. They insure us."

"I realize that. But I also know our publisher wants a new book, and at the moment we are lacking content."

"Book content won't mean squat if you're dead, darling."

"You're exactly right, milady Lemoyne. Which leads me to letting you in on something I've been researching since we got back from Paris. Something that will give us more control over our tracking and getting the content we need to flesh out another book."

She sat up in bed, grabbed her eyeglasses from the night table.

"Something safer than going to Idaho with Jackson the jackass?"

"Yes." He looked at the bedside clock. "It's late and there's a lot to go into. Are you sure you want to discuss it tonight?"

"Absolutely," Nora said, getting out of bed and putting on her bathrobe and house slippers. "I'll meet you in the kitchen with a fresh pot of coffee.

They talked into the wee hours of the night, Hayden laying out his business plan and Nora asking the occasional question. When they were done, they went back to bed and made love until the sun came up.

Exemplary Behavior and Aviation Startups

June 8: The Lacroix Residence
Missoula, Montana

PETER SAT AT THE KITCHEN TABLE next to Brinshou. Brin's mother, Kachina, sat across from them with Kimi beside her, elevated in her booster seat. Brin had picked up their dinner at Doc's Gourmet Sandwich Shop after she left work at her downtown jewelry boutique: Brinshou's Baubles & Jewelry. Doc's was a favorite Lacroix family eatery that offered sandwiches named after celebrities, both real and fictional. Peter enjoyed his Dr. Frankenstein (roast beef, turkey, ham, and salami piled thick on a French roll), and Brin her Dr. Ruth egg salad. Kachina nibbled on her Dr. Albert Einstein tuna sandwich while trying to control Kimi's out of control eating routine. As per usual, Peter and Brin's two-year-old daughter was enjoying making a mess. She had flung her sweet potato tots and chicken pasta everywhere. Cranberry juice dribbled from her sippy cup and down her chin. Her white bib looked like a modern art painting gone bad.

Today being Saturday, Peter had the day off. He'd spent hours perusing job sites looking for piloting opportunities, carefully deleting the search history from his laptop so Brin wouldn't discover his desire for new employment. He'd applied to two companies. The first excited him. It was right here in Missoula. Minuteman Aviation was looking for Bell 407 pilots. Full time. Utility flying and firefighting work that included prescribed burning. Vertical reference/longline experience. Full health insurance with dental, vision, and life insurance. Retirement account.

Year-end bonus. It was a perfect fit and Peter felt a wave of new hope wash over him when he sent his application. He'd also applied to Central Copters in Belgrade, a company looking for a UH-60 utility helicopter pilot. Requirements were 2,500 hours of flight experience and precision longline piloting skills. Check. Duties included power line patrol, crew transport, and wildland fire suppression. He checked those boxes as well. The big negative was the location; he didn't want to uproot his family and move three hours away to Belgrade. Brin had a successful business here and he loved life in Missoula. But he applied anyway to see what kind of response he would get.

He didn't dare say anything to Brin about it. His beautiful wife suffered from anxiety and she already had a lot to deal with. They had just learned six weeks ago she was pregnant with their second child.

"Anything new at work?" he asked her.

Brin nodded, swallowing her egg salad. "We got a large order for our engraved sterling eagle cuff bracelets today. From a big retailer."

"Who was that?"

"A dealer selling on Etsy. They've bought from us before. Mostly Salish beaded brooches and pendants. This is the first time they've ordered bracelets."

"So business is good then?"

"It's been steady. But I don't think we'll ever reach the kind of numbers we did when we first opened and had a good supply of that Cretaceous meteorite stone."

Peter thought about the dinosaur meteorite he and Rob Winkle had found near Yellowstone. He hadn't told Brin about it for fear she would get her hopes up about obtaining more of the profitable rock for her business. He wasn't sure yet whether he'd be able to help Gilliam retrieve any more of it.

He watched Brin finish her sandwich and chips. He couldn't get over how beautiful she was, with her dark Kootenai features. Long coal-black hair that traversed her back to her waist. Smoky, sensual eyes like a pair of buttered chocolates. Chiseled cheekbones. Full mouth with large straight teeth that gleamed against silken cocoa-brown skin. A dazzling smile. He'd known she was the one the first time he laid eyes on her. Nearly eight years ago now, in the Shore-line Smokehouse, a popular BBQ restaurant on Flathead Lake. Brin was waitressing there, serving him and a few fellow helicopter pilots. They were doing U.S. Forest Service water collection train-ing on the lake and just happened to stop in for lunch that day. One glance at Brinshou Taleka was all it took to win his heart. And she was even more beautiful now that she was pregnant. It might just be Peter's imagination, but he thought she was positively glowing the past few weeks.

These past eight years with Brinshou had been the best years of his life. The Brin years even topped the five years he'd skated as a top prospect in the Toronto Maple Leafs organization. Playing hockey in the high minor leagues of a National Hockey League franchise certainly had its benefits, but nothing could compare with the highs he felt when he was with Brin. He'd been thirty, she twenty-two, when they met that momentous day at the Shoreline Smokehouse. He was less than six months into his new career as a helicopter pilot and past the two knee surgeries that had prematurely ended his hockey career. This gorgeous Kootenai woman, Brinshou Taleka, had captivated him from the beginning, and still did to this day.

Kimi had lapsed into fussy mode, flinging bits of food around and exhorting "Boom-boom" with each toss. Kachina removed Kimi's bib and grabbed a sponge and towel, started cleaning up around her granddaughter's place.

"What'd you do on your day off, Petey?" Brin asked.

"Oh, I read a little and watched the Mariners game." It wasn't a lie. He had the Seattle-New York Yankees game on as he searched the internet for work.

"Are you still reading that book about the helicopter pilot?"

"Yeah, I am," he said, embarrassed about the length of time he was spending on it. For the past two weeks Peter had been chipping away at a book he'd picked up in Fact and Fiction, his favorite used bookstore located near Brin's shop downtown. *Heart of the Storm:*

My Adventures as a Helicopter Rescue Pilot and Commander by Colonel Edward Fleming had caught his interest, but he was having difficulty concentrating on his reading lately, being preoccupied as he was with his job woes.

"Ice cweam, ice cweam!" Kimi suddenly screamed at ear-piercing levels while pounding her plastic spoon against the table. "I want ice cweam, gwanny! Gimme ice cweam, gwanny!"

"Settle down, Kimi," Brin said, raising her voice over the din. "Your grandmother isn't your slave, you know."

Dutifully, Kachina put a fresh bib on Kimi and went to the fridge. She pulled the tub of strawberry ice cream from the freezer and spooned two scoops into a bowl, set it in front of the child. The kitchen quieted. Strawberry ice cream worked on Kimi like a strong sedative.

Kachina sat back down. They all silently watched Kimi shovel ice cream into her mouth, strawberry streaks staining her bib. Peter wondered if he was that sloppy when he was a toddler.

Out of the blue, Kachina said, "I heard from him yesterday."

Brin said, "Who, Mom?"

"Nashota. Your father."

Brin huffed. "He stopped being my father the day I saw him hit you. Actually long before that."

The mention of Nash Taleka's name made Peter tense up. "I thought he was in jail."

"He was," Kachina said. "But Lake County Jail has an over-crowding issue and they let out some of the inmates who had lesser offenses. As Nash told me, *Those of us showing exemplary behavior.*"

"Exemplary behavior?" Peter said, astonished. "Since when is assault considered good behavior or a lesser offense?"

"I know, I know," Kachina said. "He also told me the casino gave him his old job back."

"*What?*" Peter was aghast. "Jesus! There's no such thing as accountability anymore. And I suppose he's demanding that you go back to Polson to live with him, right?"

Kachina hesitated, then said, "Well, not really *demanding,* but—"

"I think we need to cut this conversation short," Brin said, nodding at Kimi, who had finished her ice cream and watched them with wide-eyed curiosity.

Peter was raging inside. There had been bad blood between him and Brin's father for years. Nash had made it clear he didn't think Peter was good enough for his daughter, which boiled down to Peter not being of Salish or Kootenai heritage. The man was a hateful misogynist racist who had been locked up last year after attacking Kachina, his third domestic assault charge against his wife in six months.

Exemplary behavior my ass!

Peter's phone buzzed on the table. He looked at the display. Hayden Fowler's name and number appeared.

"Hey, Hayden," he said, standing and moving out of the kitchen and into the living room. "Long time no hear." He plopped down on the couch.

"Yeah, I know. Sorry for being a stranger, my friend. How's that lovely wife of yours? I hear you guys are preggers."

"Where'd you hear that?"

"Nora talks with Brin on a regular basis."

"Oh, right. Brin's doing fine, thanks for asking. She's nine weeks along and working six days a week at her jewelry shop."

"Good to hear. And you, Pete? You still flying the friendly skies of Montana?"

"Sure am."

"Are you happy there?"

"Why would you ask me that?"

"Well, because I have a business proposition for you."

"Oh? What kind of business proposition, Hayden?"

"How would you like to fly for Fowler-Lemoyne Aviation?"

"What the hell are you talking about?"

"Nora and I have a lot of money coming in from our book sales and our employment with the Smithsonian. We're looking for sound investments."

"So you're starting up an airline?"

"Not an airline. A helicopter service. And we want you as our lead pilot."

"Wow! This is crazy, Hayden. Are you being serious right now? I know how you like practical jokes."

"This is no joke. Nora and I can't cover our dinosaur tracking territory on the ground anymore. Takes too much time and energy. We need air access. Helicopter access. Whaddaya say?"

Peter was stunned by this development. He stretched out on the couch, thinking.

It's out of the blue. So sudden.

"You still with me, Pete?"

"Yeah, I'm here. Just thinkin' that you're the second person who's contacted me about a flying job in the past few days."

"Really? Who else contacted you?"

"Bryan Gilliam. I've been meaning to call you about it, in fact. I was out on assignment checking out a burn site when I found one of the six missing dinosaur meteorites last week. I took samples to Gilliam and he flipped out. Wanted me to fly him out there to pick up as much as possible. I told him I didn't think my employer would approve of an undertaking like that and he started talking about maybe renting a chopper and doing an off the clock job."

"You're sure it was Cretaceous rock, Pete?"

"Never been more sure of anything. Gilliam was sure, too."

Peter explained all the details of finding the big black stones lining the bluff in Custer Gallatin National Forest. The glazed hatchout fissures and eggshell fragments. The dino tracks leading into the woods.

Hayden's tone betrayed his excitement. "You've gotta take me there."

"I'd be more than happy to. I just can't do it with Montana Forest Service aircraft or on their time."

"I understand. What if I supply the helicopter?"

"Do you know how much a helicopter costs?"

"I do. I've researched it. I've been pondering this for quite a while, Pete. I've sold Nora on the idea. We're serious about it."

"And you can afford it?"

"We can, yes. There's also a possibility of the Smithsonian Institution picking up part of the cost. Nora is most persuasive and the museum folks love her. And now that I know Gilliam wants your services, I'm gonna call him and get him on board. He's got money to burn. He's got land for a heliport. Who knows, maybe we'll build us a fleet of whirlybirds."

Peter looked around to be sure he was alone. "Um, are you interested in hiring me on a job-by-job basis or as a full time employee?"

"Oh, definitely fulltime. But not as an employee. We want you as an equal business partner."

"Now I know you're bullshittin' me, Hayden."

"But I'm not. We've seen your flying skills in action, under extreme duress. The way you handled that flight through hell at Gilliam's Guidepost last summer was amazing."

Peter realized Hayden was deadly serious. *Time to play the negotiation game.*

"You know, Hayden, I doubt you can top my Forest Service salary."

"I know approximately how much you make. Our offer would be well above that."

"And benefits?"

"Yes. A comprehensive family insurance package and profit sharing."

"Would I be office bound doing paperwork or out flying?"

"We want you for your piloting skills. Not paperwork. We'll have enough assignments to keep you airborne as often as you like. And you'll have final say in the choppers we purchase. We need your mechanical expertise in that area. Please consider it, Pete. We need you."

It sounded almost too good to be true. He didn't really know Hayden Fowler all that well, but if the paleontologist was being honest, the deal was tempting.

"Send me a written offer and I'll consider it," he said. "It's going to take a lot to pry me away from forestry flying. I'm about to celebrate my eighth year there and I'm expecting a big raise." He knew it was a lie and hoped he sounded convincing.

"You got it, partner," Hayden said without hesitation. "Give me your e-mail info. You'll have our offer tomorrow. Monday at the latest."

Hope bloomed in Peter's chest as he recited his e-mail address.

The Iridium Factor

June 9: Gilliam's Guidepost
Heart Butte, Montana

LORETTA REINED CLANCY INTO A SLOW TROT through the east pastureland, riding along the retention pond where their zoo dinosaurs were penned last summer. She pulled up to the stand of sycamore trees where her older brother Jimmy had been taken by a Tyrannosaurus Rex. Reverently, she touched her forehead then brought her hand down to her chest, swiping left to right, making the sign of the Catholic cross.

"Bless you, dear brother," she said. "I hope God is treating you well in heaven. I miss you so much."

Tears glistened in her eyes.

She and Jimmy had spent a lot of time riding together. Horseback rides through Gilliam ranchland just weren't the same without him.

Why do you punish yourself like this, Loretta? You know you could have taken the western trail.

Since Jimmy's death, Loretta's usual riding companion was Lianne. Her daughter, always eager to take her horse Beauregard out for a run, had turned Loretta down the past three days. Since witnessing the heated argument between her parents, Lianne had been distant, going out of her way to avoid her. When Loretta attempted to have a conversation with her, Lianne would stare at her with a nervous fear and retreat to her bedroom.

It was upsetting, but Loretta knew she had let too much time go by before trying to set things right. Three days later, she was still grappling with what to say to Lianne, who was a very sensitive girl. How do you explain to an eight-year-old child that you are suffering severe depression over the tragic loss of a brother, your only sibling? How can you make it clear that such a grievous loss affects your relationships with other people? Of course, Loretta remained aware that Lianne had lost her beloved uncle and was also hurting, and that only complicated the situation.

And Bryan? He'd had the misfortune of watching a T-Rex rip Jimmy to shreds. He had lost his longtime best friend. Bryan hadn't talked about his loss since the family sessions with Dr. Krickstad ended, but she knew he was still suffering as well.

Why did I go off on him the way I did the other night? What got into me? Am I a bad person? How do I fix this mess?

She leaned forward and said into Clancy's ear, "Let's go, my sweet baby." She ran her hand along the horse's muzzle and squeezed her thighs against his flanks, getting him to move. "Let's head back to the stables and I'll give you a good brushing. I know how much you like that."

She rode through the east meadow, swinging wide around the three-foot deep crater where the meteorite struck last year. The trench had also served as the fire pit for their ill-fated barbecue party. She took Clancy up on the east meadow road, where she and the kids had encountered the Dromaeosaurs that caused Loretta to wreck their pickup truck.

Too many terrible memories here. Why do you put yourself through this, girlfriend? I must be a masochist.

She would be quite happy if she never saw another meteorite or dinosaur the rest of her days.

As she rode, Loretta thought about the triggers that led to her confrontation with Bryan. After a long, frigid winter with no news of dinosaurs, she had almost forgotten about the prehistoric creatures. Then on family movie night they caught the TV news report about Tyrannosaurs killing a man in an Idaho cave. Then Peter Lacroix flies in unannounced with more of those damned Cretaceous meteorite stones. She watched her husband go into his dreamy-eyed entrepreneurial trance, the same eager-for-fame-and-fortune look he'd assumed last summer while putting the family in harm's way. When Bryan started coaxing Peter into retrieving more of the dinosaur stone, she lost it. It was all too much for her. She would not allow him to pull them back into the traumatic world they'd lived through last summer.

Still, did it warrant me being that hard on him?

She arrived at the stables and dismounted. Clancy had worked up a good sweat. The horse huffed and snorted as she led him into the barn. She loosened the cinch and removed the bit, bridle, and reins, allowing him to breathe easier. She slid the saddle and blanket off and took him to the trough to drink, sliding her hand along his back as he lapped the water. When he finished, she guided him to the wash rack to hose him down.

Leading Clancy to his stall, she noticed the stables were a mess. Apisi and Chogan had become lax about mucking out the stalls. The smell in here was getting pretty rank and it wasn't healthy for the horses. Her anger flared. She would have to talk to their ranch hands about it; just one more unpleasant thing to have to deal with.

She dried Clancy, checking his hooves with a hoof pick, then combed his mane and brushed his coat with a curry comb. The fifteen-year-old gelding cooperated, appreciating the full grooming experience. Clancy craved the personal attention more than a couple of their other five horses, namely Blackie and Max, who were younger and much more high spirited.

As she brushed Clancy, her mind went back to last week's family movie night, with Loretta laying into Bryan, then discovering Lianne standing in the doorway taking in the appalling scene. She would never forget the expression of open-mouthed disbelief on her child's face at that moment. Lianne had looked helpless, vulnerable. *Frightened.*

This has gone on too long. Time to make things right, Loretta, starting with your husband.

She steeled herself and marched out into the quad, finding him in the utility barn, sitting at a worktable tinkering with a tractor motor.

"Hey, Bry, we need to talk," she said, approaching him with a cautious smile.

He remained focused on the motor. "Do we? I believe you did

enough talking the other night." He unscrewed the gearbox and tugged it free, examined it.

She pulled up a stool next to him. "Look, I feel awful about the things I said to you. I didn't really mean—"

"Yes, you did, Loretta," he said sharply, turning to look at her. "You meant every word of it."

She was alarmed by his anger even though she'd expected it. She touched his wrist. "Oh, god, Bryan. I'm so sorry. I never meant to hurt you, sweetheart."

"You didn't hurt me. You hurt Lee-lee. You terrified our daughter. She was traumatized by your outburst. Lianne is who you need to talk to, not me."

"Don't do that, Bryan."

"Don't do what?"

"Don't use our child to avoid discussing this with me."

"I'm not avoiding anything."

"Oh no? Then why have you slept out in The Cellar the last three nights?" she said, referring to the underground shelter at the rear of Gilliam's Guidepost, a good distance from the house. "Why is it every time I say something to you, you just shrug your shoulders and shut me out?"

His narrowed stare reflected his ire. "I'm still angry with you, Loretta. Calling me all kinds of hateful loser names in front of Lianne. Using nasty language and—"

"I didn't know Lee was standing there."

"Why should that matter?"

He had a point. "Yeah, you're right."

"Lee's been asking me a million questions," Bryan said. "*Do you still love Mama?* she says. *Are you and Mama gonna get a divorce? Is Mama crazy? Is she on drugs?* She's upset and more than a little afraid of you, Lor. You need to talk to her."

"She said those things? Really?"

He went back to working on the motor. "Yeah, she did. She even said she didn't think she wanted to watch movies with you anymore."

Loretta was crushed. Wednesday family movie night was

sacred to her. She brought her hands to her face, struggling to hold back the tears. Her voice broke as she said, "I've been having a lot of problems lately. They boiled over after movie night. I'm so sorry, honey. I really think I need help—with my anger, my self-control."

There was no hiding her tears now. She propped her elbows on the worktable and sobbed over the worktable, spluttering, wiping at her eyes.

Bryan turned to her, his angry scowl softening into sympathetic concern. "What's wrong, Lor?"

"It's Jimmy. He's gone forever," she muttered between sniffles. "I'm having trouble dealing with it, Bryan. I realize it's been almost a year but I—I miss him. More than ever. I try to stop thinking about him, but I . . . I just can't." She sat there, crying into her hands, her shoulders shaking with each sob. "It's like a huge piece has been cut out of me. Goddamn how I miss him, Bry."

Bryan wheeled his stool closer, snaked his arm around her. "Hey, it's okay," he said consolingly. "I miss him, too. I understand completely." He kissed her cheek. "I've got you, sweetheart. You can lean on me. What say we help each other through our grief over Jimmy?"

"I'd like that," she said, giving him a sad smile. "I can't stand us being apart like this, Bry. It only makes things worse for Lianne, us taking sides."

"I agree," Bryan said, reaching over and wiping tears from her cheeks. "We haven't exactly been good role models for our girl. Truth be told, our separation has been ripping me apart."

"Really?"

"Absolutely. I've missed you so much, Lor. It gets lonely out in The Cellar. I haven't slept much the past few nights."

"Me either. I thought you hated me, Bryan."

"I could *never* hate you. I can be pissed off as hell at you, but it never lasts long. I don't have it in me to hate you. You're my *life*, Loretta. You're my dreamcatcher, remember?"

She let out a throaty giggle. "You're so weird, Bryan Gilliam, but I love you anyway." She leaned in and kissed him, tasting the salt of her tears on her lips. "Speaking of your dreams," she said, sitting back and studying his face for a beat, "I refuse to go through another summer like last year. That's one dream of yours I refuse to catch again."

"What're you talking about?"

"I saw the way your entire being lit up when Peter Lacroix flew in with those meteorite rocks. I followed your dream last summer and, quite frankly, it led us into the heart of darkness. It got Jimmy and a lot of our friends killed. I nearly lost *you*. Your vision of a dinosaur zoo and quest for fame came close to being the death of us all. I love you, Bry, but I won't let it happen again."

He sat up straighter and pulled back from her. "You're blaming me for all that?"

"No. I'm at fault, too. For not being stronger."

"But you misunderstood me the other night, Loretta. It's different now. There aren't any dinosaurs. At least not on our property. I don't ever wanna get anywhere near those creatures again. I also have no desire to be hounded by the press again twenty-four-seven. This is about the Cretaceous stones. Those meteorite rocks are valuable. I've just made an amazing discovery about them."

"What's that?"

"They're shot through with iridium ore, which is one of the rarest metals on Earth. I didn't know it last year but iridium metal sells for more than six thousand dollars an ounce, far more than we were getting for the jewelry and trinkets we were cutting out of the rocks. Iridium is used to make chemical crucibles and satellite communication systems and high-grade aircraft spark plugs. I believe iridium was the driving force behind the government's interest in those meteorites. Peter Lacroix knows where the iridium motherlode is and we'd be crazy not to pursue it, Lor . . ."

She listened to him talk, hearing the enthusiastic lilt in his voice and seeing the eager glint in his eyes. "You've obviously done some research on this, haven't you?" she said.

"Yeah. After Pete showed up with those rocks, I realized I didn't know enough about that meteorite that hit our property. I read some of the online stuff posted by geologists and other geo-scientists, and they all pointed out the heavy concentration of iridium ore in the dino meteorites. I learned of iridium's extremely high melting point and corrosion resistance that protected the dinosaur eggs and shielded them from burning up when the meteorites entered Earth's atmosphere. Did you know that iridium ore is worth more than gold and platinum?"

"No. But I do remember the scientists talking about it on some of the documentaries I've watched. Have you talked more with Peter?"

Bryan nodded. "Friday night. He didn't know about the iridium angle. When I told him, he became even more gung-ho. He's on board if we can supply him with a helicopter."

Loretta sighed. "I hate to sound like a skipping record, but we can't afford to lease a helicopter. Not for an hour, let alone how many hours it would take. How far away from here did Peter say the location was?"

"Three hundred miles, give or take a few."

"So that's six hundred miles round trip. For just a *single* trip. And I remember him saying leasing a helicopter goes for upwards of four hundred an hour. So do the math, Bry. It'll take a boatload of iridium to pay for it."

He seemed to deflate right in front of her. She thought he might be on the verge of shedding a few tears of his own, and suddenly was sorry she pointed out the obvious to him.

He looked at her earnestly and said, "You know, Loretta, ever since my injuries and long recovery, I've felt useless. I'm a cripple—a handicapped old man at the age of forty three. I can't do the heavy mechanic work I used to do. Can't really ride a horse anymore or do much of anything physical. All I do day after day is sit around watching TV and drink beer. The highlight of most days is tottering out to the barn to watch Paul and his band rehearse, and most of the time I get the feeling he doesn't want me there. Soon there will be Ethan's baseball games to go to. But I need something bigger in my life to make me feel worthwhile again. Something meaningful. Something like this Cretaceous meteorite find."

"But you *are* worthwhile to me, dear," she said, taking his hand. "You and me together? That's meaningful. Has been for more than twenty years now. And you mean everything to the kids, too. We all realize how important you are to us."

"But you don't want to get involved with this meteorite retrieval thing, right?" He looked at her expectantly.

She thought about how to address this without getting embroiled in another fight. Finally she said, "The thing is, Bry, we are land rich and cash poor. Well, not poor exactly. We do have some cash liquidity. I see the promise in what you're talking about, but that is a substantial operation that will require lots of time and money. Even if you could get those boulders back here, how are you going to extract the iridium from the rock?"

He frowned, disappointed. Looked away, brooding.

Loretta knew she had to make some concessions. "I tell you what," she said, "let's take care of our family crisis and get you back sleeping in our bed. Let's help each other through our grief over Jimmy. That's what we have always done—helped pull each other through. Once we get all of us back on track, I promise we'll look into moving forward with this meteorite thing."

"You mean that?"

"Yes. I want to see you be happy again, my love."

He kissed her and she pulled him into a tight hug, saying, "I think it would be best if we talked to Lianne together. Can we do that?"

"Let's do it. Tonight after dinner," he said, feeling his phone buzzing in his shirt pocket. He reached for it, checked the display. "It's Hayden Fowler."

"Hayden?" she said. "I wonder what he wants."

Bryan answered. "Hey, Hayden. Long time no hear."

A Whirlybird Gift

June 9: Gilliam's Guidepost
Heart Butte, Montana

"YEAH, NORA AND I HAVE BEEN BUSY," Bryan heard Hayden say. "We spent a week in Paris and we've been working on the new book since we returned home."

"Paris? Must be nice."

"It was. *Paris est un rêve romantique.*"

"I'm not as worldly as you, Hayden. You'll have to tell me what that means."

"It means 'Paris is a romantic dream.' If you ever need to revive your relationship with Loretta, take her to Paris. The City of Lights will put starch back in your love muscle. The place recharges your libido, if you know what I mean."

Hayden Fowler displaying his usual crudeness.

Bryan glanced at Loretta, imagining her in a frilly French maid outfit. *Paris might be just what Lor and I need at this point.*

"Speaking of Loretta, how *is* that beautiful wife of yours doing?"

"She's fine," Bryan said, winking at her.

Loretta smiled at him, stood and backed away from the work-table, mouthed the words "Remember our talk with Lianne tonight." He gave her a thumbs-up and watched her saunter out of the barn.

"How about you?" Hayden said. "Are you getting around better now?"

"Well, you know. Some days are better than others. So why'd you call, Hayden? You returning to Montana now that the dinosaurs are coming back out?"

"Soon, yes. But that's not the reason for my call. I've got an offer for you, Gilliam. How'd you like to be general manager of a startup aviation company?"

"Say what?"

"Yeah. I've been talking with Pete Lacroix about starting up a private helicopter service, mostly to give Nora and me better access to the dinosaurs we're tracking. Of course, we'll have to fly jobs for other clients to pay the bills. But our initial business model will be flying in and out of areas where our dino creatures gather. Lacroix told me he found another Cretaceous meteorite and that you were chomping at the bit to bring it back to your ranch."

"Very true. Peter says it's twice as big as the meteorite that hit our pasture. I believe there's a lot of money in that stone and I'm just achin' to retrieve it, but Loretta isn't thrilled with the idea."

"Well, we could pick up a lot of that rock for you, if not all of it. And with air access, we might find another one or two of those missing meteorites for you. If your wife needs convincing, I could have Nora speak with her. Loretta and her seem to get along well."

"That would be great. But what are you saying, Hayden? You want me to manage this new aviation venture?"

"Nora and I want you to oversee day-to-day flight operations. And we want you to be an executive partner in a four-way split— you, me, Nora, and Pete Lacroix."

Bryan sat back and thought for a moment, then barked out a chuckle. "You must be omniscient, Hayden."

"Whaddaya mean?"

"Well, I just got through complaining to Loretta about how useless I've been feeling, with my injuries and all. I was bemoaning the fact that I can't do a lot of the things I used to be able to do. Truth is, I've been bored out of my gourd. Now, ten minutes later, you call me with an employment offer."

"It's not just employment. It's a ground floor investment opportunity."

"I'm flattered, Hayden, I really am. But I've talked with Pete about acquiring a chopper, and he informs me it's almost cost prohibitive. I don't have much capital to invest. As Loretta likes to say, we're land rich but cash poor. At least until we get settlement money from those murderous assholes in the Animal Emancipation Faction."

"This would require relatively little cash investment on your part, Bryan. Here's how it works. Nora and I would finance most of the business and maintain fifty-two percent of the company. Lacroix would do much of the flying and be our technical advisor. He'd also be in charge of recruiting the additional pilots and mechanics we'd need. For this he would get a twenty-four percent cut of the business, a salary, and full benefits."

"If my math is correct, that leaves twenty-four percent," Bryan said. "What would be my role? You said general manager?"

"Yes. You said you were land rich. For your twenty-four percent, you would be donating part of your property on which we'd build a heliport. We'd also need a hangar with offices. The inexpensive way would be to convert one of your existing barns. Or if you wanted to keep the heliport out and away from your house, we could build a new hangar from scratch in your outer pastureland. Seeing as how you've got a twelve-hundred-acre spread, I think you can afford to give up a small plot. We could even build it in your east meadow, on the twenty-seven acres where you housed the dinosaurs last year. The good thing about helicopters is we won't need long runways. Don't need a whole lotta space. As with Pete, we'd give you a generous salary and a full medical benefit package. And your twenty-four percent ownership of the company will bring you additional earnings once we start showing a profit."

Bryan couldn't believe what he was hearing. "Wow! That's mighty generous. But I don't know anything about helicopters."

"You don't need to. Lacroix will take care of all things involving aviation and aircraft. We need you to run daily operations on the ground—you know, manage the ground crew, dispatch, and office staff. You'd keep track of the books and deal with the public. Advertising and marketing would be a big part of your duties, also, which I know you're good at. It's general management. Making sure things run smoothly. Nora and I think you can bring what we need to this effort."

"So Pete has already signed on then?"

"Not yet. But I've had a long chat with him, feeling him out. I think he's more than ready to leave the Forest Service and strike out on his own. This afternoon we sent him an offer he won't possibly be able to refuse. We'll know soon."

Bryan felt like he was floating on a silver-lined cloud. "Man, Hayden, your book must be selling like gangbusters for you to be able to afford this."

"It is selling well, thanks to the fickle fates of the publishing world. Penguin-Random House paid us an obscene amount of advance money for *Cretaceous Stones* and we just received our advance checks for the followup book. It's an embarrassment of riches, I'm tellin' you. The advance money alone is more than enough to get our aviation business off the ground, if you'll pardon my bad pun. In a few months our royalty checks will start rolling in, and they should be substantial based on the sales figures we're getting. Plus, we're both drawing decent paychecks working for the Smithsonian. Pool that together with the money we already had saved, and I guess you could say we are just the opposite of you and Loretta—we're cash rich and land poor. This undertaking will give Nora and me some much needed tax shelters in addition to making our dinosaur tracking jobs quicker and more efficient. We want to put our money to work for us, and I have supreme confidence that you and Pete Lacroix can help us make this thing a roaring success."

"Damn, man," Bryan said, marveling that the day could go from the lowest of lows to the highest of highs in a matter of a few hours. "Thank you so much, Hayden. You're a godsend."

"You're welcome, Gilliam. But don't count your blessings quite yet. It won't be easy. Lots of red tape and legal hoops to jump through on the front end while the bureaucrats haggle over everything. But we do think the folks at the Smithsonian will fast-track through some of the needed building permits and rezoning licenses for us. I'll get a written offer out to you tomorrow with specs on the heliport requirements. Look it over closely and get back to me with any questions. If everything goes well, and you accept, I'll fly out next week to meet with you and Lacroix. Sound good?"

"Like a sweet love song, Hayden," he said, a wide grin spreading across his face.

Bryan disconnected and returned the phone to his shirt pocket. A gift from the whirlybird gods had just been laid in his lap.

Amazing how the tides of life flow.

He let out a happy whoop as he grabbed his cane and hurried out of the barn. He couldn't wait to tell Loretta.

Dance of the Carnivores

June 12: Rendaya Ranch
Flathead National Forest, Montana

A LIGHT MIST HUNG OVER THE VALLEY, draping the pines in ghostly strands of gossamer. Holland Peak stood like a great granite sentinel in the west.

Kelton Rendaya walked the wooden drawbridge over the south fork of the Flathead River, on his way to check on his newest acquisitions—a pair of Dromaeosaurs. The Prescotts had delivered the manic creatures a week ago, the animals filled with furious rage after the sedation wore off. Mick and Claire Prescott—a husband and wife team heading up a large organization spanning the globe— were his go-to wildlife trackers. They specialized in dangerous and difficult-to-trap species. Kelton could count on them to deliver prize specimens at favorable prices. More importantly, their operations were covert and discreet, which meant everything in the shadowy world of illegal animal trafficking.

He crossed the bridge carrying a cooler full of ground beef and a rifle, the river hissing and gurgling below. The rifle was to ward off any curious bears. This was grizzly country, and Kelton had met up with more than his share of ill-tempered bruins. The beef was for tiding the Dromaeosaurs over until Tank made it here with the hogs.

Tank Mahaffey was running true to form. Three hours late and just now leaving Maynard Farms. Nothing new there. Kelton had known Tank since grade school, and he'd always operated on his own timeclock. Kelton wondered sometimes if Tank even knew what a clock was.

This dinosaur business was a new venture for Kelton. He had

shied away from bringing in prehistoric animals last summer, even though he'd had many requests from clients. He could have easily filled a dozen dinosaur orders, but there were too many eyes on those prizes. The world had been watching. The meteorite dinosaurs were featured in nearly every daily newscast; the public couldn't get enough of the ancient wonders. And the feds had tracked them, citing them as a perilous invasive species, putting out bounties that attracted big game hunters far and wide.

Kelton had followed the struggles of the poor sap rancher 70 miles north in Heart Butte. That Gilliam fellow had suffered mightily by advertising his dinosaur zoo to the world. Kelton wasn't about to make that mistake. The last thing he needed was his ranch being invaded by the media and dumbass curiosity seekers. He wouldn't stand for a bunch of bounty hunters traipsing across his property shooting at anything that moved. And he certainly didn't need any of those murdering, pillaging animal rights yahoos bulldozing his habitats and gunning him down for the "sin" of keeping a few dinosaurs in captivity.

The product was just too hot to handle last summer.

This summer was a different story. Things had loosened up somewhat. Dinosaurs weren't as center stage as they were last year. Kelton figured the time was right to add prehistoric carnivores to his animal trafficking catalogue.

He took great pride in the business he'd built on his 1,500-acre spread in the southern end of the Bob Marshall Wilderness, one of the most remote areas in western Montana. His rambling farmhouse and four spacious outbuildings provided the perfect hideaway for his unlawful trade. And now he had the spacious dino enclosures out beyond the river.

Rendaya Ranch had been in his family for three generations. His great grandfather, Sturgis Rendaya, purchased the land near the end of the Great Depression with the money he'd made bootlegging rum and bathtub gin during the prohibition. Due to depressed economic times, he'd bought the land for pennies on the dollar. After Sturgis passed, Kelton's parents got rid of most of the stills and built a legal horse and livestock breeding business. Kelton and his sister

Kelsey worked on the ranch when they were old enough.

At age 18, Kelton headed to Washington State University to study veterinary medicine. Eight long years later, he earned his graduate degree in Veterinary Medicine, and moved back to Montana, opening his own practice in Great Falls, specializing in equine medicine and surgery. Over the next fourteen years, he worked to build up his vet clinic, finally selling out to a large veterinary management consortium in Missoula when his parents died unexpectedly. His father went first by heart attack followed a few months later by his mother via a massive stroke. By then, his sister Kelsey had made a family in Boston. She was happily married to a banking executive and raising three kids. Younger sis had no desire to return to Montana to work the stud farm. So Kelton came home to take over the business.

Two years in, he knew he didn't want to breed animals anymore. The money was good but the hassle just wasn't worth it. Caring for expensive stud animals and dealing with snooty ultra-rich clientele was an ulcer-inducing business. His marriage fell apart. Marianne, his wife of ten years, left him. She never felt comfortable living in the remote wilderness, and moved back to Great Falls and the luxuries of city life. He'd known it wasn't just the remoteness of the Flathead National Forest that got to her. It was the remoteness in *him*. Kelton had always related better to animals than people. Human relationships just weren't his thing. Though he had never been officially diagnosed as such, he felt pretty sure he was autistic in some way. It was a fatal flaw that cost him his marriage to a fine woman. Their failed relationship certainly wasn't Marianne's doing. She had tried hard to make it work. He had not. He was surprised it had lasted ten years.

At age 42, Kelton found himself alone and miserable, suffering what he could only call a midlife crisis. He needed excitement in his life. He sold off all the livestock and most of the stallions, and started up his animal trafficking business, following great grandpa Sturgis's journey into the illicit world of black market sales. Now, at age 50, Kelton was an established smuggler, making piles of money in an all-cash business. He was still alone, but not lonely. He was surrounded by the animals that he felt gave his life meaning. He dealt with people only when he had to. Life was good.

Private collectors paid top dollar for his product. At any given time, he housed some of the most exotic and dangerous animals on the planet. He preferred small reptiles, which were low cost and easy to transport. Low maintenance/high profit, that was his thing. He specialized in snakes. Kelton understood his clients' obsession with serpents. Snakes fascinated him, too. The sinuous way they moved. Their ability to blend into their environment. The way they slept with their eyes open. Their stealth when hunting. The primal beauty of the act when they struck their prey. He'd acquired and sold some of the most venomous snakes in the world: Indian saw-scaled vipers, Mohave rattlesnakes, Australian inland taipans, black-necked spitting cobras, Asian king cobras, Gaboon vipers, African black mambas, South American fer-de-lances, Asian banded kraits, eastern and western diamondback rattlers. He also had just received a shipment of a dozen Utah banded Gila monsters that would fetch upwards of $2,000 apiece. His Saharan deathstalker scorpions also fetched a good price. And he had some Brazilian wandering spiders and Tunisian fat-tailed scorpions coming to satisfy a few client orders. He never inquired as to what his buyers did with their purchases. He respected their privacy. To ask questions would be professional suicide. Once the animals left the compound and the cash collected, he didn't care to know anything more.

Kelton continued out to the glen and his Dromaeosaurs, walking under the thick canopy of trees that shut out the sun. The pathway was murky and the humidity clung to him. The surrounding woods were quiet, absent the usual birdsongs, the birds having sensed alpha predators now inhabiting the area. He strolled slowly, trying to walk off his anger at Tank. He paid the man well. The least he could do was be on time. Dromaeosaurs didn't like to be kept waiting on meals.

Maybe I'll feed Tank to them. That would be a juicy three-hundred pound gourmet dinner for my newest residents.

He stepped down into a shallow tree-shrouded ravine, hearing

the Dromaeosaurs screeching and clucking as they picked up Kelton's scent. The gentle breeze carried a gamy, wild animal odor that
he found pleasing.

Another hundred yards and he stood at the gates. He set the
cooler down and peered through the heavy chain link. Hog bones
and clumps of dung littered one side of the enclosure. The
Dromaeosaurs stood stock still and glared at him from the far side
of the clearing. The creatures' otherworldly visage sent a thrill
through him.

They're beautiful in a strange, alien way.

He'd been working on this place since February with Tank,
Thorn, and Hoops. It had been a bitch to construct this enclosure
and surroundings. They'd had to carve a path through the thick
forest wide enough for vehicles to get through. They'd hacked out
bushy vegetation in the lowland glen before erecting the fencing.
Building the drawbridge had been particularly daunting. They'd had
to work in the cold swift waters of the Flathead River, drilling
through dense limestone to set the support posts, then getting the
balky mechanical components to function properly. It would have
been easier and cheaper to build a conventional bridge, but Kelton
wanted a way to cut off would-be interlopers at the river.

He admired their workmanship of the caged-in glen, taking in
the reinforced steel fencing and the three-foot concrete base running
around the perimeter. He gazed up at the thick nylon mesh ceiling
secured to the upper branches of the ponderosa pines. A tall barricade separated the Dromaeosaur area from a larger space reserved
for the prize he had yet to obtain—Tyrannosaurus Rex. Beyond that
were two more expansive holding pens reserved for other large
prehistoric species that might become available.

Suddenly one of the Dromaeosaurs let out a high-pitched
scream and charged the front gates, taking a flying leap and slamming the barrier with tremendous force. The gates trembled.

Kelton jumped back, alarmed by the animal's brute strength.
"Easy there, boy."

The strange looking beast snarled at him and sprinted in circles,
then crashed against the fence again. The second Dromaeosaur

joined in the attack.

"Settle down, fellas, I'm not your supper, okay? But I did bring a snack for you."

He opened the cooler and dug out a hunk of ground beef, pushed it through a small hinged door they had engineered specifically for small feedings. Both carnivores pounced on it, fighting each other for the small mound of raw meat. The larger of the two won the battle, gobbling it down in two swift swallows. Kelton pushed more meat through the opening. The second creature got it, sliding the beef slab down its gullet in a quick gulp.

Amazing. This meat is nothing but hors d'oeuvres for them.

Kelton continued to feed the insatiable animals, taking in the animals' muscular hind legs, deep powerful jaws, large sharp teeth, and rugged build. Standing just three feet tall and weighing in at seventy pounds, they weren't that big, but Kelton found their massive strength and revved-up demeanor to be intimidating. *Exciting.* Paleontologists called Dromaeosaurus *running lizard.* It was an apt moniker. These guys had been in constant motion since the day the Prescotts delivered them. They'd dashed around the enclosure using their long tails for balance and to propel their jumps. And they could really leap. Eight feet off the ground from a standing still position. Their jaws were deadly. Kelton learned they had a crushing bite force of 3,700 pounds per square inch, similar to that of a mature crocodile.

All muscle and cartilage; not an ounce of fat on them. And they've got some wicked dental work to boot. We need to BEWARE! he reminded himself.

He had an order for both of them from a wealthy Chinese capitalist who owned agricultural concerns in Wyoming and Kansas. Kelton had already collected from Mr. Wu and the China-man was preparing a site for the transfer. Wu was also paying for feeding and safekeeping of his Dromaeosaurs until such time the animals were delivered. Kelton was in the process of negotiating the sale of another, as yet unpurchased Dromaeosaur with a longtime client on the dark web. His net take on the three dinos would be low six figures, which put a smile on his face.

The satphone buzzed on his hip, He unclipped it from his belt, answered. "Zookeeper here," he said, knowing that only his trusted trafficking contacts had this number. "What can I do for you?"

"Hey, it's Graywolf."

Kelton grinned. Graywolf and his team had been hunting Tyrannosaurus Rex. "Gray, my man! What's shakin'? You got some good news for me?"

"Indeed I do, snake man. We've got a line on one of those Rexes you wanted."

"Excellent! Where are you?"

"We're in west bumfuck Idaho. The middle of nowhere. I'm surprised I was even able to get through to you."

"Whaddaya mean you've got a line on one? Have you bagged it?"

"Not yet. But that won't be a problem. This place is crawling with 'em. Big sonsabitches they are, too."

"Do I get a discount if I request more than one?"

Graywolf let out a garbled chortle. "I like your sense of humor, Zookeeper."

"I'm not laughing, Gray. In most walks of life the buyer gets a discount when he purchases in volume."

"Well this isn't *most walks of life*. We're putting our lives on the line out here."

"Understood. I appreciate that. But that said, I've gotta tell you, one of your competitors offered me a better price."

"Have they delivered yet?"

"No. But neither have you. You're gonna have to sharpen your pencil and give me a better deal before I give the go-ahead, Graywolf. I can't put food on my table if I go with that price you quoted me. It's laughable."

"I'll see what I can do."

"You better hustle. I'm expecting a call any minute from your competitor."

"What's with this *competitor* shit, snake man? Why don't you just say the Prescotts and be done with it?"

"Gotta go, Gray," he said, pissed that Graywolf would mention the Prescotts by name on a call, a huge violation of trafficking communications protocol. "Call me back when you have an offer that isn't a punchline for a joke."

Kelton disconnected and placed the satphone in the holster, went back to shoving wads of ground beef through the fence. The animals fought viciously over the mounds of meat, growling and scrapping and grunting. He was down to the bottom when he felt the phone vibrating against his hip again. He glanced at the display and saw it was Tank.

"You better not be callin' with another excuse, because if—"

"Relax, chief. I'm here. We're unloading at the hog pens."

"How many'd you pick up?"

"Five fat white-banded Hampshires. Lotta meat on these suckers. They average around three-fifty"

"Bring two of 'em out to the glen. My boys are hungry today. And leave the bridge up after you drive in."

"Jesus, you are *so* paranoid."

"My paranoia is a good thing. It's why we're still able to do business eight years down the line and why you still have your cushy job."

"No need to get testy, boss."

Kelton sighed deeply. "Just get the pigs out here, Tank. You've wasted enough time already today."

"Gimme a friggin' break. We'll be out there in a few."

Twenty minutes later Kelton heard the mechanical screech of the drawbridge and the whine of the truck's engine as the vehicle rumbled toward the glen in low gear. He heard the hogs squealing over the rock music drifting from the cab.

Tank pulled into the clearing in a smoky fog of transmission grease and crankcase oil. He backed the truck up to the gates, the brakes hissing like an angry snake. Two roly-poly black-and-white Hampshire hogs shuffled agitatedly in the cargo bed.

Tank shut down the engine. The music stopped. The hogs shrieked and banged against the truck bed walls, as if they were aware of their impending fate. Tank dropped down out of the cab and shut his door. Hoops got out on the passenger side, a cloud of smoke trailing him from the cigarette that always seemed to be a part of him.

"About time you two showed up," Kelton said, his anger returning.

"Give it a rest, Kel. We're here, ain't we?" Tank said, working with Hoops to pull out the cargo bed slide.

Kelton checked his watch. "Four hours late doesn't cut it, Tank. If it happens again there'll be repercussions."

"Yeah, yeah, yeah," Tank retorted. "You're getting to be more like your dearly departed dad every day. A real slave driver."

Tank's cheekiness irked Kelton. Especially when he brought up his father. The man just didn't know when to keep his mouth shut.

Gordon "Tank" Mahaffey and Tommy "Hoops" Terrell had worked as cowboys on the Rendaya Ranch for as long as Kelton could remember. They were both his age, and had hired on here with Kelton's parents when Kelton left home for college. Tank and Hoops had earned their long-running nicknames from their high school athletic glory days, Tank in football as a massive 300-pound defensive tackle, and Hoops as a skinny-as-a-rail, six-foot-five basketball player. Both had starred in their respective sports at Flathead High School in Kalispell. Neither had wanted to continue their education, only wanting to work as cowboys, and they'd had good careers doing just that. When Kelton took over the ranch, he'd kept them on the payroll, along with Mark "Thorn" Thornberry. They knew the ranch and the area, had made some valuable contacts over the years. When he'd switched the business model from legitimate stud farming to trafficking black market animals, all three had stayed with him, seeming to enjoy the thrill of life on the wrong side of the law.

Tank and Hoops wrestled the shrieking, grunting hogs down the slide. The Dromaeosaurs, anticipating the main course about to be served, squawked and drooled on the inside of the enclosure.

The dance is about to begin, Kelton thought, woozy with anticipation.

They opened the front gates and pushed the reluctant hogs into a small screened-in area, designed as a holding pen for live prey feeding. Kelton kept his rifle at the ready as a precaution. Tank closed the gates and pushed a button mounted on a post. The walls of the inner pen slid up, exposing the panicky hogs. The Dromaeosaurs immediately went after them, making strange cooing-honking noises while attempting to grasp the much larger animals with their slender, three-clawed hands. Kelton noticed their wrist joints that allowed them more flexibility in their clutching motions. But the hogs were too big to be corralled that way, and they escaped, running out into the center of the habitat.

The hogs squealed in terror, realizing they were trapped. The much quicker Dromaeosaurs pursued, one of them sinking its teeth into a hog from behind, bringing it down in flying clumps of turf. The second Dromaeosaur chased the other spooked hog around the perimeter, finally pinning it against the fence and dipping its massive head to feed, ripping it apart with its powerful jaws.

Terrified squeals echoed across the clearing.

Growling and slurping and satisfied cooing as the dinos feasted.

Pools of swine blood darkened the dirt around the fallen hogs.

The squeals abated, replaced by anguished groans of pain.

And then they heard only the sounds of gorging dinosaurs.

So beautiful, so primal. Kelton thought.

He watched in wide-eyed fascination as the Dromaeosaurs shredded the hogs with their sharp teeth and gulped down chunks of bloody pork.

The predator-prey relationship had long fascinated Kelton. *Excited* him. The act was a passionate tango, a primordial food chain give-and-take that had been sustaining life on this planet since the beginning of time.

"It's a beautiful thing, isn't it, guys?" he said, staring into the enclosure, mesmerized. "The primal dance of the carnivores."

"Beauty is in the eyes of the beholder," Hoops said, his back to the action, sucking furiously on his cigarette and refusing to look.

Tank said, "Those hogs ain't happy with their dance partners."

"Neither of you have an appreciation for nature," Kelton said.

"Oh, I appreciate nature plenty," Hoops said. "I'm just not a big fan of slaughter."

The Good, the Bad,
and the Ugly

June 13: The Lacroix Residence
Missoula, Montana

"**WHAT DID I TELL YOU ABOUT WATCHING** the news?" Peter said to Brinshou, arriving home from work.

Brin had just put Kimi to bed and sat with her mother Kachina in the living room watching the seven o'clock news. A gruesome video clip played: yesterday's Tyrannosaurus Rex attack on a crowd attending a baseball game in Boise. Four rampaging Rexes. Seven deaths. A dozen wounded.

Brin flushed in embarrassment. "I know, I know, Petey," she said, apologetic. "I can't help it. I want to know what's going on in the world. I *need* to know."

"Sweetheart," he said, going to her, taking a seat next to her on the sofa, "you know how much this dinosaur news affects you." He rubbed her stomach with one hand and caressed her forearm with the other. "You've got a bun in the oven. A growing child to protect. You can't be watching this stuff that upsets you."

The dinosaurs were making a return appearance, coming out of an eight-month hibernation in large numbers. And Brinshou had been keeping up with all of it.

First there was the nature photographer who had been killed by a Tyrannosaurus Rex in an Idaho cave ten days ago. Since then there had been multiple sightings of Dromaeosaurs and T-Rexes, with several reported attacks on livestock and herds of elk. A wheat farmer in Montana had killed a large Triceratops when he came upon a half dozen of them consuming his crops. Other farmers in the area also reported decimation of their barley and wheat acreage. Multiple videos proved Triceratopses were the culprits. And then there were two Tyrannosaurus Rex attacks on humans around Boise, yesterday and today. These first confrontations with humanity since last August had killed a total of thirteen and wounded twice as many.

The national media was back on the scene and Brin was taking it all in. Try as she might, she couldn't help herself. Something about these prehistoric creatures brought out her dark side. Some masochistic compulsion deep within her made her seek out things she knew were not good for her. She believed it explained her fixation on the dangers of helicopter flight. It fed her need to read about the risks of childbirth even though she was ten weeks pregnant. It was why she obsessed over dinosaur attacks. Peter told her repeatedly that this habit of hers was the fuel that ignited her anxieties.

She knew he was right.

But she still felt powerless to stop.

She heard Peter say, "And Kimi certainly doesn't need to be exposed to this kind of insanity."

"Kimi *hasn't* been exposed to it, Peter. I've been careful."

Peter looked at Kachina, who sat in one of the recliners knitting. "Hello, Kachina. What are you working on there?"

She kept the knitting needles in motion. "A sweater for Kimi."

Peter smiled. "Nice. I have to ask. What do you think of your daughter watching this dinosaur porn," he said, grabbing the remote and shutting off the TV.

"Dinosaur porn?" Brin looked at him through narrowed eyes. "C'mon, Peter, that's not fair."

Kachina looked up from her craftwork and smiled. "My Brinny is her own woman. She's a grownup with a curious intellect. You should treasure that, Peter."

The Kootenai woman went back to her knitting. Brin winked at her, appreciating her mother's support.

No dinosaur sightings for almost eight months and suddenly the animals seemed to be everywhere. They hadn't died off as many had hoped. Hibernation through the harsh winter and colder-than-usual spring seemed to be the consensus for their lengthy disappearance. But some scientists—their friends Hayden Fowler and Nora Lemoyne included—maintained that creatures with high metabolisms like these would not sleep for long periods as bears and other mammals did. They postulated that the dinos had found food sources well away from human activity to sustain them through the frigid, icy winter. Hayden Fowler had even made the prediction last fall that Idaho's vast cave networks would be an ideal place for them to hole up. He was right. He'd also stated that when the weather started warming up, the dinos—particularly the carnivores—would be back on the hunt in populated areas where there was a more plentiful food supply. The past week proved Dr. Fowler correct again.

Peter kissed Brin's hair and stood. "I'm gonna go grab a beer. I've got something I need to discuss with you."

"Do I need to make myself scarce?" Kachina asked.

"No. You can stay. This affects us all."

Brin raised her eyebrows at her mother, wondering what this could be about.

"Can I bring you ladies anything?"

Brin and her mother shook their heads no.

He returned with a can of Bud and settled in the second recliner, next to Kachina, facing Brin.

"Okay," he said, "I want to run something by you. Let's see. What's the best way to get into this?" He took a long gulp of beer.

The way he hesitated worried her. *It has to be something bad, doesn't it?* "Just tell me, Petey."

"Why are you looking at me like that, Brin?"

"Because I have a feeling I'm not going to like this."

"Oh, it's nothing like that."

"Then why the big production? Just tell me."

"Okay. Well . . . I'm planning on quitting the Forest Service." He paused to take a sip of his beer, checking her reaction. When she didn't respond, he continued. "Things haven't been good for me there the past few months. They've got me training younger pilots and I'm flying drones more than I'm in the air piloting helicopters. I can see what's ahead. My future there as a pilot is limited."

Brin felt herself being lifted. This was fantastic news. "Oh, hallelujah, Petey! I'm so glad you've finally seen the light. Flying those choppers is so dangerous. I worry so much every time—"

"Whoa, hold on a second, honey. I have no plans to stop flying. I've been looking for other piloting jobs and I've received an incredible offer."

"Oh," she said, her disappointment evident in that one syllable. "What kind of offer? From who?"

"Hayden and Nora have thrown in with Bryan Gilliam to start up a new aviation company—a helicopter air service. They want me to be the lead pilot and fleet commander. I would hire and manage other pilots and mechanics as well as being the aircraft technical advisor. And get a load of this. The offer is twice my current salary! It comes with a nice benefit package that includes profit sharing. They've offered me a twenty-four percent ownership of the company, Brin! It's *amazing*!"

Brin heard the excitement in his voice, saw the sparkle in his eyes. It had been a while since she'd seen him this happy. But he would just be exchanging one risky flying job for another. The notion deflated her.

She said, "Why would Hayden, Nora, and Bryan want to get involved with an aviation company?"

"Well, Hayden tells me they need quicker and better access to the dinosaurs they're tracking for the Smithsonian. Plus he thinks it will be a great long term investment. Lots of farmers and ranchers hire out helicopter services."

"So you'd be flying them out to where dinosaurs roam?"

"Yes. Initially at least."

She eyed him warily. "I'm not real crazy about this, Peter. What about Bryan Gilliam? What's his interest in all this?"

Peter took a long slug of beer, then said, "A week ago I was out on a burn site inspection flight. I was training one of the new pilots, Rob Winkle. We found one of the missing dinosaur meteorites, in the heart of Custer Gallatin National Forest. I took several samples to Bryan Gilliam and I thought he was gonna have an orgasm." He looked at Kachina, said, "Sorry, Mom."

Kachina laughed. "For God's sake, Peter, I'm far from being a prude. Honestly, you tickle me."

Peter felt his face flush.

Brin thought about Peter's news. "So you're just telling me about all this *now*? Looking for a new job? Finding another Cretaceous meteorite? Getting this offer?"

"We've both been busy, sweetie. You've been working a lot. Me too. I just received the written offer yesterday. I wanted all the facts before I discussed it with you."

"So Bryan wants a way to get more of that rock for his jewelry business?"

Peter nodded. "This will benefit you as well, Brin. He says he'll contract a lot of that business out to your store. You ladies have experience working with it."

"And Bryan will be part owner of the aviation business?"

"Yes. He and Loretta will get twenty-four percent, just like us. They're going to build the heliport in the quadrangle of Gilliam's Guidepost, and convert one of their barns into a hangar with offices."

Brin couldn't help but frown. "The Gilliam ranch is tainted. It's drenched in blood. The ghosts of our friends haunt that place."

"Don't be ridiculous, Brin. There's no such thing as ghosts."

She gave him the evil eye. "Don't ever tell a Kootenai there are no such things as ghosts, Peter. We know better. I'm betting the entire Gilliam ranch is haunted with them after what happened there last summer."

"Get real, love," Peter said, waving his hand at her. "This is an unbelievable opportunity for us. Please don't let your superstitions get in the way."

"*Superstitions*?" She glanced at Kachina, who was focused on her knitting, not wanting to get involved. Brin turned back to Peter. "Call it what you want, but I'll never feel comfortable with you flying in and out of Gilliam's Guidepost. That ranch is jinxed. It's haunted. And what about living arrangements? Heart Butte is more than two-hundred miles away. I've got my business to run here in Missoula. How would we manage that?"

Peter looked exasperated. "We can work out the details, Brin. This is way too good to turn down."

"And you're sure Hayden and Nora have the money to launch this company? To keep it solvent?"

"Yes. With some assistance from the Smithsonian Institution. Hayden was kind enough to show me his and Nora's financial statements. They're both quite wealthy."

"Well, that's good because—"

Brin stopped talking, hearing the sound of a car pulling into the driveway. They weren't expecting anybody tonight. She got up to look through the living room window and felt a stabbing sensation in her chest.

It was her father.

"We've got a visitor." Her words were ominous. "It's Nashota."

Peter set his beer aside and stood, saw Nash getting out of his Range Rover. "C'mon, Kachina," he said, grabbing Brin's mother by the hand and pulling her up out of the recliner. "Let's get you back in the bedroom."

The doorbell rang followed by aggressive knocking.

Brin shivered, thinking about her last meeting with her father. Last summer at her parents' house in Polson, when Nash had attacked Kachina. Brin had looked on in horror as Nash pummeled her mother, both fists flailing, Brin finally jumping into the fray, trying to protect Kachina. Brin wanted to kill him that awful night. She remembered the weight of him as she pounced on his back and brought him down on the floor. Wrapped her arms around his neck and squeezed with a red hot rage generated by a tidal wave of adrenaline. She had come close to strangling him that night before the tribal police arrived to arrest him.

And now, here he was again.

Another doorbell ring chimed through the house. More insistent knocking.

Brin stood by the door, fear congealing in her throat, a lightheadedness making her feel queasy.

Peter reappeared with his homemade weapon—a hockey stick with a thick iron spike bolted into the blade. Peter hated guns. He'd told her many times that gun nuts who quoted the second amendment like it was biblical verse turned his stomach. He refused to have one in the house and claimed his hockey stick weapon was just as effective as a firearm.

"I know you're in there, Brinshou," she heard Nash yell. "Open up this door right now! I didn't drive a goddamn hour and a half to stare at your front door."

His words were slurred, demanding. Brin's heart raced. A wave of dizziness washed over her.

Peter stepped up to the door clutching his hockey stick, said, "Whaddaya want, Nash?"

"Well, if it isn't the heroic forest ranger Canuck," came the reply. "Ain't no way you're gonna stop me from takin' Kachina back to Polson with me. A wife belongs with her husband. Kachina belongs to me."

Brin huddled behind Peter as she heard him say, "By being here you're violating the restraining order Kachina brought against you."

"Don't feed me that legal bullshit, Lacroix. We both know that shit ain't worth the paper it's printed on. Now open up this fuckin' door before I kick it in! I'll take Kachina by force if I have to."

Peter mouthed the words "Call 9-1-1" to Brin and she went to retrieve her cell phone, made the call.

Nash boomed, "I hear my daughter in there talkin' to somebody. You better not be callin' the police, because—"

"Settle down, Nash. We've got neighbors who'll call the cops if you don't stop yelling."

"Then open the goddamned door!"

Peter unlocked the door, then opened it slowly. Nashota Taleka stood there brandishing a handgun, his eyes glazed with a drunken anger. He eyed Peter's weapon and laughed. "You brought a *hockey stick* to a gunfight? You're more retarded than I thought."

Peter maintained his cool. "And with that gun you are violating your parole, Nash. That could get you another ten years in Montana

State Prison without early release for *exemplary behavior*. That bullshit that got your release this time won't work again."

"Where is she?" Nash said, his stance unsteady, his gun hand shaky. "Where is my Kachina?"

"Listen," Peter said more calmly than Brin ever could have managed, "the best thing for everybody is if you get yourself a hotel room and sleep it off before driving back to Polson. You've obviously had a lot to drink and you shouldn't be behind the wheel tonight. I'll even pay for your room."

"You have a lot of nerve tellin' me what to do, you dumb-cluck Canuck." Nash looked around Peter at Brin, who was still on the phone giving the 911 operator information. "And I still owe you one my terribly lost daughter. I haven't forgotten what you did to me last year, you sorry-assed bitch—"

"Okay, that's quite enough," Peter said. "Time for you to leave, Nash."

"Not until I have my Kachina, Lacroix. I know she's here. Bring her to me. Now!"

Brin saw Kachina emerge from the hallway and grab her two knitting needles, then race toward Nash, hurrying past a startled Peter and shouting, "Here I am, you son of a bitch! Take this, you sorry piece of shit!"

She rushed Nash, yelling like a madwoman and slashing the air with the knitting needles, connecting on her second lunge, planting them deep in her husband's chest. Nash cried out in pain and surprise, dropping to the ground. The gun clattered on the concrete.

Blood stained the front stoop.

Brin felt faint. She sat on the sofa listening to Nash struggling to breathe and her mother sobbing. She caught a peek at her father's body sprawled out on the stoop, the two knitting needles sticking out of his chest like small aluminum harpoons.

Sirens wailed in the distance.

She felt a ripping pinch in her uterus.

Please, God, not the baby!

Taking Flight

June 14: Gilliam's Guidepost
Heart Butte, Montana

LORETTA'S FRIDAY WAS A WHIRLWIND of activity. Nora had sent her the Federal Aviation Administration specs for constructing an authorized heliport and Loretta started early this morning, researching contractors, selecting the companies best suited to meet their needs. She'd called four paving companies to get quotes for laying the heliport pad, and five general construction firms for the conversion of the utility barn into an aircraft hangar. The helipad was basic concrete work and could be done immediately. The barn conversion was much more complicated, especially with the need for attached office space. Loretta also spent an hour dealing with aerospace lighting companies. The helipad was required to be equipped with lighting for final approach/takeoff and touchdown/ liftoff areas, as well as directional landing lights. She had read through the Montana Secretary of State's rules for fuel dispensing and contacted several aviation fuel suppliers for prices on installing the necessary pumps and underground storage tanks. She also filled out the FAA 7480-1 Notice of Landing Area Construction and the associated heliport application. After construction, the state would send an inspection team for final approval of the layout. Nora told her the Smithsonian had agreed to use their influence to get the bureaucracy moving and get things done quickly.

It had been a long, exhausting day. She sat at the kitchen table with her fourth cup of coffee and thought about how quickly it was all coming together. Gilliam's Guidepost would soon become the home of Fowler-Lemoyne Aviation, LLC.

Hayden Fowler had pitched the offer to Bryan just five days ago, the same day Peter Lacroix had been made an offer. Peter had not yet accepted, but Nora assured her that his signing would be forthcoming. "We made him an offer nobody in their right mind could refuse," Nora had told her.

Bryan had spent the day out in the utility barn where he once worked as a mechanic. He oversaw the cleanup effort, getting the structure ready for a construction team to come in and transform the place into a working aircraft hangar. Unable to do any heavy lifting, he advised Apisi and Chogan on what needed to go and what could be kept. One of the first things to go was the *GILLIAM'S GLADE PREHISTORIC ZOO* sign with its gaudy blood-red medieval lettering. Bryan had put up a stink about wanting to keep it, but Loretta insisted it be gone. She did not want any lingering memories of last summer's tragedy. Apisi and Chogan worked hard, hauling out tractor parts, engine components, rusted mufflers, old tires, plow heads, combine attachments, seeders, balers, suspension systems. They also removed the dog crates and aquarium tanks they'd used to house the Dromaeosaur hatchlings early last summer. They loaded up Bryan's pickup, and he'd made three trips to Butch's Salvage Yard in Browning to sell the discards.

If she was being honest, Loretta was grateful for this aviation opportunity. It gave her and Bryan something productive to focus on while they were still in the throes of grief for her brother Jimmy. Since last August when they had lost literally everything they owned, they were like two sinking ships, trying to stay afloat while navigating turbulent waters.

Loretta had been reluctant about the heliport at first, but after several calls, Nora finally convinced her that the aviation company would eventually become a lucrative business, and that she would be smart to accept their offer. She was onboard, but before agreeing to Nora and Hayden's generous offer, Loretta laid out a few hard and fast rules for Bryan.

"I'm fine with using our land as an air strip," she'd told him. "I'm also fine with hauling Cretaceous meteorite rocks here. But I am totally against bringing in dinosaurs. I will absolutely *not* go through that again, Bryan. The only animals I want here are our horses."

"Dinosaurs?" he'd said, surprised. "That's not gonna happen, Lor."

"How do you know? I'm quite sure Hayden Fowler wants a place where he can pen those beasts. A place where he can study them. I'm telling you, that's not going to happen anywhere near where I'm living. Never again, Bry."

Bryan nodded. "I've already discussed that with Hayden. He says after what went down here last summer, he wouldn't think of doing that to us."

"That all sounds good on the surface. But I know how fast things can change. I'm warning you, if Hayden goes back on his word and brings in more of those monsters, I'm taking the kids to Shelby to live with Olivia. You'll be on your own."

"Hayden says I'm the general manager of this heliport. What I say goes. If I mandate no dinosaurs at our ranch, he says he'll honor that."

"Hayden Fowler says a lot of things. I'll only believe that if we get it in writing and it's witnessed and certified by the attorneys."

Bryan had looked at her thoughtfully. "Okay, no worries," he said slowly. "If I get it in writing and certified, are you good to go on this?"

"Yeah. But one more thing. I want you to promise me you'll never go up in one of those choppers. Not even to go out on Cretaceous stones pickups."

"No problem, Lor. I got my fill of helicopters in Afghanistan. I'm more than fine staying grounded."

Bryan brought her the written promise yesterday, signed by Hayden, Nora, and the two lawyers they had on retainer.

Amazing. Just a week ago she and Bryan hadn't been talking to each other. Now, here they were getting into a new business together.

She e-mailed Nora the last of the estimates and closed her laptop. She sat, drinking her coffee, thinking, recalling the conversation they'd had with their daughter the night they settled their differences.

Lianne had been standoffish and reticent to talk when they first approached her. She seemed fearful of them—especially Loretta—and refused to sit on the couch with them, electing instead to curl up in an easy chair in the corner.

Bryan started if off. "Your mother and I want to talk with you about what happened on movie night, Lee."

No response. She eyed them suspiciously.

"You saw your mom shouting at me, right? Saying some bad words?"

Lianne nodded tentatively.

"She had a right to be mad at me, Lee. I was being selfish. I was thinking only of myself. Do you understand that?"

No response.

Loretta said, "Sometimes husbands and wives—*parents*—have disagreements. They fight. But that doesn't mean they don't still love each other. Just the opposite, really. When we get angry it's *because* we love each other and want to work things out. That's what happened between your daddy and me, Lianne. It doesn't mean we're getting a divorce. We will always be together and here for you kids. Do you understand?"

Lianne slouched in her chair, covered her eyes. She spoke quietly, guardedly. "You scared me, Mama, when you yelled at Daddy. When you said those bad words."

"I know, and I'm so sorry, Lee-lee. I'm sorry you had to see me acting like that. It was very immature of me. I saw how much my actions bothered you and I should have apologized sooner. Your father and I have worked things out." Loretta shifted closer to Bryan, rubbed his thigh. "We love each other and we love you. Please don't ever doubt that, honey."

Bryan said, "I didn't act very mature either, Lee. We have forgiven each other and we hope you'll forgive us. Part of growing up is understanding that people have misunderstandings. They argue. It doesn't mean they hate each other. It means they are trying to understand each other. Your mother and I understand each other now. And she's right. We both love you very much. Can you please look at us, Lianne?"

She didn't move for a long moment, just sat curled in a protective ball, keeping her face hidden behind her arms. Then finally, she lifted her head and Loretta's heart broke. Tears streamed down Lianne's cheeks and she wept in blubbering gushes. "I didn't know what to think, Mama. I was all mixed up," she said through loud sniffles.

Loretta went to her, took her in her arms, repeating "Oh, my sweet baby," over and over and over, and hugging her close. "Of course you were confused, darling. I'm so sorry, Lee."

"I didn't wanna hate you, Mama."

"I never thought you did, sweetheart," Loretta said, rubbing Lianne's back.

Bryan rose and came to them. They engaged in a three-way hug around the easy chair, with Lianne weeping and Loretta and Bryan whispering words of love to her. Soon Lianne stopped crying and said, "I love both of you. I love Mama and I love Daddy." That confession made Loretta's emotional dam burst wide open, and it took several long minutes for her to regain her composure.

Lianne was back watching a movie with them Wednesday night (no *Flicka* this time but rather the animated *Zootopia*). Loretta didn't care what movie they watched as long as they were together. Yesterday—Lianne on her horse Beauregard, and Loretta on Clancy—mother and daughter rode together for the first time in a week. They rode the western trails of the property, staying well away from the east meadow and memories of Jimmy Enright. It had been a fun ride albeit a bit chilly.

All seemed to be getting back to normal with their daughter. As Dr. Krickstad pointed out, most children showed a remarkable capacity for rebounding quickly from upsetting experiences.

Loretta took the last sip of her coffee, feeling drained. The house was quiet but for the soft ticking of the wall clock and the occasional thump of the fridge icemaker. She could also hear Bryan's occasional snores from the living room where he'd been napping the past hour. Lianne was spending the day with her cousin Marnie in Shelby and Ethan was at baseball practice. Paul and his

Moonrise bandmates had left an hour ago for their regular Friday night gig at Browning High School. They had won a battle of the bands there in April and were now the house band for the school's Friday night dances. Moonrise had quickly won over a small but growing legion of young followers by playing VFW posts that Bryan had gotten them into, and school talent shows that Paul had booked himself.

She took her coffee cup to the sink and washed it out. Put her laptop away and pocketed her cell phone. She collected the garbage bag from the waste bin, put a twist tie on it and hauled it out to the quad, headed toward the dumpster next to Paul's rehearsal barn.

She heard something banging around behind the dumpster and froze.

Too big for a racoon or possum. Not big enough for a bear, she hoped and prayed.

She stood still as a statue, listening, eyes laser focused on the dumpster, her heartbeat thumping in her throat.

The banging ceased, replaced by sounds Loretta knew all too well—angry, wheezy snorts and screeches that took her back to last summer.

Oh, please NO! This can't be happening.

More banging against the back of the dumpster.

Chuffing noises.

The sounds petrified her. She couldn't move.

A large Dromaeosaur leaped up on top of the dumpster, the lid rattling under its weight. A second Dromaeosaur came around the side. Both animals glowered at her. Loretta recalled seeing those same evil crimson eyes in her rearview mirror last year just before a Dromaeosaur caused her to wreck her pickup truck.

Their screeches and bellows sent a chill through her. Long strands of drool dripped from their wide shovel mouths. One of them hissed and lowered its head, going into an attack position.

She screamed. Dropped the trash bag, turned and ran back to the house, yelling until she thought her lungs would burst.

She heard them behind her, predators on the hunt.

She made it to the sunroom's sliding glass door, her hands

shaking as she slipped inside and slammed the door shut. A split second later one of the animals slammed into the glass with a thunderous blow, falling back, stunned.

Bryan entered the sunroom, leaning on his cane. "What's going on?" he shouted. "What's wrong, Lor?"

"We're gonna have to move the horses again, Bry," she said through labored breaths.

"Why? What happened?"

She moved aside so Bryan could see the struggling creature on the patio. "The monsters have returned."

They both watched in shock as the Dromaeosaur got back on its feet and sprinted through the quad, disappearing behind the barns. They could hear frightened neighing and whickering coming from the horse barn.

Loretta fell to her knees, her breaths coming hard and fast. "Why us?" she yelled. "Jesus Christ, Bryan, why can't they leave us alone!"

"I don't know," he said, "but I'm going after them."

She watched Bryan leave the sunroom, heard him open the lockbox in the den where he kept his Smith and Wesson revolver.

She tried to yell out to him, "Don't!" but couldn't find her voice.

Dragons In the Quad

June 14: Gilliam's Guidepost
Heart Butte, Montana

BRYAN SHAMBLED OUT INTO THE YARD, cane in his left hand, gun in his right. The sun sat low on the horizon, casting long shadows across the quad that reminded him of dark, misshapen fingers.

He scanned the dim yard. Stopped and listened. His heart galloped in his chest. He heard Loretta behind him, imploring him to come back, that he was no match for these creatures and to not do anything crazy. A nauseating unease fluttered in his gut, but the frightened squealing and blowing coming from the horses in the stables drove him forward.

He approached the dumpster, alert, his head on a swivel. Gun raised, he looked behind the heavy duty polyethylene bin. Saw the spotted three-toed tracks in the dirt and a pile of fresh scat. He poked his way with the cane to the utility barn that he and his ranch hands had cleaned out earlier, moving carefully along the length of the building. Peeked around the corner, which gave him a clear view of Paul's rehearsal barn and front of the horse stables.

No sign of the Dromes, but the horses are still worked up.

He caned his way across the open area to the band rehearsal barn, moving as fast as his broken body would carry him. The boys had closed and locked the swinging front doors after they'd loaded out their equipment. No need to check inside.

He went around to the side wall, seeing more tracks etched in the soft earth. Followed the wall to the rear of the barn. Looked around the corner and gasped. Two Dromaeosaurs were doing their damnedest to bust through the stable's sidewall vents. The horses bucked furiously against the stall walls, banging, nickering, and neighing. From where he stood, Bryan could see Max and Blackie through the open vents, their ears pinned back, nostrils flaring, eyes wide, blowing and snorting in utter terror. One of the beasts clung to the vent frame with grasping forelimbs and took swipes at Max with a forelimb killing claw. The other creature had ripped part of Blackie's Dutch door loose.

If these beasts get into the stables, our horses are goners.

Loretta's question came back to him: *Why us?*

He had to act fast.

He stepped into the open and shouted, trying to distract them. The animal going after Blackie stopped, spun its big head around and stared him down with a malicious gaze.

Bryan felt an icy chill race through him.

The creature turned and charged him, snorting and growling as it sprinted across the yard.

The beast was shockingly fast and agile.

The Dromaeosaur left the ground in an impossibly long leap. Bryan barely had time to raise his gun, firing off three shots in quick succession, *Boom! Boom! Boom!* striking it in the throat and chest as it took him down.

He hit the turf hard, losing his cane but managing to hold on to the gun. Warm blood sprayed across his face and neck. The panicked animal had him pinned and Bryan was unable to raise the gun to get off another shot. It couldn't have weighed more than seventy pounds, but it was all hardbody, leathery muscle, smothering him. A foul odor of rotted meat and wild animal hit him and he thought he would be sick as he was able to move his left arm up and push at its snout, trying valiantly to keep the creature's powerful jaws and razor edged teeth away from him..

Though maintaining its immense strength, the Dromaeosaur was struggling. Labored wheezing and bubbling came from the creature's damaged throat as it struggled to breathe.

Bryan's strength was flagging, his left arm trembling with fatigue, but he had two fingers of his left hand in a nostril of the squealing beast, pushing its snout away from him with all the power he could summon.

Just when he felt he couldn't hold out any longer, the Dromaeo-saur shifted, and Bryan was able to swing his gun hand into position.

He fired a shot into its right eye.

Boom!

The blast blew open the right side of the beast's head. Gushy blobs of brain matter speckled Bryan's face and arms. The Drome took one long last gasp and died on top of him, its great might ebbing quickly through its final death spasms.

The lifeless animal felt thirty pounds lighter as Bryan pushed the carcass away. He wiped sticky brain goo from his face and lay there, next to the shot-up Dromaeosaur body, completely exhausted, his mind frazzled, his thoughts hazy.

An angry hissing shriek brought him back to reality.

In the confusion of his tussle, he'd forgotten about the second Dromaeosaur.

He turned his head toward the horse stables, his low view from the ground disorienting. As if lost in a dream, he watched the beast approach slowly, cautiously, studying its dead companion lying in puddles of blood, half its face shot off. It tilted its head as if considering the risk in attacking.

Bryan tried to get to his feet. Couldn't move.

Tried to grab his revolver. His arm was unresponsive.

He freaked, thinking what he'd just been through had paralyzed him somehow.

The Dromaeosaur seemed to sense his helplessness and charged, moving at an impossible rate across the quad, its wide jaws snapping as it ran at him.

This is it, Bryan fretted. *I'm going to die here!*

The animal swooped in, snorting, head lowered, gaping mouth open wide.

Bryan squeezed his eyes shut, realizing this was the end.

And then he heard three rapid-fire gunshots. Heard the creature squeal out in pain, followed by retreating footsteps plodding across the yard.

He opened his eyes to see the Dromaeosaur running toward the woods, noticing one of its forearms had been reduced to a bloody stump. He listened to its wounded cries, watching its long tail sweeping the turf behind it before disappearing into the thick grove of hemlock behind the stables.

Painfully, Bryan turned his head to see Loretta standing there, cradling a rifle, thin wisps of smoke drifting from the barrel.

"Are you okay, dear?" she asked.

"Thanks to you I am," he said, his voice weak and shaky. "You really saved the day, Lor. You put a hurtin' on that thing."

A grim determination tightened her face. "I meant to *kill* the bastard!"

She went to him and took a knee, looked him over. "Quite the mess here, Bry. Did it get you anywhere?"

"Just some cuts on my left hand where I was trying to hold him off." He looked at her, thinking he'd never loved her more than he did at this moment. "Jesus, Loretta, if you hadn't come along—"

"Don't say it, Bry. Let's just get you inside and cleaned up. Can you stand up?"

"I think so, if you give me a hand."

She helped him up, glancing at the butchered Dromaeosaur carcass heaped next to him. "Those things sure are ugly," she said. "I'll get Apisi and Chogan to move the remains into the utility barn. And not a word of this to anyone, Bryan. Understand?"

"Yes," he said, dizziness hitting him as he got to his feet.

He picked up his cane and gun, feeling weak and wobbly as she walked him back to the house.

"I cannot believe those goddamned beasts are back trolling our property," she said. "When oh when is this gonna end?"

Bryan didn't know how to answer that.

Breeding Grounds

June 16: Gilliam's Guidepost
Heart Butte, Montana

NEWS OF THE DROMAEOSAUR KILLING brought Hayden Fowler to the Gilliam ranch. He'd taken an early flight this morning from Minneapolis to Great Falls, then rented a car for the two-hour drive to Heart Butte.

The Gilliams made him swear an oath of secrecy about the Dromaeosaur carcass they held on their property. Loretta had been particularly stern about the privacy issue. The paleontologist could write about it in his and Nora's next bestseller, but she didn't want news of it leaking to the press. Loretta demanded the same secrecy from the wildlife veterinarian—Dr. Horace Barton—who yesterday made the hour drive from Choteau to check the dead animal for zoonotic diseases such as rabies, blastomycosis, and trichinosis. The vet had doused samples of the Dromaeosaur's brain tissue with chemicals, examining the results under a fluorescence microscope. Fortunately for Bryan, the animal was clean. If Bryan had contacted rabies, they would have been under legal obligation to report it to the authorities.

Late afternoon now. Hayden stood next to Bryan, peering down at the Dromaeosaur corpse laid out on a long worktable. They were in what Gilliam called the music rehearsal barn, where his son Paul and his band practiced. On their way in, they had passed by the small elevated stage with the large drum kit, speaker cabinets, and microphone stands.

"You made quite a mess of this guy," Hayden said, bending over the Drome carcass.

Gilliam emitted a nervous chuckle. "Yeah. He came close to making an even bigger mess out of me."

"So I see," Hayden said, pulling back, looking at Bryan's bandaged left hand, the nasty scrapes along his forearm. "I can't imagine tangling with one of these beasts. Pound for pound, they're every bit as vicious as Tyrannosaurus Rex."

"Believe me, I *know*."

"You say he leaped on you?"

"Yeah."

"I'm surprised you were able to keep him from sinking those teeth into you."

Bryan's grin lacked mirth. "Adrenaline is a great thing."

"You're lucky. If it had been a Rex you'd be a dead man."

"I'd definitely be dead if Loretta hadn't saved my ass. She shot the arm off the second one that tried to eat me."

"The one that ran off into the woods?"

Bryan nodded.

"And you said none of the horses were hurt?"

"They were plenty shook up, but they're okay. Fortunately, our stable vent windows are small. Just enough room for the horses to stick their muzzles out to get fresh air. Difficult for the creatures to get at them."

Hayden looked down at the cadaver. "You've kept this bad boy on ice the past forty-eight hours?"

"Yeah." Gilliam lifted his chin toward the large stainless steel refrigerator in the corner. "In one of the commercial freezers left over from our general store. It's where we stored the meat by-product cubes we fed the dinosaurs last summer."

"That's good. If you hadn't kept it cool, you'd never clear the smell out of here."

Hayden snapped on a pair of latex gloves and began doing a physical examination of the theropod. "It's impressive how much these things have grown since we last saw them." He lifted a muscular hind leg and pushed out the second toe, the lethal looking killing claw. "They've added an inch or two to their sickle claws. Their tails are thicker and longer. Means they have better balance and more power in their leaps than they had last summer." He moved up to the shattered cranium, turning it to the left side that was still mostly intact. "Look at the jaw hinges," he said, opening and closing the wide mouth. "They are much more developed. Gives these growing juveniles stronger bite and crush force. For their size, Dromaeosaurs have some of the most powerful jaws of all Cretaceous carnivores. And the teeth?" Hayden ran a finger lightly along the ridges of the lethal teeth. "Twice the size of the choppers on the Dromaeosaurs you had here." He looked at Bryan. "You're quite the stud, Gilliam, taking this predator down. You're a lot stronger than you look."

Bryan made a show of flexing his biceps, then laughed.

It gave Hayden a smile. "You know, I'm going to be bluntly honest with you, Gilliam. I wasn't real sure about you when we first met. But you've grown on me. You showed me a lot last summer with your courage. The way you held off those psycho terrorists, the empathy you showed for your lost Blackfoot friends. I know you and your family have been through a lot. You survived so much adversity, and you have my utmost respect for that."

"Thanks. I appreciate you saying that. It means a lot coming from you."

"I wouldn't go into business with just any schmuck. You're a good man and I'm proud to be working with you." He gave Bryan a friendly poke on the arm. "What say we get this guy back in the freezer so you can show me the plans for the heliport. Nora has kept me in the loop, but now that I'm here, I'd like to see it."

"Sure thing."

Hayden said, "I forget. Is this the barn where we hatched out the Dromaeosaurs in the chicken incubator?"

"No. That was the utility barn. That's the building we're gonna convert into a hangar."

"Let's start there. But let me get some blood samples before we put this guy back in the box."

Hayden drew three small vials of blood. The samples would be skewed somewhat since the animal had been dead and refrigerated for more than 48 hours, but he could get some valuable hematological and serological comparisons against the data he'd collected from the Dromaeosaur hatchlings here last summer. He would look at enzymes, hormones, proteins, immunoglobulins, antigens, and antibodies. All would help in determining the growth patterns and health of these animals.

As they were returning the carcass and blood samples to the freezer, an inner voice bombarded him with questions.

What drew the two Dromaeosaurs to Gilliam's Guidepost?

Were the six horses in the stables the target?

There are many other ranches and farms in the area that have far more livestock.

So what attracted these Dromaeosaurs? Certainly not a half dozen horses.

Hayden considered a theory he'd long held about Cretaceous dinosaur breeding practices. Maybe, hopefully, he could prove it here today.

As they left the barn and passed the stage, Hayden said, "You say this is your son's band? Is he the one who played deejay at your cookout last year?"

"Yeah, my oldest. Paul. He's got a power trio rock band. He plays guitar and sings. Two of his Blackfoot buddies are the rhythm section."

"They any good?"

"They're *really* good. They call themselves Moonrise and they're starting to make a name for themselves around these parts. Loretta and I are proud of them."

"Cool. I'd like to hear them play sometime."

"You'll get to. They rehearse out here almost every night. They're dedicated kids. Really into their craft."

They walked the hundred yards through the quadrangle to the utility barn. Gilliam clasped a rifle under his right arm, using his left hand to plod along with the cane. It pained Hayden to have to walk so slow.

Gilliam swung open the doors, leading Hayden inside. "This will be the heliport hangar. The offices will be built out along that far wall. We kept my two hydraulic lifts because Pete Lacroix says they'll be needed for helicopter maintenance work."

"Good deal," Hayden said, taking in the cavernous interior. The smell of motor oil, aged rubber, and sheet metal hit him. *The perfect space and ambiance for an aircraft hangar.* "So this is where we raised the Dromaeosaur hatchlings?"

"New building, same foundation."

"But it's the same location, right?"

"Yep. If you remember, it's where I did my mechanic work. We cleaned it out a couple days ago. Long day. Three trips to the salvage yard."

Hayden scratched at his beard, thinking. He scanned the walls and ceiling. "How easy would it be for Dromaeosaurs to get in here?"

"Critters got into our old wooden barn, no problem. Lots of holes and cracks and entry points. But when we rebuilt, we went with prefab steel. Better protection against fire and pests. Also cheaper to insure. The only way even the smallest of dinosaurs could get in is through the front doors. But that's unlikely. The sliding doors overlap the opening by several inches so the gaps are closed off. And the only time the doors are open is when someone is here."

Hayden nodded his understanding. He went to the nearest corner, checked the panel seams. Walked along the wall to the adjacent corner, checking the floor along the way.

He heard Bryan say, "What are you looking for?"

"Nests . . . Eggs."

"What? Why would there be eggs in here?"

Hayden continued to circle the interior, inspecting the walls, top to bottom. "Probably no reason," he said, his back to Bryan. "One of the more difficult-to-prove theories I have is that Cretaceous animals were in the habit of returning to their birth site to breed and lay their eggs. I believe they had some kind of innate natal homing instinct like our sea turtles and salmon. I'd like to find out if it holds true for Dromaeosaurs." He came to the end of the far wall, turned and looked at Bryan. "Doesn't look like they returned here to lay eggs. At least not inside. Let's go check the exterior."

They walked around the perimeter of the barn, Hayden stopping periodically to sweep brush and weeds aside, or to overturn rocks. Bryan followed, wielding the rifle, nervously eyeing the edge of the woods and the horse barn.

Hayden spent fifteen minutes searching, finally giving up in disappointment. "Looks like my natal homing theory struck out here." He hated when one of his hypotheses didn't prove out. Failure had never been an option for him. "Show me where the helipad is going."

Bryan led him to the wide area of lawn between the hangar barn and the horse stables. "We're gonna lay down two concrete landing pads here with a broad asphalt track leading to the hangar. Rows of LED runway lights will mark the boundaries. Peter guided us on the layout."

"Excellent. What about a fueling station?"

"We'll be contracting a deep dig on the south side of the hangar for the underground storage tanks. The fuel pumps will sit on top. Probably have to take down some of those hemlock trees to fit it all in."

Hayden was pleased. "Sounds like you're on top of things here."

"Loretta's been obsessed with it the past few days and I've been in frequent contact with Lacroix."

"That's one fine woman you've got there, Gilliam."

"Don't I know it, partner. Your lady is pretty special, too. How is Nora doing?"

"She's got a lot on her plate right now. We both do, trying to meet publisher deadlines while jumpstarting this aviation company. Hardly have any time or energy to get in a decent lay since we got back from Paris."

Bryan shook his head and gave him an amused smile. "Hey," he said, "it's getting late and I'm sure you're tired after your trip. Whaddaya say we head back to the house and chat over a beer or two?"

Did Gilliam forget that I'm a teetotaler now? "Well, I'll gladly sit with you and sip a ginger ale."

"Oh, yeah. My bad. Sorry," Bryan responded, embarrassed. "You gave up the firewater for Nora, right?"

"Well, for her *and* me. A decision I have never once regretted."

"That's good. I'm happy for you, Hayden."

They walked across the quad toward the house, Hayden having to walk with baby steps to stay with Bryan. They were halfway across the quad when Hayden stopped in his tracks, an epiphany coming to him. "Wait a minute. Your hangar barn is where we hatched out Dromaeosaurs in the incubator. But that was an artificial hatching process. Your east meadow is where they hatched out naturally. Is that meteorite crater still out there? That firepit where you barbecued last summer?"

"Yeah. It hasn't gone anywhere."

"You been out there recently?"

"Not recently, no. I avoid it. Bad memories and all. Loretta and my kids ride their horses out that way, but I think they stay pretty clear of the meteorite strike area."

"How about we head out there now? Before it gets dark. Do you mind?"

"No, not at all. We can take my truck."

They drove out to the east grassland, jouncing along the bumpy dirt road, dust billowing into the cab of the pickup. Bryan steered the truck down into the hollow, the meadow newly green and splashed with yellow cinquefoil, blue larkspur, and red paintbrush wildflowers. Hayden had forgotten how beautiful western Montana was when the rains of spring gave way to the early summer bloom.

Bryan pulled up to the meteorite pit and shut off the engine. They got out and approached the three-foot-deep trench that had served as a barbecue firepit where Bryan smoked meats last summer at the doomed Gilliam cookout.

Hayden hardly recognized the place. The area possessed a lonely, abandoned quality. Gone were the dinosaur habitats with their high fences and raucous occupants. Absent was the soaring observation tower and viewing bleachers. The pasture was now a flat expanse of verdant grasses and colorful wildflowers as far as the eye could see. A soft warm breeze blew in a susurrating whisper, the only discernable sound on this secluded plain.

Hayden searched the periphery of the fire-blackened pit. Bryan stood well away, rifle in hand, watching, worry lines creasing his forehead. Nothing but prairie grass and small rocks. Hayden peered over the edge, seeing the remnants of charred mesquite wood chips and burnt charcoal bricks lining the base. The walls were coated with a solidified layer of ash. He saw nothing out of the ordinary. He walked to the opposite side of the firepit, seeking a different perspective. Dropped down on his knees to get a closer look.

And then he saw it.

The low-angled sunlight reflected the tip of an egg peeking out from under a mound of crusty ash. An egg with the same blue-green color swirls as the Dromaeosaur eggs they'd hatched out in the chicken incubator.

Well, I'll be damned! I was right, Hayden thought, excitement building in him. He got to his feet. "I believe we've got something here, Gilliam. Come take a look."

Bryan caned his way over, looked down to where Hayden pointed.

"See it?"

"Sure do," Bryan said with a frown.

"I'll bet good money on it there's more than just the one. I'm going in."

Hayden stepped down into the pit, careful where he put his boots, trying to avoid crushing any concealed eggs.

Bryan said, "Be ready to run. If mama Dromaeosaur shows up, we'll be in deep shit. I don't wanna tangle with another one of those things."

"Roger that," Hayden replied, poking around the floor of the pit. He bent and lifted the veil of charcoal residue that hid the egg.

An electric charge zipped through him.

He counted seven brightly colored eggs dusted with ash. Hayden picked one up, felt the heft of it in his hand, the soft, leathery texture of its surface. They were heavy but smaller than the T-Rex eggs he'd seen in Jackson Lattimer's video. Identical to the eggs they'd hatched in Gilliam's chicken incubator last summer.

"Holy mother of god, look at this!"

Bryan's shadow darkened the pit. Hayden heard Gilliam say, "Fuck me! Not again! Loretta's gonna be pissed."

Hayden returned the egg to the nest and looked up. "Sorry, but this is a frickin' miracle. It's a blessing. My breeding theory is correct!"

He pulled himself up out of the pit to see Gilliam staring morosely at the eggs, shaking his head in disbelief. "C'mon, Gilliam, cheer up," he said, clapping Bryan on the back. "This is a great day, *mon ami*."

Bryan continued gawking into the pit, stunned, looking like he'd just lost his best friend.

Hayden left him there and went to the truck, plucked his cell phone off the seat and called Nora. "Hey, sexy lady, I have great news."

"I've been wondering when I would hear from you. How was your flight?"

"Well, it was on time and they didn't lose my luggage, but the goddamn seats were too small and the only food they served was a bag of stale pretzels and a pack of peanuts."

"Welcome to the world of modern travel, Hayden. How is our friend Bryan faring after his close encounter with the raptors?"

Hayden looked at Gilliam, who remained standing on the edge of the meteorite crater. "He's doing amazingly well. I can't believe he held off that Dromaeosaur and then killed it. I told him he was a lot stronger than he looked. I don't think he appreciated my comment."

"That man has been through so much," Nora said. "Bryan and Loretta, they're both determined survivors. I just got off the phone with her. They're doing a great job with the heliport planning. Loretta is so organized and things are proceeding much quicker and smoother than I thought they would."

"Yeah, I know. Gilliam gave me the guided tour."

"You sound really excited, Hayden. What's your great news?"

"I've got new material for our book," he said jubilantly. "A chapter's worth, maybe two. We found a nest of Dromaeosaur eggs in Gilliam's east meadow."

"Wow! That's terrific. So your Cretaceous natal homing theory rings true then."

"It would seem that way, yes. At least for Dromes."

"That's fantastic. It's also quite extraordinary that these animals are able to reproduce at such a young age, don't you think?"

"Yeah," Hayden said. He knew that paleontology wisdom held that reproductive maturity in Cretaceous animals would have been at seven or eight years. "That's largely due to the time it takes for the medullary bone to fully grow."

Nora said, "The medullary bone? The bone that contains the tissue in its marrow cavities that provides the needed calcium carbonate for eggshells?"

Hayden smiled. "Damn, you're good, my love. Yes. The medullary bone would need to be fully mature to produce durable and fertile eggs. This egg laying is happening at *one year*, Nora. To put it in human terms, it's comparable to kids six and seven years old having sex and producing children. It's unbelievable!"

"What do you attribute it to?"

"Well, my best guess is that the females are endowed with abnormal amounts of estrogen at a very early stage in their development. Similarly, the males must also develop large supplies of spermatozoa early. It's like these animals have been granted supercharged procreation sex drives as toddlers, and given the equipment to handle it. It's fascinating. I guess those of us in the paleontological sciences have been wrong about dinosaur reproduction. This is a major new find, *mon amour*."

"You're right. Dinosaur estrogen and sperm. That's not something we've checked before."

"Well, obviously there hasn't been any way to check it until now. I took some blood samples from the dead Dromaeosaur, and I'll look at those things."

"That's right in your wheelhouse, Hayden, sex being your favorite subject and all."

He smiled, imagining her grinning on the other end. Hayden got a kick out of Nora's playful sense of humor. He had a tendency to get overly serious when discussing his work, and her wry wit had a way of balancing him out. "Funny girl, aren't you, Lady Lemoyne?"

"Hey, I'm not complaining. In fact, I wish you were here right now. I'm feeling the itch coming on. The itch that only you can scratch."

"Keep talking like that and I'll be on the next flight home."

"I think I'll live. If my itch gets too bad, I have Mr. Happy in my nightstand drawer to keep me satisfied."

"But Mr. Happy doesn't have my charm and charisma. He's just a stick in the mud."

She laughed, her gleeful giggle warming him. "Two points for that one. Mr. Happy has his place. But I miss the hell out of you already. Do you realize we've rarely been apart the past year?"

"I do, sweets. I miss you, too. It's gonna be tough sleeping without you tonight."

"Same here. But this'll all be worth it if you keep uncovering new discoveries for our book."

"Yeah, I've gotten lucky this first day out."

"It's not luck, Hayden. It's your knowledge and experience."

"Aw, shucks, ma'am."

"Will you have time to do a writeup of what you've encountered today and e-mail it to me? If you can, I'll polish it and get it into the manuscript. The publisher needs two chapters next week."

"Yeah, I'll try to get something to you. Probably be tomorrow though."

"That's okay. You still planning on staying with the Gilliams for a few days?"

"I am now. This ranch is loaded with Cretaceous phenomena."

"Just be careful. I know how *into it* you can get. The last thing I need is for my man to get hurt, or worse. I'd hate to have to rely on Mr. Happy the rest of my life."

He was about to reply with a clever quip about competing with a hard rubber dildo when he heard Bryan Gilliam let out a shriek.

"Hayden, get over here!" Gilliam shouted breathlessly. "One of 'em's hatching. Oh, Jesus! It's déjà vu all over again!"

Hayden said to Nora, "Gotta go, love. We've got another Cretaceous phenomenon developing."

He told Nora he loved her and clicked off the call, went to where Gilliam stood alongside the edge of the pit.

A small claw had broken out of one of the eggs. A second egg jiggled at the top of the nest. Hayden wished he had his camcorder with him; his cell phone camera would have to do. He started shooting, hoping there was enough light in the bottom of the pit to pick up the images.

The yolk-drenched hatchling broke out of the shell, squeaking like a mouse. Its head was twice the size of its body and was unstable on its elongated neck. Its small wide jaws snapped at the air as it moved. A claw burst through a second egg, and another creature covered in glaze broke out.

Definitely Dromaeosaurs. Hayden filmed, transfixed by the sight of the hatchout-in-progress.

Gilliam stood next to him, nervously shifting his weight from one foot to the other, as if making a decision. After a long moment of gazing into the nest, he turned and hobbled toward his truck. "I'm getting my gun. I can't have these things on my property."

"No Gilliam!" Hayden yelled, continuing to film the activity in the nest. "You can't kill 'em. They're an endangered species."

Bryan got to his truck and pulled his rifle from the gun rack. "You're right," he said. "They're endangering my family." He approached the pit. "Get outta the way, Hayden."

Four of the creatures broke through their shells. A thick yolky fluid glazed the nest. The hatchlings trod over shell fragments as they clumsily negotiated the pit walls. Hayden didn't want to stop filming. *This hatchout is incredible!*

Two of the creatures cleared the rim of the pit and took off sprinting, disappearing into the tall prairie grass. A third Drome followed close behind.

"Get the hell outta there, Hayden! You're gonna get bit, sure as shit."

Hayden pocketed his phone and jumped up out of the pit.

Bryan leaned into the pit and opened fire—*Blam, Blam, Blam, Blam!*—blasting the nest and decimating four of the hatchlings.

"Take that you evil little motherfuckers!" he screamed between shots.

Silence ensued after the shooting. Bryan stood on the lip of the pit, breathing heavily, rifle barrel smoking.

"Jesus, Gilliam. This isn't a war, fer Chrissakes," Hayden said glumly, surveying the nest ruins.

"Oh, it's *definitely* a war," he said, eyeing the grassland where three of the hatchlings had disappeared. "Loretta's not going to like this at all."

They walked back to the truck in silence, Hayden masking his disappointment over the killing of four Dromaeosaur hatchlings. Gilliam's rage had been so red hot there wasn't enough left of the Drome carcasses for research. But Hayden was happy he had gotten some terrific video footage of the hatchout. He only hoped there was enough light.

Bryan's hands were tight on the wheel as he drove through the east meadow up to the dirt service road. He looked across the seat at Hayden. "With all the millions of square miles in Montana, why do these monsters find Gilliam's Guidepost so inviting?"

Hayden responded with a smirk. "Maybe it's because you are gracious hosts."

Bryan stared at him as if to say, *I can't believe you actually just said that?* "Not funny, Dr. Fowler, not funny at all."

Hayden said, "Well, you asked."

Hello, Goodbye

June 19: USDA Forest Service Offices
Missoula, Montana

"IS THIS FOR REAL?" Gary Ralston asked from behind his desk, looking up from Peter's resignation letter.

"I'm afraid so, yes."

"Are you sure?"

"Very."

"May I ask why? I mean, you've been flying for us eight years and I thought you were happy."

"I *have* been happy, Gary. This is no reflection on you, if that's what you're worried about."

"You know I'm not—"

"My wife and I have a second child on the way and so lately I've had to think more about our future. You and I both know there have been some big changes around here since the first of the year, and I'm not quite sure how I fit in anymore."

Ralston studied Peter over his half-rim reading glasses, gray eyes steady, his shock of silver hair shining in the overhead fluorescent lighting. "You are one of our best pilots, Peter. That's why I tapped you for the flight instructor position. The positive feedback I'm getting from our young recruits tells me I made the right decision. You have a solid future with the Forest Service."

"Maybe so. But it's not the kind of future I want."

Peter scanned the plaques lining the wall boasting of Gary Ralston's achievements—Professional Excellence; Line Officer Award; Fire Containment Merit; Aerial Fleet Manager of Distinction; multiple Northern Montana Forest Service Pilot of the Year awards. His boss had done quite well in his storied career.

"So what is it you want, Peter?"

"I'm a helicopter pilot, Gary, not a drone operator. I want to fly choppers, not play with toys. And if I wanted to be a flight instructor I'd be in Kalispell working at Red Eagle Aviation or Central Copters in Belgrade."

He saw Ralston's shoulders droop, the disappointment clouding his manager's face. He actually looked hurt. Thinking he might have laid it on too thick, Peter followed up with, "Look, you have been an excellent boss, Gary. You have done so much for me. You gave me my first piloting job. You were my first flight instructor and I have learned so much about flying fire containment missions and emergency rescue operations from you. But it's time for me to move on. I've received the proverbial offer I can't refuse."

"With who?"

"It's a startup with some people I met last summer working the Operation Hot Rocks detail with the Air Force."

"Those people at the Heart Butte ranch?"

"A few of them, yeah."

"Come on, Peter. Surely you remember the kind of trouble they brought down on you?"

"This is different. This is a private sector air freight company with big plans and they're giving me a part ownership position. A piece of the pie. A *big* piece of the pie. And I'll be the lead pilot, flying as much as I want."

Ralston stared at Peter for a long beat, then said, "I'm sure you are aware that startups are notoriously unstable. Most of them close their doors in a year or two after burning through the venture capital."

"Please don't make this more difficult than it already is," Peter said. "I have a lot of friends here that I'm gonna miss. This isn't easy for me, Gary."

"I understand," Ralston said. He sighed deeply and peered out the window at three Northrup Grumman fixed wing planes and two Bell Super Huey helicopters parked on the tarmac. He turned back to Peter. "Please forgive me, but I have to ask. I know you had some pretty shocking family trouble last week. Does that have anything to do with this?"

"No, absolutely not," he responded, thinking about Brin's father Nashota, who'd spent three days in Community Medical Center being treated for chest wounds under the watchful custody of the Missoula Police Department. Nash was released Monday and held at the Missoula County Detention Center jail pending a hearing for his numerous parole violations (carrying a firearm, breach of registered restraining order, threatening with a deadly weapon, criminal trespass). Kachina was not charged for her attack on Nash, but she was still paying a heavy emotional toll. Peter remained quite shaken at having a loaded gun pointed at him on his front doorstep. He was still angry as hell and wanted to personally murder Nashota Taleka for his threatening intrusion into their lives. *Just how is it that someone as beautiful and kindhearted as Brinshou can come from someone so wretchedly ugly and hateful?* Fortunately for everyone, Kimi never woke up to witness the violent encounter. And Peter was greatly relieved that the night's upset hadn't caused any problems with their unborn baby. Brin's gynecologist, Dr. Linda Masterson, had given Brin a thorough examination and pronounced her healthy and the baby fine and growing according to schedule.

"If it's a question of money, Peter, I can—"

"No, Gary. It's not the money. It's just time for a change."

"Would it help if I took you off of drone training?"

"No."

"How about if I said no more flight training duties with the young guys, that you could go back to flying your usual routes five days a week?"

Peter felt like he'd been run through the wringer the past week, beginning with the Nash incident. He'd also had to deal with Brin's standoffish attitude about him taking another helicopter pilot job, flying out of Gilliam's Guidepost, which she crazily thought was haunted. Now his boss was making his resignation difficult. He was tired of threats and pushback. He tried to keep the anger and frustration out of his voice. "Nothing you can offer will change my mind, Gary. It's time for me to get out of government work and move into the private sector. I'm going through with it. Sorry."

Ralston, tense, squeezed the bridge of his nose. "This is really bad timing, what with heavy fire season upon us."

"I know. And I'm sorry about that. But from what I've seen, you have a good freshman class of young pilots. They'll be able to handle it."

"You've always been tough and headstrong, Peter. That must come from your hockey playing days."

"Some of it does, yeah."

Ralston smiled for the first time. "You're a gifted pilot, a real natural. I knew that the first time I sat in the cockpit with you. You've got special skills."

Peter returned the smile. "My wife loves to tell people I was a bird in a previous life."

"I wouldn't doubt that. You'll be hard to replace, and I know I speak for everyone when I say we're all going to miss you. I wish you the best of luck in your new endeavors. And with your new baby."

"Thanks, Gary. I appreciate all you've done for me. I really do."

Ralston slipped Peter's resignation letter into a folder. "You'll be paid through the end of the month. Can you give me another week? Of course, department regulations concerning resignations means I can't let you fly, but Dispatch needs some help right now."

"Absolutely, I can help out," Peter said with false enthusiasm. The thought of being cooped up in the cramped Dispatch Center that reeked of coffee, cigarettes, and stress disheartened him. But he could survive anything for a week. And then he would be his own boss.

"Super!" Ralston said, coming around the desk to shake his hand. "Thanks for your service, Peter."

Peter left Ralston's office and went to the employee lounge. He was pouring himself a cup of coffee, his head in the clouds thinking about the make and model of the first helicopter they would purchase, when he heard a familiar voice behind him.

"Hey, old man. What are you doing here?"

He turned to see George Dantley, his young friend who had

nearly died last year when one of the dinosaur meteorites toppled the Forest Service fire watchtower he was manning as a part-time summer employee.

"Georgie! Fancy meeting you here," he said, turning and leaning into him for a man hug.

"I'm in my second week of training downstairs. I'm on my way to becoming a conservation ranger. Can you believe it?"

"Not hardly," Peter said. "When I saw you last you were a wet-behind-the-ears college student with a trophy girlfriend. How is Emma?"

"She's great. We're talking about gettin' hitched after she graduates."

"Hey, that's wonderful! I'm happy for you, Georgie."

George Dantley was a smart, twenty-two-year-old recent graduate of the University of Montana's College of Forestry and Conservation. A good looking kid, despite the burn scars along the left side of his face that plastic surgery couldn't completely erase.

"Thanks. But seriously, Pete. What are you doing here? I've never seen you here in HQ."

Peter took a sip of his coffee. "I'll be working in Dispatch for a bit. I'm a short timer, my friend."

George wrinkled his brow, confused. "Whaddaya mean short timer?"

"I'm leaving, Georgie. Moving on. Goin' to a new job in a few weeks."

"New job? Where?"

"In Heart Butte."

"You're leaving Missoula?" George looked crestfallen.

Peter nodded. "I'll be heading up a new helicopter air freight business at the Gilliam Guidepost ranch."

"You mean the place where they kept all those dinosaurs last year? The ranch those animal activists shot up and burned down?"

"One and the same."

"And your wife is okay with it?"

"Brin put up a hell of a fuss, but I can be very persuasive. It's an outstanding opportunity."

"Well, damn," George said. "Who am I gonna go to Missoula Bruins hockey games with now?"

"Heart Butte is only four hours away by car, Georgie. It's not like I'm going to another universe. And don't forget. I'm a pilot with access to a helicopter. I can make it there in under two hours in a chopper."

"But the question is, *will* you?"

"Of course I will. You can count on it."

George wore a look of distress. "Man, so many things are changing so fast, Pete. It's dizzying."

"Get used to it, my young friend. That's life in a nutshell. It's called becoming an adult."

"I'm not sure I want to enter adulthood."

"Too late for that. It's inevitable, Georgie," Peter said, thinking back to sixteen years ago, when he'd harbored similar thoughts about making his way into the adult world, recalling how everything was moving too fast to comprehend. "It'll be a while before we move. We'll have you and Emma over for dinner soon. Kimi's been asking about you, wanting to play with *Unca Jaw*. She can almost say *Uncle* now, but she still struggles with *George*."

George broke into a wide grin. "She is such a darling little thing, Pete. *Unca Jaw*," he said, shaking his head in wonderment. "So cute. It's nice that she thinks I'm her uncle."

"Yeah, let's keep that going as long as we can, shall we?"

"You've got it, old man."

"Do I have to keep reminding you that I'm only thirty-eight. I'm nowhere near ready for Bingo and shuffleboard just yet."

"You just keep telling yourself that, Mr. Methuselah," George said laughing and playfully slapping Peter on the back.

Salties

June 21: Adelaide River
Northern Territory, Australia

SALTWATER CROCODILES ARE THE WORLD'S largest reptile. Fully mature males average eighteen feet in length and weigh in at 2,200 pounds. Dubbed "salties" by biologists, they are much bigger and more nasty bad-assed than their cousins, the alligator. Hunted nearly to extinction in the 1970s, conservation laws were enacted to protect the crocs, allowing them to proliferate.

Jackson Lattimer stared out over the bow of their dive boat, breathing in the mix of briny algae river scent, marine gas, and cigar smoke drifting from the boat's bridge. A brisk wind whipped at his face. The temperature was in the low eighties and the sun warmed the deck beneath his neoprene dive booties. It was an hour boat ride to their entry site, a section of the Adelaide River known to have the largest concentration of salties anywhere in the world. They had left the port of Darwin (the capital of Australia's Northern Territory) forty-five minutes ago, they being the grizzled dive operator Oscar who loved his cigars, safety divemaster Maurice, and Jackson Lattimer with his fellow videographer, Caleb Campbell.

As they motored to their destination, Jackson watched a dozen or more pairs of eyes breaking the surface of the muddy water, peering at the trolling boat. Several salties swam along the starboard side and snapped their wide maws, showing off their frightfully outsized teeth in a threatening gesture. He marveled at how similar the salties' mouth structures were to those of the T-Rexes he'd encountered in the Idaho caves. Both saltwater crocs and Tyranno-saurs were capable of generating thousands of pounds of crushing power with their jaws, and could slice through thick bone with their razor-sharp teeth. Their eyes were the big difference. Tyrannosaurs had large, widely spaced, blood-red eyes while salties possessed close-set green eyes with narrow, vertical-slit pupils.

Jackson felt a nervous tingle in his gut as he scanned the river ahead. The number of reptilian eyes observing them increased the further upriver they traveled. The tingle grew into a sharp sting as he considered the additional threat of bull sharks in the area.

If there are no pre-shoot jitters, the subject isn't worth videoing.

This was his first filming excursion since the tragedy in Idaho three weeks ago. Yes, that Idaho shoot had been a good payday, bringing him lots of money from the television networks and cable news outlets. But he'd paid a big price. Jackson doubted he'd ever be able to get over witnessing Milton Haynes being ripped apart limb from limb and devoured by a hungry Tyrannosaur. His surviving employee, Sam Beeson, was taking a paid leave of absence to deal with the emotional fallout. Jackson, however, had contracts to honor, like this one with National Geographic. He was a pro and had to soldier on regardless of his frazzled spirit.

They puttered upriver, heading for their entry destination. Thick stands of northern salmon gum trees blanketed both sides of the wide waterway. Jackson heard deep yowling cries overhead, *ra-ra-ra-raurau*. He looked up to see three white-bellied sea eagles gliding effortlessly on the thermals with their impressive seven foot wingspans.

He glanced at the dive gear hanging from racks on the foredeck—scuba tanks and regulators, dive masks, fins, buoyancy vests, wetsuits. He, Caleb, and Maurice would be diving into the middle of these salties, swimming with these creatures of antiquity. National Geographic had hired him to do his usual daredevil videography and were paying him well for his services. Jackson Lattimer had never let a client down, and he had no intention of short-changing Nat Geo on this videography outing, no matter the risks. After all, he had his Gonzo Shutterbug reputation to uphold.

Plenty of saltwater crocodile videos were available to the masses on YouTube and Instagram, video Jackson called *amateur tourist crap.* Adelaide River jumping saltwater croc cruises were a big tourist attraction in these parts. River cruise companies took tourists out to photograph salties leaping five feet in the air to snag buffalo meat strung from poles suspended over the sides of the boats. Jackson regarded them as cheap images. Any fool able to point and click a cell phone camera could film salties from the safety of a boat deck.

Jackson didn't know safe. Didn't *like* safe.

He wanted to capture salties up close in their natural setting.

He wanted to be in the water with them.

He wanted to capture them swimming straight at the camera.

That's why they paid him the big bucks.

Jackson Lattimer had been attracted to dangerous wild animals as far back as he could remember. It started when he was six years old during his first trip to the San Diego Zoo. His parents had taken him and his older sister Lilly, hoping to give their children an introduction to the wild kingdom. While visiting the reptile house, his parents had taken their eyes off their hyperactive son for the few minutes it took Jackson to climb over the low railing and into the baby alligator enclosure. He screamed as he was repeatedly bitten on the arms and legs. Zoo officials rushed in to pull him out. Fortunately they were juvenile gators, and their bites inflicted only minor damage. When his father asked him why he would do something like that, Jackson replied simply, "I just wanted a closer look at the little dinosaurs."

Young Jackson became obsessed with the reptile house on subsequent zoo trips. Mom and Dad had learned their lesson and made sure to keep a close eye on him on those visits. And of course, Jackson being Jackson, he developed a yen for the most dangerous of the animals housed there: the two-foot long New Zealand tuatara lizards, Komodo dragons, slender-snouted crocodiles, Gila monsters, king cobra and black mamba snakes.

When Jackson was seventeen and just starting to take an interest in photography, he and one of his friends broke into the San Diego Zoo at night and scaled the fence at the Safari Park lion exhibit. The African lions didn't sniff them out, but zoo security did, having them arrested on trespassing charges. Teenager Jackson told the police at booking that he only wanted to try out his new night vision camera. The arresting officer could only shake his head.

And then there was Jackson's infamous post college Kenyan safari. After earning a double-major degree in Photography and Zoology from the University of California San Diego, Jackson's parents gave him a graduation gift of an African safari trip. While observing white rhinoceros in central Kenya, he caused a stir when he jumped out of the safari truck before the guides could stop him, and, showing no fear, walked briskly toward a rhino cow and her calves, his videocam whirring. African officials shouted at him from the safari caravan and lifted their rifles, prepared to protect the crazy American tourist. When Jackson got within thirty yards of the small herd, the rhino cow made a growling trumpet sound, and dipped her snout horn low to the ground. She sniffed the air and dug into the turf with her front hoof, once, twice, three times, aggressively plowing up clods of earth. Jackson stopped his approach, steadied his camera, and casually continued filming, ignoring the shouts urging him to return to the caravan.

The rhino charged, 3,500 pounds of muscle and maternal anger thundering toward him. He flopped to the ground and rolled out of the way as the surging beast thrashed past him, pounding the ground inches from his head. He never stopped filming as screams and gunshots rang out, Jackson thinking, *Please don't kill her.* Still splayed out on the ground, he calmly turned and filmed the rhino plowing into one of the safari vehicles, the explosive impact nearly flipping the customized Land Rover.

More screams.

Gunshots.

Complete chaos.

The misadventure got Jackson sent back to San Diego with a heavy fine for damages and violating safari rules. He also faced several lawsuits from tourists who were injured due to his transgression. The setback didn't affect him much. He believed, even at that young age, that all publicity, both positive and negative, was *good* publicity. He learned a lot about marketing himself and selling his work to the media. The footage of the charging white rhinoceros brought him his initial fame and the beginning of his notoriety. The media clamored for his daring video of the rhino attack, along with some other sensational footage he'd shot on the trip (amazing videos of leopards climbing across the roofs of covered safari wagons, and rare closeups of elephants mating, which he referred to as his "elephant porn"). He was paid substantial sums of money for those photos and videos, and his reputation for being a risk-taking wildlife photojournalist was born.

Twenty-three years old and he had made a splash that put him on the national stage.

He became a much sought after guest on TV talk shows. Eight years later and thousands more perilous wildlife images under his belt, *Rolling Stone* did their feature cover story that labeled him *America's Gonzo Shutterbug.*

In the years he'd been crisscrossing the globe photographing dangerous animals up close, his impressive résumé included grizzly bears, polar bears, Indian sloth bears, Sumatran and Bengal tigers, African elephants, white and black rhinos, great white sharks, killer whales, Amazon piranha, hippos, South African spitting thick-tailed scorpions, Middle Eastern deathstalker scorpions, Cape buffalo, and a wide variety of highly venomous snakes. A month ago he'd added Tyrannosaurus Rex to his list of videoed conquests. His near-term goal was to film the smaller, but no less deadly, Dromaeosaurus and the herbivorous Triceratops. What would really set him apart would be to find a unique dinosaur species that had hatched out of the meteorites last year, but had yet to be seen.

Strangely, he had never before had a chance to photograph salt-water crocodiles. He was about to get that opportunity now. He bubbled with anticipation.

They floated past a group of tour boats, the guides extending bait poles out over the river. Hungry crocs leaped five feet in the air to rip the buffalo meat from the poles. Oohs and aahs of the appreciative tour group guests followed the crocs' loud belly flop splashes as they hit the water.

"Those're some big crocs, eh, CC?" he said to his dive partner

Caleb Campbell as they looked out over the bow observing the tour boat activity. The nerves in his gut tightened, equal parts excitement and wariness.

"You bet. Can't wait to get in the drink with 'em," Caleb responded in his thick Aussie accent.

Jackson had worked with Caleb on several of his Australian trips, most recently in February filming great white sharks in the Neptune Islands. The man was a competent scuba diver and he exuded a quiet professionalism Jackson found reassuring. The man known as CC was also a superb underwater videographer, utilizing a filming style close to his own.

"Time to suit up, gents," Oscar yelled from the helm, cigar stub planted in the side of his mouth. "Our entry site is just around the curve."

Jackson had been briefed they would be diving in a private river inlet, well away from where the commercial tour boats were permitted to go. He, Caleb, and boat divemaster Maurice grabbed their equipment from the racks. They wriggled into their skintight wetsuits and slipped on their flippers. Prepared their masks by rubbing small dabs of Soft Scrub cleanser over the lenses, rinsing them, drying them, then spitting into them and rubbing in the saliva. This would prevent their masks from fogging up in the river.

Jackson opened the two camera cases and pulled out two Sony Dive Buddy high-def videocams, both encased in Amphibico underwater housings. They had used these same cameras to film sharks with great results on two previous occasions. Maurice, whose job it was to direct the dive and watch their backs in the water, pulled out his pneumatic speargun and attached the quiver of extra spears to his dive belt. Salties were a seriously protected species in northern Australia, and the fines for killing one without proper authorization were in the tens of thousands of dollars. Jackson had applied for, and received, the necessary permits to defend themselves in the water should the need arise. Of course, none of them wanted to harm the creatures, but if it came to kill or be killed, Maurice would be their protector.

"Let's not do anything crazy down there, guys," Maurice said, looking out over the placid water of the inlet. "It'll mean tons of red tape and hassle if I have to use this thing," he said, raising the speargun.

Jackson gave the safety diver a glance that said, *Do you have any clue about who you're diving with?*

Caleb spoke. "We promise to be good boys, mate."

Jackson scoffed. "Don't bullshit our divemaster, CC. We're going for the cinematic masterpiece of saltwater croc films. If it means stirring up a bit of trouble to get that, then so be it."

This was the kind of arrogance that made many wildlife photographers refuse to work with Jackson Lattimer. He paid his people well and his outings were high visibility, but his ambition and recklessness made other top professionals shy away from him.

Maurice gave him the stink eye. "Listen, Jack. I won't stand for any nonsense down there. If I see things goin' buggy, I'll have no choice but to call the dive. And when I do call the dive, I don't want any hesitation or push back. My call means *out of the water immediately*. Got it?"

Jackson knew he was insanely reckless at times, but he wasn't stupid. This was Oscar's boat and divemaster Maurice called the shots when they were in the water. To go against him could jeopardize future dives. He said, "Got it, Mo. You're the boss when we're under."

They motored around a wide bend in the river and entered a small brackish bay. The water was calm and clear, the brown hue turning to a dark green. Jackson no longer saw any croc eyes piercing the surface, but he knew the salties were here. He could *feel* them the same way he'd felt those Tyrannosaurs in the caves. He scanned the crescent shoreline, ringed by eucalyptus trees. As they got closer, what he initially thought were tree roots were actually sunning crocodiles. Two of them slithered into the water as Oscar steered the boat to the entry point.

Oscar dropped anchor, the chain thumping the stern deck as it played out. Jackson went in first, backrolling off the dive platform, keeping his mask tight with his left hand while clutching the camera—tethered to his waist—in his right hand. The water enveloped him and he felt the initial chill through the neoprene, the squeeze of the mask against his face. The wetsuit tightened around his shoulders, restricting his upper body movement. He kicked and swam through a surge of bubbles. He heard Caleb and Maurice crash the surface above him. Visibility was better than expected and he checked his surroundings, spiraling to get an all-around perspective.

No salties in the immediate vicinity.

Oscar informed them the depth here was sixty feet. Jackson stroked downward, toward the bottom. Salties could lower their heart rate to three beats per minute and stay submerged for as many as two hours. He knew they liked to lay on river floors to let the swift undercurrents wash over them. He felt the pressure building in his ears as he descended, and tensed his throat, thrust his jaw forward, and swallowed a couple of times to clear the pressure. Caleb and Maurice caught up with him and he gave them the thumbs-up as they swam as a trio.

Suddenly a large croc approached on the left flank, whipping its thick tail and paddling furiously with its short webbed feet to propel it swiftly through the water. The animal circled them, checking them out. It soon was joined by a second salty swimming in from out of the murky depths. The three divers stopped their descent, treading in place, Jackson and Caleb filming the circling creatures that moved in closer with each pass. Maurice kept the speargun in a ready firing position.

Such magnificent animals, Jackson thought as he worked the zoom lens to get a closer view. *They have to be twenty-two feet! More than a ton each! Marvelous throwbacks to the dinosaur age.*

Soon two more salties entered the area and began circling with the other pair. The four big crocs opened their mouths on each pass, displaying all 66 of their large, curved teeth in threatening gesticulations. This predator circling put Jackson in mind of shark movement preceding a feeding frenzy.

He knew he should be fearful, but he wasn't. He felt calm. He was in his element. Time seemed to slow down and a sense of elation overcame him as he followed the salties' languid movements with his camcorder.

It's like they're just checking us out. Not aggressive. At least not yet.

What good is this if they're only going to swim in circles? He and CC might as well be tourists shooting video from a cruise boat.

He swam closer to the largest croc, swinging his arms, provoking it, trying to get it to come at him. The croc stopped its circling, seeming to hang suspended in the water, sizing him up with those freakish, slitted green eyes.

It was a standoff, diver and croc staring each other down for several protracted beats.

And then the beast went on the attack.

The croc swam directly at him, folding its legs in close to its streamlined body and coming in like a moss-covered torpedo. The creature snapped its deadly jaws at him, just missing taking a chunk out of his side as Jackson kicked his flippered feet, backing out of its path. The animal whooshed past with the weight of a mini submarine. The powerful backwash of the huge reptile's wake hit him like a solid wall, slamming him, stunning him, but he managed to keep the camcorder focused on his fearsome subject.

Wow, such enormous power!

His heart hammered so hard he thought it might burst through his wetsuit. He felt revved up and supercharged.

The croc looped back around and came at him a second time.

Jackson knew he could never outswim one of these salties, but he also knew they had poor eyesight underwater. They detected their prey through motion sensors in pits around their mouths, but their efficiency in hunting their quarry was limited to floating on the surface. They were less effective predators when submerged in deep water.

But that didn't mean he could take them lightly.

He quickly peeled off his diving gloves and flung them. They fluttered in the river currents like disembodied hands. The croc swept in and scooped up one of the gloves while Jackson remained stock still and captured it all digitally.

He looked for the other two divers and picked them up about

twenty feet away. He filmed a croc taking a run at Caleb, Maurice distracting it with big movements. Another croc came in from the opposite side and Jackson filmed the two divers tag-teaming the beast, all the while on high alert, keeping an eye out for more salties possibly moving in on him.

A shadow darkened the water above him. He looked up, seeing a big croc, webbed feet spread wide, floating on the surface near the dive boat. Jackson kicked upward, camera zooming in on its white underbelly. With eyes on top of its head, the reptile couldn't see him coming from below. Zoologists theorized that the light colored undersides of crocs and gators protected them from attacks underneath as it allowed them to blend in with the sunlight.

Jackson swam up under the croc and gave it a hard poke in the belly, then surfaced to video the startled animal's reaction. The reptile thrashed and rolled over, jaws snapping, water spraying, chaotically attempting to locate the annoyance. Much more adept at locating prey above the surface, the angry croc found Jackson and literally leaped out of the water at him. Jackson backstroked to avoid getting chomped. Continuing to operate the camera with his right hand, he got in a solid punch to the creature's eye with his left hand, knowing the eyes were the only vulnerable areas on a crocodile. Stunned, the creature hissed and clicked in pain, then submerged and disappeared into the depths.

The water calmed. Jackson heard Oscar yelling from the boat, "You okay? Everything cool, Jack?"

He waved to the skipper and removed his regulator mouthpiece, shouted, "Yeah, I'm fine. But holy shit, Oscar! What a rush!"

He popped the mouthpiece back in and dove, wanting to get more footage below. Descending, he saw more crocs had gathered around Caleb and Maurice. So strange how they circled the divers, as if the salties were in a trance. Occasionally, one would break away from the circle and advance on Caleb or Maurice, the other creating a distraction to ward them off. Jackson floated in place and videoed the scene below.

He saw three more crocs swim in from the murky depths.

Too many salties patrolling the area now. Maurice pointed to the surface, calling an end to the dive. Caleb followed the dive-master up, both men twirling, watching their flanks and backs on their ascent. Jackson was disappointed but understood the need to get out of the water. He certainly didn't want another death tainting this photoshoot. And this was just the first of three days they would be on the river. He'd already gotten a lot of impressive footage and no one had been hurt, so he was happy with the day's production. He ascended slowly with Caleb and Maurice up to the boat, stopping and checking their nitrogen levels along the way so as to avoid the bends.

Back on deck, the men removed their masks and tanks, and stripped off their wetsuits.

"What'd you think, CC?" he said to Caleb. "Life changing experience, wasn't it?"

Caleb nodded enthusiastically. "Bloody sick it was, Jack. Wicked gnarly, I say, mate."

Jackson said, "Yeah, I believe I saw my entire life flash in front of me on one of those croc approaches."

"I know what you mean. They got my nuts all twisted up as well. Scary creatures, those things."

"Did you get some good shots?"

"Yeah. Did some good framing. Solid perspectives and angles. The lighting was better than I thought it would be, too."

Jackson was pleased. "Yeah, same for me. Can't wait to edit it down. It was a good first day out, eh?"

"That it was."

Dressed now in a polo shirt, clam diggers, and sandals, the boat on its way back to Darwin, Jackson checked his phone messages. There were four voicemails, but the one that intrigued him most was from the paleontologist, Hayden Fowler. He listened to it.

"Hey, Jack. It's your old dinosaur pal, Hayden Fowler. I hope you're enjoying your land down under trip swimmin' with the crocodiles. I don't know if you've heard, but things are really pop-ping here in the western states. Our Cretaceous friends are comin' out in force now. Seems as though you got things rolling on your Idaho trip. There have been five attacks on humans in these parts

this week, three of them by Tyrannosaurs. I've lost count as to the number of dead. Lots of raids on livestock, too. And Montana wheat and barley farmers haven't been able to keep Triceratopses out of their fields. Idaho potato farmers are being overrun by the herbivores, too, and one of our dear rancher friends—Bryan Gilliam— was attacked by two Dromaeosaurs. We even found Dromaeosaur eggs on his property and saw them hatch out. I hope you get back here soon to film the goings-on. I've been able to shoot some video, but I'm sure you'd call my work pieces of amateur shit.

"But the main reason I'm calling is to let you know Nora Lemoyne and I have launched a new aviation company. We'll be getting our first helicopter in a couple of weeks so we'll be better able to track these beasts from the air. I'm willing to offer you free air travel to the sites if you'll work with us and promote us. How about it, Jack? Interested? Call me when you come up for air."

Jackson smiled. He liked Fowler's moxie. He was somebody he could respect because he had balls and said what was on his mind. And free helicopter transport? How could he turn that down? As good as today had gone filming salties, he now desperately wanted to get back stateside and get in on recording Cretaceous creatures in the wild. This was beginning to feel like last summer, being stuck overseas while one of the greatest (and weirdest) events in zoological wildlife history was unfolding in the United States. He checked the local time on his satellite phone: 3:12 pm. He did the math in his head. It would be 8:42 pm the previous day in Montana.

He called Fowler, listened to the ring.

Two more days in Australia diving with the salties, then home to Wyoming.

He couldn't wait to get back to filming dinosaurs.

And he could learn so much working with Hayden Fowler.

Hot Librarian Stripper, Chopper Talk, and Dowsing for Dinosaurs

June 24-25: Eden Prairie, Minnesota

NORA FELT ON TOP OF THE WORLD now that Hayden was home. He returned last night on a late flight from Boise after nine days in Montana and Idaho following up on dinosaur sightings. He'd only been gone a little more than a week, but it marked the longest stretch they had been apart in their one year relationship.

She hadn't slept well during his absence, tossing and turning night after night in their bed. She missed his big warm bearish body lying next to her. His empty space in the bed felt like an amputation of sorts, like she had lost a critical part of her anatomy. She missed cuddling with him after hot sex. She missed him whispering naughty things to her and playfully nibbling on her ear lobe. She missed his enthusiastic eagerness to please her orally, which she enjoyed even more than intercourse, both giving and receiving.

Does all of this missing mean I love him?

Nora still grappled with her *being in love* conundrum. Did great chemistry in bed equate to everlasting love? She wanted to believe it but her two failed marriages told her otherwise.

Regardless, she was happy to have Hayden back home with her.

She wanted to give him a special homecoming, so last night, after two glasses of wine, she met him at the door wearing a crotchless black silk teddy, black velvet choker, and flesh-colored stockings with garters, then proceeded to show him just how much she missed him.

Hayden had dropped his luggage where he stood and exclaimed, "*Oh mon Dieu! Vous êtes un beau cul,* Lady Lemoyne."

"Enough of the froggy talk, dear," she said, taking his hand. "Talk to me in English."

"Loosely translated it means I think you are one hot piece of ass. You're my hot librarian fantasy, and . . . Wow! You're gonna make me come in my pants!"

She gave him a droll smile. "You have such a sweet way with words, Hayden." Nora tried to conceal her thrill at being called hot. No man had ever desired her the way Hayden Fowler did.

He looked her over approvingly and smiled. "Looks like my lady has been doing some shopping at Victoria's Secret while I've been gone."

"Guilty," she said." She went up on her tippy toes, wrapped her arms around his neck and pulled his head down to her. Kissed him.

"God how I've missed you, baby," he said, scooping her up and taking her to the sofa.

"Wait," she said, pushing him away as he fumbled with her satin drawstring. "I want to give you a little show before the main event."

He sighed. "You're killing me here, Nora."

"Cool your jets, big boy," she said with a wink. "You're going to like this."

She grabbed her cell phone and called up her Spotify playlist, beginning with "More Than Words" by Extreme. Nora strutted toward him, slowly, seductively, in time with the ballad. She loosened her garters and slowly peeled off her nylons. The lust in his eyes emboldened her as she danced close to him, then backed away, teasing him as he reached for her. She loved drawing out the anticipation, making him wait. This kind of slow foreplay always heightened the sex for her, holding off his urge to sprint to orgasm. She had trained him during their year together, convincing him that her slower buildup techniques and her tantric sex mindfulness led to much more explosive and enjoyable couplings.

She slipped the spaghetti straps off her shoulders and untied the drawstring, giving him a quick flash of her breasts. She turned so he could see her rubbing her nipples underneath the teddy.

If my colleagues saw me now they would be shocked. Strait-laced, no-nonsense, intellectual paleontologist Nora Lemoyne doing a striptease? Say it isn't so! The only thing missing is the stripper pole and lecherous men stuffing my garter with dollar bills.

She dropped her hands between her legs and fondled herself.

Nora was cooking with fire. Wet, turned on.

She ran her tongue along her upper lip and fluffed out her coal-black bob, letting a few stray strands fall over her glasses. "More Than Words" ended. "Sex On Fire" by Kings of Leon filled the living room. Nora glided across the floor, mouthing the lyrics, pointing at Hayden when the chorus rolled around: "You—your sex is on fire!"

She went to remove her glasses and he told her to keep them on. (In her excitement she had forgotten her eyewear was a key item in his hot librarian fetish.) Slowly, seductively, she stepped out of her baby doll teddy and let it drop to the floor. Nora stood before him, completely naked but for her black velvet choker. She made a face of mock embarrassment as she rubbed her crotch with one hand and caressed her breasts with the other. She continued to grind and mouth the lyrics of "Sex On Fire," her burning green eyes never leaving him.

"Stop!" Hayden boomed over the music. "Oh please, love, I can't take any more. My cock is so hard it could cut diamonds!"

He grabbed her and pulled her down on the couch.

Nora fell on top of him with a groan. She could feel his erection through his pants, pushing against her leg. She unbuckled his belt, tugged his zipper down, reached in and grasped him through his boxer shorts, gave him several slow strokes before helping him wiggle out of his pants and slip off his shirt. They were all hands in a feverish rush to get at each other. A week of pent-up desire came pouring out of them, with mouths and tongues and hands and fingers all searching, probing, feeling, tasting. All sense of slowed-down tantric sex was now gone as she mounted him, emitting a small gasp as she took him in. She rode him, moving her hips frantically as he thrust deep and hard below her.

She felt him expanding, on the verge of exploding. "I'm so close, baby," she breathed into his ear. "Wait for me and we'll go over the cliff together."

Nora felt him slowing his thrusts, easing up. She fell into a gentle rhythm with him, slippery and measured.

She rode the edge of ecstasy for long sensuous minutes, Hayden tantalizingly changing up his pace, teasing her, keeping her on the thrilling brink of climax like the expert lover he was.

Finally she couldn't hold back any longer. "I'm ready, honey!" she cried out. "Give it to me! Come with me!"

She shuddered and let go, tremors racing through her in waves of blissful release. Hayden grunted loudly and bucked, once, twice, giving a final hard push and holding his position as he came deep inside her.

Nora straddled him, motionless, trying to catch her runaway breath, every one of her nerve endings spent. She and Hayden were dazed, lost in the wake of their intense lovemaking, too exhausted to move or speak.

They remained in postcoital clutch, their ramped up breathing loud in the small bedroom. She lay on top of him for several long minutes. Neither one stirred as Nora's playlist songs cycled on her cell phone. When "Come Together" by the Beatles played, they broke the spell, sharing a hearty laugh.

Hayden mumbled beneath her, "You sure know how to pick 'em. You shoulda been a DJ."

"What? Not a stripper?"

He laughed. "Good god, babe, you're gonna kill this old man sooner or later."

"Old man?" she said. "You could have fooled me."

"Maybe I should go away more often. I love you, Nora."

"Welcome home, sweetheart," she said, stroking his beard before sliding off of him and gathering up her discarded apparel.

* * *

Last night's sex had been fantastic. It reminded her of that

Carole King song—she'd felt the earth move. Maybe Hayden was right. Maybe he *should* go away more often.

Nora slept soundly, her first night of being able to sleep straight through in a week. She woke up this morning feeling sore but refreshed and rejuvenated.

Her man was back.

All was good with the world.

Leaving a snoring Hayden in bed, she went downstairs to the kitchen and made scrambled eggs and bacon, English muffins slathered with butter, orange juice, and coffee. While preparing breakfast she reflected on where she was last year at this time, thinking about the monumental changes that brought her here to Minnesota to cohabitate with Hayden. She had been leading a Smithsonian sponsored paleontology dig in Choteau, Montana, her first big commercial expedition, managing a team of seventeen scientists and interns, and overseeing several tons of earthmoving equipment. It was her dream job, a position she had been working toward for nearly twenty years.

The expedition started with a bang, her team unearthing the intact skeleton of a Maiasaura with an accompanying nest of fossilized eggs. Then they received word of meteorites hitting western Montana and Idaho, hatching out hundreds of Cretaceous Period dinosaurs. Crazy times ensued. The Smithsonian pulled her and Hayden (her lead paleontologist) off the dig and paid them to track dinosaur hatchlings that were causing havoc on both sides of the Continental Divide. She and Hayden traveled thousands of miles across the two-state area, filming the creatures in the wild and capturing young dinosaurs, transporting them to the Gilliam ranch in Heart Butte for scientific study. They visited with dozens of ranchers and farmers, documenting the aftermath of livestock slaughters and crop devastation caused by these invasive Cretaceous species. On two separate occasions they witnessed horrific Tyrannosaurus Rex and Dromaeosaur attacks on humans. Those gruesome sights and sounds would forever haunt her.

But these days, Nora preferred to think about her relationship with Hayden, and the way it grew into something much more than a professional friendship between two highly educated scientists. She smiled knowingly as she thought about the night she first slept with him, almost a year ago to the day, in that trashy motel room in Bozeman after one too many glasses of wine.

Life's fates have certainly led me down some weird paths the past year.

But it's taken me to some wonderful places, too, like getting a lucrative book deal and co-authoring a bestselling book with Hayden. Doing a coast-to-coast book-signing tour. Earning obscene amounts of money as a writer and dinosaur scout.

Ending up in Hayden's bed.

She put their breakfast on a large serving tray and took it upstairs to the bedroom. Sat on the edge of the bed and ate with him. The food and coffee energized them, and soon they were back pawing at each other's naked bodies. Afterward, they hopped in the shower together for some slippery intimacy.

Forty-five years old and I'm acting like a horny teenager, she thought as she soaped his broad back with a sponge.

They spent the rest of the morning and afternoon sitting in the den, catching up, drinking coffee, soft orchestral music playing in the background. The heliport project was the first order of business.

"Things are progressing rapidly," she told Hayden. "I spoke with Bryan and Loretta yesterday. Contractors are scheduled to lay down the helipad tomorrow. Once the concrete dries they'll be back to paint the surface and install the landing lights. And our Smithsonian friends have helped tremendously, getting the FAA paperwork pushed through quickly so that we'll be flying in accordance with federal aviation regulations."

"Excellent," Hayden said. "What about the hangar and fueling station?"

"Those are moving more slowly. The blueprints are final, but the Gilliams are still in the process of selecting contractors to convert the barn and build out the offices. Peter tells me we can use the barn as is. I agree. The office space is a nice-to-have, but we can wait on it. The barn entrance will need to be enlarged to allow helicopter access.

"The fueling station is another thing. As you know, we first looked at underground storage tanks. But we'd need powerful, top-of-the-line pumps since the tanks have to be buried thirty feet deep. Also, subterranean pumping systems are less safe than above-ground fuel storage, and there is more red tape getting approval from fire departments. The only requirements on above-ground systems are a covering—a lean-to overhang—to protect tanks from the heat of the sun, and the pumps must be a minimum of twenty-five feet from the nearest structure. Far cheaper and less hassle all the way around. When I ran this by Peter, he said our worst case was we'd have to park our chopper outside on the pad for a while and fuel up at offsite locations."

"Okay, no worries there. What about the aircraft? Lacroix told me about a couple of helicopters he's interested in. Said he sent you the specs."

Nora clicked open a several files on her iPad, read from her notes. "Yes. To start with, both his favored models run on turbine engines."

"What does that mean? Turbine as opposed to what?"

"Piston driven. Peter says piston helicopters are shorter range and less powerful when carrying cargo. He says turbine choppers provide superior flight performance and better fuel mileage, and they handle heavy load transport and high-altitude flying better. He also says turbines are more reliable and safer than piston engines. The clincher is that most of his experience has been flying turbine helicopters."

"Okay. Give me the skinny on the models he's looking at."

"Come sit beside me and I'll show you," she said. He joined her on the couch and Nora read from her iPad as they looked at photos. "He likes the Bell 206L-4 LongRanger, one of the more popular commercial copters. It can carry up to seven passengers with a range of four-hundred miles and flight endurance of four hours per trip. His other choice is the Bell 407, which is derived from the Bell 206, and has similar performance stats. It's a flexible utility chopper that is often used for movie filming due to its spacious cabin and Plexiglas windows all the way around. Makes for panoramic visibility and excellent camera perspectives. Both models are manufactured by Bell Textron out of Quebec, Canada."

Hayden scanned the pictures and nodded. "The 407 looks like a good fit. Especially now that I've been in touch with Jackson Lattimer."

"That lunatic wildlife photographer? You mean he hasn't been devoured by some carnivorous animal yet?"

"I know you don't like him, Nora, but—"

"What does Lattimer have to do with our helicopter purchase?"

Hayden said, "Jack can be a huge boon to our startup business, my love. His fame has given him solid connections with the media and the big corporate world. I offered him free air transport for his photoshoots if he'll agree to promote us. He agreed immediately. I checked and he's got close to a million followers on his Instagram account. His videos on YouTube and TikTok are getting hundreds of thousands of views. He told me he'd include an *Air transport provided by Fowler-Lemoyne Aviation* tagline on every video he shoots using our services. He also agreed to talk us up on Twitter and Instagram. His involvement is a good thing, Nora. Jackson Lattimer is guaranteed money in the bank for us."

"I have to be honest, Hayden. I think the man is trouble. I've done some research on him while you've been gone. Two of his assistants have been killed on his shoots the past year due to his irresponsible ways. He's negative karma and I think he would do us more harm than good. America's Gonzo Shutterbug? It's the perfect moniker for him."

Hayden rolled his eyes and waved off her comment as though she was talking nonsense. "For the record, I don't believe in karma, negative or otherwise. It's almost as dumb as astrology. As far as Lattimer goes, he's in a risky profession. There're bound to be some accidents along the way. He'll be the perfect pitchman for our company, Nora. Colorful and exciting. Daring. Hugely popular with the masses."

His defense of the photojournalist irritated her. "Yeah, well, I think he's an accident just waiting to happen, and I don't want that accident coming our way."

"What's the matter, sweets?" he said, staring at her, confused. "You seem really uptight. Things are going great for us. We're on easy street and yet somethin' tells me you're not happy. You're acting a whole lot different than you did last night when you did your stripper dance for me."

She set her iPad on the coffee table and turned to him. Cleared her throat and said, "Okay, I'll level with you, Hayden. I'm having second thoughts about our aviation startup. It's making me crazy. I mean, the kind of money we're talking about is mindboggling. Do you have any idea what a Bell 407 costs?"

"Sure I do. Three million new, half that used, depending on upkeep and maintenance."

She peered at him over the top of her glasses. "And that doesn't make you lose sleep at night?"

"No, it doesn't. We've been over this before. We talked about leasing the first helicopter and financing a second on a six percent, ten-year loan. You said you were okay with that."

"I did, but the more I think about it, you've been talking like we're playing with Monopoly money. Or like we're printing crisp new Benjamins on a press in the basement."

Hayden took a sip of his coffee, set the mug on a saucer, spoke evenly. "Lacroix tells me he's friends with the guy that owns the flight school where he trained. He sells and rents out helicopters. Pete says this guy can cut us a good deal on a lease. Ten thousand a month. I've checked around and that's as good as we'll get any-where. That'll get us started."

"But, Hayden, that's just for a single used copter. You said we'd need two aircraft, minimum. We've also got to build out the hangar, hire and train employees, pay salaries and benefits, purchase insurance, and about a million other incidental expenses."

He laughed. "Methinks you worry too much, milady. You did a great job negotiating with the Smithsonian folks to get them to chip in on the helicopter lease. In fact, you're doing a marvelous job all around in getting our aviation company going," he said, leaning over and kissing her forehead. "Your organizing and team manage-ment skills are off the charts, babe."

Nora blushed, embarrassed, unable to take compliments gracefully. "Thanks. But I have to say it's been taking me away from work on our book."

He touched her wrist. "We'll get the book written in due time, and it's going to be superb. It'll be an even bigger seller than our first book. But look, let me talk you down off the ledge here. We're still on the Smithsonian payroll, both of us earning good incomes. Yes, we're paying out big sums to Lacroix and Gilliam, but we're getting a hell of a lot in return with what they have to offer. They're good business partners, both of them. There's no doubt we have an exorbitant initial cash outlay. But as we discussed a few weeks back, I'm looking at this as a long-term investment. I expect we'll lose money the first few years, but it will be a good tax write-off for our book money that's pouring in. And this is going to make work on our second book so much easier, being able to fly in and out of dinosaur territories on a moment's notice to film and do our research. It's a win-win for us."

"I know what you're saying is true, Hayden. But I still get panicky when looking at all the big dollars we'll be dishing out."

He shook his head in consternation. "I love you, babe, but you're just too cerebral for your own good sometimes. Quit doin' the math and loosen up. Enjoy life. Live a little. I predict that three or four years from now, we'll be wealthy aviation moguls."

She gave him a weak smile. "I wish I shared your confidence."

"You will in time," he said, standing. "Just trust me. I know what I'm doing."

"I know you do. But you *are* clueless about Jackson Lattimer."

He went to the dining room table and picked up his laptop. "Let's just forget about him for a while, shall we? What say we look at the videos I shot on my trip?" he said, returning to the sofa.

"Yes, absolutely," she said. "I'm looking forward to seeing what you have. It might pull me out of my writer's block."

"I got some outstanding recordings, but I need to do some serious editing before I send them to the Smithsonian. I'd like your suggestions on how best to edit these. You have a good eye for that kind of stuff."

"You got it," she said, picking up her empty coffee mug. "I need more caffeine. You want a refill?"

He nodded while sorting through files on his laptop.

Nora returned minutes later with two steaming mugs of coffee. Hayden cued up his first clip and they watched the miraculous hatching out of baby Dromaeosaurs at Gilliam's Guidepost ranch, the newborn dinos climbing up out of the meteorite trench.

Hayden said, "I've got three different clips of this, starting with Gilliam and me finding and uncovering the nest, then the second segment showing three of the eggs breaking apart, then finally this clip showing the Dromes scaling the walls of the pit. I stopped filming when Gilliam started shooting, blasting four of them to smithereens. Damn shame that was. Anyway, I'd like to merge the three files into a single time-lapse sequence, a three-to-four-minute video of discovery to hatchout to ambulatory dinos running off into the prairie grass."

"This is really good," she said, rubbing his arm.

"Well, it's not Jackson Lattimer quality, but—"

"I thought we were going to forget about him. Stop idolizing that maniac, Hayden."

He gave her a sidelong glance. "Don't you mean our meal ticket?"

"If you say so. Show me what else you've got."

She looked over a group of his still shots: the corpse of the Dromaeosaur that attacked Bryan Gilliam; the remains of a Tyrannosaurus Rex that had been hit by a train outside Pocatello; a pack of T-Rexes advancing on a herd of bison near Bozeman (he also had some startling video of the attack). She also watched impressive videos of Triceratops raiding Idaho potato farms and eating up acres of vines to get at the choice spuds underneath.

"I shot plenty of footage of Triceratops ravaging Montana wheat fields, just like we saw them do last year. But it looks like our gluttonous Cretaceous herbivores have found another favorite diet staple," Hayden said as they watched a group of Triceratops using their snout horns to dig out immature potatoes. "I've also got interviews with two irate farmers who grow the cherished Idaho Russet potatoes. They want the government to reimburse them for their losses. And they're just in the middle of their growing season. It's going to get much worse. One farmer shot and killed two of them."

"That's illegal, isn't it?" Nora asked.

"It is in Idaho. The state imposed protections on Triceratops since they are herbivores and don't maim and kill humans. And they weren't as big a pest in Idaho last year as they were for wheat and barley farmers in Montana. You can still legally bag Triceratops in Montana, which only pisses off the Idaho farmers more. I've got photos of those carcasses somewhere here. I promised not to use the potato farmer's name in any reporting we do."

They watched another incredible video of three Tyrannosaurs taking down a couple of big elk in Glacier National Park, Montana. Another one of a T-Rex taking down a huge moose and feasting on it on the banks of the Snake River in Idaho. He showed her several videos of newly hatched Dromaeosaurs and T-Rexes that he'd located in mountainous woodland areas in both states.

"You got a lot done in nine days," she told him while he searched for more material. "You have an uncanny knack for knowing where these creatures are. How do you do that?"

"Well, I had some help in Idaho," he said, pulling at his beard. "A Forest Service wildlife biologist by the name of Bill Carlton. He'd been doing some dino scouting of his own before I arrived, so he knew where the best places were."

"What about Montana?"

"I kind of knew where to look east of the Rockies since we spent most of our time in Montana last year."

She smiled at him. "You're being uncharacteristically humble, Hayden. Admit it, you have a gift, a special sixth sense that leads you to Cretaceous creatures. Like a divining rod or something. Dowsing for dinosaurs," she said with a chuckle.

"That's good, Nora," he said, laughing along with her. "I don't know how I do it really. I guess I just follow my instincts . . . take everything we've learned about them and try to think like pre-historic animals who find themselves in an alien environment."

"This is exciting stuff, Hayden," she said, viewing several other clips of Triceratops hatchlings waddling into the forest for cover, and juvenile Tyrannosaurs running along a riverbank. "It looks like they're coming out in even bigger numbers than last year. You were right about the dinos laying low for the winter. And the fact that they are reproducing this young is a magnificent discovery."

"Yeah, it was a worthwhile trip. It proved two big theories of mine. As you said, it's truly remarkable how these Cretaceous animals mature at warp speed. Their ability to produce offspring in their first year is phenomenal. It's thought that some breeds of sharks and snakes and lizards can do this, but it hasn't really been scientifically confirmed. My other proven theory is that these animals—at least the Dromaeosaurs—return to their place of birth to lay their eggs. We saw that innate natal homing instinct at Gilliam's place. They built their nest in the bottom of the crater where the egg-bearing meteorite hit! It doesn't get more *natal homing* than that. All of this will surely stun zoology and paleontology scholars. This is groundbreaking stuff, Nora."

"Yes, it absolutely is," she said. "Lots of stirring, engaging science and human interest angles for our book. I liked those two writeups you did on the Gilliams confronting the hungry Dromaeosaurs and the hatchout at the meteorite site. I didn't have to do much polishing to flesh it out into two new chapters."

He smiled. "Oh, thanks. It's easier to write about events when they're fresh."

"I sent them to the publisher last Friday and Molly was impressed. I just wish we had video of the Dromaeosaurs trying to get in the Gilliams' horse stables."

Hayden nodded. "Me, too. But I learned a great deal from studying the carcass of the one Bryan killed. I've got some pretty extensive notes on that."

"Good. Send them to me and I'll start working on it. Molly says she needs another chapter by Friday."

"I think you're starting to enjoy this author gig."

"It pays really well and I like books. After all, I'm a hot librarian, remember?"

"How could I ever forget!"

The Heliport, The Cellar, Sin, and Missing Persons

June 28: Gilliam's Guidepost
Heart Butte, Montana

INITIAL CONSTRUCTION OF THE HELIPORT was progressing rapidly. The quadrangle—the spacious grassy courtyard that stretched between the three barns and the Gilliam's farmhouse—had been a beehive of activity the past few days. A pair of cement mixers rolled in two days ago, laying out a level concrete pad in the middle of the yard. Yesterday, another crew spent the day varnishing the surface with a non-skid coating and sealing it with light green fluorescent paint. The finishing touch had been the 50-foot crimson **H** emblazoned in the center of the helipad that one of the workers referred to as *the chopper pilot's bullseye.* Today a team of electricians came to install the necessary lighting.

Bryan leaned on his cane and looked out over the quad, watching the men install the surface-mounted perimeter lights, the center-line landing lights that outlined the **H** landing mark, the mounted floodlights along the barn eaves, and the parallel rows of approach signal beacons leading far out into the grasslands beyond the barns. They were then going to wire the circuitry to a power grid control panel. They worked quickly, efficiently, and were a vocal bunch. Their shouts carried across the quad. Bryan heard terms like amperage, lumens, ballast, illuminance, photometry, kilowatts, voltage, as though they were communicating in some obtuse foreign tongue. He took in all the chatter, understanding some of the jargon. It sent him back some twenty years, when he and Jimmy Enright had converted the old zinc mine at the rear of the property into a luxurious, three-tiered, subterranean survival bunker they named The Cellar. He and Jimmy had done all the electrical work, installing and wiring the light fixtures, appliances, and HVAC system, learning as they went.

Damn how he missed Jimmy! Those were some good days back then, when they were young studs and the world was theirs for the taking.

He was momentarily overcome by a melancholy that descended on him like a misty, dark cloud. He stood there, wobbling on his cane, his leg aching more than usual, the realization hitting him like a hammer blow to the head that he would never again see his brother-in-law. He felt sad knowing that the good old days of his past were shrinking in the rearview mirror of his mind. Jimmy was gone forever. His one and only male friend. Someone other than Loretta he could confide in.

Loretta was having problems, too, dealing with the loss of her brother, and had started seeing Dr. Krickstad again. The sessions seemed to be helping her.

Maybe I need to get back with the good doctor, too?

What is it about nostalgia? Why does the past always seem so much better than the present?

Bryan shook his head vigorously, trying to chase the blues. He focused on the lighting techs scurrying about, pulling tools from their work belts, pounding and drilling, securing beacon covers, mounting lighting brackets, testing, shouting out instructions, measurements, results. But today there was no escaping The Cellar and memories of his times with Jimmy Enright.

His and Jimmy's subterranean dwelling had been one of their proudest accomplishments. They had turned the dark, dusty zinc mine into three well ventilated floors with central heating and air. Four spacious apartment suites equipped with kitchenettes, indoor plumbing, modern amenities, and strong WI-FI connectivity. He and Jimmy had poured their hearts and souls and bodies into The Cellar not long after they'd returned from their second Afghanistan tour of duty. They thought the well-appointed survival bunker would be good insurance, a place for the Gilliam and Enright families to live in if, and more likely *when*, the power hungry idiots ruling the world unleashed their missiles of doom. Thankfully there hadn't been a need to use the space for survival purposes. At least not yet.

Over the years, The Cellar had been a comfortable place for guests to stay when the 12-room Gilliam Inn—destroyed in last summer's fires—was booked solid. But the belowground domicile saw its most use over the past year. Hayden Fowler stayed there during his last visit. It's also where Hayden and Nora Lemoyne resided last summer when they were here researching the dinosaurs penned in Gilliam's Glade and writing their bestselling book. Peter Lacroix's family had also occupied two suites for a month so Brin could work as lead jeweler on Bryan's Cretaceous Stones jewelry operation, an ambitious venture that took up the entire basement tier of The Cellar. Peter and his family would be moving back into their same two suites permanently next week, as Peter was to begin his employment with Fowler-Lemoyne Aviation.

In many respects, The Cellar was more comfortable and spacious than their new farmhouse that had been constructed after the fires. Bryan would be fine with the family living out there permanently, but Loretta and the kids—especially Lianne—felt claustrophobic underground without windows and natural sunlight. And he had to admit, the balky old mining freight elevator could be a bit of a hassle.

He was looking forward to getting the heliport up and running. And he wanted to get his Cretaceous Stone jewelry operation ramped up again. But for that to happen they needed an abundant supply of dinosaur meteorite rock. Peter knew where it was. It was frustrating having to wait on their first helicopter before they could make pickup runs to Southern Montana. It had been three long weeks since Peter had discovered the Cretaceous boulders. Would the meteorite rocks still be there? Peter told him it was a remote area, a place with little flyover air traffic. But still. Bryan fretted about losing out on the valuable rock almost every day. He was chomping at the bit and impatient, wanting to get their first helicopter in operation. Its inaugural flight would be the 450-mile round trip to southern Montana to pick up pieces of the valuable meteorite. Hayden, Nora, and Peter all agreed that the long flight to bring back heavy cargo would be a good initial test of their new aircraft.

As he watched the lighting techs scurry around the quad and out into the field, Bryan recalled his terrifying encounter with the Dromaeosaurs here two weeks ago. He'd stood in this very spot, watching the pair of Cretaceous carnivores attempting to get at the horses in the stables.

While there had been increasing dinosaur confrontations with humans in western Montana since then, there had been no sign of Dromaeosaurs—or any other dinos—here at Gilliam's Guidepost the past two weeks. True to his promise, Hayden had kept the attack on Bryan and the dead Dromaeosaur under wraps. Fortunately the public never caught wind of it.

Earlier this week, armed with rifle and revolver, he drove out to the east meadow to check the meteorite pit, and was relieved to see that there was no new nest or eggs.

But as much as he would have liked to keep the attack from his boys and Lianne, he couldn't. It would have been negligent of him and Loretta to keep quiet. They couldn't just let their kids go about their days as if nothing happened. The Cretaceous beasts were back on the prowl, bigger and more fierce than they were last summer. Paul and Ethan—and especially Lianne—were vulnerable. The night after the attack, Bryan and Loretta decided they would talk to the kids the next day. However, Paul got to Bryan before they could get the family together for a discussion. Late the next afternoon, he came storming into the house from the rehearsal barn, wild-eyed and accusatory. Bryan was relaxing with a beer, watching TV in the den, still trying to process how he'd gotten so damned lucky, how it was that he had escaped death.

"What in the hell is that *thing* you've got in the freezer?" Paul bellowed.

Taken by surprise, Bryan mumbled something about having no idea what Paul was talking about, which he knew sounded lame.

"Sin just got back from the store and was putting our pizzas in for later," Paul started. "She screamed bloody murder when she opened the freezer door. I thought maybe she was bein' attacked or something. Kit and I put our guitars down and hustled over to see what was happening. The three of us stared at the ugliest creature I ever saw, half its head blown off. One a those Dromes like we had here last year, only a lot bigger. What gives, Pops?"

Bryan cursed himself: *I should have known Pauley and his bandmates would be using that freezer.*

But maybe it was best they *had* seen the Dromaeosaur carcass. The sight of the bloodied Drome would certainly put the fear of God in the teens, make them proceed with utmost caution.

Bryan had no choice but to lay everything out for Paul. He described the Dromaeosaur attack, with Loretta being chased back to the house and him stepping out to hunt the pair of Dromes down. Him killing the one in the freezer and Loretta winging the second animal, and them watching the wounded creature lope off into the forest.

"Yeah, I saw those cuts on your hand earlier," Paul said. "I wondered where they came from. And I wondered why you and Mom were acting so . . . nervous. You both had the heebie-jeebies somethin' fierce."

My oldest child certainly doesn't miss much.

"It was a pretty nasty tangle, Pauley. They're back, stronger than ever. Incredible really, how quick and stout they are. If it hadn't been for your mother," he looked away for a long beat, "well, let's just say I might not be sitting here talking with you right now."

"Jesus, Dad."

"Yeah, I believe Jesus himself might have been lookin' out for me."

"Does this mean we're gonna have to move the horses again?"

"No. The horses are better protected in their new stables, but I'll need you and Ethan to help me reinforce the Dutch doors in the stalls."

"No problem. But are we gonna have to hide out indoors like we did for a while last summer? Because I refuse—"

"No, Pauley. You and your brother are old enough and responsible enough to look out for yourselves. Lianne is another story.

Your sister isn't going to like this one bit. Your mother and I will speak with your brother and Lee tonight, but I'm telling you right now, you need to be on the alert again. If you go riding, take your rifle with you and stay eagle-eyed. These things can come out of nowhere really fast. You and your band can still rehearse, but keep the barn locked up tight when you're inside. When you're coming and going, you and your friends need to be armed. Do your band-mates carry guns?"

"Kit and Ox do. But Sin doesn't. She doesn't like guns. Her weapon of choice is a canister of pepper spray she keeps in her purse."

Bryan let out an amused chuckle. "Pepper spray against these animals? Your girlfriend needs a gun. I can help her purchase the right weapon and teach her safety and proper maintenance."

"She's gonna push back on that, Pops. Sin's pretty stubborn."

"You think she's still stubborn after seein' that monster in the freezer?"

"Yeah, now that you mention it, maybe that *has* changed her mind." Paul looked at him curiously. "You make it sound like we're going to war."

"It *is* a war, Pauley. A war against an enemy that can tear you apart and devour you in minutes."

"You're scaring me, Dad."

"That's my intention. You *should* be scared. Fear means survival. That's what our Army drill sergeants used to tell us grunts to prepare us for battle. I want you to be safe. I want you to watch your back, and for your friends to have each other's backs. Surely I don't have to remind you how many good people were killed by those beasts here last year. They're even bigger and faster this year."

Paul nodded slowly. "We'll be careful. But why did you freeze the corpse? Why didn't you bury it out in the field?"

"Because that scientist, Hayden Fowler, is visiting. Day after tomorrow. I want him to examine it."

"Cool. He's a big celebrity now with that book of his. He's a big music fan, too, I can tell. But this new dinosaur invasion sucks," Paul said, shaking his head. "It's like déjà vu. Like these monsters have a grudge against us or something."

"It does seem that way, yes. Just promise me you'll be careful."

Paul groaned. "I promise already."

"Good. How's everything going with Moonrise? The band's been sounding good lately."

"Thanks. We've been working on a few originals. A guy in an expensive suit approached me at our gig last night and said he wants to record us. Just a single at first, but then an EP and maybe a full-length album once we get enough material."

Bryan saw the hopeful shine in his son's eyes, the optimistic lilt in his voice. *The boy is hopelessly naïve. Still a child really.* "Be careful with that, Pauley. Dinosaurs aren't the only predators lurking about."

"I know, I know," Paul said, obviously annoyed with Bryan's unsolicited advice. "The guy was a smooth talker, but we mostly thought he was full of shit."

"Well, please come talk to me before you boys go signing anything."

"Don't worry, I will," he said with a roll of his eyes.

"Things goin' good with Sin?"

"Yeah. Things are great between her and me, but the guys are gettin' a bit sick of her hanging out with us all the time. She's been pushing to get in the band. She wrote the lyrics to a couple of our new originals and now she fancies herself as a lead singer. Her lyrics are really good but she can't carry a tune. I love her, and I know she's crazy about me, but it might be becoming a problem. Kit and Ox tell me in private they don't want to do girly songs. Especially not with her doing lead vocals."

All Bryan heard was that his son was in love with Sinopa Harwood. The girl was a beautiful, dark skinned Blackfoot who oozed seventeen-years-young sensuality with every smile and strut. Sin was a passionate girl with simmering ebony eyes and a spill of long brunette hair that she kept draped over one delicate shoulder. They had only been dating a couple of months, but things had become serious quickly.

"Are you protecting yourself, Pauley?"

"Christ, Dad! Do you always have to give me *The Talk* every time Sin's name comes up? And what makes you think we've done the deed?"

"Well, have you?"

"It's none of your damn business!"

"Oh, but it *is* my business. Look, I just want you to be careful, okay? This is your first real relationship and I know how gorgeous girls can make a young man's head spin. They can make you do things you might regret later. Trust me on this."

Paul stared at him defiantly, his face flushed in anger. "I don't regret anything I've done with Sin."

"I'm sure you don't. But let me put it another way. I'm not ready to be a grandpa yet."

"Jesus, you're a friggin' trip. Goodbye, Pops," Paul said, turning and walking out of the den in a huff.

"I love you, son," Bryan said to his back, watching Paul disappear into the kitchen without a response. He heard the door leading out to the sunroom slam shut.

The following day Paul came to him and said, "I'm super glad that beast didn't take you down, Dad," which Bryan knew was his son's way of telling him he loved him.

The recollection brought a smile to his face.

He was yanked out of his reverie and brought back to present day by a loud male voice calling his name, the calls rising above the workers' hammering and drilling. Bryan looked across the quad to see Apisi approaching. The man walked with a determined purpose, a look of concern pinching his weathered face. The red and gold snake tattoo encircling his forearm gleamed in the afternoon sun.

"*Oki*, boss," Apisi said in his usual Blackfoot greeting.

Ap had always reminded Bryan of a jack-o-lantern with his moon face and wide gaps in his teeth. Apisi was a good man, a dedicated and loyal ranch hand who had been with them fifteen years, and Bryan felt shame every time he equated the Blackfoot cowpoke with a Halloween pumpkin.

"Hey, Ap," he replied, bumping fists with him.

Apisi fingered one of his two long braids of hair and looked around at the workers doing their thing. "Your airport is really taking shape, *napi.*"

"Yeah. Surprising how fast it's all coming together," Bryan said, noticing strands of wet grass on Apisi's boots, the caked mud on his jeans. "You been out grazing the horses?"

"Yes. They've been restless lately. Especially Beauregard. I haven't seen your daughter riding the past couple of weeks. Is that because of the attack on you and Mrs. Gilliam?"

"Yeah. We're keeping a close watch on Lianne. Tryin' to keep her safe. She spent a lot of last week with her cousin Marnie in Shelby, helping her Aunt Olivia on the farm. The only dinos they've been seein' out there are Triceratops. No carnivores." He eyed Apisi, who was scratching at his neck and looking nervous. "Just curious, Ap. You haven't told anybody about the attack, have you?"

Apisi shook his head as if offended. "Oh no, sir! I would never do that. You told me to keep it to myself and I have. I haven't even told Chogan."

"I didn't think you did, but I had to ask. The horses all back in the barn?"

"Yes, sir."

"Good. We can't leave them out in the pasture unprotected this summer."

"Yes, I know. But if I may say so, Mr. Gilliam, the horses need more attention. They need to be ridden more. With all due respect it's not good to keep 'em cooped up inside all the time."

"I'm well aware of that, Ap. That Dromaeosaur attack on the stables really shook us up. But we'll get back to letting them out soon. You know that you and Chogan are welcome to ride anytime you want. Same applies to your friends and family. Just be sure that whoever goes out takes a firearm with them and grooms the horse and cleans the stall afterward."

"Yes, thank you, sir. I appreciate your generosity."

An awkward silence ensued. Apisi shifted his weight from one foot to the other, nervously fidgeted with his braids. His eyes had a hollowed-out, spooked quality about them.

It prompted Bryan to say, "It's obvious you didn't search me out to talk about our horses, Ap. What's on your mind? You need money?"

"Oh no, sir. You pay me plenty good."

"Then what is it?"

"It's my wife, Mr. Gilliam."

"Kanti?" Bryan said, recalling Apisi's sweet, quiet, roly-poly wife. "What about her? Is she sick?"

Apisi hung his head. "No. I'm afraid it might be worse than that," he said, his words whistling softly through the gaps in his teeth.

"Worse? How so?" Bryan asked, a feeling of dread grabbing him. "What's wrong with Kanti?"

"She's missing."

"Missing?"

"Yeah, gone. AWOL. Lost. Disappeared into the night."

"Shit, Ap. I'm sorry. How long?"

"Two days. More than forty-eight hours. Last I heard from her she was shopping at the trading post. I'm really worried."

"Have you notified the police?"

"Oh, I absolutely did. I called the state police. As soon as they knew Kanti was Blackfoot, they started talking in circles, finally passing me off to the Blackfeet tribal police, telling me it was their jurisdiction. The officer I spoke with told me there was a good possibility my precious Kanti had been dragged off by a dinosaur, and asked if I had been keeping up with the news about attacks on humans. Can you believe that, Mr. Gilliam? I got very angry and started yelling at the man, saying how could he possibly know that without investigating. The police don't want anything to do with this. I contacted the Bureau of Indian Affairs yesterday but I haven't heard anything back. I'm frustrated," Apisi said, tears wetting his eyes. "My Kanti is out there somewhere, lost and I'm sure, terrified. I fear something really bad has happened to my wife, Mr. Gilliam. These people we pay to protect us aren't doin' their jobs. At least not for us Blackfeet. They treat us like we're subhuman . . . like we're diseased dogs running wild in the streets. I don't know what else to do. I feel so helpless. I normally wouldn't ask, but this is really serious. Can you please help me, Mr. Gilliam? I don't know where else to turn."

Bryan knew that missing and murdered Indigenous women had long been an epidemic in Montana. The authorities, to their ever-lasting shame, were reluctant to investigate missing Native women, preferring to spend their time and policing budgets on crimes against white people. Knowing this, kidnappers operated with near free latitude. Based on statistics, he didn't have high hopes for rescuing Apisi's wife. But he couldn't, in good conscience, ignore the man who had given the Gilliams fifteen-plus years of steady, hard work. And Ap—along with Chogan and Jimmy Enright—had risked his life helping Bryan hold off the Animal Emancipation Faction terrorists who invaded Gilliam's Guidepost last summer.

Bryan stepped forward, reached out and cupped Apisi's shoulder. "I'm so sorry this has happened to you, Ap. I'm not a detective and I don't have the stamina I once did, but I'll do what I can to help."

Taipans, Tank, T-Rex

July 1: Rendaya Ranch
Flathead National Forest, Montana

KELTON RENDAYA FED HIS SNAKES every Monday. He looked forward to the task, seeing it as the best possible way to kick off the week.

Live snake feedings stimulated him in ways he could not explain. It was almost sexual for him. A warped fetish, he supposed. Maybe a few twisted genes that had shaken loose from his veterinarian roots? Whatever it was, he couldn't deny it. He was mesmerized watching the interplay between predator and prey. It was the food chain hierarchy in action, the law of the natural world. Why fight it? Nature's ballet of death providing sustenance had been going on since life first formed on this planet, animals dancing their choreographed steps leading to the inevitable coda.

Predator and prey.

Dominance and submission.

As ancient as the sun, the moon, and the stars.

It was primordial.

It was *beautiful*.

He sat in the darkness of the snake barn, the only light coming from the ring of high-walled aquarium tanks surrounding him. Ventilation fans whispered. Vacuum pumps wheezed. The 125-gallon tank he faced contained a six-foot inland taipan, the world's deadliest snake. The Australian serpent lay in a tight coil, its dark obsidian eyes like tiny chips of polished lava rock. Unlike most of Kelton's snake menagerie, this guy wasn't for sale. But he *was* a big moneymaker. Twice a month he milked this snake along with his seven-foot coastal taipan, and sold the venom to antivenom manufacturers at $4,000 a gram. He milked some of his other snakes, too—black mambas, king cobras, vipers, rattlers—but the taipan venom was by far the most profitable. Only scorpion venom—highly sought after by big pharmaceutical labs to help detect and cure diseases—brought higher prices. Venom from the aptly named deathstalker scorpion brought double the price of taipan venom. But the little buggers were a pain in the ass to milk. Kelton had to use tongs and a pair of tweezers for the venom extraction. It was time consuming, dangerous work. So much so that he was thinking of selling the scorpions to the labs directly, and letting them deal with the venom extraction. Less revenue, but much easier and far safer. His snake venom sales provided him with more than enough legal income. It kept the IRS hounds at bay while he racked up lucrative cash-under-the-table sales from his illicit operations.

To keep the venom flowing, Kelton kept his snakes well nourished. He rolled up his sleeves and donned heavy leather gloves, reached into a wooden crate and pulled a plump, long-haired rat out by the tail. The rodent squirmed mightily, its high-pitched squeals bright and urgent. He opened the top of the tank and dropped the rat inside. The snake came alive, uncoiling, flicking its forked tongue, sensing a chemical change in its environment. The rat scurried into the opposite corner, screeching and chittering, slamming against the glass, trying in vain to escape. Finally realizing it was trapped, it turned to face its adversary, twitching its whiskers, its beady little eyes wide with fear. The taipan slithered along the tempered glass bottom, getting into striking position, its movement languid, calculating. Sinuous. The rat scrambled to an adjacent corner, shrieking wildly.

Kelton watched the primitive dance, a dizzying euphoria coming over him.

The taipan ceased movement, laying splayed out in an s-shaped curve, its bullet-shaped head pointed at the frightened rodent. The snake flicked its tongue repeatedly, compensating for its poor eyesight, locating the rat's exact position by picking up its scent.

Such a beautiful specimen, he thought, admiring the snake's honey gold and black markings.

The taipan struck.

A lightning quick jab, its fangs plunging into the rat's belly and holding there, jaws squeezing, opening, squeezing again, biting repeatedly, injecting the rat with its potent venom. The rodent's wild squealing lessened to a barely audible whimpering, and then silence as paralysis set in.

The snake lay immobile with its lifeless prey secured in its mouth, as if the taipan was savoring the taste of his catch. After a minute or two of stillness, the snake swished its tail aggressively, opened its mouth wide, and took in the rat in one swift jerk, working it into the back of its throat, swallowing the rodent whole. Kelton watched in fascination as the snake's body stretched to accommodate the rat, the meal making its slow way down the taipan's digestive track to its stomach.

"Good show, my friend," he muttered to the gorged taipan. "Five-star cuisine, isn't it? A gourmet dinner I know you'll thank me for with a rich batch of venom."

He stood and picked up his crate full of screeching rats, moving on to repeat the hand-feeding process for his other snakes. He moved down the rows of aquariums, listening as the hisses and rattles increased in volume. His snakes always knew when it was feeding time.

Kelton plopped rats into tanks, looking on as the snakes feasted. His mind was at peace. He felt blessed. His venomous snake and scorpion trade was doing well. So was his banded Gila business. He'd also recently made an exorbitant profit on a handful of African clawed frogs, which were highly illegal in Montana. Kelton was sometimes amazed at the huge demand for his reptiles, amphibians, and arachnids. It was smooth, almost hassle-free animal trafficking commerce. The smaller animals were easy to transport and conceal from the authorities.

The mammals brought higher prices, but the size and temperament of many of them required more caution. He'd sold a pair of Costa Rican howler monkeys last week to an unlicensed backyard zoo. And he had orders for his three South American spider monkeys. Close contacts with tiger farms in Thailand and Vietnam had allowed him to bring in some of the big cats over the years—highly endangered Bengal and Malayan tigers that fetched $20,000 apiece. Congolese lions. Cheetahs and leopards. Locally he'd brokered mountain lions and bobcats, even a couple of mature grizzly bears that went to a Montana wildlife casting agency. And his Chinese connections had allowed him to traffic in more pangolins than he could count. Asian pangolins had become a larger part of his U.S. business, with Americans craving their scaled leather for boots, handbags, and belts. All of it prohibited in the States as the pangolin numbers were in great decline. And there were the illegal animal parts he dealt in—bear gallbladders (a huge moneymaker due to harvested bear bile being in high demand for treatments of human gallstones, hypertension and some cancers), and bear paws that Taiwanese restaurants desired for their bear paw soup delicacy they sold for $1,500 a cup.

His dinosaur trafficking operation was just starting to ramp up. To be honest, Kelton was a little nervous about it. More so than any of his past illicit trafficking. The dinos were large animals that the authorities were watching closely. Housing them and transporting them created all kinds of security and logistical issues. A bust now would blow his entire operation wide open, destroy everything he'd worked so hard for. He was proceeding, but with great caution.

He'd turned over three Dromaeosaurs the past couple of weeks, selling two to a rich Chinese capitalist in Nebraska—Henry Wu—for $120,000, and a third to a wealthy rancher in Wyola, Montana for $50,000. Both were cash deals netting Kelton 140K. Last week he'd purchased his first Tyrannosaurus Rex from his go-to trappers, Mick and Claire Prescott. Delivery was expected today. Tank Mahaffey and Hoops Terrell left yesterday for Idaho to make the pickup. Kelton was expecting word from them at any time. He'd had to shell out $35,000, but he already had a longtime client in Kansas—Frederick Lawson—promising to pay $150,000 for the animal. Lawson had already laid down fifty percent in earnest money.

Kelton had been working through his channels to buy two more T-Rexes. The Prescotts told him they could get him a pair within a week, but they doubled their price to $70,000 apiece, citing the risks involved: trapping the animals and having to pay off government officials. Kelton knew the bribe to the authorities claim was bullshit. Citing fear of government fines and arrest had become a common negotiating ploy by trappers trying to raise their prices in this new dinosaur age. Be that as it may, things *were* getting hot along these parts of the Continental Divide. Kelton knew that much was true. But he'd called Mick Prescott out for the bribe nonsense.

"Don't try to play me, Mickey," Kelton warned him on his encrypted phone line. "We've been doing business a long time, and I'd hate to have to cut you and Claire off."

"Sorry, Kel. But you're an astute businessman. You know all about bottom line economics. You can't blame me for trying to increase my profit margin."

"I'm not blaming you for that. Just saying you should pick your spots better, that you shouldn't get greedy with one of your longtime loyal clients. That gets a little dicey, you ask me. Jeopardizes our relationship. Starts making me look closer at what your competitors have to offer."

"Yeah, you're right, Kel. Sorry, I should have known better than to pull the federal shuffle on someone like you. But I gotta say, there're a lot of strange things going on with the government concerning these dinosaurs."

"Oh yeah? How so?"

"Well, the Idaho and Montana state governments have reinstituted their cash bounties for Dromaeosaur and Tyrannosaurus Rex kills since attacks against humans are on the rise again. But the feds are fining and jailing people who are trying to trap and sell them. They've got small armies of Fish and Game agents running around like headless chickens tracking folks like us. They let the hunters go wild, and even reward them. But they target us, like we're criminals or something."

Kelton had laughed. "We *are* criminals, Mickey. You keep deceiving yourself into thinking we're not. The sooner you accept it the better you'll sleep at night. Do what I do. Count your money and don't think too much about where it comes from. Practice the criminal creed and wear the badge proudly, my friend."

"Yeah, maybe you're right."

"I'm *absolutely* right. And find a way to get your price down on those Rexes, Mickey. I can't go that high."

"I'll see what I can do."

* * *

Kelton was feeding one of the black mambas when his satellite phone buzzed. He saw it was Tank Mahaffey.

"You make the pickup?" he asked.

"Yep. A coupla hours ago. We're stopped for lunch right now."

"I told you not to stop for anything but refueling."

"Hey, Hoops and me are growing boys. We can't go without nourishment for six hours."

"And I told you to call me when you were leaving with the merchandise."

"I *am* calling when we're leaving," Mahaffey said smugly. "Just a coupla hours *after* we left. What's two hours in the overall scheme of things, anyway?"

Kelton felt his anger rising. "Why do you always have to be so difficult?"

"Keeps life exciting."

"Anybody see you loading Rexy?"

"Christ, Kel. This ain't my first dino rodeo. We were next to the Salmon River. Surrounded by the Sawtooth Mountains. Nobody but bears and elk out there for fifty miles."

"What about the delivery guys?"

"What about them?"

"Who made the delivery?"

"The same dudes who delivered our Dromaeosaurs. Bradwich and Felton."

"Any problems with the exchange?"

"Nope, other than this is one humongous Rex."

"How humongous?"

"Eleven feet three inches, not counting the tail. Gotta weigh close to six- or seven-hundred pounds, I'd say. All scaly muscle and a nasty disposition. It took all four of us to wrangle him into the truck."

Eleven feet? Fred Lawson will be pleased.

"Nasty disposition?" Kelton asked. "Wasn't it sedated?"

"Of *course* it was."

"So how'd you know it had a nasty disposition?"

"I don't know, Kel. Because it looked mean, okay? It's a T-Rex for Chrissakes. Gimme a fuckin' break."

Kelton knew the return trip was approximately six hours. "So did you tranq it properly for the long ride? Shoot it up with the prescribed dosage?"

He heard Tank sigh. "Goddamnit, Kel, why're you always doubtin' on me the way you do?"

"Because you have a track record of monumental screwups, that's why."

"Oh ye of so little faith. Yes, Hoops shot the beast up good. He'll be sleepin' until Christmas."

"Who? Hoops or the Rex?"

"Good one, chief," Tank said, chuckling.

"The exchange went well?"

"Yep. Bradwich counted every bill, checked to make sure each one was legal tender. It took forever. You know how long it takes to check thirty-five grand in small bills?"

"Anybody suspicious tailing you on the highway?"

"Damnit, Kel, why the twenty questions? You wanna know the brand of underwear I'm wearin' too?"

"Not particularly. Just if you spotted anybody who's overly curious."

"I don't know. Let me ask my navigator," Tank said, his words dripping in sarcasm. "Hey, Hoops, has there been anybody on our ass?"

Kelton heard Tommy 'Hoops' Terrell say "Nope."

He said, "You two get on back here before dark so we can get our newest addition in the pen and acclimated."

"Ten-four, Kel. We'll be there in three or four hours, give or take a few."

"I don't want to hear that *give or take a few* horseshit, Tank." Kelton checked his watch. "It's two o'clock now. I want you back here no later than six."

"Is that six Mountain Daylight Time or Mountain Standard Time? Or would it be Pacific Daylight Time perhaps?"

Why the hell do I put up with him?

"See you at six," Kelton said, exasperated. "And obey the speed limits, Tank."

He disconnected and went back to feeding his snakes.

The truck rolled in at 6:35, its chassis squeaking as it crossed the bridge, arriving in the glen on a cloud of exhaust. Kelton felt a lump of excitement lodge in his throat. He'd been waiting at the enclosures with Thorn for the past hour. It was going to take him and all three of his ranch hands to wrangle the beast into the holding pens.

His first Tyrannosaurus Rex had finally arrived and he was hopped up. Giddy even.

Tank Mahaffey shut down the engine and creaked open his door. He lifted his brawny form out of the cab and stepped down. Hoops did the same on the passenger side, his slender, six-foot-five frame casting a long, spindly shadow. Both men stretched their legs. Hoops lit up a smoke and pocketed his lighter. Tank, wearing a *Get Lost In Montana* baseball cap, went to the edge of the woods to take a leak.

"About time you jokers showed up," Kelton said with a sneer.

"You try driving Idaho backroads keeping to the speed limit," Tank quipped over his shoulder as he relieved himself. "We'll see how fast you make it."

Kelton frowned. "Well if you hadn't stopped for lunch—"

"Why're you always on my case, Rendaya?" Tank said, zipping up and turning, a flush of anger darkening his beefy face. "I do your dirty work for you and you treat me like I'm nothing but a steaming pile of diarrhea you stepped in." He took a couple of long strides toward Kelton, fists clenched.

"Now let's not go gettin' hostile, Tank," Thorn said. "We've got some serious offloading to do here."

"Indeed we do," Kelton said, irritated with Tank's disrespectful insolence in front of the other two. "Don't you ever forget who pays your salary, Gordon," he said, using Mahaffey's first name that he knew Tank hated. "Now let's take a look at our newest acquisition, shall we?" He went to his Dodge Ram and grabbed the DanInject tranquilizer dart rifle from the cargo bed.

"You won't need that," Hoops said, moving around to the rear of the truck, cigarette dangling from his lips.

Kelton flaunted the rifle. "Just a precaution in case our sleeping beauty Rex needs another jolt."

"We'll need to get the ramp out first," Hoops said, unlocking the padlock on the rollup door.

Hoops threw his cigarette butt on the ground, pulled the grab handle and yanked. The door juddered as it rolled upward on its tracks.

Like a rocket shot from a missile launcher, the Tyrannosaur charged out of the truck's cargo hold, fully alert, bounding off the back of the truck. A prehistoric demon possessed.

All four men stood there, mouths agape, paralyzed by shock.

For a flash of an instant, Kelton saw a fearsome shovel mouth of pointed teeth come at him.

Before he could raise the rifle to fire a dart, the beast struck, flattening him like he'd been hit by a freight train.

He hit the ground hard, the beast's clawed toes gouging him as it ran over him, braying like an insane donkey.

Steamrolled, his brain rattled, he lay there, dazed, hearing chaotic shouts all around him. He frantically tried to locate the tranq gun.

In his peripheral vision he saw Hoops and Tank on the ground, Thorn running away. Everything had a jagged, disjointed quality to it, like looking through a kaleidoscope.

Kelton found his rifle and reeled it in.

He got into a sitting position, his head spinning madly.

Saw the Tyrannosaur sprinting, its powerful legs churning.

He took quick aim and fired off a shot. Missed badly, the dart sticking the trunk of a ponderosa pine.

He watched the creature's thick, leathery tail, raised up behind it, flipping side to side like a rudder as the animal lumbered into the woods. After several prolonged minutes, he heard it splashing in the shallows of the river.

Full of rage, Kelton got to his feet. He was shaky, dizzy. Despite his queasiness, he advanced on Tank, who groaned and writhed on the ground ten yards away, his cap lying in the dirt beside him.

"You're a goddamned nitwit, Gordon!" he screamed, doing his best to refrain from killing the idiot. "You didn't dose the animal right. You could've killed us all, you fucking moron!"

"I did the dosing , Kel," Hoops said calmly, getting to his feet and studying his bleeding arm. "And I did it right, didn't I, Tank?"

Kelton, seething, looked down at Tank. "You were in charge, Gordy. This is on you. No way that Rex was sedated properly. If at all." He looked at Hoops. "How much tranq did you give it?"

"Exactly what you told us to give it, Kel. I emptied a full dart into him. At the pickup site, when we made the transfer."

"Just the one dart?"

"Well, yeah. That was your instruction, wadn't it?"

Kelton shook his head in disgust. "You brain-dead moron! Ever stop to think why I gave you two loaded darts?"

Hoops looked to Tank for support, but none was forthcoming. He tried his best to explain. "Well, I um . . . I thought the Rex was plenty conked after I shot it. It was already completely under from the zap and I thought a second dart might kill it. That stuff is strong. I didn't wanna bring you a dead T-Rex."

Kelton couldn't believe what he was hearing. He looked back at Tank. "The ride back was six hours, Gordon. One dose of xylazine is only good for five hours, max. Really more like three or four hours. You knew that. I assigned you to do the injection, not Tommy. You were supposed to hit the Rex with the second dart when you stopped to gas up. We discussed this before you left."

Tank looked up at him from where he lay. "The gas station was too crowded. Too dangerous to try it there."

"Then you could've pulled off to the side of one of those country roads and done it. Jesus, Gordon, sometimes I think there's nothing but air between your ears."

Tank sat up, looking hurt, but he fired back. "If the tranq was that weak, why didn't you get a stronger dart so we'd only hafta shoot it once?"

Kelton definitely wanted to kill him. "Goddamnit, Tank! Don't you *dare* try to bring this back around on me! Your ignorance just cost me a hundred and fifty grand!"

"You're fulla shit, Kel. You and me and Hoops all know you only laid out thirty-five thou for that Rex."

"I'm talking about profit, not cost. And the fact remains—your stupidity could have killed somebody!"

He stared down at Tank Mahaffey, pulling in deep breaths, trying to control his anger. Tank had made more than his share of mistakes over the years, but none this costly. Certainly none this potentially deadly.

Finally he said, "I'm going to sleep on it tonight, see if I want to fire you. That goes for you as well, Hoops. I want to see both of you first thing in the morning up at the house."

He turned on his heel and walked to his pickup, threw the tranq rifle in the back, and drove out of the glen.

He needed to get away before he murdered somebody.

Kelton drove around the bend and saw the lowered drawbridge, spotted Mark Thornberry walking briskly down the path on the other side of the river. Kelton crossed the bridge and pulled up alongside him.

"I've never seen you run that fast, Thorn," he said.

"Yeah, that was a heavy scene. Didn't mean to bug out on you, but . . ." he looked off into the trees, "well, you know."

"Yes, I *do* know." Kelton said, still extremely pissed off at Tank and trying to control his breathing. He wanted to scream out his rage but he knew better than to badmouth one employee to another. "You want a lift back?"

"Yeah sure."

Kelton leaned across the seat and pushed open the passenger door.

Thorn climbed in. "Everybody okay back there?" he said.

"Okay is a relative term. Nobody died, if that's what you mean."

They were silent as Kelton drove the tree-lined corridor, headed back to the living quarters. He noticed Thorn continuing to stare at him from under the brim of his brown buckskin cattleman hat, those bulging dark eyes of his unnerving him.

"What? What is it, Thorn?"

"You're bleeding, Kel. Did you know that?"

Kelton looked down at his midsection where Thorn was focused. Saw three dark crimson splotches of blood staining his shirt and leaking onto the seat belt. He unbuckled the belt and pulled his shirt up, seeing three weeping wounds across his stomach. There was still so much adrenaline pumping through his veins he hadn't felt it.

"Christ," he said, "that Rex must've clawed me when it plowed over me."

"Those things are ferocious," Thorn told him.

"That they are. We're lucky nobody was killed."

"Yeah," Thorn said, still looking at Kelton's wounds. "That doesn't look good."

Now that he was aware of the injury, Kelton started feeling the deep burn and sharp, needlelike ache. "You're right," he said. "I need to stick myself with a rabies shot. Maybe a tetanus as well."

"I'd say that might also call for a coupla stitches, Kel."

Kelton pulled his shirt back down and drove, aspen branches slapping the side of his pickup as they jounced over the earthen path. The pain in his gut intensified with each bounce.

On the way back to the house, he fantasized about the escaped Tyrannosaur taking down Tank Mahaffey.

Now that's a predator-prey dance I'd pay to watch.

Changes in Latitudes
Changes in Attitudes

July 3: The Cellar Suites
Gilliam's Guidepost, Heart Butte, Montana

RAIN HAD FINALLY HIT WESTERN MONTANA after a long drought that had farmers and ranchers second guessing their chosen occupations. Peter Lacroix was oblivious of the torrential showers. He remained dry and comfortable deep in the bowels of The Cellar, the lavish subterranean apartments on the back forty of Gilliam's Guidepost. This was his new home. His *family's* new home. It was a homecoming of sorts as they had spent a month in this same apartment suite last August, when Brin worked for Bryan Gilliam, leaving to go back to Missoula when the AEF terrorists had freed the dinosaurs and burned the ranch to the ground.

But that was then.

So much had changed the past year.

Especially the past month.

Peter and his young family were embarking on an exciting new chapter in their lives. At least he saw it as exciting. He wasn't so sure Brin saw it that way.

Yesterday, he and Brin had put in a fifteen-hour day packing and relocating the family here to the Gilliam ranch. Peter drove the U-Haul van with Brin's mother, Kachina, following in her car, and Brin pulling up the rear in their car with Kimi strapped into her child's seat. The 215-mile trip took them nearly five hours with stops.

The rent-free occupancy in the Gilliams' stylish apartments

came as part of Peter's compensation package as a partner in Fowler-Lemoyne Aviation, Inc. Kachina got one apartment to herself while Peter, Brin, and Kimi resided in the larger suite across the hall from her. The only difference from last year was that Hayden and Nora were no longer occupying the suite next door.

Peter had listed their Missoula house with an agent, offering it as a fully furnished rental. Their home for the foreseeable future would be this spacious Gilliam's Guidepost underground dwelling on the southern edge of the Blackfeet Indian reservation. Peter's change of employers and this move had happened at a dizzying speed, and often over the past three weeks, he thought he was living in an amphetamine-fueled dream.

Last week—his first full week after leaving the Forest Service—he spent two long days shopping for a helicopter. His first call was to Rocky Mountain Rotors and Ed Callahan, the flight instructor who had trained him.

"Pete Lacroix, as I live and breathe!" Callahan had said, surprised at hearing from Peter after nine years. "How's my favorite hockey phenom slash chopper jock?"

Peter grinned, recalling how Callahan had always called him *Hat Trick* during his training. "I'm good, Ed. How's the wife?"

"Uh—we divorced five years ago."

"Oh, I'm sorry to hear that."

"Don't be. It was for the best. I've got a new young lady in my life now. Michelle is a wonderful woman. Changed my life for the better."

"Good to hear."

"What about you, Pete? You hitched yet?"

"Yeah. Almost five years now. To an amazing Indian woman—Brinshou. We have a daughter who's two-and-a-half and a baby on the way."

"That's fantastic." An awkward pause, then, "I know you didn't call me to talk about our families. What's up?"

"I'm looking to purchase a bird, Ed."

"A bird? You mean like a parrot or a macaw?"

Peter snorted a laugh through his nose. "No. A *whirly*bird. A helicopter. Thought I'd check with you first, see if you had any old training choppers on hand you'd be willing to let go for a bargain price."

"Holy crap! Did you win the lottery or something?"

"Something like that, yeah."

Ed Callahan whistled. "Wow! I knew I should have been investing in those Powerball and Mega Millions scratch off tickets."

"It's not like that, Ed. I've entered into a business partnership with a couple of wealthy entrepreneurs. Maybe you've heard of them—Hayden Fowler and Nora Lemoyne?"

"The famous dinosaur scientists? That couple who wrote that mega-popular book?"

"Yes. One and the same."

"Jesus, Pete. They're bigtime celebrities! How'd you get hooked up with them?"

Peter didn't want to get into a long conversation about it, so he said, "It's a long story, Ed. But listen, I'm looking for a Bell helicopter. Preferably a four-oh-seven."

Callahan told him Rocky Mountain Rotors didn't have any choppers for sale or lease, but gave him contact information of three places he might find one. Peter thanked him and made the calls, negotiating with two sellers, asking the pertinent questions—model year, maintenance history, engine mileage, flight capabilities—but he failed to work an affordable deal. The third call was the charm. The seller was right in Peter's back yard: Minuteman Aviation in Missoula, near the airport. The purchase price was higher than what Hayden and Nora wanted, and try as he might, Peter couldn't get the guy to come down off that price. But the lease-to-own deal was something they could handle. Peter made a verbal commitment over the phone for a well maintained 2014 Bell 407. With its four-blade main rotor, cruising speed of 150 miles per hour, seating capacity of seven, and large touring windows for easy-access photography, the ten-year-old chopper matched all of Hayden's requirements. It also fit the company budget, not to mention a model Peter had experience piloting.

Peter went out there the next day and took a test flight, fell in love with the aircraft. So easy to operate, the pitch and collective sticks smooth, the rudder pedals very responsive. So smooth in the air. Hovering and landing a breeze. Rapid ascension and pinpoint turning. Efficient high altitude handling. He felt revitalized, flying again after being grounded for two weeks. Several Zoom sessions with Hayden and Nora later, he was given the green light to enter into a one-year lease/five-year purchase plan. This time next week Fowler-Lemoyne Aviation would have a Bell 407 on their helipad, hopefully flight ready. Peter would drive a rental car back to Missoula Saturday to finalize the deal, then fly the chopper to the Gilliam ranch. He hoped the weather would be clear for his flight. He'd be flying solo and didn't want to give Brin another reason to worry. If all went well, the inaugural flight would be on Monday, July 8, to southern Montana to pick up a first load of Cretaceous meteorite rock.

Peter had also been working as a recruiting agent for Bryan Gilliam, signing up personnel he knew and trusted for the heliport staff. He recommended Nancy Diehl, whom he worked with at the Forest Service, for lead dispatcher. Bryan hired her after one quick interview that was mostly a formality. She would be starting in two weeks. They'd also hired another Missoula based Forest Service veteran—fleet mechanic Carl Lacey—which prompted an angry call from Gary Ralston, Peter's former boss, accusing him of stealing his best employees. It didn't bother Peter in the least.

All's fair in the cutthroat world of capitalistic commerce. Look at me, I'm already a devious, scheming corporate pirate! The thought made him smile.

Brin and he had worked side by side this morning, unpacking and getting settled in while Kachina took care of Kimi. Brin had worked diligently, quiet, focused. Peter knew she was dealing with a lot right now—pregnancy, rampaging hormones, the move, saying goodbye to her Missoula friends, bowing out of her jewelry business, the fallout from Kachina's stabbing of Nashota, Brin's wife-beating father. And the uptick in dinosaur attacks on humans that news channels insisted on feeding the public daily didn't help. Much to Peter's chagrin, his wife had become a certified news junkie over the past year. Highly sensitive woman that she was, she took each assault to heart, usually having a long cry after watching reports of people being mauled and devoured by prehistoric carnivores. These ghastly encounters affected Peter, too, as it did most people. But the dino feeding frenzies seemed to hit Brin much harder. And she just couldn't bring herself to stay away from the horrific newsfeeds. She was tangled up in an inexplicable addiction.

Peter tried to keep her away from her angst triggers, but hadn't had much success. Every time he told her to shut off the TV and think happy thoughts, she became angry with him. Her anxieties had elevated the past few weeks, and he was having a difficult time keeping her level. But thankfully, the past few days she remained calm and focused on the move. There had been no time to watch television news or think about much other than getting them and their belongings to Heart Butte.

Her most consuming anxiety seemed to be leaving her business behind. Peter had been doing his best to convince her that Brinshou's Baubles & Jewelry was in good hands with Luana and Nuna running things. They were hardworking, competent, honest women and Brin could Zoom with them as often as she wanted. After all, she was still the owner. But Brin's control side wouldn't let her accept that. She was a hands-on woman when it came to her jewelry. She complained that she would miss face-to-face dealings with her customers and of being able to handcraft the jewelry she loved making. She grumbled about not having "a meaningful place to go every day." Peter reminded her that she could soon be leading Bryan Gilliam's Cretaceous Stone jewelry operation once again after they brought back meteorite rock from Southern Montana. It didn't seem to console her. Brin viewed it as a hollow promise.

And then last week came the big confrontation that had been brewing since the day a month ago that Hayden Fowler made Peter the partnership offer. Brin was in one of her cantankerous moods, peevish once again about having to leave her jewelry shop behind.

"I have worked so hard to build my brand, only to have it yanked out from under me," she'd said. "I'll never get that back."

Peter had lost his cool and made the mistake of responding,

"You still have that brand, honey. It's your name on the shop marquee, your name behind your pieces. But let's not forget how you got that national reputation—from working on the Gilliam Cretaceous Stone product line. Bryan Gilliam made you who you are."

Peter regretted saying it as soon as it left his mouth.

Brin struck back, furious. "Damn you, Peter Edward Lacroix! Everything is always about you! Your career. The kids you want. What you want to do with our money. This crappy move out to the middle of nowhere, living underground like freakin' groundhogs. It's always everything you want with me tagging along like I'm the family pet or something. I'm sick of it! Sick, sick, sick, damn you!"

Brin had locked herself in their bathroom and cried for a couple of hours. He finally coaxed her out and apologized, tried to smooth things over, but it took a day or two before she would talk to him again.

And if being distanced from her business was her number one anxiety trigger, then the dangers of Peter's profession was a close second. Brin was still panicky about him flying in and out of Gilliam's Guidepost, where they had witnessed so much horror last summer. For the past two weeks she'd constantly harped about Gilliam's Guidepost being haunted, that there was some kind of negative karmic juju infiltrating the ranch.

"Look what happened there last summer, Peter. These Gilliam grounds are jinxed," she told him. "It's a bad omen for a pilot flying an unstable deathtrap."

He thought her fears of Gilliam's Guidepost being haunted in some tragic way was nothing but a Kootenai conspiracy theory superstition, though he would never be so crass to verbalize it that way to her. And her mind was made up about helicopters being unsafe. He would never be able to talk her down off that cliff of high anxiety. Nearly every time she voiced her perception of the hazardous nature of helicopters, she would include disparaging references, calling them *hellchoppers, eggbeaters, deathtraps,* or *heligrinders.*

Brin will come around once we get settled in here, he kept telling himself.

Peter tried to get her focused on helping her mother. Kachina was still struggling to come to terms with her attack on her wayward husband.

"She needs you more than ever right now, Brin. That was one hell of a shock to her, what she did."

"I know," she'd say, "but she's really buttoned up about it. Doesn't want to talk about it no matter how much wine I give her. And to be honest, I'm not in a real great place right now myself. I'm in no condition to be of much help for Mother."

No doubt Brin was hurting these last few weeks, lashing out, angry, feeling cheated and playing the victim card. He couldn't hardly blame her, really. He was asking a lot of her. It was hard, but it was hard on all of them. He'd kiss Brin and hold her close and tell her he loved her, and she would smile at him with that faraway gaze in her dark eyes, lost in her world of worry. She looked like a woman waiting for the proverbial other shoe to drop. It was a vacant look that saddened him greatly.

She'll come back around, he'd think.

He was, however, thankful for the last two days. They worked together peacefully, like a happily married couple taking care of family needs. Getting on with their new life.

Maybe Brin is starting to turn it around, he thought, a surge of hope elevating him.

Yesterday and this morning had exhausted him and Brin. After putting Kimi down, she retreated to the bedroom to take a well-deserved nap. Peter would have liked to join her, but he had some company business to attend to. Some calls to make.

The immediate staffing need was finding two more skilled helicopter pilots. His first choice was Larry Bing, the Montana Forest Service pilot who had partnered with him last year in the Air Force Operation Hot Rocks meteorite roundup. Bing was laid back and steady, an excellent pilot. They had worked well together. Peter first met him when they were enrolled in the Rocky Mountain Rotors flight training program back in the day. Both had been trained by Ed Callahan. Bing was five years younger than Peter and single as far as he knew. Living four hours south of Heart Butte, in Bozeman. A perfect candidate for relocation.

Peter sat in the alcove off the hallway that connected the two bedrooms with the living area and made the call. Surprisingly, Bing picked up after two rings.

"Hello?"

"Larry? Is that you?"

"Yeah. Who is this?"

"Peter. Peter Lacroix. Your old meteorite roundup flying partner."

"Lacroix?" Peter heard the surprise in his voice. "Goddamn, man. How the hell have you been?"

"I'm fine, thanks. You still flying for the Forest Service?"

"Yeah." Short pause, then, "This is so weird. I was just thinking about you a few days ago. Thought about calling you but I couldn't find your number."

"You were going to call *me*?"

"Yeah. I guess you probably haven't heard, but our old nemesis, Colonel Glick got his sawed-off self booted out of the Air Force. The brass drop-kicked the midget off the base after he was court martialed for a couple of unreported felonies. The online reports said it was one of those *for the good of the service* dismissals."

"Really? Glick is gone from Mount Bennett?"

"Yep. High ranking officers usually aren't let go like that unless it's really bad."

"I wonder what he did," Peter said.

"I don't know. But I'm betting some of it was due to the way Glick messed up Operation Hot Rocks. The sonofabitch got what he deserved, I'd say."

The news made Peter smile. "Yeah, Thaddeus Glick put us through some uncomfortable moments last summer, for sure. Not real competent, that guy."

"You got that right. He'll never realize his Pentagon dream. He'll never see that Brigadier General rank that he wanted so bad."

"Couldn't happen to a nicer fella," Peter said. "Hey, how're things with the Forest Service down there in Bozeman, Larry?"

"I'd be lyin' if I said it was good. We got a new management team in January. Things haven't been the same since. You still flyin' outta Missoula?"

"No. I left forestry work a coupla weeks ago. No more USDA work for me."

"What? I thought you were a lifer, Pete."

"Naw. I got out. I didn't want to be a drone operator."

"Drones? That was going on in Missoula?"

"Yeah. They tried to convince me it would be a safer way to earn a living. I was miserable."

"That's what they're doing here in Bozeman, too. Won't be long they'll be bringing in artificial intelligence to fly 'em. Won't need us chopper jocks at all anymore."

"So I take it you're not happy there?"

"No, Pete. Like you, I've been miserable. These schmucks in management think we would be perfectly satisfied to fly model aircraft from the ground. Shows how clueless they are. They have no idea about a helicopter pilot's makeup . . ."

Peter's smile widened as he listened to Bing bitch about his workplace. "Well, Larry. How would you like a new start flying independent and making more money."

"What're you talkin' about?"

"My wife Brinshou and I moved to Heart Butte yesterday. We'll be living on that ranch where you and I picked up those wedges of Cretaceous meteorite last summer. Gilliam's Guidepost. I'm sure you remember Bryan Gilliam, the guy who was getting all the media attention?"

"Sure, I remember him. Colorful guy with the dinosaur zoo. Almost got killed by those crazed animal lovers. I'm confused, Pete. Why are you living there?"

"I'm a partner in a new air freight company. An independent helicopter service. We're building a heliport on the Gilliam ranch. Bryan and his wife Loretta are partners. Hayden Fowler and Nora Lemoyne—the two paleontologists turned bigtime authors—are the controlling partners. They manage the purse strings, and they have deep pockets. Until we get established we'll mostly be chasing after dinosaurs and picking up meteorite rock."

"Meteorite rock? You mean the *dinosaur* rocks?"

"Yes, the Cretaceous stones of Fowler's and Lemoyne's book title."

"I thought there weren't any left."

"Oh, they've been around. Just under heavy cover. Six of them were never found. The Air Force gave up looking for them after they called off Operation Hot Rocks. I located one. Bigger than any of the ones we came across."

"Really? Where?"

"Down south of you, in the Custer Gallatin Forest. Just north of the Wyoming border. The thing's got to be worth a small fortune."

"What were you doing flyin' that far south? That's our territory."

"Me and a trainee got the call to check out an old burn site. We were told Bozeman fire corps were tied up with an active wildfire in Yellowstone and didn't have the staffing to cover it."

"Yeah. *That* mess. It spawned a few offshoot conflagrations we're still fighting."

"Using drones?"

Bing laughed. "No, they haven't got those things that sophisticated yet, but they're workin' on it."

"So, Larry, do you think a change in latitude would help your attitude?"

"Sounds like you might be making me an offer, Pete. Are you?"

"I am. Well, the official offer would have to come from Bryan Gilliam. He's the hiring manager. But if I say you're a good fit, it would be a done deal. I liked flying with you last summer. You're a hell of a pilot, my friend, and I'd love to have you on board. And I know you don't want to be a drone operator any more than I do."

"This is unbelievable! Your timing is perfect, Pete. How do we proceed?"

Peter told Bing he would have Bryan contact him for a phone interview, and that Bryan more than likely would extend him an offer on that phone call.

"After all," he said to Bing, "Bryan Gilliam met you last year and he knows what kind of pilot you are. Besides, he still owes us for not ratting on him about all the meteorite rock he pilfered."

The two of them shared a hearty laugh.

Bing said, "I remember. The guy had zero skill as a liar."

"Yeah," Peter agreed. "We should have let him keep the entire meteorite just for trying to play us."

"Colonel Glick would have been furious," Bing intoned. "He would have shit his junior-size pants."

"Don't you mean his Depends?"

More laughter.

When the laughter died down, Bing said, "I remember reading that Bryan Gilliam was almost killed by those terrorists who laid waste to his ranch. How's he doin' these days?"

"He's been to hell and back. Spent more than a month in the hospital. He's a little worse for wear, walking with a cane and not as spry as he was when we dealt with him. And he's been avoiding the media. But he still has the same impresario mindset. He'll be a good general manager for the heliport. I'm glad to be partnering with him in this venture."

"And you say the money is good?"

"Better than good. A full benefit package as well."

"Wow. This sounds too good to be true."

"That's what I thought, too, when I got my offer. But I guarantee you, Larry, it's all very real and above board. I'd love to fly with you again, my friend."

"The feeling's mutual, Pete. Hey, a million thanks for getting in touch with me."

"Don't mention it."

"Please have Bryan Gilliam call me."

"Will do."

He disconnected and leaned back in his chair. Peter thought about calling Bryan but realized he was too tired to keep up a coherent conversation. The last few days had left him completely drained.

He yawned and closed his eyes. Drifted to the edge of sleep where reality melted away and dreams took over. He thought he might be dreaming when he felt Brin's nimble-fingered hands massaging his shoulders from behind. Her long black hair fell across his face and the sweet flowery scent of her perfume wafted over him. He luxuriated in the smell of her, the way she caressed him, her dexterous jeweler fingers rubbing the soreness out of his shoulders and neck.

Her voice was husky with sleep. "Kimi will be out for another hour. What do you say we retreat to the bedroom, love."

He opened his eyes, turned in his chair to look up at her. Her smile was genuine, intimate. The vacant, distant stare was gone, her dark eyes now flashing with a hopeful desire. She had shunned sex for more than two weeks, but there was no mistaking what she wanted now.

"Are you sure?" he asked.

She pulled her hand across his chest. Stepped around in front of him. "Yes, I'm *very* sure."

He glanced at her slightly distended belly.

"Come on," she said, urgent, her look suggesting her pregnancy was nothing to worry about. She took his hand and pulled him up from the chair. "I need you, Petey."

"Music to my ears," he said, letting her pull him along.

"I love you so much," she said.

"I love you, too, Brinny."

Maybe my wife is coming back to me. Maybe this will all work out yet.

More Growl Than Howl

July 5: Jackson Hole Valley
Teton County, Wyoming

"YOU HAVE A BEAUTIFUL PLACE HERE," Hayden said.

Jackson Lattimer sat next to him in a matching Adirondack chair, drinking scotch. Hayden sipped lemonade from a plastic tumbler. They were on Lattimer's covered deck, looking out over the rear of his property, taking in the large cedar pergola built over a garden of colorful flowers, and the wide grassy lawn leading to the edge of the forest.

Hayden had taken an early afternoon flight from Minneapolis to Jackson Wyoming, then rented a car at Jackson Hole Airport and drove thirty-five minutes to Lattimer's place. The day had been picture postcard perfect, temperature in the high seventies, the sun blazing gloriously, the cloudless sky a brilliant cerulean blue tapestry that provided a stunning backdrop for the breathtaking Teton mountains.

"Glad you could make it out for a visit, Hayden. I finally get to meet the world famous dinosaur expert."

"You're the famous one, Mr. Gonzo Shutterbug," Hayden said with a wide grin. "I've never been on the cover of *Rolling Stone* or *People* magazine. They've never done a feature segment with me on *Entertainment Tonight.*"

Lattimer smirked. "Count your blessings, partner," he said, taking a sip of his scotch.

Hayden laughed, gazing at the snowcapped peaks surrounding them on three sides, the leafy carpet of lodgepole pine and Engelmann spruce rolling out to the foothills, the Snake River winding along the west boundary. "I tell ya, it's a whole other universe from Minneapolis," he said. "Puts me in mind of that Eagles song, 'Peaceful Easy Feeling'."

"Yeah, this place has a way of relaxing folks," Lattimer said, standing, scotch in hand. He leaned against the deck railing and scanned the horizon. "I've been to Minneapolis. Great city, but cities are too crowded for my liking. I'm a little claustrophobic that way. Need me some wide open spaces. This area *is* gorgeous. It's why all the celebrities invest in property out here. Harrison Ford, Sandra Bullock, Matthew McConaughey—they're my neighbors. At least part of the year."

"I'm impressed."

"Don't be. They're just regular folks."

"How much land do you have here, Jack?"

"Not much. Most of what you see is the edge of the Bridger-Teton National Forest. We're in the southern end of Grand Teton National Park. Land is ultra-expensive out here. I put my money into the house, not the acreage."

No lie there. Jackson had spared no expense on his Mountain Modern home. The exterior was constructed of western quarried stone with teak and mahogany trim. Marbled kitchen floor, counters, and bathrooms. Spacious, open floor plan with vaulted ceilings ribbed with exposed mountain timber beams. Floor-to-ceiling windows offering sweeping views of the impressive landscape. Smoked glass sculptural chandeliers in every room. Navajo and cowhide rugs over hickory floors polished to a high sheen. Distressed wood-and-leather furniture. A few original Georgia O'Keefe paintings and framed Thomas Mangelsen landscape photos adorning the walls. Surprisingly Hayden didn't see Lattimer's photography or any of his many awards displayed.

Jackson turned and looked at him. "You know, with the way your book is selling, you and Nora could probably afford a place here."

"I would love that, but right now we have our money invested in our new aviation venture."

Jackson took a drink, nodded. "Yeah. So how is that going?

How soon can we fly out and chase down a few of those Rexes?"

"It'll be another week or two. We're expecting our first helicopter Monday. The first few flights will be test runs to pick up some Cretaceous meteorite rock north of Yellowstone. Our lead pilot located it and it could turn out to be one hell of a cash cow. If that goes well, we'll start tracking dinos the following week. Believe me, I'm as eager as you are to get started."

"But we're still going out tomorrow in my truck, right?"

"Absolutely. I've scoped out a map and it looks like you're only about twenty minutes from the Idaho border, right?"

"Correct."

"Great. I've got some ideas where we might find a Rex or two. We'll plant GPS trackers on any we find, get some data on their movements . . . their migratory habits."

"Awesome. You know I'm all about getting close to my subjects." Jackson took a swallow of scotch, gave him a reflective look. "I guess it's true what they say about you on social media."

"What do they say about me?"

"That you're like a dinosaur diviner or something. A magnet for prehistoric animals."

Hayden smiled. It made him think of Nora. She had half-teasingly told him, *"Admit it, you have a gift, a special sixth sense that leads you to Cretaceous creatures. Like a divining rod. Dowsing for dinosaurs."*

"Look, Jack, don't get your hopes up. I can't divine anything. I'm not clairvoyant. I said we *might* find a Rex or two, not that we *will*."

"Okay. If you say so." Jackson shook his glass, the ice cubes rattling. "I need a refill. You sure I can't get you something with more zip than that lemonade?"

"I'm sure. Lemonade's fine."

The photographer gave Hayden a quizzical look. "You know, after reading your books, I never would have taken you for a teetotaler."

"You sound disappointed. Maybe you expected some party animal coming to visit you? Somebody more fun? A drinking buddy, perhaps?"

"No. Not at all. I just—"

"A year ago I would have taken you up on that, Jack. Probably would have finished off a whole bottle of scotch myself. I was a falling down drunk, getting into scraps in bars. Arrested twice for assault. Three failed marriages and a pair of DUIs, one after a pretty serious car wreck. On top of that baggage, I could have been labeled a sexual predator. Screwed young girls indiscriminately. Had a thing for hot chicks young enough to be my daughter. I was one hot mess. And then Nora came into my life. She is the difference. Nora Lemoyne saved my life. She tamed me. She got me off the sauce and I intend to stay on the wagon. For her. For *me*."

Jackson gave him a knowing look. "I was just asking about your drink. I didn't mean anything by it. The only thing I'm expecting from you is good company and the possibility of you leading me to a few dinos I can film. And I wanted to meet the man behind the books I have learned so much from."

Hayden felt a stab of guilt, looked down at his feet. "Sorry. I get a little overly sensitive about my sobriety."

"No harm, no foul," the photographer said, returning to his seat. "The truth of the matter is maybe I'm a bit envious. Your struggles sound familiar. I have a wild side similar to what you describe as your past. I'm restless. I have a lustful itch. I love young pussy. I guess I'm an incurable pussy hound. Unfortunately, with my desire for playing the field and my travel schedule, it's nearly impossible for me to keep up a serious relationship. I have yet to meet the woman who can tame me. Trust me, there isn't any shortage of available, willing women. Most of them just want to get close to the famous videographer. Groupies really. Most of them just want to sleep with the myth. That's what I've become, Hayden. A myth. A media creation. I'm growing tired of these fawning young chicks who jump into bed with me just because I've reached a certain level of fame. I just turned forty and I'm starting to realize I need something more substantial in my life. Something more stable than drunken one night stands with embarrassing mornings of regret after. I just haven't found my Nora yet."

There was a repentant sadness in Jackson's tone. Hayden saw a middle-aged man struggling with loneliness and masking it through the haze of alcohol. He'd been there himself a year ago.

"You'll meet your Nora when you least expect it, Jack."

Maybe America's Gonzo Shutterbug isn't the shallow celebrity I thought he was.

They locked eyes for an extended, awkward moment, then Jackson, looking a bit discomfited by his confession, shook his head and said, "Well, I need to get a refill. You want more lemonade?"

"Yeah sure. Thanks." Hayden handed the tumbler to him.

He heard the sliding glass door open and close behind him as his new friend went inside to refresh their drinks. The talk about Nora got him thinking. He'd been away from her for just eight hours but he missed her so much it hurt, like a section of his heart had been excised. He and Nora had spent the past nine days together working on the book and attending to the numerous details of launching Fowler-Lemoyne Aviation, Inc. They put in long days, working side by side, writing, editing, discussing book content, making phone calls, participating in Zoom sessions, meeting with bankers and insurance people, attending appointments with their financial analyst and accountant. The book was progressing nicely, working title—*Dragons of the Great Divide: Running with the Cretaceous Beasts.* Hayden wasn't crazy about the title but Nora was resolute about keeping it, and their editor Molly Barnes, and publicist Nick Fiore, both loved it. He and Nora also had things pretty much ready for the official opening of their company on Monday, when the four partners would meet at Gilliam's Guidepost to kick things off. He'd reunite with Nora there. Three days away.

Hayden was counting the minutes.

He recalled their recent evenings together, eating home delivery pizza, chicken wings, and Thai food. Rekindling the closeness they had shared on their Paris trip. He'd loved the homey intimacy, cuddling with her on the couch, bingeing on their favorite old TV shows—"ER" and "Ally McBeal" for her; "Seinfeld" and "The X-Files" for him. They'd also shared a few laughs watching the *Jurassic Park* and *The Lost World: Jurassic Park* movies, calling out the numerous paleozoological errors and the implausibility of the plots. It became a fun competition, seeing who could find the most outrageous gaffes in the films.

And of course they'd had sex—crazy, uninhibited, mind-blowing sex—nearly every night of those nine days. They'd enjoyed a few morning wakeup booty calls as well.

And then came yesterday, which marked the anniversary of the July 4th Livingston Roundup disaster, the popular Montana rodeo where sixteen people were killed and two dozen injured by a pack of voracious Tyrannosaurs during the fireworks show. He and Nora had been there. Those tragic memories still troubled her. Last night Hayden wanted to venture downtown to the riverfront to watch the fireworks from the Stone Arch Bridge with hundreds of other Minneapolitans. Nora didn't want any part of it.

"I'm sorry, Hayden, but I just can't do it," she'd told him. "I know how much you love your fireworks, so you go on without me if you want. Another fireworks show could possibly bring all those horrible memories rushing back. I don't need to experience a panic attack in the middle of a crowd downtown."

At first he'd been disappointed. It was the first time he'd missed an Independence Day fireworks celebration in twenty years or more. But then he realized he was being selfish, conveniently forgetting what Nora had been through since that tragic event. She'd had a couple of scary panic attacks and a handful of nightmares that brought her awake screaming in the middle of the night. He didn't want to stir up those demons again. He also didn't want to leave her in the house and go by himself, knowing he would be flying to Wyoming today, so they stayed in and watched a movie together— *Silver Linings Playbook*—with the sound turned way up to drown out the explosions of the neighborhood fireworks.

He thought it strange for Nora to be frightened by fireworks but not bothered by the *Jurassic Park* flicks. He knew there was usually very little rhyme or reason to phobias and fears. But really? She was okay with movies showing marauding dinosaurs but scared of bright flashes of light and explosions? That said, she did wince and excuse herself to go to the bathroom after the T-Rex plucked the lawyer off an outhouse toilet in its immense jaws, shook him violently, then swallowed him whole. He had paused the movie, waiting on her return for close to ten minutes, finally going to see if she was okay, hearing her sniffling sobs behind the door.

His thoughts scattered when Jackson returned with their drinks.

"Here you are," he said, handing Hayden his lemonade and retaking his seat next to him.

They sat and talked for the next hour as the sun dipped below the highest summits of the Tetons. The sky blazed with vivid streaks of pink, purple, and orange.

Hayden was awestruck. "We sure don't get sunsets like this back home."

"Beautiful, isn't it?" Jackson said. "I never get tired of it. Wait until full dark. You've never seen so many stars in your life as you'll see out here."

They drank and talked.

Jackson spoke excitedly about his recent trip to Australia. "I love the Aussie people. Downright friendly folks. They're all 'G'day, mate' and 'Would you like some snags with yer brekkie?' Most of them are really chill and unpretentious. The country is wild and beautiful, home to many exotic indigenous species. It's my home away from home, a heavenly place for wildlife photographers. Here, I'll show you a few vids from the trip." Jackson opened his laptop.

Hayden scooted his chair closer. The clips were closeup films of strange looking creatures one could only see in the Australian outback, all captured with Jackson Lattimer's skilled eye and assured hand. A kangaroo carrying its young in its pouch; a family of koalas playing in eucalyptus treetops; a platypus building a nest in a riverbank preparing to lay her eggs; a three-foot wombat coming out of its burrow, displaying its powerful jaws and sharp teeth; a pair of carnivorous kookaburras spreading their wings and squawking their laughing call. Their haunting cries reminded Hayden of loons he'd heard on Minnesota lakes.

Jackson then went into the main reason for his trip down under: diving with saltwater crocodiles.

"They're fearsome fuckers, Hayden. They're big. Mature adults weigh in at over two-thousand pounds. And they're fast, both on land and in the water. They can outswim humans. They're unpredictable as hell. If they're hungry enough and they get you in the water, you're almost assuredly a goner. I tell ya, it was a hell of a rush, those dives in the Adelaide River. Much scarier than swimming with the great whites."

"Yeah, I'll bet," Hayden said, watching a big croc swim directly at the camera. "They're definitely a throwback to our Cretaceous dinos. How is it you're able to hang in there when they get that close? I'd be shittin' my britches."

"I don't know really. I've always had a sense of calm around dangerous animals. I figure most creatures, especially predators, can sense fear in humans. I have a way of subconsciously tamping down my fear so they see me as an equal—as another predator, not their prey. It basically involves shutting off my nervous system. It's always come naturally to me."

"Interesting."

They watched another ten minutes of saltwater croc videos, Hayden impressed by the videographer's poise underwater, swimming among one of the most dangerous animals on the planet.

Then it was Hayden's turn for show and tell. He went inside to take a leak and retrieve his laptop from the dining room table. He returned to his deck chair and flipped up the lid, showed his videos of the baby Dromaeosaurs hatching out in Gilliam's east meadow.

"Look at those little buggers move," Jackson said, eyes glued to the screen.

"They won't be little for long," Hayden replied. "If you can believe it, the nest was down in the trench dug out by one of the Cretaceous meteorites. The exact location of where the original Dromaeosaurs hatched out last year. It goes a long way in proving my natal homing theory."

"Which is?"

"That Cretaceous dinosaurs return to their place of birth to lay their eggs."

"Fascinating,"

"Granted, it's a very random sampling. A limited case study. An absolutely lucky find, if you will. But it's rock solid and concrete."

Hayden showed him more videos of his nine day trip through Montana and Idaho. Triceratops eating their way through wheat fields, leaving behind nothing but stubby stalks and grain dust; the two Triceratops shot and killed by an Idaho potato farmer; Hayden dissecting the body of one to learn of the herbivores' anatomical structure. Two T-Rex attacks he'd been able to catch as they happened, with three Tyrannosaurs taking down a couple of big elk in Glacier National Park, and a T-Rex running down a moose and feasting on it along the bank of the Snake River in Idaho.

"I've got a lot more, but those are the highlights."

"Thanks for sharing with me. I'm absolutely gobsmacked, Fowler! And I must say, your videography skills have improved mightily since your footage from last year."

"Thanks, that means a lot coming from you, Jack."

"You've got some incredible clips here. Why haven't I seen them in news reports?"

"You will soon. Nora and I are under contract with the Smithsonian Institution. They get first right of refusal on any visual media we generate. They haven't gotten back with me yet to let me know which clips they're interested in and how they plan to use them. We *are* allowed to use still shots in our book, but the book won't be published until next spring."

"All this just proves further that you are indeed a dinosaur diviner, good buddy. Deny it all you want, Hayden, but you have a knack for finding them."

As the sun set behind the mountains, Hayden described the Dromaeosaur attack on Bryan Gilliam, how Gilliam had faced off with one and killed it while his wife Loretta wounded a second animal.

"Wow! Rugged Montana ranchers, those two," Jackson said with respect. "I remember reading a little about them in your book."

"Yeah, they're a tough couple."

Hayden went on to share the zoological data he'd learned from his autopsy of the Dromaeosaur carcass, Jackson listening attentively.

Darkness cloaked the valley when Hayden finished reciting his Dromaeosaur postmortem findings. The temperature had dropped a good fifteen degrees and a light breeze carried a crisp mountain breeze across the deck. The sky had opened up to a million pinpoints of light. So many stars it was almost overwhelming in its vastness.

Hayden closed his laptop and said, "It's getting chilly. I'm gonna go in and grab my jacket."

"Yeah, me, too," Jackson said, standing and stretching. "I'm ready for a refill. Can I get you something to warm you up? Coffee? Hot chocolate?"

"Coffee's good. Black. Thanks."

Hayden got his windbreaker out of his luggage and returned to the deck. Jackson soon followed, wearing a fleece jacket and carrying a tray with their drinks.

"Here's your coffee," he said, Hayden relishing the heat in his fingers as he took the cup from him. "I also have a little nighttime treat for us. Please tell me your sobriety doesn't make you shun the holy herb."

Hayden glanced at the baggie of weed, pack of Zig-Zag rolling papers, and two tightly rolled joints on the tray next to the scotch glass. He watched as Jackson sat down and fired one up, inhaled a deep hit, the skunky pine-sweet smoke drifting towards him.

"It's illegal in Minnesota, and I haven't indulged in a while, but I'm all in for it, yeah."

"It's not legal here, either, but that's never stopped me," Jackson rasped, holding the smoke in his lungs. He passed the jib to Hayden, who took a tentative drag.

Jackson exhaled. "Jesus, Fowler, you'll never get high that way. Smoke it like you mean it, brother!"

Hayden took another, deeper pull, feeling the burn in his throat, the smoky expansion in his lungs. He held it in, trying to keep from coughing. He immediately felt like he was floating. On the exhale, he said, "Strong stuff, Jack. Mighty fine."

Jackson took the joint from him. "Yeah, it's a Godfather OG

strain. Very potent. Thirty-four percent THC content. I get it from a dispensary in Steamboat Springs, Colorado." He pointed the joint out into the darkness of his back yard. "Been trying to grow some myself out there under my pergola, but not having much luck. Climate and soil just aren't right for it." He took in another deep lungful of smoke.

Hayden, already feeling buzzy, said, "I see now how it is you stay so calm around dangerous animals."

Jackson waited a beat, then exhaled a fog of smoke. "Oh, I never toke up on the job. I need my full awareness and all my motor skills in the work I do."

He passed the doob. Hayden, not wanting to show weakness in front of his host, took a long, deep rip, which led to an extended coughing jag.

"Easy there, Fowler. We've got all night."

Hayden's eyes burned and itched. Tears streamed down into his beard. He couldn't stop the coughing. It took several gulps of coffee to chase the scratchy tickle in his throat.

"You okay?"

"Yeah, I'll make it," Hayden croaked.

They passed the doob twice before Hayden opted out and watched Jackson finish it between drinks of his scotch.

Amazing how much weed and liquor the man can consume.

Hayden was completely wrecked, blazed, baked, the deck taking on a pleasant surreal visage. It reminded him of being in a carnival house of mirrors, everything stretching and shrinking, warping and twisting, his eyes and mind playing games with him. Despite the cold, he felt warm, safe, comfortable. He tried to remember the last time he'd been high. Couldn't. Decided it didn't matter. He felt really good in this moment. Looked up at the vivid light show spread across the expansive sky, knowing he was viewing ancient history, that the light from a majority of these stars and planets had traveled millions of years to reach his eyes. It was almost too much to comprehend in his current state.

An almost supernatural quiet had fallen over the valley, as if the mountains were muffling everything.

And then the night's silence was shattered by low-pitched bellowing cries and deep-throated yaps. Hayden listened for a moment, the eeriness of the sounds causing him to shudder.

"You hear that, Jack?"

"Yeah. It's just coyotes. They get cranked up after nightfall."

Hayden wasn't sure. He listened a little longer, hearing distinctive rumbling growls and snorting grunts. "I've got news for you, Jack. Those aren't coyotes."

"No? What are they then?"

"I believe you've got a few Tyrannosaurs nearby."

"Ah, you're just stoned, Fowler."

"I might be lit up, but I'd know that sound anywhere. I know my Rexes."

"You think?"

"I *know*, Jack."

Jackson listened to the animal noises coming out of the forest. "You might be right, Hayden. It has more low end to it than the racket coyotes make. Same with the grey wolves that roam these parts. Coyotes and wolves tend to have a higher-pitched howl. This is more growl than howl."

Hayden laughed. "More growl than howl. That's the truth of it right there."

"Tomorrow's gonna be a blast," Jackson said, laughing along with Hayden. "The dinosaur diviner strikes again!"

A Ghost on the Digital Timeline

July 6: Running Crane Trading Post
Heart Butte, Montana

A SECOND BLACKFOOT WOMAN HAD DISAPPEARED. Ahwee Red Crow had been missing for four days, joining Kanti Lyttle, who vanished ten days ago.

Bryan had been doing what he could to find Kanti. Then, Thursday, Huritt Red Crow came to him asking for his help in finding his wife, Ahwee. Bryan knew both women well. Ahwee and Kanti had attended the Gilliams' ill-fated barbecue last summer, running for their lives when the AEF mob invaded the ranch with their guns and bulldozers, setting free the dinosaurs and torching the Gilliam homestead.

He'd spent much of yesterday on the phone, talking to some of the same noncommittal law enforcement types he'd spoken with earlier in the week. He'd pleaded and cajoled and argued, but the authorities remained standoffish. Bryan was disappointed in their adamant refusal to serve and protect. The police had given him the same song and dance they'd given Apisi. One desk sergeant was particularly brusque and coldhearted: "*There have been a number of dinosaur attacks in this area, Mr. Gilliam. It's possible your women could have been wounded, or worse. Have you checked with local area hospitals? Have you contacted funeral homes to see if they've taken in any Jane Does? Of course, if the dinos got 'em, well . . . there might not be enough of 'em left to identify.*"

Bryan became more enraged with each unsuccessful call. It was nothing but transparent, unapologetic racism. At the very least, lazy policework. He recalled Apisi's words: *"They treat us like we're subhuman. Like we're diseased dogs running wild in the streets."*

Ap had it right. The authorities made it clear. They weren't going to spend their time, energy, and money looking for missing Indigenous women. The state police he'd dealt with were insulting and abrupt. Condescending.

"Mr. Apisi Lyttle gave us a description of his wife's car and her plate number," a bored sounding Montana State desk sergeant told him. "Says here it's a 2015 silver Ford Expedition. Our Highway Patrol has been on the lookout for it. No sign of it yet."

"You call that an investigation?" Bryan responded, angry. "I assure you, they switched the plates the first chance they got. Probably dumped the car shortly after that."

"Who are *they*, Mr. Gilliam?"

"Kanti's abductors. Who else?"

"We have no evidence Ms. Lyttle was abducted."

"You have no evidence because you're not doing anything about it," Bryan said, frustrated.

"I assure you, Mr. Gilliam, we are doing everything possible to find Kanti Lyttle. Might I suggest you contact local hospitals and funeral homes?"

"Yeah, I've heard that suggestion a couple of times now. She's been missing for over a week and you bums sit on your fat asses!"

"Mr. Gilliam, there's no need to—"

Bryan disconnected. *Thanks for absolutely nothing!*

He was certainly no detective, but Bryan knew enough to check hospitals and funeral homes. He'd called Blackfeet Community Hospital in Browning where he'd been taken after suffering gunshot wounds last summer. No female patients admitted there matching Kanti Lyttle's description. He'd also called the Northern Rockies Medical Center in Cut Bank. No luck there either. Calls to funeral homes in Shelby and Conrad produced nothing. Both places told him they had several badly mutilated Jane Does from recent dinosaur assaults, but none matched Kanti's or Ahwee's age or physical characteristics.

He tried appealing to local police. Blackfeet Law Enforcement Services told him their staffing budget had been cut and they didn't have the manpower to search for missing persons. He called the Bureau of Indian Affairs in Billings. A sanctimonious bureaucrat informed him that the BIA's responsibilities "extend only to tribal self-governance, economic development, education, social services, and natural resource management."

Bryan, infuriated at being put off, responded, "Well what the hell would you call two missing Blackfoot women if not a need for social services?"

"I'm sorry, sir, but this is a matter for your local police. I suggest you contact Blackfeet Law Enforcement Services. I can assist you with that phone number, if you need it."

Unbelievable! It's their own people being victimized and they sit on their hands!

Kanti Lyttle and Ahwee Red Crow were out there somewhere and no one wanted to help find them.

Hopefully they were still breathing.

Bryan remained angry as he pulled into the parking lot of Running Crane Trading Post, the last known whereabouts of Kanti Lyttle. Bryan kicked himself for not coming here sooner. He had been so consumed with heliport work and dealing with family issues that visiting the trading post as a followup to Kanti's disappearance simply hadn't occurred to him. Like he'd told Apisi, he wasn't a detective, and in many ways he felt he was in way over his head with this investigation stuff. But better late than never he supposed.

He entered the store and saw Marvin Running Crane, the proprietor, checking a customer out at the front register. The lean seventy-ish trading post namesake was dressed in his usual attire: dark leather vest over an open collar white dress shirt, acid washed jeans, black fedora with a large eagle feather held in place by a snakeskin band. Flowing locks of platinum hair fell across his shoulders and glowed brightly under the fluorescent lights. Silver bracelets adorned his wrists, clinking as he bagged the customer's purchase. He spotted Bryan and smiled, held up a finger, indicating he'd be with him shortly.

Bryan knew Marvin Running Crane well, though he hadn't seen him since before his accident last year. He and Loretta had shopped at the trading post for most of their twenty years in Heart Butte, coming here back when Nina Running Crane—Marvin's late wife—was a smiling presence behind the cash register. Last summer, Bryan had cut Marvin a good wholesale deal on his Cretaceous Stone jewelry line and Marvin had made a significant amount of money selling the obsidian adornments, trinkets, and accessories, particularly the enormously popular Cretaceous Egg (the small stone fashioned into a fake dinosaur egg with claws punching their way out, nestled inside a black lacquer presentation case). People flocked to the store from far away to purchase the dinosaur meteorite items. Running Crane Trading Post remained a popular tourist attraction due to its connection with Gilliam's Guidepost, which was dinosaur central last summer. Bryan knew Marvin would do anything he could to help him locate Kanti.

While he waited for Marvin to get free, he walked around the store. Soft music played, mostly drums and bells with occasional humming vocals. The interior was much larger than it appeared from the parking lot, with items displayed floor to ceiling and crammed into every nook and cranny. Half of the store was a modern grocery with large refrigeration units running along two walls, and fruit and vegetable bins lined up along the middle of the floor. The other half was dedicated to more traditional tribal merchandise. He breathed in the leathery scent of moccasins and beaded bags and admired the handcrafting of the porcupine and bird feather quillwork. There were elk and deer hides draping a section of a wall. Medicinal herbs and plants. Handmade pottery and baskets. Knives, axes, and awls. A section with Native foodstuffs— pemmican cakes, camas root, chokecherry jelly, Saskatoon berry pie, huckleberry jam and syrup, venison filets and river trout. Bryan experienced sensory overload as he poked his way along with his cane.

"*Okhi*, Bryan. *Naa'ki?*" he heard Marvin say behind him, which he knew to be the Blackfoot greeting *"Hello, Bryan, are you good?"*

"I'm well, thanks, Marv. And you?"

"This crane doesn't run as fast as he once did."

"Neither does this broken down mechanic," Bryan said, lifting his cane.

"You look better than I thought you might. Loretta has kept me updated about the hell you've gone through. Glad to see you out and about again, *náápikoan.*"

"Thanks, Marv. I had a rough go of it, but I'm better."

"Seen any thunder lizards down your way lately?"

"Yeah, a few," Bryan said. "A pair of Dromaeosaurs tried to get at our horses. We got rid of them. Have you seen any around here?"

"Fortunately none yet this summer. The news reports have been bad lately. I hope it doesn't get like last summer for us. Had more than our share of the beasts. Kept customers away for a while. Our business dropped way off. Then you saved the day with your Cretaceous Stone jewelry."

"Glad I could help you out, Marv. I've got some news on that front you might be interested in."

"What's that?"

"We found another dinosaur meteorite. A lot larger than the one that hit my property. We'll probably be making more of that jewelry, and you'll be first in line as our brick-and-mortar seller."

"*Aamsskáápipikani!*" which Bryan knew was Blackfoot for *Most excellent!* "I'll be looking forward to that, *náápikoan.* So what brings you to the Post today?"

"I know how fast news travels on the rez, so you've probably heard that two women who are regular shoppers here are missing."

"Yes, I just heard about Kanti Lyttle two days ago. There's another?"

"Ahwee Red Crow. Huritt called me yesterday. Asked if I'd look into it. I was already searching for Kanti."

"Oh no. Ahwee is such a sweet lady."

"Yeah, and according to Huritt and Apisi, both of their wives were last known to be grocery shopping here. About a week apart."

Marvin Running Crane eyed him suspiciously. "I hope you're not implying that I—"

"No, oh, Jesus, no," Bryan said laughing at the absurdity of it.

"I'm quite sure you didn't have anything to do with it, Marv. But I'm stalled in my investigation. I came to check out your surveillance tapes. I know you have security cameras."

Marvin nodded. "Sure do. Sad to say, we have a big problem with theft here. Many of our families can't afford even basic necessities, so I let a lot of the pilfering slide. But I do use security footage to pick and choose who to prosecute. It's not a fun part of the job, but it's necessary. We don't use VHS tapes anymore. It's all digital stored on a hard drive now. Much cleaner imaging and we can keep a lot more history. The tribal police come by regularly to view the video files. They go after the shoplifters to help us regain some of our lost revenue."

Hearing *tribal police* made Bryan's stomach turn. "The rez police aren't my favorite people right now. They refuse to get off their lazy asses to help us find Kanti and Ahwee."

"Don't be too hard on them, Bryan. They do pretty good by us. They're working with a skeleton staff these days. I think the feds would eliminate them entirely if they could."

"Your cameras aren't just inside are they? You have outdoor cameras as well, right?"

"Yes. Powerful cameras that capture all of the parking lot and part of Wild Gun Drive."

"Excellent. Do you keep more than two weeks of history?"

"Oh, we go back two or three *months*. We've got a twenty terabyte hard drive that gives us a round-the-clock view of the store, inside and out. Our security system is expensive, but it's paid for itself many times over."

Bryan felt a surge of optimism. "Great, Marv. Can I take a look?"

"Sure. Come on back to my office and I'll get you set up."

He followed Marvin down a narrow hallway, past the restrooms to a cluttered space that smelled of coffee, cigar smoke, and stale sweat. Marvin cleared his battered desk of paperwork and dirty mugs, sat Bryan in front of an HP EliteDesk computer and gave him a quick tutorial. He showed him how to log into the system, jump to specific days/times, increase/decrease the scroll speed. Bryan quickly learned how to freeze an image and zoom in on a selected area and offload clips to a USB flash drive. Marvin poured him a cup of coffee and went back out front. Bryan sat facing two large monitors that displayed separate frames for each camera.

Apisi and Huritt had given him recent photos of their wives. He laid the shots of Kanti and Ahwee on the desk, a little spooked that these women smiling at him had disappeared and could quite possibly be dead. He went back ten days to June 26, scanning the multi-camera views slowly, starting at noon, when Apisi thought his wife had gone to the store. It was a laborious process, slow-walking through the videos. So many faces and bodies moving through the trading post, entering and leaving the store, getting into and out of cars in the parking lot. Lots of Blackfoot women wandering around, checking out merchandise, talking with friends. No sign of Kanti as of two o'clock. Nor at three o'clock . . .

As he forwarded through the video footage, Bryan's optimism faded. Maybe Apisi was fuzzy about the time. Or maybe he got the day wrong. But that couldn't be. He knew his lead ranch hand possessed an infallible memory for dates.

He felt a headache coming on. Pain shot through his leg. He was stiffening up. But he knew he had to keep going. He slogged on through the next hour, perusing the camera frames, moving past four o'clock. And then, with 4:14 pm showing on the timeline, he saw a woman who looked like Kanti Lyttle enter the store. He froze the shot, zoomed in.

It was her! No doubt about it.

Kanti picked up a handbasket and went to the grocery section, picking out fry bread, assorted fruits and vegetables, what looked like packs of beef jerky. Green beans, milk, cheese. He followed her movement around the store as she checked items off her list. He lost her a couple of times behind high shelving, then saw her stop to talk to a younger woman with a toddler in a stroller. Kanti seemed happy and unconcerned. Just a housewife out shopping for her family. Twenty minutes later, her basket full, she went to the front counter where a young Blackfoot girl rang up her purchases.

Bryan followed her as she grabbed her bags and walked to the front door. An old man held the door for her and she nodded her thanks to him. She exited the store, walking out into the sunshine. Bryan swiveled in his chair to scan the panel of parking lot cameras, following Kanti's progress. She walked past a couple of rusted out Ford pickups, a Jeep Wrangler, and an early model Chevy Tahoe, then disappeared behind a row of ten-foot tall juniper hedges.

Damn! You're not helping me here, Kanti.

He checked each camera angle, hoping for a clean view. There were none. The hedges cut off his line of sight. That small corner of the lot was obscured.

He cursed his bad luck.

Why the hell did you have to park there, Kanti?

Bryan knew there was only one way in and out of the trading post, and whoever parked in that obstructed view section would have to drive out in the open to leave. He waited. Three minutes. Five minutes. Eight minutes . . .

What's taking so long?

Then, twelve minutes later, at 5:23 pm, he watched Kanti's silver Ford Expedition come into view. A man wearing a wide brimmed slouch hat pulled low drove. Bryan could see Kanti on the far side, in the passenger seat, slumped over, her head leaning against the window. She looked unconscious. The car moved slowly through the lot and exited onto Wild Gun Drive.

Bryan backed the video up and watched it again, zooming in on the man. He could only make out lower facial features from his profile. Strong jawline, hollowed out cheeks sprouting a three-day grayish stubble. Nothing definitive. The hat covered his most distinguishing characteristics—eyes, nose, ears, hair. Bryan ran through the sequence again and this time noticed a tattoo on the man's left forearm. It looked like a human fist and an animal paw superimposed over a triangle with lettering. No matter how close he zoomed in, he couldn't make out the lettering. He ran it a third time, zooming in on Kanti. She looked dazed, a vacant stare on her round face. He couldn't see any visible wounds. It appeared as though she'd been drugged.

Bryan knew the abductor had to have had transportation to

Running Crane's, so he let the video play further. At 5:29 pm—six minutes after Kanti and her abductor drove out of the parking lot— a mud-streaked Army green Toyota 4Runner pulled out from behind the hedgerow, and turned onto Wild Gun Drive, headed in the opposite direction that Kanti's abductor had gone. The male driver wore a paper surgical mask and a floppy cowboy hat, completely hiding his face and head. The pandemic was in the past, but a few people still elected to wear masks, so this guy wearing one wouldn't necessarily draw attention. Bryan zoomed in on the license plate above the rear bumper. A Montana Centennial plate: ADU4?? in dark blue with the last two numbers obscured by mud. He knew the Centennial specialty plates were all three letters followed by three numbers.

Bryan felt a rising tide of elation. He finally had something to work with. But just as quickly, his excitement turned to fear as Kanti's wrecked condition floated across his mind's eye. This video was from ten days ago.

Am I too late?

Bryan sighed and copied the footage to a flash drive, then jumped the video ahead six days to July second, the day Huritt said Ahwee had been in the store, the last day he'd seen or heard from her. Bryan worked through the moving images for the next three hours, covering July second and third, then backing it up to July first. downing two more cups of bitter coffee, seeing many familiar faces, but no sign of Ahwee Red Crow.

Bryan pushed away from the desk, stood. He was stiff and his lower back and leg hurt. He thanked Marvin as he caned his way out.

Time to get home to his own family.

The Dragons of Willow Pond

July 7: National Elk Refuge
Jackson Hole, Wyoming

THEY DIDN'T HAVE TO TRAVEL FAR to find Tyrannosaurs. The troubling growls and cries they'd heard on Jackson's rear deck the night before last were definitely not coyotes or wolves. They were the real deal.

Tyrannosaurus Rex roamed nearby.

The news broke early this morning as he and Hayden Fowler ate breakfast in Jackson's alpine kitchen. More than forty mature elk had been slaughtered and devoured during the night in the National Elk Refuge, the 25,000 acre wildlife preserve just five miles from Jackson's house. Tyrannosaurs were the killers, with one T-Rex taken down in the onslaught. As soon as they heard the news, they left their breakfasts unfinished and scrambled to get their gear together, then left for the preserve.

They were now parked high on a bluff overlooking the dale where the attack occurred. The sun crept up over the eastern peaks, throwing splashes of gold and amber across the valley floor. The scene—with a dozen or more U.S. Fish and Wildlife agents milling about—had a surreal, gilded ambiance about it.

Jackson stood outside his pickup, peering through the zoom of his Canon PowerShot camera, snapping off a succession of shots. He spoke to Hayden through the open driver's side window while continuing to shoot. "There aren't many elk out here now, and that's not just because of the Rex attack. Most of the big herds head up into the mountains to graze during the summer. Then they come back to lower ground during the winter. Six to eight thousand of 'em. It's quite an impressive sight. I filmed their seasonal migration three years ago for a *Mutual of Omaha's Wild Kingdom* special. Last check it had over eight-hundred-thousand views on YouTube."

"That's awesome, Jack," Hayden said from where he sat in the passenger seat, scoping the valley with binoculars.

Jackson stopped shooting, leaned down and looked across the seat. "You picking up anything useful?"

Hayden shook his head. "Not really. Just a lot of blood and bones. I wish we could get down there to check out that dead Rex."

The Fish and Wildlife agents were keeping curiosity seekers away. Jackson had tried to drive in, past the barricade, but had been denied access by some hardcase federal agents wielding menacing guns. One guy even toted an AR-15. Hayden and Jackson's position up here on the bluff was the closest they were going to get. The authorities were taking no chances on more humans becoming dinosaur prey. It probably wouldn't be much longer before they closed off the entire sanctuary.

Hayden set his binoculars on the dash. "To the best of my knowledge, this is the farthest south Rexes have been spotted. They're branching out this summer. No better time to start my migration tracking program."

Jackson climbed behind the wheel and looked through the windshield, taking in the spread of bones littering the grassland and the small group of elk gathered at the western end. "Those elk are huge. How many Rexes you figure it took to kill forty of 'em?"

Hayden raked his beard with his fingers, thinking. "Eight, maybe a dozen. Tyrannosaurs can take down animals three to four times their size and devour them quickly. Nora and I visited a ranch in Greenfield, Montana last year when this whole thing started. Looked really similar to this. Fifty head of cattle were taken that night, and the Rexes were much smaller then. There's no stopping 'em when they're hungry, which is most of the time." He gazed out over the carnage below, seeing the sets of intact ribcages that had been stripped clean. "Looks like their intestinal systems aren't able to digest bones yet, however."

Jackson nodded. "Yeah I see that."

"The only reason there aren't more human deaths, I think, is because Rex has learned to fear guns. I think Tyrannosaurs associate guns with humans. They're smart creatures. They're evolved from their ancestors that ruled this planet for millions of years. Survival like that takes intelligence. Much easier and safer to go after defenseless animals and stay clear of humans. That said, their appetites are so colossal they'll attack humans if they think they've got a safe shot."

Jackson sat behind the wheel, mulling that over. He thought about being with Milt Haynes in the Idaho cave, facing off against three angry T-Rexes, watching Haynes being eaten alive. He'd replayed that horrific scene many times and still couldn't comprehend how he and Sam Beeson had escaped when Milty hadn't.

Survivor's guilt maybe?

He said, "So what do you think killed that Rex down there?"

Hayden picked up the binoculars, glassed the area where the downed Tyrannosaur lay. "Judging by its wounds I'd say he was trampled. Elk are usually only aggressive when threatened. This was a threat on steroids. I could see a few of them teaming up on this Rex, bringing him down and stomping him flat."

They sat in silence, watching the federal agents doing their thing, kneeling and sorting through mounds of bones, bagging remains, making plaster molds of tracks. Four agents stood around the T-Rex carcass talking, one of them writing something on a clipboard.

After several minutes, Jackson said, "You know, I've been thinking about your natal homing theory, Hayden. I know you covered some of it in your book, but it has me wondering. All those meteorites containing dino eggs came down in the same exact region where they disappeared millions of years ago. Rexes, Dromaeosaurs, and Triceratops—correct me if I'm wrong, but weren't those the three main species that ruled this part of the planet at the end of the Cretaceous?"

"Yeah. I see you've been doing your homework, Jack. It's estimated that tens of thousands of those species roamed what is now the Continental Divide and parts of southern Canada when the big boom wiped them out. Triceratops were especially abundant. They provided a plentiful food source for the carnivores."

Jackson said, "Well, that couldn't be an accident. That's like the grand kahuna of natal homing isn't it? To be brought back to this specific geographical area?"

"You're right. It's not an accident."

"So how do you explain it?"

"I can't."

"I mean is it divine intervention? Satan's work? A force of nature where all the stars and planets line up just right?"

"I opt for the latter. It was some kind of a natural world anomaly. The theory those astrophysicists—Mallory, Rayburn, and Britton—came up with dovetails nicely with what you call the big kahuna of natal homing. I don't completely buy into it, but who the hell am I to question it?"

Jackson had read a few things about the MRB Theory of Cretaceous Terrestrial Rebirth. Millions of people had. It dominated the worldwide news media last year. Jackson was a photographer and not a scientist, so much of it was above his level of comprehension. He had read about the catapulting of lava/magma/ iridium-encased dinosaur nests into deep space when the cataclysmic asteroid hit; the cryonic freezing of the eggs in interstellar space; the wormhole that transported the eggs through the space-time continuum back to Earth sealed in meteorites.

"Yeah, I'm with you on that. I don't understand a lot of it, but I find it fascinating."

Hayden replied, "Our publisher wants me to include a chapter in our next book about my thoughts on the MRB Theory, how I think it might be horseshit. I keep pushing back. I tell them we don't want to lose any of our readership. Anthony Mallory, Walton Rayburn, and Cornella Britton are three very bright scientists. The public and the astrophysics community largely support their findings, and I don't feel like I'm the one who should challenge it. But our publisher keeps telling me that controversy sells books."

"So are you going to write that chapter?"

"No. I'm not an astrophysicist. My training is in Earth sciences: paleontology, geology, paleozoology. I don't have the science cred to refute theories outside of my scientific acumen. I admit I don't know much about interstellar space or physics. My dissing the MRB Theory would surely hurt Nora's and my popularity with our readers. The three astrophysicists have their own books coming out soon. I'll let them stand or fall on their own. Meanwhile, I'm thankful for whatever brought the dinosaurs back to us. I'm enjoying getting to know them. It's a dream come true for a paleontologist like me who has a passion for zoology."

"Makes sense," Jackson said, staring down at the activity taking place in the valley. A van had motored in and the wildlife agents were lifting the dead Tyrannosaur into the back. "They should have let us in down there, Hayden."

"Why so?"

"Because you're the world famous dinosaur tracker and bestselling author, and I'm America's Gonzo Shutterbug."

Hayden laughed. "Knowing your wild man reputation is probably *why* they turned us away, Jack."

"I would say it's more likely they read your book, Fowler, and didn't want your dinosaur-magnet ass bringing the Rexes back for an encore."

Both men laughed easily and high-fived each other.

Jackson was starting to realize he liked spending time with his new friend. Hayden Fowler was like a brother from another mother. He suspected that underneath Hayden's prestigious university degrees, professional success, and social sophistication, the man was just as loony-tune crazy as Jackson himself.

Hayden said, "Hey, we're not getting much accomplished here. What say we cut bait and drive out to that pond we found yesterday? Our Rexes have sated their appetites. Just a hunch, but they're gonna need a lot of hydration while they digest their elk dinner."

They had spent most of yesterday afternoon in the refuge looking for Tyrannosaurs. It had been an afternoon of frustration, driving several miles into the reserve, parking Jackson's truck on the side of the main gravel road and hiking into thickets of cottonwood trees. They'd seen mule deer and bald eagles and plenty of squirrels, but no living, breathing Cretaceous creatures. Jackson had some good-natured fun ragging Hayden about having lost his dino divining magic. Hayden grew prickly tromping through thick underbrush in the heat, huffing and puffing, being in nowhere near Jackson's peak physical condition, to which Jackson had more fun busting Hayden's chops about not attending his fitness camp.

"I don't feel the need to train for the Olympics, Jack," Hayden, had retorted, hot and irritable. "I'm a paleontologist, not a decathlon athlete for Chrissakes!"

"No need to get huffy, Fowler," Jackson replied. "I'm just sayin' a little conditioning would help you in your field work. As with me, your work takes you into some very difficult terrain."

"That's why I bought a helicopter."

Jackson smiled. "I'm just lookin' out for you, my friend."

Then, late yesterday, after an unproductive afternoon, Hayden spotted a large pond through a veil of willow trees and suggested they follow an old game trail down to the water's edge. Towering willows, fifty to sixty feet high, surrounded the pond, their drooping branches creating a leafy canopy. They'd found fresh tracks etched into the muddy banks. Wide, deep, three-toed imprints with two large curved claws and the first smaller digit that Hayden called the *hallux*. Unmistakably Tyrannosaurus Rex. They'd found piles of fresh scat amongst the fireweed and mountain bluebells at the edge of the woods. Hayden collected samples of the droppings while Jackson photographed the footprints, both men on alert for trouble. The big predators had been there recently, but apparently had moved on.

They retraced their steps from yesterday, heading down the game trail to the pond. Hayden was armed with two DanInject tranquilizer rifles, tranq darts, and satellite tracking tags. Jackson was loaded down with his assortment of cameras. Both of them carried Smith and Wesson revolvers, powerful enough to take down big game. Just in case.

About halfway down the path, Hayden came to an abrupt stop and flung his arm out, halting Jackson.

"Hear that?" he whispered.

Jackson nodded.

Low growls and grunts.

Hisses and snorts.

Slow, plodding steps through the underbrush.

They ducked down along the side of the trail, taking cover behind a patch of wild rose bushes. Through the thick curtain of willow branches, Jackson caught sight of movement fifty yards away. A well camouflaged greenish-taupe form, crashing through the dense forest.

"They're here," Hayden whispered, excitement evident in his voice. He unstrapped the two rifles. Handed one to Jackson along with extra tranquilizer darts.

Jackson frowned, said quietly, "I'm a photographer, not a gunslinger."

Hayden muttered, "You might be a *dead* photographer if you don't take this."

Reluctantly, Jackson took the tranq gun from him, put the extra darts in his hunting vest. "Just so you know, I'm no sharpshooter."

"You don't need to be. They're big targets. Hit 'em anywhere and they'll collapse in minutes. How are you at climbing trees?"

"Okay, I guess. Why?"

"Rexes can't climb. Not like bears. Their tiny forearms can't grasp and hold. We're safe in the treetops, so we'll climb up high and take our shots from the treetops. C'mon, let's get down closer where we can scope 'em and take our shots."

Jackson fumbled with the rifle. "How do you expect me to shoot video when I have to deal with this thing?"

"Quit your bitchin' and let's go, Jack!"

Jackson was put off by Hayden's dictatorial tone, but he figured the guy knew what he was doing around carnivorous dinosaurs. Probably best to follow his lead.

Cautiously they moved down the trail, stopping when the pond came into view. Jackson felt that old heart-fluttering exhilaration return as he saw two mature T-Rexes, backs to them, bending over and slurping pondwater. They looked like giant muscular birds in the way they lowered their heads and dipped their long snout-like mouths to draw in water, then pulled back and stood erect to swallow. They repeated the action—*dip, slurp, stand, swallow . . . dip, slurp, stand, swallow*—oblivious of him and Hayden, taking in large volumes of water with each dip of their oversized heads.

Hayden pointed to a thicket of large willows and went to a tree. He started climbing. Up, up he went, Jackson staring up the trunk of the stately tree, watching him disappear into the canopy. He followed, going to an adjacent willow and shimmying his way up to an intersection of thick branches. From here he had an unobstructed view of the drinking Rexes below and a clear sightline to Hayden lodged in the treetops twenty feet away.

Jackson started up his videocam, getting clear shots of the Tyrannosaurs dipping and slurping. After several minutes he paused and glanced through the leafy foliage at Hayden, who waved frantically, pantomiming shooting a gun, nodding vigorously, indicating it was time to fire the tranq darts. Further hand signals told him that Hayden would take the one on the right while the Rex on the left was his.

Jackson shut down the videocam and set it aside on a shelf of dense branches. He unstrapped the rifle and took aim at the broad back of his T-Rex.

Almost simultaneously, both rifles discharged with twin cracks. *Pop! Pow!*

He watched the feathered darts zing through the air and strike the beasts, both solid hits, embedding along the ridges of their spinal columns. The Rexes yelped and turned in tandem, their blood-red eyes searching for the deliverers of their pain. Jackson grabbed his camera, capturing them leaving the water's edge and stumbling up the slippery bank, growling and snorting, using their thick tails to help them negotiate the muddy earth.

Jackson shuddered, reminded of that dark night in the Idaho cave five weeks ago, facing off against a trio of Tyrannosaurs. These Rexes were much bigger. *Gotta be eleven feet tall and tip the scales at eight-hundred pounds!* He filmed them struggling to keep their balance, snapping their deep shovel mouths open and closed as they shrieked maniacally, stumbling about in blind anger, confused about their loss of coordination. Through the viewfinder Jackson saw their crushing jaws lined with rows of wickedly curved, guillotine-sharp teeth. Jackson thought of them as land roving saltwater crocs.

Tyrant lizards.

Man-eating dragons.

Terrifying and yet magnificent!

The sedative worked quickly. Dazed, they walked in circles, bumping into each other, their cries quieting. Within three minutes their powerful legs gave out and they dropped, their heavy bodies crumpling, slapping against the muddy turf.

Laying on their sides, they jerked and quivered with seizure-like spasms.

Jackson kept filming until the Rexes ceased moving.

Serene quiet settled over the pond for a couple of long minutes. Then, a flock of Canada geese honked overhead. A pair of mallards quacked from the far bank.

He heard Hayden call out, "Let's go, Jack. Time to tag those bad boys."

They came down out of the trees, revolvers in hand, guardedly making their way to the fallen beasts. The air was heavier and more humid at the water's edge. Jackson breathed in the mossy fungal scent of the pond and an overwhelming sulfurous odor that was immediately repulsive.

"What's that horrible smell?" he asked Hayden.

"It's decayed meat. Rotting prey," Hayden said, taking a knee next to one of the sedated Rexes and grabbing a satellite tag from his pack. "I believe we're smelling the remains of a few of those elk. Decomposed meat is a common stench with carnivores."

Jackson watched Hayden produce a large tube of epoxy and glue the wildlife GPS tag to the animal's flank.

Jackson got his videocam out. "We should be documenting this," he said, beginning to film Hayden's work, moving in to get some closeup shots. "Those're a couple of big dudes."

Hayden moved to the second animal and attached the tracking

tag. "They *are* big, but they're not both dudes."

"Whaddaya mean?"

"This one here is a female."

"How can you tell?"

"She's smaller with wider hip bones and a larger pelvic section to produce and house her eggs. Her coloring is duller and she has a shorter tail. The male is bigger. Probably has sixty or seventy pounds on her. He's a much more vibrant green with distinct earthy-brown marbling and has a longer tail. Males usually have brighter coloration and longer tails to attract females."

"Interesting. So size *does* matter then."

Hayden gave him an amused scowl. "Your standup routine needs a lot of work, Jack."

"So I've been told. Pry the male's mouth open so I can get some shots of those killer teeth."

"No can do," Hayden said, standing. "Even sedated, these guys can reflexively snap those deadly jaws. I don't cherish losing any fingers or hands."

"Okay, how about a few selfies then? The two of us kneeling by our tranquilized Rexes?"

Hayden complied and Jackson had reeled off a half-dozen selfies when they heard a raucous noise start up from the underbrush in the willows—a chorus of deep guttural grunts punctuated by loud rhythmic thumps. The sound reminded Jackson of the wild emus he'd encountered in the Australian outback. Especially the booming thumps that carried across the pond. When sensing danger, Australian emus vibrated their throats, making a low-frequency, percussive sound.

"What the hell is that?" Jackson said, tilting his head in the direction of the clatter.

"I believe we have a problem," Hayden said.

"Problem?"

Hayden pointed at the downed Tyrannosaurs. "I think we just sedated the parents of some juvenile hatchlings."

"So what? If they're just hatchlings then let's—"

"Those calls are going out to other Rexes in the area, Jack. Big animals like these guys. We need to move out. Now."

"Hell, we've got the tranq rifles and our Smith and Wesson cannons. Let's find the hatchlings. I want to get some footage." Jackson walked through a patch of wildflowers and entered the woods.

"I'm telling you, Jack, you don't want to tangle with the juveniles. They can be vicious. And it won't be long until a few mature Rexes show up."

Jackson stopped and turned, looked at Hayden. "Well then we'll tag a few more. I thought that's why we came here, Fowler."

"It is, but we need to stay safe."

Jackson waved him off as if the comment was nonsense. He turned and walked deeper into the woods, toward the growls and syncopated thumps.

He heard Hayden shout at his back, "I'm headed back to the truck and I advise you do the same."

Fowler can be such a pantywaist sometimes, he thought, ignoring him, kicking through the underbrush, videoing his trek while remaining alert for snakes.

The drumming thumps and hissing growls increased in volume.

He walked slowly through the tufted hairgrass, pushed around low growing mountain snowberry shrubs, winding his way through the thick willow forest, camera in one hand, revolver in the other.

He came upon a rockpile covered with fuzzy greenish-yellow moss, heard the hatchlings thrumming and growling behind it.

Jackson put his foot on the rocks and stepped up, leaned over, his videocam whirring as he looked down the backside of the pile.

Four miniature Tyrannosaurs squawked and thumped and hissed and growled at him, their watchful little cherry eyes blazing in anger. Long strips of bloody meat draped the rock, which Jackson took to be elk leftovers.

This will make a fantastic video, he thought as he filmed.

And then he heard a high-pitched hiss behind him. He turned in time to see another T-Rex hatchling take a running leap at him, its tiny jaws wide open.

He lost his footing on the slick mossy surface and tumbled off the rocks, banged his knee against the hard ground. He lost the gun but managed to hold on to the camera and keep filming, capturing the Rex clamping on to his left ankle and biting into the bone. Intense pain traveled up his leg. The surprise attack from behind had stunned him, but he had the wherewithal to use his good leg to push himself up and kick-shake the ornery little bastard off. The hatchling squealed as it slammed against the base of a big willow, then came at him again.

In pain, his heart galloping, Jackson ran on his damaged ankle to the nearest tree, three Rex hatchlings after him now in growling pursuit. Just as he hit the tree, one of the hatchlings caught up with him, snapping its jaws, its teeth ripping his pantleg but fortunately missing his flesh.

Jackson scrambled up the knotty trunk of the willow, getting as high up in the tree as he could. Out of breath, he glanced down to see five Tyrannosaurus Rex hatchlings circling below, determined to get at him.

His left foot was on fire. He pulled off his shoe. Blood soaked his sock. Pain radiated up his leg. He wondered how long he'd have to stay up here. He called out for Hayden. Heard only the relentless growling and hissing from the mini-dragons below.

As he waited for escape, he checked his videocam footage. It was all there, crystal clear definition. *National Geographic* quality. He'd even maintained a steady hand when he'd taken the fall.

Though he was hurting, he smiled.

The world is going to love this stuff!

Christening the Bird

July 9: Gilliam's Guidepost
Heart Butte, Montana

NORA SEETHED AS SHE WATCHED HAYDEN address the small gathering on the helipad. He stood in front of their gleaming new Bell 407 helicopter, speaking of the plans and ambitions of Fowler-Lemoyne Aviation, Inc. This official launch of their startup company was supposed to have taken place yesterday, but had to be rescheduled due to Hayden's AWOL status.

You have a lot of nerve to stand up there and yammer on as though you haven't let these people down, she thought, watching his prideful delivery.

Sunday Nora had taken a nonstop flight from Minneapolis to Great Falls and rented a car, driving two hours here to settle in and prepare for Monday's commemoration. Four times she had tried to reach Hayden through the day Sunday with no success. *Where is he?* became her disquieting mantra. He was supposed to arrive a few hours before her. Then, finally, she heard from him as she was unpacking in their Guidepost Cellar suite. He informed her he had run into a problem in Wyoming and couldn't get to Heart Butte until the following evening, and would she please reschedule the event for Tuesday? Her incessant worry for him soured into a burning anger, but she held her tongue. She entertained ideas of spiting him, pushing ahead with the company launch as planned and giving the dedication speech herself. But she changed her mind. Doing that would surely cause a major rift in their relationship. Nora thought it would be best to deal with him in person. So she spent much of Sunday evening making calls, informing everyone involved that she had to move the event to Tuesday, doing her best not to reveal her resentment.

The problem had to be Jackson Lattimer. The man was trouble. She saw it but Hayden didn't. He absolutely refused to acknowledge any downside to a friendship with the famous wildlife photographer known for his reckless lifestyle.

Nora's stomach churned as she watched him talk to the small crowd. He didn't mention his absence. He didn't issue an apology. His cavalier attitude and complete disregard for the people who had worked so hard to make this happen rankled her. His actions were not those of an effective leader.

He's certainly not getting this thing off to a positive start.

". . . and I'd like to thank Peter Lacroix for finding a super deal on this beautiful aircraft, which he is about to take to the skies on its inaugural flight for Fowler-Lemoyne Aviation . . ."

Nora scanned faces to see if others shared her disappointment with Hayden. A few yawns and a couple of bored expressions, but most looked interested, smiling, nodding in agreement, hanging on Hayden's every word. Peter Lacroix stood with his family near the tail rotor. Bryan and Loretta Gilliam and their three kids congregated in the grass well back of the helipad. Newly hired dispatcher Nancy Diehl and mechanic Carl Lacey, and ranch hands Apisi Lyttle and Chogan Stimson stood around the perimeter of the landing pad. The only missing employee was second pilot Larry Bing, who was finishing out his employment with the U.S. Forest Service. He would be joining them next week.

A small contingent of local media congregated at the far left of the helicopter. Madison Donnelly—the popular news anchor from KECI-TV, the NBC affiliate out of Missoula—sat in a director's chair, looking over her interview notes as her makeup assistant fussed with her platinum blonde hair. Her cameraman focused a boxy videocam on a sturdy tripod while the audio tech worked the boom mic that hung above Hayden's head, just out of frame. Also here were two print journalists: Business reporter Justin Contraldo from the *Great Falls Tribune*, and community news director Robert Dressler from the Kalispell *Flathead Beacon*. Bryan had developed a good rapport with this group last summer when the Gilliams were overseeing their dinosaur zoo habitats. He had banned all other members of the media today, telling Nora he didn't want a repeat of the paparazzi three-ring circus that had reporters tromping all over the ranch last summer.

As Nora listened to Hayden thanking all who had worked hard to get their fledgling company up and running quickly, she replayed their conversation from yesterday. Hayden had dragged in at five-thirty without apology, without thanking her for taking care of the rescheduling.

"Nice of you to finally show up, Mr. *CEO!*" she said, avoiding his embrace, unable to control her temper that had been simmering all day. "I hope it didn't put you out too much."

He threw up his hands in surprise. "What the hell, Nora. We've been apart four days and this is how you greet me?"

"In case you forgot, I was supposed to greet you twenty-four hours ago."

He reacted like he'd been slapped. "I explained to you why I'd be delayed."

"No you didn't. You only told me you had a problem you needed to take care of. You didn't tell me what the problem was, but I have a good idea."

"Now don't go off blaming Jack again."

"I didn't mention his name."

"No, but I know you were thinking it. Why do you hate him so much? You've never even met him, Nora. Jack's a great guy. He's fun and he's a world class nature photographer. He's smart. He possesses a deep intellectual curiosity. And he loves our book. He thinks we're geniuses. How can you hate a guy like that?"

"I never said I hated him. I just don't trust him. He's careless, a feral wild man, and I don't think he has other people's safety in mind on his shoots. Two deaths in the last fourteen months on his watch speaks for itself. You know I didn't want you to go to Jackson Hole. I begged you not to go but you went anyway. And so when yesterday went by and you didn't respond to my calls and texts, I got worried. I was terrified you might be death number three on

Jackson Lattimer's hit parade. And then when I finally heard from you—a couple of hours *after* you said you'd be here—you sounded like you didn't have a care in the world . . . like you weren't even aware of how concerned I was. I wondered if you even cared about our company launch."

"That's ridiculous! Of *course* I care about our launch. I care about Fowler-Lemoyne Aviation. Lord knows I've pumped a lot of money into it and—"

"*We* have pumped a lot of money into it. You and *me*, Hayden. Don't you ever forget we're a team here. And we now have employees who need us to provide stable and responsible leadership. Right out of the gate you have committed a supreme act of irresponsibility, oh lover boy of mine. We have a ton of work to do for the company. We're facing aggressive publishing deadlines and you're off goofing around in Wyoming on your bromance with America's Gonzo Shutterbug and demanding everybody else rearrange their schedules to accommodate your whims."

"Goofing around? I'll have you know it was a working trip and I worked my ass off, thank you very much. Jackson Hole was a productive outing. We tagged two Tyrannosaurs with GPS chips to start my migration study. I got some great new material for the book. And what's with this *bromance* shit? Jesus, Nora!"

She raised an eyebrow. "Well? It's true, isn't it?"

He gave her a hard stare.

She said, "Just answer one question for me?"

"Ask away."

"The problem in Wyoming was Lattimer, wasn't it?"

"Yeah, but—"

"I rest my case. We'll talk more tomorrow. You're sleeping in the other bedroom tonight, Hayden. I don't want to share a bed with you."

Leaving him stunned, she'd walked away and locked herself in the master bedroom. Turned on the TV to drown out his persistent knocking and lame apologies.

Nora didn't sleep much for worrying that she might have taken her outrage too far. This morning she came out of the bedroom expecting the worst, but Hayden wasn't there. She went to the kitchen nook and noticed a half pot of coffee on the burner, a crusty skillet and dirty dishes in the sink. Her anger bubbled up all over again. And it wasn't due to the soiled dishes.

The bastard! He doesn't even have the backbone to stick around and discuss things with me. At the least he could have left me a note.

She'd checked the digital clock on the microwave. 8:12. The festivities were scheduled to start at nine-thirty. Just enough time for a breakfast of Danish and coffee and a quick shower before heading out to the helipad.

And now Hayden was wrapping up his comments with the christening of the aircraft. He held the champagne bottle aloft as his voice carried across the quad. "And so it is my pleasure to now commemorate the inaugural flight of our new helicopter with the ceremonial breaking of the champagne bottle. With this action I also christen the official opening of Gilliam Heliport. Thank you Bryan and Loretta for donating a piece of your land to the cause and for all of your hard work in turning your quadrangle into this beautiful air strip. May this bottle of bubbly spirits protect our new chopper and give our pilots and crew eternal good luck."

With that, Hayden turned and dramatically broke the bottle against the fuselage, holding up the jagged bottleneck with a look of triumph. Cheers and whistles and applause followed. Nora felt goosebumps race across her arms, her anger momentarily softened. She couldn't help but feel a creeping sense of pride. They had done this. Her and Hayden and Peter Lacroix and the Gilliams. It had seemed like an impossible challenge just a short five weeks ago. Now here they were, with a million-dollar aircraft sitting on the tarmac of Gilliam Heliport. She breathed in the dusty ammonia scent of the twin concrete landing pads, the tarry odor of the asphalt track leading to the barn that would become the Fowler-Lemoyne Aviation hangar.

It's truly a miracle, she thought, watching Bryan, Loretta, Peter, and Hayden go through their interviews.

"Hi, Nora," Brinshou Lacroix said from behind her, stepping around to face her. "It's quite the celebration isn't it? How have you been?"

Nora smiled at her, struck as she always was by the dusky beauty of the woman. Pregnancy had only added depth to Brin's loveliness. Her flawless, soft cocoa skin was radiant in the mid-morning light. Nora would kill for skin like hers.

"Oh, hi, Brin. I'm good. Just tired. Too much work and not enough rest, y'know. How are you doing? When is your baby due?"

"The second week of January. I'm feeling fine right now, but it's going to be a tough year." She looked at Nora, her dark eyes searching Nora's face, questioning. "Can I confide in you, Nora?"

"Of course. Anytime."

"I hate to admit it, but I'm scared."

Nora looked across the quad at little Kimi Lacroix, holding her grandmother Kachina's hand. "Why? You didn't have any problems delivering your daughter did you?"

"No. I'm not worried about the pregnancy. There'll be some uncomfortable times ahead, but that's not it."

Nora touched her shoulder. "What is it then, dear?"

"It's my Peter," she said, nervously fidgeting with the silver chain of her Cretaceous Stone necklace. "I have a bad feeling about him flying for your company. No offense," she added as an after-thought.

"None taken."

"I was hoping that when Peter resigned from the Forest Service he would come to his senses and take a safer job. Instead he signed up for this," she said, pointing at the group of people crowding around the helicopter. "I would never tell the Gilliams this because they have been so nice to us. But I feel this ranch is a troubled land after what happened here last summer. I believe malevolent spirits inhabit this place, the ghosts of those who died here. They are warning us. I can feel them right now. My husband doesn't believe in my clairvoyance. He says my visions are nothing but Kootenai nonsense, which really hurts me."

"Yes," Nora said, thinking of her issues with Hayden, "men can certainly be insensitive at times."

"Oh don't get me wrong. My Petey is a wonderful man, a caring husband and a very devoted father for Kimi. I love him with all of my heart and soul." Brin looked away. She focused on Peter, who was answering questions Madison Donnelly fired at him. "Sometimes I think I love him too much, if that's possible. Every second he's in that cockpit, I worry. Helicopters are an unsafe aircraft to begin with and now my Petey will be flying in and out of a heliport on cursed land. It was hard enough when he was flying over forest fires, but now he'll be out searching for dinosaurs. Man-*eating* dinosaurs. That doesn't bode well, Nora."

Nora knew of Brin's problem with anxiety. Peter had discussed it with her and Hayden when they talked employment with him.

She said, "Your husband has a perfect flight record over his eight years with the Forest Service, Brin. He's a superb pilot as he showed us last summer, flying us out of that trouble you mentioned. Hayden and I wouldn't have selected him to partner with us if we didn't believe in his skills. Peter will be fine. And I'm quite sure that helicopter he chose is perfectly safe. Flying helicopters is what he loves doing. It's his lifeblood. It's as important to him as the air he breathes. My advice is to put more of your trust in him. Trust that his love of what he is doing and his love for you and his family will keep him safe. In other words, trust your trust. It will lessen your anxiety about his flying."

No sooner did those words of wisdom leave her mouth than Nora felt like a hypocrite. Did she put her trust in Hayden? Did she trust her own trust in him?

Brin ran her hand through her long midnight-black hair. "What you say makes sense, Nora. I'll try, but it's hard for me. I'm not claiming to be a soothsayer, but my strong visions feed my worries. Personal visions are a big thing among the Kootenai people."

Hayden's booming voice interrupted their conversation. "Okay, folks, we're off to see the wizard. On this inaugural flight we are heading three hundred miles south to pick up more of the Cretaceous meteorite rock . . ."

"We?" Nora said aloud. "Hayden is going with them?" She watched Peter climb into the cockpit. Apisi and Chogan loaded hammers, picks, chisels, and battery-powered drills into the cargo section.

"You didn't know?" Brin said.

"It's a surprise to me. But Hayden's been in Wyoming. We haven't talked much the past week."

"Hayden told Petey it was his helicopter, goddamnit. His words, not mine. Hayden said he bought it and he would be on that inaugural flight no matter what."

Hayden's voice again: ". . . and with any luck we'll bring back enough rock to restart the Gilliam Cretaceous Stone jewelry operation . . ."

Nora heard Brin say, "That's one of the carrots my Petey dangled in front of me."

"What, the jewelry business? Oh, that's right. You worked as the lead jeweler."

"Yes. And I loved it. It brought me a lot of new customers and helped me start up my store in Missoula. Peter knew that. What he didn't know was that I wasn't eager to return to this place after what happened last August. All the fire and death that occurred on this disturbed land. I wanted so much to stay in Missoula and manage my store. And I must say, I don't think smashing a bottle of champagne is going to bring us the luck we're going to need."

Nora watched Hayden give the crowd a double thumbs-up then jump up into the chopper behind Apisi and Chogan. The doors slid shut. Any attempt at further conversation was cut off as Peter fired up the copter. The engine roared. The rotor blades whirled. A stiff downdraft breeze blew across the quadrangle. The chopper lifted off the pad and rose above the barns and horse stables, turning due south.

Nora shielded the sun with her hand, following the chopper's flight. As the copter flew over the southeast border of Gilliam's Guidepost, Nora saw what looked like a trio of Dromaeosaurs run out of a grove of sycamore trees and look up at the aircraft passing overhead. She realized it was the last thing Brin needed to see. Nora moved quickly to cut off Brin's view, but realized her attentions were on trying to locate her mother and daughter.

Nora looked back at the distant sycamores. The Dromaeosaurs

were gone. She knew two Dromes had attacked the Gilliams three weeks ago. She also knew Hayden had found a nest in the Gilliam's east meadow containing seven eggs. She thought about Hayden's natal homing theory and what that implied.

As Nora watched the Fowler-Lemoyne helicopter disappear beyond the treetops on its maiden flight, she thought there might be a hint of truth to what Brinshou Lacroix had said.

Maybe this land *is* troubled.

Perhaps Gilliam's Guidepost really *is* cursed.

Please be careful, Hayden.

Millions of Reasons to Settle

July 10: Gilliam's Guidepost
Heart Butte, Montana

"THE COMPANY KICKOFF WENT WELL, don't you think?" Loretta heard Bryan say.

She took a seat across from him at the kitchen table. "Yeah, Hayden gave a good speech. And the new helicopter is impressive."

"It is, but it doesn't have as much cargo space as we needed," Bryan said. "Not nearly as much as *I* wanted. It's really more of a passenger aircraft. They brought back as much meteorite rock as they could, but it's barely enough to restart my jewelry line. Pete said he and Carl Lacey could take out the seats for the next run. That would triple our freight capacity. The good news is, there are thick bands of iridium in this rock, much more than we saw in our first meteorite. Pure iridium is going for six grand an ounce and we've got close to two pounds in this first haul alone!"

"Iridium? It's *that* valuable?"

"Oh, yeah. It's used in medical lab crucibles and satellite communication systems. High-performance spark plugs and electrical contacts, too. Also, iridium is used in high-tech products like observatory telescopes and satellites and space exploration equipment. I did the math. We could clear a hundred-and-eighty *thousand* just moving what we already have! I talked to Nora about setting up sales and distribution channels. She said she would look into it when she got a chance."

Loretta saw Bryan's eyes blaze with the entrepreneurial excitement that had been missing for so long. She was happy for him that he had something to focus on that was meaningful to him, something that made him feel whole again. But his exhaustion showed in the deep lines on his face, the weariness in his voice.

She gave him a thin smile. "That poor woman has enough on her plate, Bry. And so do you. How about letting me handle it?"

"Are you sure? You're busy, too."

"Not as busy as Nora. Let me handle iridium sales."

"Okay, that's cool! After you research it, let me know the sizes and weights buyers prefer."

"Will do."

"Thanks, hon."

The conversation shifted to the missing Blackfoot women. Bryan's enthusiastic tone turned pessimistic. "There are no less than one-hundred possible number combinations for those two hidden digits of the license plate I'm chasing, It's so frustrating, Lor. Especially with no help from the police."

Bryan had been putting in many long hours the past few weeks, getting the heliport up to code and searching for Kanti Lyttle and Ahwee Red Crow. Yesterday a third Blackfoot friend, Kai Laverdure, asked for Bryan's help in finding his girlfriend, Aiyana Halfmoon, who had been missing for three days now.

"You look drained, Bry. Totally wiped out. You should slow down and get some rest."

"I would if I could, but my conscience won't let me. Those women—our *friends*—are out there somewhere, I'm sure they're terrified and I'm the only one looking for them. It falls on me to find them. I owe all three of those families."

Loretta felt a wave of compassion for her husband in that moment. He had a big heart and would go to the ends of the Earth to help anyone he considered his friend. She loved him and admired him for his dedication, but she wondered if he wasn't chasing after ghosts. After all, Kanti Lyttle had been missing for more than two weeks. The odds of Apisi's wife still being alive were slim. Loretta's heart ached for their disappeared friends, for Bryan's search that had tested his resolve and worn him down.

She said, "Those security clips from the trading post you showed me are solid evidence. I can't believe the authorities aren't following up."

"I know, right? The Blackfeet tribal police and Montana DCI both give me the same old song and dance about not having the manpower. Budget cuts. You know, the old standard excuse for not getting off their lazy asses to serve and protect. A couple of cops even had the audacity to say our Native friends could possibly have been eaten by dinosaurs, so what would be the use in looking. Can you believe that shit, Lor?"

"That's tragically lame."

"If these were white women they'd be all over it. They'd have no problem finding the manpower then."

"You're right, Bry. But the fact remains, you have *got* to get some help from the authorities. You can't keep going it alone. You need to take this to the FBI."

"No! I hate those pricks. They didn't do anything for us last year, even after we sent them damning voicemail evidence. When they finally took action, I was half dead and our ranch was in flames."

"You're exhausted, dear. You haven't gotten a decent night's sleep in a week. You need some help. Maybe—"

"Actually, I got some help this morning. A private investigator that Atlee Pinnaker set me up with. Name of Mike Mathews. He does a lot of footwork for Atlee and specializes in missing persons cases—bail jumpers, extradition subjects, scammers, thieves, kidnappers. I sent him the clips and he got back with me right away. He says the tattoo on the abductor's arm—the animal paw and human fist—is a common symbol with animal rights activists."

"Animal rights groups? You don't think—"

"Yes I *do* think," Bryan replied with a slow grin. "All three of the women—Kanti, Ahwee, and Aiyana—were at our barbecue last summer. They're Native American and therefore easy targets. I checked the Animal Emancipation Faction website, and although the paw-fist tat we saw in the security video is not an official symbol of the AEF, a Google search turned up a few animal rights people showing off that same tattoo. No faces or identification, just photos of arms and chests bearing the tattoo."

"Interesting," Loretta said.

"Isn't it though? I don't know why I didn't connect all of this sooner. Mathews says the license plate with the covered-up last two digits will be difficult to track down, but he has contacts in the Motor Vehicle Division. He's going to get me a list of car and truck owners based on those hundred possible number combinations."

"That's a long list of suspects."

"It is. And it might all be for naught when you consider it could be a stolen plate. But it's a start."

"What have you told Apisi?"

"I've been honest with Ap. I told him all of this."

"How's he holding up?"

"Pretty good, considering. I told him he didn't have to fly out with Peter yesterday to retrieve that meteorite rock, but he insisted. Said he needed to keep busy. The Blackfeet are strong-willed people, Lor."

"What do you think their motive is? I mean, why abduct three women off the reservation. Those families don't have any money for ransom. And they certainly don't have anything to do with the mistreatment of animals."

"You're right. But it's possible the kidnappers might view us Gilliams as animal abusers, a view they would share with the AEF. The AEF thought we were evil for keeping those dinosaurs penned up in our zoo. And in these kidnapper's own warped Neanderthal minds, they might hold us responsible for the deaths of the terrorists who invaded our property, and for the imprisonment of Leonard Sheridan. Taking women close to us sends a not-so-subtle message. I know you don't wanna believe it, Loretta, but the world is full of sick human beings."

"Oh, if last summer didn't convince me of that, nothing will. But why send us an indirect message? Why not come after us directly?"

"Because we're white and well known. Much less risk going after Indigenous women."

It dawned on her that Bryan had possibly hit on the truth. "Jesus, Bry," she said, failing to keep the panic out of her voice. "We have *got* to get some security for us and the kids."

"I agree. I'm working on that. Mike Mathews recommended a couple of good private security firms I'm going to call. I shudder thinking about Pauley and his band playing public gigs and Ethan out in the open on baseball fields. We can keep a tight leash on Lianne no matter how much backtalk she gives us." He shook his head in dismay. "As if the dinosaur threat isn't enough. Christ!"

"Are we going to have to corral Paul and Ethan, too?"

"No. They both have a good sense of situational awareness. I've preached to them about the potential for dinosaur attacks and being mindful of their surroundings. They're both carrying, so if there's trouble, they can protect themselves."

"Paul and Ethan carrying guns makes me nervous, Bry. They're so young."

"I've been training them since they were eight or nine. You know that."

"I know, but—"

"They're responsible, Loretta. I feel better about them having some protection. This is Montana, not one of those candy-assed liberal states with ridiculous gun laws that only help criminals."

"True that," she said.

Loretta felt that now was a good time to mention the discussion she'd had with younger son Ethan this afternoon. Bryan had been in The Cellar basement checking out the Cretaceous meteorite rocks Peter Lacroix and crew had brought in when Ethan approached her as she was reading in the den.

"Speaking of the boys," she said, "Ethan gave me an earful today."

"Ethan? An earful? He's usually so quiet."

"Not today he wasn't."

"What's his problem?"

"He's jealous of his big brother."

"Jealous of Pauley? Why?"

"He says we're paying a lot more attention to Paul than him. Ethan thinks we're more interested in Pauley's band than his baseball. He says we've stopped giving a damn about him. He claims you have been going overboard with your praise of Pauley's guitar playing and singing, but that you ignore him. He reminded me we haven't been to a single one of his games this season. He's leading his team in hitting and the team is riding high in first place, but we would never know it because we just don't care enough to come see him play. Sibling jealousy at its finest," she said with a tight smile. "It was a real pity party, Bry."

"Wow!" Bryan said. "That hurts a little. Especially since he didn't come to me with it."

"Well, Ethan's always been the sensitive one. For whatever reason, he always comes to me first."

"That's because you're an easy mark when it comes to dishing out sympathy," he said, smiling, and giving her a wink.

"Well he's right. We have been shutting him out lately."

Bryan reached across the table and took her hand, caressed her wrist. "This raising children thing never gets any easier does it?"

"No it doesn't. The teen years are the hardest, when they're on the edge of adulthood with all that raging testosterone and their bodies changing and everything in their lives magnified a hundred-fold. It's a confusing, insecure time for them." She shot him a sad smile. "Too bad they can't stay our cute little darlings forever, huh?"

"So true. I'll talk to Ethan," he said. "When is his next game?"

"Friday night."

"Let's make it a date, no matter what. Our future Hall of Famer needs us."

"I'm putting it on my calendar now," Loretta said, entering it in her phone.

Bryan said, "I sure wish we could get the boys interested in family movie night again. We were a lot tighter group then."

"I think they've outgrown it, honey," Loretta said, thinking that both boys had spread their independent wings and flown from the Gilliam nest this summer. She felt a pang of melancholy as that realization hit her.

Bryan said, "Has Lee picked out a movie for tonight?"

"Yes. Lee-lee wants *The Princess Diaries*."

"What, no horse movie?"

Loretta chuckled. "Our little girl is growing up, Bry. She's moving on to more sophisticated films."

"You call *The Princess Diaries* sophisticated?"

"Compared to her *Flicka* movies, yes I do."

Bryan groaned. "I'll try to stay awake."

"Remember, this is for her, not us."

Bryan's phone vibrated on the tabletop, the display showing it was their lawyer, Atlee Pinnaker.

Bryan picked up. "Hey, Atlee. Been meaning to call to thank you for that investigator you recommended."

Loretta could hear the tinny garble of the lawyer's voice but couldn't make out any words.

Bryan nodded and said 'yeah' a few times before his face lit up with a big grin. "What? *Really?*" he said. "Wow, that's *tremendous* news, Atlee. Listen, my wife is here with me. She needs to hear this. I'm going to put you on speakerphone."

"Hello, Mrs. Gilliam," she heard the attorney say. "How have you been?"

"I'm good, thanks. Very busy with the opening of our new heliport and playing mom to three active kids." *And still going through therapy over the death of my brother,* she wanted to add, but didn't.

"I heard about your heliport. Congratulations. I'm sure my firm will start booking flights with you in the near future."

"Excellent. So what is this tremendous news you have for us?"

"Well I was just telling your husband that I heard from AEF's legal team this morning. They don't want this to go to trial. They said they want to avoid further negative publicity. They don't want the actions of a few rogue members to tarnish their sterling reputation for all the good they do for the animal kingdom."

Bryan said, "I guess they don't consider human beings to be part of the animal kingdom."

"Indeed. A most cogent point, Mr. Gilliam. What I hear them saying is the Animal Emancipation Faction doesn't want to damage their recruiting process or lose donations from their deep and extremely wealthy donor base."

"How much are they willing to settle for?" Bryan asked.

"It's not chump change. They're authorized by the board to pay you seven million."

"*Dollars?*" Bryan exclaimed.

"Absolutely. I'm in the process of setting up your remuneration distribution now."

Loretta heard the figure and thought it couldn't possibly be real. She looked across the table at Bryan, who wore the same astonished expression she was sure she had plastered on her face. "*What?*" she exclaimed. "Who the hell can afford to dish out that kind of money?"

"Don't be fooled, Mrs. Gilliam. AEF is a huge global operation. Millions of animal lovers see them as doing good work and donate generously. They have more money than Elon Musk. Seven mil is basically their petty cash fund. How do you think they get away with some of the more nefarious things they do?"

Loretta and Bryan stared at each other for a long, silent beat, stunned.

Atlee Pinnaker said, "Are you folks still there?"

Bryan answered. "Uh, yeah, we're here, Atlee. What's the catch? Surely there must be some downside to all of this."

"There is. They want a nondisclosure agreement signed by you both stating you will not publicly defame the AEF or any of its members and that you will not discuss this settlement with any other person or party. That's completely doable and reasonable. What's not reasonable is they want you to sign a binding declaration that you will drop all criminal charges and any resulting proceedings, which means no trial—civil or criminal. This is a fairly common practice we see from wealthy defendants. If you'll pardon my talking up the other side, it's a very smart ploy on their part."

"No criminal charges?" Bryan said.

"Only if you sign that specific declaration. They know they were in the wrong and would lose much more than the seven million in a civil trial. More than likely they'd have to pay out three times that in a followup criminal trial. They're aware of your past relationship with the press, Mr. Gilliam. You have been a celebrity mouthpiece that has the public's collective ear. The settlement with its stipulations allows AEF to sweep this under the rug, prevent future costly litigation, and maintain their lucrative donor revenue stream."

Bryan said, "So they wouldn't have to admit their guilt publicly?"

"That's right. And you would be required to keep quiet about anything that happened last August the eighth on your property. Nothing on social media. No discussing it with TV and print journalists. No podcasts. No mention about it in any book deals you might get."

Bryan scowled. "I'm not sure I like being censored like that. It's un-American."

"It's the American legal system, Mr. Gilliam. There are always tradeoffs."

"It's seven *million* dollars, Bry!" Loretta nearly screamed. "Other people can tell that story. Just not us. Isn't that right, Mr. Pinnaker?"

"Yes, you're correct."

Bryan said, "So what are our options here, Atlee?"

"You can go a couple of ways with this. The most hassle-free way is you take the seven million payoff and keep quiet. The tricky part is if you violate the terms of the settlement NDA and speak out, you would be financially liable for damages. They could turn around and hit you with defamation or slander charges. The second way is to turn down the payment and take AEF to court. As I mentioned before, you could proceed with the lawsuit we had planned and win much more than the seven million Both the civil and criminal suits would be slam dunk wins for us. But it could take a year—probably two—just to get into a courtroom before a judge and present your case to a jury. The civil trial could take a couple of years, a criminal trial most likely longer. Their legal team would tie things up in endless appeals and you and your family would have to relive the entire experience all over again, with you and other witnesses having to testify. You could be looking at being involved for the next five or six years. And not just you. Any and all of the other people you had at your cookout would also be on call to testify."

Loretta said, "What is your advice, Mr. Pinnaker?"

"Well, obviously, it would be in my firm's best interests to follow through with the lawsuits. It would give us hundreds—perhaps *thousands*—of additional billable hours. And you would receive additional millions of dollars in recompense. But you will have to wait much longer for your money and revisit the heartbreak and pain of that day. You folks will have to make that decision."

Bryan asked, "Out of that seven million, how much would we actually get? I mean after your firm's fees and taxes."

"As we agreed to, my contingency fee is thirty percent, which comes to a little over two million. That would leave your taxable income at just under five million. There is no state tax in Montana so you would be liable for only the federal. But that's where things get tricky. Since much of your claim was for personal injury and destruction of personal property, you could possibly be exempt from all taxes. If not all, certainly a large chunk of it. I can look into it for you and get back to you with real figures."

"Please do," Bryan said.

"In the meantime, how about the two of you talk it over and let me know which way you want to go with this."

Loretta said, "How much time do we have to make a decision?"

"Oh you have some time, Mrs. Gilliam. The settlement offer as it stands is good for thirty days. I'll send you folks the Settlement Agreement Proposal and you can put your heads together."

Bryan said, "are we allowed to make a counteroffer, Atlee?"

"I'm so glad you brought that up. In this case I would highly recommend that you do. You have them over a barrel. Their reputation is important to them and they were most definitely in the wrong. Based on my experience in these kinds of settlements, I would say they would probably be willing to pay out twelve to fifteen million to avoid a couple of embarrassing public courtroom trials. I can do some more feeling out of their attorneys, but I say we should come back with a request for fifteen million, of which they will talk us down. We'll hold firm at twelve million. That's where we can get them. However, I do believe they are steadfastly non-negotiable on the nondisclosure agreement and their desire for a declaration that you will drop all criminal charges. All of this, of course, only if you folks decide to go with the settlement."

"Good to know, Atlee. Send us the paperwork and we'll talk it over."

"Remember, as far as the criminal charges go, if you want, we can still go after Leonard Sheridan and the other surviving AEF terrorists. Those would be slam dunks, too, with all the evidence we have in hand. I just thought it was prudent to hit the organization that has the funds first."

They signed off with Pinnaker and sat there looking at each other in a stunned silence. Yesterday at this time, Loretta thought Atlee Pinnaker was just another incompetent, greedy shyster lawyer of the ambulance chaser variety. Now she thought he was a legal genius. Still greedy, but far from incompetent.

A razor-sharp legal genius.

Bryan closed his eyes and leaned back in his chair, taking in and letting out deep breaths.

Loretta thought: *We're going to be multi-millionaires!*
Am I dreaming this or is this real?

Blues In the Badlands

July 13: Tyrannosaurus Rex Delivery
Western North Dakota

KELTON RENDAYA GLANCED AT THE DASHBOARD CLOCK. 4:13 AM. He gripped the steering wheel tighter and yawned, trying to keep from nodding off. He and Thorn had been on the road in this creaky rental truck for eight-plus hours. They'd taken U.S. Route 2 East across northern Montana and picked up I-94 into North Dakota, thirty miles south of the Canadian border.

The headlights flashed on a road sign: MEDORA 17 MILES. They had another two hours east to Bismarck, then south along the Missouri River for another hour to their destination, a sprawling cattle ranch owned by one of Kelton's wealthiest clients. There they would deliver the two heavily sedated Tyrannosaurs being transported in the rear cargo hold.

Kelton continued to be astonished by the strange requests (needs?) of his clientele. *Why does a prosperous cattleman want large prehistoric carnivores anywhere near his herds?* Certainly a perplexing question, but he had learned long ago to keep his curiosity in check. In this business, the less he knew about the motivations of his paying customers, the better. Their money was the only thing that interested him.

Three hours ago, they had stopped near Wolf Point to tranq the Rexes with a second dose. The efficacy of even the strongest doses was five hours max on these creatures. This trip being near twelve hours, they would have to pull off the road and tranq them a third time somewhere south of Bismarck. The timing and strength of the dosages was tricky. Any errors could be disastrous as Kelton well knew from Tank Mahaffey's recent fuckup.

He thought back to the incident two weeks ago, when he'd lost his first T-Rex. His longtime ranch hands—Tank Mahaffey and Hoops Terrell—had failed to follow proper sedation instructions. That fiasco had been a huge financial loss and near human tragedy. It was all on Tank really. Kelton had put him in charge, mistakenly thinking Mahaffey could carry out simple instructions. But no. It had quickly turned into a disaster. Two weeks later, Kelton was still beating himself up over it.

He recalled the fully-awake Rex rumbling out of the back of the truck, screaming shrilly, steamrolling him, then flattening Tank and Hoops. Felt like he'd been hit by a freight train. Kelton had been clawed in the gut and Hoops suffered an arm wound that kept him out of action for ten days. Tank, as luck would have it, got away without injury.

The next day, the wound in his midsection burning and stinging, Kelton fired Tank. It wasn't easy. Kelton had known Gordon "Tank" Mahaffey since fourth grade, and Tank had been a hired hand on the family ranch for more than thirty years. Booting his old friend out of the bunkhouse was one of the hardest things he'd ever had to do. But it was necessary. The loss of the under-sedated Rex was Tank's final misdeed in a long career of incompetency. Kelton had excused Mahaffey's blunders many times in the past, but there was no excusing this one.

Tank Mahaffey had been his primary delivery driver. Firing Tank, and having Hoops out for a week-and-a-half, doubled the workload for Kelton and Thorn. A day after firing Tank, Kelton hired two new ranch hands and gave them quickie training sessions. Both new hires seemed competent and trustworthy, but they weren't ready to make long distance deliveries of illicit wildlife across state lines. Hence the reason why he and Thorn were out here in the North Dakota badlands in the darkest of night with a pair of mature Tyrannosaurs in the back.

They had made two other deliveries last week. Two Dromaeosaurs, one to southern Wyoming, the other to northern Utah. Both trips required overnight stays and went without a hitch. As with this excursion, they traveled under the cover of night in rental trucks. And they rode incommunicado, leaving their satellite phones behind. Kelton knew sat phones could be easily tracked, contrary to popular belief.

He looked over at Thorn, who was asleep in the passenger seat, his ever-present buckskin cattleman hat covering his face. Thorn's sleeping on the job pissed him off.

The least the man could do is stay awake and offer some conversation. After all, he's on the clock and I'm paying him extra for this trip.

Kelton decided to shake him up. He opened his sleeve of CDs, in the mood for some vintage Aerosmith. Pulled out *Toys In the Attic* and slid the disc into the player. Cranked the volume. Joe Perry's thundering guitar ripped through the cab. The dash pulsated. The bench seat vibrated.

Thorn woke with a start, his hat falling to the floor. "Christ, Kel! What the hell, man!" He reached out and turned down the raucous music.

Kelton looked at him askance. "You have no appreciation of great rock n' roll, Thorn. I need some heavy head bangin' to keep my eyes open since my poor excuse of a navigator has spent the last hour in dreamland."

"Navigator? There ain't nothin' out here to navigate. Nothin' but our headlight beams on the asphalt in front of us."

"Granted. But it's still your job to keep me awake. Be tragic if I fell asleep at the wheel, what with our high-priced cargo in back."

Thorn shook his head and looked out his window at the passing night.

Aerosmith played on at a low volume, Kelton keeping time, tapping his thumbs against the steering wheel, singing along with the choruses. Thorn stared straight ahead at the road rolling out in front of them. The dark night surrounded them like black curtains.

They came upon a large billboard:

WELCOME TO MEDORA
POPULATION 131
GATEWAY TO THEODORE ROOSEVELT NATIONAL PARK

Kelton drove through Medora, slowing down, well aware that some of these small North Dakota towns were speed traps. A few feeble streetlights cast hazy illumination on a collection of wooden, old-western buildings—U.S. post office, a café and a diner, two western wear boutiques, an art gallery—all closed up tight and dark at this hour.

He pushed on into the night. Five miles east of Medora Thorn started talking.

"Why do you think rich people want these dinosaurs? They ain't nothin' but trouble. I mean, they ain't pets. Not like dogs or cats. You can't sleep with 'em or take 'em on walks. They're man-eaters."

"That's a big part of the attraction," Kelton answered. "The danger. But a truer part of it is that the wealthy always want something unique to show other rich assholes they've got something they don't. That they're better than them. It becomes a pissing contest among the absurdly rich."

Thorn thought that over for a minute, then said, "If I'm not mistaken, you're rich, too, Kel."

Kelton gave him a doleful side eye. "At least you didn't call me an asshole. Thanks for that."

Thorn smiled. Staring out his window, he said, "I learned a long time ago it's never good to bite the hand that feeds. Tank never understood that logic." Kelton felt his eyes on him. "You know, Hoops and me, we were both surprised you fired him. No disrespect, but we didn't think you had it in you."

"No? Why would you think that?"

"Because you're a veterinarian. Aren't you supposed to be kind to animals?"

It took Kelton a long second, but then he got it. He burst out laughing and Thorn joined him. Kelton laughing so hard it brought tears to his eyes. He knew he was overreacting. The off-the-cuff comment wasn't that funny, but all the hours behind the wheel hauling a couple of 900-pound Tyrannosaurs had left him slap-happy, and more vulnerable to Mark Thornberry's understated wit.

The Aerosmith CD ended and Kelton ejected it from the player, slipped it back in the sleeve. He was searching for another disc when he heard a thump behind him, coming from the cargo section.

Another loud thump, followed by a dragging sound.

"You hear that, Thorn?"

"Indeed I do. Sounds like one or both of our boys might be awake."

"But that's impossible. We just drugged them a few hours ago. Hit them with full strength xylazine. Almost enough to put down an elephant or rhino."

"Yeah, but these ain't elephants or rhinos. We've never seen these kinds of animals before."

They went silent, heads back, listening, the drone of the engine and rubber meeting the road producing a dull hum in the cab. No more thumping or scuffling in back. Kelton thought perhaps he'd been hearing things.

Just road weary hallucinations?

Thorn said, "Maybe they just shifted around when we went into that curve back there."

Kelton hoped that was true, but doubted it. He remained hyper alert, listening closely for any strange noises.

He was about to suggest stopping to take a look when he noticed the flashing blue-and-red lights of a police cruiser in his sideview mirror, gaining on them quickly.

Then he heard the siren.

"Looks like we've got company," he said, frowning.

Thorn glanced at his side mirror. "What the hell do they want? We ain't been pushing the limits."

"Probably just bored. Most likely just wanna have some fun with us out-of-staters," Kelton said, feeling more uneasy than he let on.

"Think we can outrun them?"

"Are you crazed? We're carrying close to a ton and this is a rattletrap rental." He kept his eyes on the mirror. "Running is the worst thing we could do. Let's see what's on their mind."

Kelton steered the truck off the road and onto the gravel shoulder, thinking about what he would say. The cab lit up in swirl-

ing purplish light as the cruiser pulled in behind them. He shut off
the ignition and waited, his nerves in a tangle.

In his mirror he saw the black North Dakota Highway Patrol
sedan strobing colorful waves of light across the interstate. Two
cops got out. The taller one came to his window, the other
approached on Thorn's side. Kelton pushed the button to lower both
windows. The cop on his side shined a flashlight into the cab, blinding him momentarily.

"What's the problem, officer?" Kelton said, squinting into the
harsh glare.

"License and registration please," came the gruff reply. "And
you over there, midnight cowboy," he said directing the flash at
Thorn, "keep your hands where I can see them."

Kelton produced his fake ID and rental truck paperwork. His
fake driver's license showed him as Brad Anderson with a Helena,
Montana address.

The patrolman spread out Kelton's information on a clipboard
and shined the flash on it, looking over his identification while his
partner on the other side watched him and Thorn closely. The cops
wore those Smokey Bear campaign-style hats with the strap secured
under the chin that Kelton had always found comical.

Nothing comical about this, Kel old boy.

"Have you been drinking, Mr. Anderson?"

"What? No sir, I—"

"What is the nature of your business here in North Dakota?"

"We're making a delivery in Bismarck."

"What kind of delivery?"

Kelton was prepared for this. "Farming implements of all
kinds—plow heads, tractor attachments, feed grinders . . . those
kinds of things."

"You got any documentation for what you're hauling?"

"Sure do. The shipping manifest is under my seat. If you'll
permit me to—"

"I'll find it myself. I want you both to please step out of the
vehicle."

"Officer, with all due respect, we haven't violated any rules of the road, and I don't think—"

"Out of the truck NOW! Both of you. And no funny business."

Oh, this is bad, Kelton thought as he reluctantly opened his door and dropped down on the gravel. *Just our luck we run into a pair of by-the-book Lethal Weapon types.*

Thorn opened his door and climbed out. The second officer escorted him around to the driver's side. The cops positioned them against the side of the truck.

"Mr. Anderson, how about you open up the back and let us have a look."

Kelton tried to keep the agitation he felt out of his voice. "It's all listed in the manifest, if you'll just look—"

"That's just paper. I want to see the physical goods for myself. Open it up."

Bad went quickly to worse as the thumping noise started again in the cargo area, followed by loud wheezy gasps.

"That doesn't sound like farm implements to me," the lead cop said. Kelton read his nameplate: **State Trooper Francis Darby— North Dakota Highway Patrol**. "You wouldn't happen to be transporting illegal migrants now would you?"

"Migrants?" Kelton said with a snicker. "We're two thousand miles away from the Mexican border."

"A lot of illegals are coming across the Canadian border these days. It's more open and easier to cross. They're learning ways to avoid that logjam down in Mexico. Now enough of the immigration lesson. If you refuse to open the back, we'll do it for you."

Thorn spoke up. "Don't you need a search warrant, officer?"

"Listen, cowboy, the noises coming out of your cargo hold give us probable cause that a crime is being committed. With probable cause, we don't need a warrant."

Another loud thump against the inside cargo wall. More husky gasping.

"Okay, that's it." Sergeant Darby motioned to his partner. "Open it up, Irv. I didn't see any lock on the door."

Patrolman Irv moved to the rear of the truck.

Panic began to grip Kelton. "I wouldn't advise that, officer."

Darby said, "Let's join Officer Irving shall we, gentlemen? See what we've got here."

Darby prodded Kelton and Thorn to the rear of the truck. Kelton had not seen any other traffic out here since they were stopped, which was a good thing as he considered what was about to happen. He gave Thorn a gentle nudge with his elbow, a subtle message to be ready, and backed up a step. Thorn backed away, too.

"You guys stay where you are," Darby said. "I don't wanna hafta cuff you."

They watched patrolman Irving lift the cargo door.

Irving's "WHAT THE F—!" was smothered mid-syllable by the Rex that jumped off the back of the truck. The charging Tyrannosaur snapped him up in its powerful jaws and shook him side to side, once, twice, Irving's screams quickly weakening as he flopped helplessly in the creature's mouth. The Rex then chomped him in half with a sickening crunch. A fountain of blood spurted across the gravel shoulder, a spray of it wetting Kel's face before the Tyrannosaur tilted its head back and swallowed patrolman Irving in two swift gulps.

Kelton wiped the blood off his face as he ran. Thorn followed. They hustled to the cab and climbed in. Slammed the doors shut and watched their sideview mirrors.

Officer Darby seemed frozen, stunned by the sudden demise of his partner. The Rex was on him before he could snap out of it and go for his gun. The frenzied beast opened its shovel mouth wide and went in high, decapitating him with a bite of terrifying power, swallowing his head whole, Smokey Bear hat and all. The creature trotted into the woods, carrying Darby's headless body in its mouth, the officer's legs kicking a couple of times in postmortem spasms before going still.

"Oh my fucking god!" Kelton said, sitting behind the wheel, watching it all go down, trying to catch his runaway breath. He'd seen a lot of predator-on-prey attacks in nature, and even appreciated them for their primal, sustenance-giving beauty. But he'd never witnessed anything like this. What just happened shook him to his core. He'd never seen human beings mauled and devoured like that.

Two state cops no less.

He hoped to never see anything like it again.

"You okay, Thorn?" he said after regaining a few of his wits.

"Not sure. You?"

"Well, we're still here. That's a good thing, I reckon."

Thorn said, "What happened with that Rex? It didn't seem like he'd been drugged at all. In fact, he seemed supercharged."

"You're right. But unless we dreamed it, we sedated them just a few hours ago. And unless my eyes deceived me, the other one is still back there. Something's not right with this. Get my pistol out of the glovebox, will you? Let's go have a look."

They got out of the cab and cautiously walked around back, Kelton leading the way with his gun. A gruesome tableau greeted them. The gravel shoulder was stained dark with splattered blood. A tattered state police hat and Officer Darby's nametag was mired in a pool of blood. Bones draped with tangles of gristly tendons and ligaments were scattered about.

A cool breeze brought a strong metallic scent of blood to Kelton's nose. He felt bile rise into his throat. Fighting to hold the sickness down, he moved a safe distance from the rear of the truck and peered into the cargo space. The swirling lights of the patrol car illuminated the interior like the undulating neon of a carnival midway. The second Tyrannosaur was still out cold, asleep on its side. He gave Thorn a questioning glance.

"Don't know. Your guess is as good as mine, Kel."

"This Rex is the slightly smaller of the two," Kelton said, hopping up into the cargo section. "Maybe his constitution is such that he is more susceptible to the xylazine. I need to check this guy's vital signs. We're probably going to have to tranq this guy again to ensure a safe delivery."

Thorn said, "You mean we're actually gonna go through with this?"

Kelton turned and looked down at Thorn, who cut a dark outline against the police lights whirling behind him. "Hell *yes* we're going through with it! I'm damned sick of losing my investments. That Rex that just disappeared into the woods cost me a bunch. Our client is gonna be pissed that he's only getting half of what he paid for. But at least we didn't lose both of them. I'm gonna deliver this guy if it kills me."

"We need to get a move on, Kel. I'm sure they reported our truck when they pulled us over. We just killed two state cops. There might already be a BOLO out on us."

Kelton breathed in the warm gamey smell of the cargo hold. He kneeled down next to the sedated Tyrannosaur in the dim light and checked its pulse and breathing rate. "We didn't kill anybody, Thorn. It was death by dinosaur."

"You're dealing in semantics, Kel."

"Quit your yapping and do something useful," Kelton said, opening the tackle box where he kept his tranq darts. "Lucky for us the cops weren't wearing body cams, but I did see a dash cam in the patrol car. Go shut off the lights and grab that camera. Smash it up and toss it down in the gulley. Here, put on these gloves first." He stood and tossed a pair of latex medical gloves down to Thorn, then slipped on a pair himself. Picked up his DanInject rifle and loaded a tranq dart.

A random thought popped into his mind. The Rex that got away didn't seem drugged at all. He thought about the sedation chemical, xylazine. Was it past its effective date? Kelton felt sure he hadn't been that careless. Was it possible this batch had somehow lost its potency? Temperature change? Contamination?

Thorn shut off the patrol car lights. The cargo area went dark.

Kelton laid his gun down and pulled a small penlight from his pocket. Shined it on the hypodermic cartridge of one of the darts. Tapped the cylinder a few times. The fluid inside appeared cloudy. He checked other darts. They were all milky as well. He tore the dart off the end of one of them and pulled the cap off the hypo-dermic reservoir. Carefully spilled a dollop of fluid into the palm of his glove. Sniffed it. No scent. He dabbed a little on the tip of his tongue. It had an extreme bitter taste. Not pure xylazine the way it should be. Xylazine is a colorless, odorless, tasteless drug. This batch of tranq darts had been compromised, diluted with a pow-dered agent. He took another taste and cringed at the bitterness.

Kelton suspected some type of amphetamine. A sulfate or dextro-amphetamine of some type had been added. That would explain the out of control violence displayed by the attacking T-Rex.

But what about this Tyrannosaur? he thought, glancing at the dozing giant. *Why would he have a different reaction?*

Xylazine is an inexpensive veterinary non-opioid tranquilizer that had become popular with American drug dealers. In order to boost profits, they cut their heroin with xylazine as well as fentanyl. So much so that test strips were now available to check xylazine levels in drug samples. Kelton had never had a need for the quick response strips, but he had a supply just in case. He needed them now. He took one out of the package and soaked it with the liquid from a second hypodermic dart. Waited impatiently, time becoming a factor.

Finally, after four agonizing minutes, the strip revealed its results. Less than thirty-five percent xylazine.

His face burned in anger.

He heard Thorn calling to him. "I trashed the camera, Kel. We need to get the hell outta here, man. Fast. Their dispatchers are going crazy on the patrol car radio, wondering where their cops are."

"Got it," he said. "Somebody set us up, Thorn."

"Whaddaya mean set us up?"

"You take the wheel. I'm too pissed off to drive. I'll tell you about it on the way. We need to deliver this Rex fast."

He removed the gloves and picked up the DanInject rifle. Fired the loaded dart into the animal's hind quarters. He prayed the weak-ened sedative would keep the animal down for another three hours.

He jumped down out of the cargo hold and pulled the rear door shut. An eighteen wheeler blew past, the first vehicle he'd seen since the start of all this. He left the gravel shoulder and grabbed a handful of mud, brought it back and smeared it across the license plate as a precaution. The law surely had a description of their truck, but why make it easier for them.

As Thorn drove, Kelton fumed over the sabotage of his tranquilizer kit. He had a good idea who was behind it. The same guy who lost his first Tyrannosaur. Kelton would deal with him when they got back home.

That is, if the law didn't catch up with him and Thorn first.

Pennywise Visits Kanti's Tomb

Mid July

Location Unknown

TIME HAD BECOME AN ALIEN CONCEPT TO HER. This dim cold root cellar had been her prison for an unknowable stretch. Kanti could have been down here a week or more, she wasn't sure. They had taken her cell phone so she had no idea of the date or time of day. And without sunlit days or starry nights to guide her, it was impossible to gauge the passage of time. Her location remained a mystery as well. She could still be in Montana, on the Moon, or somewhere in between.

Whatever they drugged her with had kept her suspended in this murky state of unknowing.

She had come to know her two kidnappers. Sort of. They checked in on her periodically, bringing her food and water. At first she refused to eat or drink for fear of being poisoned. But soon her hunger and thirst demanded that she take a chance, and she was thankful that poisoning was not their intention. But with the sustenance came the injections. Drugs that left her mind foggy and her body weak. The men always showed up cloaked in long sleeve shirts, hats, gloves, and masks. Neither of them appeared without a frightening Halloween mask: Leatherface, Darth Vader, zombie walkers from *The Walking Dead* series, the Ghostface mask from the *Scream* movies. The masks escalated her fears to new levels, which she was sure was their intent. The only way she could differentiate between the two men was by their physical builds and the timbre of their voices.

Kanti leaned back against the plywood wall and looked around the cellar, a place she was beginning to think of as her tomb. A dim lightbulb hung from the low-slung ceiling, casting shadowy light on racks of fruits and vegetables and canned preserves. She sighed deeply, breathing in the damp earth, the sweet aroma of ripe apples, the vinegary tang of pickled cucumbers.

She was alone, cold, and terrified.

Was anybody searching for her?

Would they even know where to start looking?

The bigger question had dogged her from the beginning: *Why me?* She wasn't wealthy. She wasn't a celebrity. Kanti knew she was far from beautiful. She didn't have any enemies as far as she knew. She was just a plain-looking, overweight, middle-aged Blackfoot housewife and mother scraping by on the rez. She couldn't think of a single person who would have a reason to keep her imprisoned like this.

So why me? The question continued to poke at her.

She had asked her jailers that question every time one of them dropped in with food and their painful hypodermic needles. The answer never varied. "Your day is coming," they would say. The same indecipherable message from both.

My day is coming? What does that mean exactly?

Rape? Torture? Death?

She shivered thinking about it.

Surely it couldn't mean freedom. What would be the point in keeping her imprisoned here if they were just going to let her go? They had to have an endgame. But try as she might, their reasons eluded her. They were keeping her fed and hydrated and out of the elements. They wouldn't be that hospitable if they planned on killing her, would they? And she hadn't seen their faces thanks to the creepy masks. She wouldn't be able to identify them, which was a good thing, wasn't it?

They were keeping her alive for some reason.

So why is this happening?

So far, they seemed more interested in playing head games, keeping her off balance and uncertain.

Keeping her terrified.

As she had done so many times since being brought here, she replayed the abduction in her fatigued mind. She thought about how the two men surprised her in the trading post parking lot, jumping out from behind a row of high hedges, wearing those surgical masks that were everywhere during the pandemic. Hats covered their heads, one of them similar to the green, flat-topped military cap Fidel Castro made famous. She recalled the pain she'd felt in her arm when they grabbed her forcefully, and took her purse, cell phone, and groceries. The fact that neither man said a word through the ordeal made the incident even more disturbing. They'd pushed her into the passenger seat of her own car, her screams smothered by a strong hand clamped across her mouth. She remembered the long shiny syringe and the sting of the needle in her thigh as one of them pinned her to the car seat. Within minutes, her head swam to where she couldn't make sense of things. One of the men drove her here, the tall lanky one who wore a wide brimmed slouch hat. He'd had to push the seat all the way back because of his long legs. She recalled the acrid smell of cigarette smoke on his clothes.

As the drug kicked in and she slid further into oblivion, Kanti thought: *Why is this man driving my car?*

She couldn't make out any street signs or landmarks on the drive. She'd tried to speak, but her vocal cords were paralyzed. The driver remained quiet, keeping his eyes on the road. She had no recollection of being dumped in the root cellar.

She had tried escaping several times, but found the shallow cellar to be well sealed. The cramped underground space offered only one way out—six steps up and through the slanted, reinforced concrete double doors. She had bruised her shoulder trying to bang the doors open, learning the hard way that the doors were bolted and locked from the outside.

Kanti had searched for a weapon, but the best she could do was a dull can opener, which she doubted would have much effect against two big men.

She thought of her beloved husband, Ap, and their two teenage daughters, Kippy and Nitanis. Picturing them got her through the long, uncertain hours. Kanti hoped her disappearance wasn't too hard on them.

She paid homage to Natosi, the Blackfoot sun god.

She prayed to the Great Spirit.

She had spent a lot of time walking around the tight space, reciting a few of the traditional Blackfoot proverbs that calmed her and brought her comfort.

"Nahka itaahksiyo'pii" (Nurture your inner fire and spirit, which provides you with the strength you need).

"Nisitapiyiwa" (Face adversity with bravery and resilience, and draw upon your inner powers).

"Aipia'saahsihkiiksi" (The sun will shine again; even in the darkest times, there is always hope for a new day).

She heard a scraping against the entry doors. Heard the bolt sliding back. Her heart thudded in her chest. Another visit. Time for another injection?

The doors opened, filling the cellar with blinding sunlight. Kanti shielded her eyes with her hand and squinted, saw a pair of muddy boots come down the steps.

The gruff voice of the taller man greeted her. "Good afternoon, Sacajawea," he said, entering the room, hunched over to prevent his head from knocking against the low ceiling. He wore a flame red fright wig and a Pennywise clown mask inspired by Stephen King's evil clown in his novel, *IT*. The sinister clown face with its glowing yellow eyes, spooky ear-to-ear grin, and sharp teeth unsettled her.

Always Sacajawea, she thought.

The shorter man called her Pocahontas.

Sacajawea and Pocahontas—the white man's limited frame of reference when it came to Native American women. Sacajawea was a Shoshone. Pocahontas was from the Powhatan tribe in Virginia. As different as could be from her Blackfoot heritage. Her kidnappers didn't know the difference, nor did they care.

To these men, we're all the same. Indians. Indigenous slaves. Natives subservient to the white man's wishes. Not worthy of proper tribal distinction. Unworthy of the most elementary human respect.

"I brought you some lunch," he said, his voice muffled behind the mask.

"I'm not hungry."

He let out an exasperated sigh and set the Styrofoam container on a shelf, took a seat on a stool and faced her. "You're being an ungrateful squaw bitch! After all the work I put into preparing it."

"I'd like some answers to my questions once and for all," she said, her ire rising at this man who hid behind masks.

Pennywise laughed. "You're in no position to be demanding."

Kanti was tired of playing psychological games. "Look, you and your partner keep telling me my day will come. When will that be? And what does that mean?"

"A little feisty today, aren't we?" he said. "I'm happy to report that *today* is finally your day, Kanti Lyttle." He glanced at the Styrofoam box. "I think you should eat your lunch. You'll need your strength for what's to come."

The words chilled her. She stared at him, said, "Have you finally decided to kill me?"

"Oh, no, my fat little redskin. You're much more valuable to us alive. We're not murderers like your husband."

His comment surprised her. "What? I don't understand. You must be confusing me with—"

"No, I'm not. Don't play stupid with me, squaw. Your husband Apisi Lyttle killed two of our friends."

"*What?* You're sadly mistaken. My husband is a peaceful man. He would never—"

"Come on, li'l red Injun. Don't insult me. You know damn well what I'm talking about. Your hubby killed two of our friends last August at a ranch on your reservation. Gilliam's Guidepost, owned and operated by that crazy dinosaur zookeeper. Surely you remember the night of the great dinosaur liberation, sweetheart. The night of August the eighth. I know you were there, enjoying barbecue with all your Injun friends. That bringing back any memories for you, squaw?"

A chill iced her spine with the realization that he was connected in some way with the animal rights terrorists that had invaded Bryan and Loretta's ranch. Kanti knew that Apisi—as well as Chogan Stimson and Jimmy Enright—had killed a few of them helping

Bryan defend his home. She recalled her terror as she hid with others, hearing the gunshots echo across the meadow and not knowing if her husband was dead or alive. Ap had never discussed it with her, at least not the particulars, preferring to bury the ghastly experience and keep silent about the battle in the dinosaur habitats that left eight dead bodies lying in the dirt and Bryan Gilliam severely wounded.

"Cat got your tongue, my little redskin?"

Kanti wanted to rip the mask from his face and claw his eyes out. But she sat petrified. At a loss for words. She didn't know what to say, what she *could* say.

"Your expression tells me all I need to know, squaw bitch."

Kanti found her voice. "What is it you want with me?"

"We want compensation for the loss of our two dear friends."

"Ap and I . . . we don't have any money."

"I know you don't. But your husband's boss does."

"Bryan Gilliam?"

Pennywise nodded. "The Gilliams are getting a big cash settlement from a civil lawsuit against AEF. We feel we're entitled to a large chunk of it."

This was news to her. She figured there would be legal actions taken, but Bryan and Loretta had been tight lipped about it.

"We know about Gilliam's loyalty to his Injun friends," Pennywise continued. "We know he shared a lot of the insurance money. The guy would do almost anything to bail out his friends. Too bad he doesn't have that same love for animals. It was deplorable the way he treated those dinosaurs. Anyway, we figured he would come to Apisi's rescue when he learned we had you. Thing is, it's gonna cost him dearly to get you back with your family. Just how generous is he gonna be in your case, squaw. Anything you care to share with me?"

It took all of her self control not to lash out at him. "Were you there?" Her voice was more meek than she would have liked.

"No, but I heard all about it from one of the survivors. I hear tell your husband was a regular Jesse James out there. It was definitely Apisi's sharpshooting that brought down my two friends. We have a witness."

Kanti's outrage bubbled over. "They were trespassing. They deserved to be shot. Your friends were the murderers, not my Ap."

That got to him. She saw him lean in and clench his fists. She flinched, thinking he was going to hit her. But he quickly regained control and sat back.

"You've got a lot of balls for a fat little squaw," he said, standing. "Enough of the jibber jabber. I've told you why you're here. Now I want to show you something. Get up. We're going outside. It's feeding time."

"Outside? Feeding time?" she said, worry gnawing at her stomach. They hadn't taken her out of the root cellar since she arrived.

"Yeah. C'mon, get up. You need to get some fresh air."

He offered her a gloved hand, but she refused it with a wave of her hand. "What, no shot today?" she said, standing without his assistance.

"No. We want you clearheaded for this."

"What do you mean by *this*?"

"Too many questions, my little redskin. Shut your yap and get on up them steps," he said, pushing her from behind.

She went up the creaky wooden steps and out into daylight. He led her to a golf cart, helped her in. They rode through an expanse of towering trees. Not another person or building in sight. The sun hurt her eyes as the electric cart whined along a dirt path. Her head throbbed with each bump on the uneven trail. Through the veil of her headache she searched for landmarks, but nothing stood out. Just trees and the narrow earthen track.

The air cooled as they came to a wide river with an upraised bridge. Whitewater rapids roared in her ears like an urgent whisper. Pennywise stopped the cart and went to a metal box bolted to a tree trunk. He opened the lid and punched in a combination. They waited while the drawbridge lowered, then rode across the rushing waterway.

They wound their way through a maze of hardwoods. Pennywise's red wig blew in the breeze, the shiny red nose of his clown mask shining radiantly when they went through patches of sunlight.

This is like a surreal dream gone bad, she thought. *Like the warped peyote visions I had in my wild partying days. Before Ap.*

She heard what sounded like squealing pigs in the distance, dissonant noise that alarmed her.

Pennywise steered the cart around a curve and an overpowering stench slapped her in the face. A gamy scent. Something feral. A wild animal smell mixed with something else. Blood? Decay? Death?

The squealing got louder, sounding like the hogs on her uncle's farm.

They pulled into a dusty clearing and Kanti saw two pickup trucks parked along high chainlink fencing, the length of which ran back into the woods. She noted that both trucks bore Montana plates, and committed them to memory.

Does this mean I'm still in Montana?

Three men—all wearing weird Halloween masks to rival Pennywise's disguise—stood along the front of the fence talking and gesturing at four plump black-and-white hogs waddling skittishly inside what appeared to be a large holding pen.

Pennywise parked the golf cart beside one of the trucks and shut off the ignition. Climbed out and grabbed her by the arm, thrust her toward his buddies.

That's when she saw the dinosaurs. Four of them in the rear of the enclosures. Two large, terrifying creatures lumbering around in a rear pen and separated from a pair of smaller animals that scurried energetically in their own space. She knew from news reports the big ones were Tyrannosaurus Rexes. They had to be more than twelve feet tall with broad muscular chests and long snouts with wide mouths full of lethal looking teeth. The smaller ones looked like miniature versions, hopping around on muscular hind legs. They were called Drome-*somethings* and were crazy hyper. The animals had long strings of drool dripping from their mouths as they focused their predatory inflamed eyes on the screeching hogs.

The scene took her back to last summer and the Gilliam's dinosaur zoo. These animals were much bigger. Much more menacing.

What is going on here?

Where is this place?

Kanti was lightheaded, dizzy. She felt her knees buckle.

Pennywise held her up. "C'mon, squaw. Act like an adult."

She thought she would be sick.

Did they plan to throw her in the pen with those monsters?

"Gentlemen," Pennywise said, addressing his friends, "This here is one of our tickets to the good life. This little redskin is worth a coupla mil at least."

One of their tickets? Did they abduct others besides me?

Kanti wanted to ask what this was all about but couldn't get any words out. She scanned the four men who stared at her from behind the strange masks: a burned and disfigured Freddy Krueger; Jigsaw, a face she recognized from those awful *Saw* movies; an unsettling and distorted Purge mask; and of course, Pennywise the Clown.

The Freddy Krueger character tipped his fedora at her with a flourish. Jigsaw and Purge acknowledged her with raised thumbs and weak nods.

Even though it was a bright afternoon in July, the scary masks, coupled with the salivating dinosaurs and squealing hogs, turned the clearing into an insane Halloween setting. Kanti thought she might be slipping over the edge.

Pennywise pushed her up against the fence. Told her to stand there and watch what happened next.

She observed Jigsaw walking around the perimeter of the enclosures, opening the holding pen gates, releasing the dinosaurs and hogs into the main corral. The hogs froze for a split second, assessing the danger presented by the beasts across the way, then went into a chorus of panicked snorts and grunts and took off running, zigzagging in different directions. The smaller dinosaurs immediately went after two of them, leaping on them and bringing them down in clouds of dust. They ripped into them with their hind claws, blood spewing, shrill squeals of pain drifting across the corral. She watched the Tyrannosaurs tackle a third hog and rip it apart with their frightful teeth and mighty jaws, their heads dipping to feast on the hog flesh, then raising up to gulp down the bloody strips of meat.

Kanti couldn't watch another second of the vicious slaughter. She closed her eyes. Feeling weak and nauseated, she held onto the fence for support. Unbelievably, over the din of the snorting, grunting, and squealing of the terrified hogs, and the slurping of the carnivores, she heard the men cheering and whistling, rooting on the dinosaurs as the prehistoric beasts feasted on the defenseless hogs.

I thought these people were for protecting animals.

She couldn't take any more. Using what little strength she had, she pulled her hands off the fence and plugged her ears with her fingers. It helped, but the disturbing noises still managed to get through.

She felt two big hands grip her shoulders from behind, then move to pull her hands away from her ears. She opened her eyes and turned. Pennywise stood there, staring down at her from behind the clown mask with the malicious grin and sharp yellowed teeth.

He said, "This is a warning. What's happening to those hogs out there will be your fate if your husband's boss doesn't come through for us. You got that, squaw bitch?"

Kanti gazed up at him, the hair of his red wig blowing in the breeze, the whiteface mask glowing in the afternoon sun. The strangeness of it pushed her over the edge.

She felt her legs collapse beneath her and she keeled over, fainting dead away.

Animal Trafficking
and Brin's Turnaround

July 15: The Cellar Suites, Gilliam's Guidepost
Heart Butte, Montana

THE NEWSCASTER'S VOICE FILLED the dining nook where Peter and Brin shared an early breakfast. The wall-mounted flat-screen TV showed the reporter standing on the side of a rural highway, trying in vain to keep his hair in place as big tractor-trailer rigs roared past.

> "The dinosaurs are on the move. I'm standing here along I-94, seventy miles west of Bismarck, where two days ago, two North Dakota Highway Patrol officers were attacked and killed by what authorities report was a large Tyrannosaurus Rex. Wildlife biologists have investigated the site and made the identification from the tracks left in the roadside gravel bed and the remains of one of the patrolmen. We'll zoom in to give viewers a closer look."

Please don't show dead bodies, Peter thought, chewing his bacon-egg-and-cheese muffin.

The camera scanned the gravel shoulder, showing a scattering of deep three-toed prints with broad heel marks and patches of dried blood, black as oil slicks. Fortunately body parts had been cleaned up and taken away.

The reporter continued:

"You can also see the trampled brush leading into the woods. The depth of the prints and the damage along the tree line indicate a very large animal. This is the farthest east we have seen evidence of dinosaurs. However, there is a wrinkle in this story. We're told this creature probably didn't get here on its own. The Highway Patrol tells us that the deceased officers—Francis Darby, forty three, and Edward Irving, thirty seven—pulled over a midsize truck on a routine traffic stop at about the time of the estimated dinosaur attack. Officer Irving is on record as having called in the stop at four-fifty-eight AM with the make, model, and plate number. That was the last communication the North Dakota Highway Patrol received from the officers.

"Investigators now believe the truck was part of the illegal animal trafficking trade that has escalated in these parts this summer. The vehicle—a sixteen-foot, yellow with blue trim, box truck leased through Penske Truck Rental in Kalispell, Montana—was not returned as scheduled. Lucky for law enforcement, this Penske leasing location uses Fleet InSite GPS technology, which tracks the movement of their trucks, and they have located it south of Bismarck on the banks of the Missouri River near Fort Rice. The state police are en route to retrieve the vehicle to take it to their compound to dust it for prints and to try and piece together what happened out here. The rental agency discovered after the fact that the truck was leased using false identification and paid for with a bogus credit card. The driver and any passengers are wanted for questioning in the police officers' deaths. There have been no witnesses or leads in the case. If you or anyone you know has any information, please contact the North Dakota Highway Patrol. The number is at the bottom of your screen. We will keep you informed of any further developments. This is Todd Brandywine of KBMY TV, Channel 17 News, Bismarck, signing off."

The news program shifted back to Great Falls regional news

coverage of western Montana, with the news anchor diving into a related story, reporting on another dinosaur attack that occurred yesterday at a popular campground at the West Glacier KOA Resort. Three Tyrannosaurs ripped through encampments, plucking campers out of tents amid desperate screams and gunshots. Seven people were killed. Another nine were injured and medevacked to North Valley Hospital in Whitefish. One of the Tyrannosaurs was shot dead.

Peter said, "Could you please turn this off, honey? It's not doing much for my digestion."

"Agreed," Brin said, shutting off the TV.

"So you're taking Hayden and Nora out today?" she asked.

He nodded, his mouth full of biscuit.

She eyed him warily. "You'll be careful, right?"

"Of course," he said, wiping his mouth with a napkin. "Today is easy stuff. We're flying out to the Basin Region, two hundred miles south of here. A dinosaur migration tagging trip. Hayden says Triceratops are overwhelming wheat farmers down there. You don't need to worry, Brin. They're plant eaters and don't present any danger. And the landing and liftoffs are much safer on the plains than going into forests and negotiating mountainous terrain."

Brin looked at him doubtfully. "But you *will* be tracking the meat eaters, right? That's still on the agenda, right? Flying into more difficult areas?"

"Yes. Soon. Look, I know you aren't—"

"I'm okay with it, Petey," she said, holding up a hand. "Really, I am. I know you'll handle it well. Of course I would prefer you to be making more of those meteorite rock runs. Or maybe shuttling tourists around the state. But I have come to realize my beloved husband is a gifted pilot doing what he loves. I'm starting to under-stand that when you love somebody, you let them love what they love. Let them *do* what they love and trust they can manage it, no matter how dangerous."

Where is this coming from? Peter thought. "That's pretty deep," he said. "Quite a change from the Brinny I know. So does this mean you're starting to feel more comfortable here? Are you starting to come around and admit this move was good for us?"

He saw something flash in her dark eyes. "Oh, I still think this place is cursed. But yes, I'm a lot happier than I was. Less stressed. It's done me good to be around the Gilliams. Bryan is such a nice guy. And Loretta inspires me."

He studied his lovely wife, taking in Brin's dark Kootenai beauty. If possible, she looked more gorgeous than ever in the early stages of her second trimester.

"That's great. I think pregnancy is doing wonders for you."

She smiled, sending a warm rush through him. "It has nothing to do with pregnancy," she said, her smile never leaving her face. "It's Nora. She's been giving me some good advice. She's become like my very intelligent big sister."

"Nora *is* a smart woman," he said. "Very together. She's been a good influence. I'm glad you two have been talking."

"Yeah, she is really good for me, Petey. But I don't think she's been following her own advice lately."

"What do you mean?"

"Well, Nora's been pretty frosty toward Hayden lately. You haven't noticed?"

"No. I don't usually pick up on stuff like that."

"Most men don't. I think it's a woman's intuition thing."

"You're right. Women do seem to have a sixth sense about those things. I haven't noticed. But I have long thought their relationship is a bit peculiar."

"Oh? How so?"

"They snipe at each other sometimes, though it seems to work for them. I guess it's due to them both being intense professionals. It's the competitive drive in them."

"True. They *do* pick at each other. But the sniping is done with love. However, over the past week I have detected some true distance between them. I first noticed it at the helicopter christening."

"Yeah, well, all relationships have their ups and downs, Brin."

"I realize that. I guess I'm being too nosy," she said, taking a sip of her coffee. "How are you liking the new aircraft?"

"It's a dream," he said. "Like flying a magic carpet. Smoother and much easier to pilot than the Hueys I flew for the Forest Service. Certainly better than those repurposed old Sikorsky eggbeaters Bing and I flew for the Air Force last year. And you'll be happy to know this Bell chopper has a lot more safety features."

"That's good to hear." Brin finished her coffee and glanced at her watch. "Oh, god, I'm running late. I wanted to check on Mother and Kimi before I head downstairs."

Downstairs was the spacious basement one floor below in The Cellar, where Bryan Gilliam had restarted his Cretaceous Stone jewelry operation this week. Brin worked with three inexperienced Blackfoot women who were learning stonesetting and jewelry crafting under Brin's tutelage. Peter was pleased by his wife's newfound self-confidence and positive attitude.

Brin stood and took her dishes to the sink. Kissed Peter and uttered, "Be safe out there today. I love you."

"I love you, too, babe."

Peter watched her leave the nook, heard the front door open and close. He checked his cell phone and saw he had another twenty minutes before he was due out at the helipad for liftoff. He poured himself another cup of coffee and sweetened it with hazelnut creamer and sugar. Returned to the table and sat. Thought about how well things were going now that they had settled in their Cellar suite. He contemplated his new career with Fowler-Lemoyne Aviation. Peter had flown out three times this week to the Cretaceous meteorite site in southern Montana, bringing back heavy payloads of the valuable rock. The 600-mile round trips with the grueling physical exertion involved in fragging stone and hauling the rock wedges to the chopper had made for long, exhausting days.

Peter had heard about Apisi's missing wife, Kanti, and felt a great deal of sympathy for the Gilliam ranch hand. When asked how he was holding up, Ap would just say that hard work was the best thing for him right now, and that he had all the confidence in the world that Bryan Gilliam and a private investigator would find her. It was obvious to everyone that Ap Lyttle idolized Bryan. But even so, the second day out, Peter overheard Apisi praying to the Great Spirit Napi for Kanti's safe return. It brought tears to his eyes. Peter wasn't sure how much his faith would console him if Brin had been missing for two weeks. He didn't know if he could function.

Bryan Gilliam was pleased with the poundage of Cretaceous meteorite they had retrieved. It was more than enough to relaunch the production of his famous line of dinosaur meteorite jewelry and trinkets. The bonus was the heavy concentration of iridium in the rock. It was a pain to separate the silver-white heavy metal from the darker feldspar sections, but at $6,000 an ounce, it was well worth the effort. Apisi, Chogan, and Bryan had been working long hours down in The Cellar basement—dubbed the *Cretaceous Cavern* by Bryan—chipping away weighty amounts of iridium the past three days. Peter also knew that Loretta Gilliam had begun negotiations with aerospace companies to set up iridium sales channels. Their new aviation venture was already producing revenue.

Life is good, he thought. *And in January we'll be welcoming a new family member.*

Today they would be starting Hayden's dinosaur GPS tracking program. It was also to be Larry Bing's first day with Fowler-Lemoyne Aviation, acting as co-pilot on the flight. Peter had been somewhat anxious flying solo on the three long excursions south to the Custer Gallatin National Forest for the meteorite rock. Fortunately he had not experienced any problems on those flights.

He cleaned his dishes and left the suite, walking down the hallway to the elevator. Up one flight to ground level. The doors squeaked open and he walked out into the bright new day. He had an extra kick in his step as he trekked out to the heliport and the waiting helicopter.

Life is so good, he thought again, feeling happier than he had in a long time.

Tagging the Tri-horns

July 15: The Basin Region
Jefferson County, Montana

"WE'RE FLYING OVER THREE FORKS and I'm spotting a small herd of Triceratops on our left side," Peter said over the intercom, his amplified voice loud and clear in the passenger section. "I'm taking us down for a closer look."

Hayden Fowler felt his stomach leave him as the chopper descended. He peered through the high visibility window, taking in the patchwork rectangles of golden winter wheat that seemed to go on forever. Directly below, he saw half a dozen mature Triceratops escorting three juveniles through a stretch of trampled wheat.

Adults protecting their young? he speculated. It contradicted all paleo science theories about Triceratops. Cretaceous scholars had long theorized that Triceratops—a herding species known to group in large numbers—left their juveniles to fend for themselves. The breed was nothing like the Maiasaura, known as "Good Mother Lizard," who nurtured and safeguarded their offspring. The paleo-zoological sciences community had embraced the theory that Triceratops were uncaring, neglectful parents.

"Nora, you have *got* to see this."

"What is it?" she said, unbuckling her belt and leaning over so she could see out his window. She smiled. "Oh my god, Hayden! Triceratops exhibiting maternal care? This is groundbreaking! It reverses much of what we thought about Ceratopsian behavior."

"Without a doubt," he said, mesmerized by the scene below.

He perused the landscape that rolled out beneath them, watching the small herd move across fields ravaged by the herbivores. Off in the distance, he picked up another group of Triceratops surrounding four juveniles in the same protective manner. Extensive sections of wheat had been flattened and stripped to roots and nubs, as if a giant thresher had rolled through. But Hayden knew the winter wheat wouldn't be ready for harvesting for at least a couple of weeks. This was the work of insatiable Triceratops.

He felt Nora's breath against his cheek as she leaned across him. They watched the Tri-horns waddle along, devouring everything in their paths, pulling long stalks of wheat into their beaky mouths, decimating crops at an alarming pace. The view made it clear to him why the farmers were so angry. A prehistoric invasive species had invaded their land and was jeopardizing their livelihood. It was even worse than some of the farms he and Nora had visited last summer further north, around Shelby. The animals were bigger now, their appetites more ravenous and destructive.

Nora said, "This is fantastic, and yet sad at the same time."

"Yes. Fantastic for us paleontologists, not so fantastic for the farmers."

"One thing is certain," she said with an amused grin. "These Triceratops certainly don't suffer from celiac disease."

Hayden let out a full-throated laugh. *There's that nerdy, intellectual fun I've been missing lately.* With tongue planted firmly in cheek, he said, "Yeah, the gluttons love their gluten."

Nora groaned, mocking him, then laughed along with him. "You're so weird, Hayden."

"Me? You started it."

She pulled back from the window and smiled, peering at him from behind jade-colored designer frames that animated her arresting green eyes. That look never failed to stir something deep inside him.

She kissed him, deeply, eagerly, and he kissed her back.

Jackson Lattimer, sitting on the far side of the cabin, said, "Jesus, get a room, you two!"

Hayden, tried to pull back, but Nora held on, planting a trail of kisses across his beard. Nora had been coming back around to him the last few days after their spat following his Wyoming trip. The sex had been spectacular the past few nights, and the heat between them was carrying over.

Their make out session ended when Jackson moved into the seat across from them, shouldering his bulky Sony videocam. "What are you two so giddy about?" he asked.

"Check it out, Jack," Hayden said, pointing out the window.

Jackson angled his camera down, using the wide zoom lens to better scope the activity in the wheat fields.

Hayden glanced at Nora, who rolled her eyes and circled her ear with an index finger in a *he's crazier than a loon* gesture. Hayden knew she didn't want Lattimer here. She detested the man, and had been badmouthing him at every opportunity.

Nora hadn't spoken two words to Jackson on the ninety-minute flight. But she was smart enough to know the famous wildlife videographer was good for their fledgling business. She knew the value of publicity. Lattimer's videos of the Wyoming T-Rex hatchling attacks had gone viral with more than two-hundred-thousand views in less than a week. Jackson had survived that intense encounter with a foot wound that gave him a slight limp, but his run-in with the junior Rexes had put him back in the national spotlight. He'd done two live network TV interviews this week, mentioning Fowler-Lemoyne Aviation in both. As a result, yesterday the phones started ringing. A senator and two mining executives had inquired about private charters. A travel agency wanted to lease the chopper for sightseeing tours. A geologist wanted to know rates for flying his team to mineral sites. Their new venture didn't even have a website up and running yet, but two mentions by Jackson Lattimer on national television, and bingo! His words had generated business with people who had deep pockets.

And so today, Nora had put her personal feelings about Jackson Lattimer aside and made this trip, cloaked in her business persona. She claimed she was getting cabin fever spending her days locked away in The Cellar at Gilliam's Guidepost working on their book. She'd said she needed to get back out doing fieldwork. While part of that might have been true, Hayden knew the truth. She was taking one for the team—the Fowler-Lemoyne Aviation team. Hayden loved her for making this sacrifice.

He said to Jackson, "What's happening down there is important, Jack. You need to get some footage. You see the way the adult animals have formed a barricade around the juveniles? They're protecting their young. It's unheard of in our circles."

"Yeah, I see," he said, peering through the viewfinder.

Jackson stopped filming, looked at Hayden. "Man, it doesn't take much to get you two propeller heads excited, does it? I really don't see the big deal here, folks."

He turned his attention back to his filming. Nora made a sour face, then raised her hands and pantomimed strangling him.

"Propeller heads?" Hayden said. "That's rich coming from a *gonzo shutterbug.*"

Jackson smiled, head bent over his camera, still focused on his filming. "Touché, my friend, touché."

Hayden said, "Well, since you're such a thrill junkie, I'll tell you something that might make you happy."

"What's that?"

"There's a good chance that predators are in the area. My thinking is the Rexes might be learning there are easy pickings in wheat and barley fields—herds of Triceratops."

"Awesome. I hope you're right."

"We don't," Nora said.

Peter's voice filled the passenger cabin, interrupting any further exchange. "Co-captain Bing and I are gonna take us down for a landing, let you guys do your thing. Please buckle in."

Hayden stood and opened the overhead bin, pulled down two Pneu-Dart X-Caliber tranquilizer rifles and loaded them with darts. He handed a rifle to Nora, who frowned at him as she took it. He knew she didn't like firearms, but she understood the necessity for a successful tagging and tracking operation. And these rifles wouldn't kill anything.

He dropped into his seat next to her and strapped in, his adrenaline kicking in, his pulse quickening.

An hour and a half in the air. Time to hit the ground running and tag a few dinos. He hoped it would go better than it had in

Wyoming.

Hayden looked at Nora. "You okay, *mon amour*?"

She nodded, "I'm fine." Her eyes traversed the barrel of her rifle. "We're just tagging herbivores. It's not like we're going after Tyrannosaurs or Dromes."

Jackson spoke up. "Oh, the big bad boys are out there, darlin'. You heard your boyfriend. Rexes are probably in the area with all the easy prey around."

Nora's eyes narrowed. She lifted the rifle and pointed it at Lattimer. "You call me *darlin'* again and I will pull this trigger, put you out of commission with one of these tranquilizer darts."

His face registered surprise and he raised his hands in surrender. "Easy, Nora. It was a word of endearment, that's all."

She stared him down, her eyes large and threatening behind the lenses of her glasses. "Well don't *endear* me anymore. Got it?"

"No need to get all hysterical feminist with me. Christ!"

"Hysterical *feminist?*" She lifted the barrel of the tranq gun, aiming at his head. "Why you smug—"

"Chill out, Nora," Hayden said, reaching over and nudging the rifle barrel down while looking at Jackson. "Let's not lose sight of the fact that we're a team here, about to undertake a potentially dangerous task. We need to have each other's backs. Okay?"

Jackson said, "Yeah, I hear you. Look, Nora, I'm sorry if I offended you in any way. I have nothing but the utmost respect for you. I hope you know that."

Nora didn't respond. Just turned her head and stared out the window, the rifle across her lap.

Nora's emotional outburst was more than a little over the top, but Hayden wasn't surprised. He loved her, but knew she could get up on her high horse when something stuck in her craw. And Jackson Lattimer was very much in her craw. Hayden felt trapped between his lover/business partner and his new photographer friend. A most uncomfortable position.

The helicopter set down with a soft thump. The engine shut off and the rotor blades cycled down.

"We're here," Peter said over the intercom. "You can unbuckle and move on out. It looks like our noise and downdraft scared the animals off, however. They disappeared. Be careful out there, guys."

Hayden stood, knowing they would find them. Triceratops were low-slung, bulky, and much slower than the carnivores. Protecting their young would slow them down further.

He donned his sunglasses and reached into the overhead bin, grabbed his backpack that contained spare tranq darts, GPS tracking tags, and the epoxy kit. He strapped on the rifle and pack. Unlocked the rear door and pushed it open, leading Nora and Jackson out into the fields. Peter stayed with the helicopter while co-pilot Bing followed, carrying a .375 Ruger rifle.

They were in a small clearing near a dirt road carved with tractor ruts. The day was pleasantly warm, in the mid-seventies, but the air was thick with grain dust stirred up by the feasting Triceratops. Hayden sneezed and he heard Nora answer with her own sneeze behind him.

He stopped on the other side of the farm road, just short of the standing wheat, and addressed the others. "Okay, let's be on our toes. Triceratops aren't usually aggressive, but these are looking after their young. Even docile mothers can be quite ornery when they think their toddlers are threatened."

Hayden entered the nearest field and pushed aside a curtain of wheat stalks, making his way into one of the open barren sections.

"You guys still with me?" he shouted over his shoulder.

Nora didn't answer but Jackson yelled, "If you moved any slower we'd be standing still, Fowler."

Hayden sneered, answered, "And if you were any less witty you'd be a mortician."

He heard Nora snickering behind him and Jackson muttering something indecipherable further back.

They entered the clearing they'd seen from the air, a wide stretch chewed to the ground by the Triceratops. Hayden breathed in the dusty scent of wheat pollen mixed with the odious smell of dinosaur dung. The four of them spread out, walking over the roots and stubble, sidestepping large mounds of smelly scat. Hayden and

Nora had their X-Caliber tranq rifles at the ready. Jackson balanced his boxy videocam on his shoulder. Larry Bing cradled the Ruger. They moved stealthily, listening, watching the bushy wheat for any signs of the herd. They walked the perimeter of the clearing, carefully poking and prodding to rouse any looming creatures. Waves of grain dust made Hayden's eyes water.

"What am I supposed to be filming here, Fowler?" Jackson said, impatient, his words cutting through the prolonged silence.

Jackson's voice irked Hayden. He gave Lattimer a sharp look and said, "Shut your yap, Jack! That voice of yours could—"

Nora screamed, a piercing cry that hit Hayden like a lightning bolt to the brain. He looked across the way, seeing that she had dropped her rifle and was backpedaling from a section of leveled wheat. He didn't see any charging Triceratops.

He ran to her. "What is it, Nora?"

She pointed to the wall of wheat near where her rifle lay. "In there," she said, her voice shaky.

Hayden went to where she pointed, Jackson close behind with his camcorder. Hayden separated the wheat with the barrel of his rifle. Looked down. The slaughtered bodies of two mature Triceratops lay in a bed of straw. Their horns had been carved out, leaving three ragged, bloody stumps on each of their mangled snouts. A horde of black flies buzzed around the carcasses. He estimated the creatures to be eight feet long from snout to tail. Maybe four feet tall when standing. Had to weigh close to half a ton.

"They're a hell of a lot bigger than they looked from the air," Jackson said, continuing to video the gruesome sight. "They don't look like they were attacked by carnivores."

"That's because they weren't. They were shot." Hayden took a knee, waving the flies away from his face. "It's a little hard to see because of their coarse pelts, but if you look close you can see the bullet wounds in their sides."

Nora had come up behind them. "Why would the shooter leave their bodies out here? Wouldn't hunters want to turn them in to collect their bounty money?"

Hayden turned and looked back at Nora. "You make a good

point. Killing the Tri-horns is legal in Montana. Encouraged even. If this was Idaho, I could better understand leaving the carcasses behind. Killing a Triceratops can get you a fine and jail time in Idaho. But whoever killed these two weren't interested in the bounty money. They were after the horns. I've been reading about it online. Triceratops horn is the newest rage. Some people claim there are strong aphrodisiac properties to powdered Tri-horn. Some hallucinogenic properties, too. It's being marketed as a potent mix of Viagra and Ecstasy. Authentic Tri-horn powder is selling for big bucks."

"How disgusting!" Nora exclaimed, scrutinizing the bloody remains.

Jackson chimed in, "Yeah. People are so fucked up. They'll believe any goddamned thing. There's no more truth to that than rhino horn being a sexual stimulant."

Nora said, "The internet generates its own set of truths, and all the rubes flock to it like it's gospel."

"Yeah," Jackson said, "Sometimes I think these prehistoric animals are more intelligent than we are."

"Speak for yourself," Nora said, directing a gleeful smile his way.

Jackson stopped filming and shook his head. "You don't quit, do you? What exactly do you have against me?"

She gave him a long, hard stare, then said, "I'll just say your reckless macho style rubs me the wrong way. We'll leave it at that."

"Guys," Hayden said. "This isn't the time or place for personal battles. Let's focus on the task at hand, shall we?"

Jackson shot Nora an annoyed look. Hayden was disappointed in her unprofessionalism. Jackson didn't deserve this.

Hayden steered the conversation back to the dead animals. "It looks like these are recent kills. Maybe within the last twelve hours. There's no gas bloating yet and the blood still looks pretty fresh. My guess? The killers were the farmers who own this land. I think maybe they left the animals out here as a warning to keep other Triceratops away."

"Doesn't seem to be working," Nora said.

"No, it doesn't."

Suddenly, Larry Bing cried out, "Heads up! Here they come!"

Hayden jumped to his feet and turned, saw two big Triceratops charging them, kicking up clods of dirt as they pounded across the wide clearing, snorting and yowling. He pulled up his rifle and took aim at the Tri-horn on the right. "Nora, take the one on the left," he barked.

Bing fired his Ruger into the air, trying to scare them off.

The ploy didn't work.

They kept coming.

Hayden pulled the trigger. A click, then a loud hiss as the dart discharged. The sedation barb whooshed through the air in a rigid line and struck the rightmost Triceratops in the breastbone with a solid *thwack*. Almost simultaneously, Nora's dart hit the second charging animal in one of its thick front legs.

The Tri-horns continued their charge, nearly a ton of prehistoric animals bearing down on them.

"Run!" Hayden shouted, as he loaded up another dart. "Run in zigzag patterns. Their lateral movement isn't very good. And don't shoot them, Larry. They'll be conked out in a matter of minutes."

The four of them ran in different directions.

The Tri-horns slowed their advance, momentarily confused by their targets running in all directions. Jackson Lattimer, his shoulder-mounted videocam running, yelled at one of the creatures, challenging it to chase after him, which it did. The other one went after Hayden, the dart flopping wildly from its breastplate.

Jackson whooped and hollered as the Tri-horn got close, lowering its massive head like a bull going after a matador, trying to gore him with its three-horn weaponry. Jackson taunted the animal, shouting challenges at it as he ran, all the while keeping his videocam balanced on his shoulder and continuing to film. After a couple of passes, the animal managed to catch Jackson in his upper thigh with its bottom horn. Jackson groaned loudly with the hit and dramatically fell to the ground, never losing his camera. The animal turned and came back at him. He scrambled out of the Tri-horn's path as it shambled past him. The creature's squat legs gave out while trying to make a return charge, and went down in a heap. Jackson went to the fallen animal and filmed himself telling his future audience that he was okay and that he had won this battle against the prehistoric beast. He then aimed the videocam down at his feet, filming his prostrate quarry.

Hayden ran side to side, eluding the creature that huffed and wheezed behind him, careful not to twist an ankle on the wheat stumps. Another minute or two, the animal slowed and crumpled into the dust. Hayden dropped his Pneu-dart rifle and bent over, hands on knees, trying desperately to catch his runaway breath. His chest hurt and his lungs burned. His legs felt rubbery and his hands were shaky.

He heard Jackson calling out to him. "You wouldn't be in such shitty shape if you'd attended my workout camp, Fowler. I can outrun you even with my bum foot."

Hayden continued huffing and puffing. When he finally got his wind back, he pulled a GPS tracking chip out of his pack and epoxied it to his sedated Triceratops, his trembling arms making the closeup work difficult. Then he marched over to where Jackson stood over his Tri-horn like a conquering hero, taking selfies of his wounded thigh. His pantleg was ripped, but up close, Hayden could see the wound underneath was superficial.

Larry Bing stood close by, a look of concern on his face. "You need me to go back to the chopper and get the first aid kit, Mr. Lattimer?"

Hayden said, "He doesn't need it, Larry." To Jackson he said, "You let that Tri-horn gore you, didn't you, Jack?"

"Now why would I do that?"

"I saw you slow down and let it catch you."

"I saw it, too," Nora said. "Anything for a danger shot, right, *Gonzo*? You are one reckless sonofabitch."

Jackson shut off his camcorder and smiled. "You didn't hear it from me, but yes, you're right." He pointed at the fallen Triceratops. "I *did* let that big boy catch me. I'm angling for my own syndicated TV show. The producers are looking for danger shots. They *appreciate* my reckless behavior."

"Good for you," Nora said, angry. "Maybe if your TV show doesn't pan out you can get a featured guest spot in one of those *Jackass* movies."

Hayden laughed and Larry Bing joined in.

Jackson's smile widened. "Oh, Nora, my sweet Nora. Someday you're going to love me. I guarantee it."

"Only in your wettest dream, Gonzo!"

So much for Nora keeping her resentment under cover.

"Wow! Snap!" Hayden said to Jackson. "She really hung one on you there, amigo."

Hayden dropped to his knees to attach a tracking tag to the Triceratops that would soon be famous for goring Jackson Lattimer.

Aerial Surveillance

July 18: Gilliam's Guidepost
Heart Butte, Montana

"I'VE COME UP WITH TWO VIABLE SUSPECTS," private investigator Mike Mathews said to Bryan, speaking of the Kanti Lyttle abduction. This was Bryan's first face-to-face meeting with the sleuth after communicating with him by phone and e-mail the past week. They sat in the den, Bryan in an easy chair, Mathews on the couch, paperwork spread out on the coffee table between them.

Mathews continued. "I found seventeen vehicle registrations that had Montana Centennial license plates beginning with ADU4, but only two of them were for 2021 green Toyota 4Runners, the SUV we saw in the surveillance videos. Of course, these two suspects might not have been involved at all. Either the plate or the vehicle could have been stolen. But it gives us a solid starting point."

"Excellent legwork, Mike," Bryan said, watching Mathews pull a handful of photographs from a folder and lay them out on the coffee table.

"Thanks. I had to sift through a hell of a lot of forms to arrive at these two men. But it helps to have friends at the MVD. And those trading post security clips you sent me got me started on the right track."

Bryan had done his homework on Mike Mathews after his and Loretta's lawyer, Atlee Pinnaker, had recommended him. Mathews spent fifteen years with the Billings Police Department, the last five as a detective in the Investigations Division. He'd earned a number of prestigious decorations for his work, including the Medal of

Valor, the Distinguished Service Medal, and the Police Star of Bravery. He'd been on his own as a PI for more than ten years, specializing in finding people who didn't want to be found—bail jumpers, scammers, kidnappers, thieves, teen runaways, murder suspects on the lam. Narrow faced with a crooked nose, Mathews wore the world-weary look of one who dealt with the dark underbelly of humanity. His cynical outlook spoke to the often shocking truths of human nature. People disappeared off the grid for a variety of reasons, and Mathews had seen them all. Bryan learned the man was brutally frank and averse to sugarcoating the truth. He was thorough. Deep. Dedicated. Serious and competent. Tough and gritty. Bryan bonded with him immediately, especially after learning that Mathews had done two tours in Iraq, overthrowing Saddam Hussein's regime in the Second Gulf War.

And Mathews had also done his homework on the Gilliams. He knew all about their highly publicized dinosaur zoo, Bryan's fight for the betterment of his Blackfoot friends, the AEF raid on Gilliam's Guidepost last year, and the ensuing tragedy.

Bryan felt confident that private investigator Mike Mathews was the right man for the job of finding Kanti Lyttle, Ahwee Red Crow, and now Aiyana Halfmoon.

Mathews slid a couple of photos of the first suspect toward Bryan. "This guy, Jordan Nordquist, owns a sheep farm in Bitterroot Valley. Lolo to be exact. What raised a red flag for me is his longtime membership in PETA. It checks our animal rights activist box. I couldn't, however, find any information about tattoos or body markings. And Mr. Nordquist has a clean history. There isn't even a traffic ticket in his past."

Bryan studied the photos. Didn't feel any *gotcha* vibes.

Mathews slid photos of the second suspect across the table. "This man, Kelton Rendaya, is a veterinarian who owns a large ranch that was once one of the most successful horse breeding compounds in Montana. I learned that a couple of Kentucky Derby horses came from that ranch. Unlike Jordan Nordquist, Rendaya is not affiliated with any animal rights organizations. The ranch is in Flathead National Forest, near Kalispell. I did a little digging and discovered the property was the home of a big moonshine operation back during the Prohibition. That was a long time ago and probably has nothing to do with Mr. Rendaya, who has no criminal history. I just find it interesting that there is outlaw blood coursing through the Rendaya ancestral veins.

"Lastly, I couldn't find any racist posts against Indigenous peoples or women in either man's online activity."

Bryan scrutinized the photos of Rendaya. Compared them with those of the first suspect. Both men were clean-cut and about the same age—late forties, early fifties. Both had short cropped, graying brown hair. Neither had the strong jawline he'd seen on the kidnapper driving Kanti's car away from the scene. Neither man had the threatening aura he associated with criminals. Neither of them felt right. Nothing there that jumped out at him, shouting *I'm a kidnapper*. Of course, what does a kidnapper actually look like? And no telling when these photos had been taken or under what conditions. You could only discern so much from a photograph.

"Are we on for a helicopter ride today?" Mathews asked. "We still planning to fly out to check on these guys?"

"Absolutely, I've got the chopper reserved and our pilots are ready to go," Bryan said. "I was lucky to get an opening today. Business has been great our first week, and we're fully booked all of next week."

Mathews checked his phone. "Looks like Lolo is the further trek. Two-hundred and twenty-five miles. Long way to go on a hope and a prayer. I wish we had more solid evidence to go on."

"What you've got is incentive enough to take a look," Bryan said, checking his own phone, "Flathead Forest—the Rendaya Ranch—is closer. Only a half hour by helicopter. We can do a flyover and check it out from the air. Then head to Lolo."

"Sounds like a plan. I gotta tell you, Bryan, I have a gut feeling this might just be the tip of the iceberg."

"Tip of what iceberg? Whaddaya mean, Mike?"

"Doing my research, I learned that as of yesterday, there are seven missing Indigenous women in western Montana. All of them picked clean off their reservations." He checked his notes. "Three

Blackfoot, two Salish, a Pend d'Oreille, and a Kootenai. Kanti Lyttle has been gone the longest. Missing three weeks now. The seventh—a Kootenai woman—was grabbed two days ago."

"Kootenai?" Bryan said. "Our lead pilot's wife is Kootenai. She's living here working for me as a jeweler."

"She's a lot safer here than on the rez. It's sad, the way this is turning into an epidemic."

Bryan thought about the missing Native women. Seven of them? From four tribes? "The shame of it all is that not many people seem to give shit," he said.

"Unfortunately I'm afraid that's true. I'm surprised you haven't taken this to the press, Bryan. I saw a couple of your interviews last year about the plight of the Blackfoot. You make a good case. Television exposure might get law enforcement moving on this."

"Maybe. But my wife and I don't want the media circus we had here last summer. It was hell. I discovered being a celebrity isn't all it's cracked up to be."

"Yeah. The media can swoop in like vultures, pick at you until you're a shredded mess. I've seen it happen to a few friends of mine. I'm just glad my work keeps me behind the curtain, so to speak."

"I wish we had a few more of you, Mike, so we could find all these women."

"Thanks, but you're giving me far too much credit. We haven't found Kanti Lyttle yet. And I haven't made any progress on Ahwee Red Crow."

"Well, I think we might getting close on Kanti. I hope so, anyway. She's Apisi's wife. Ap is my ranch hand foreman. He's a good man and her disappearance has devastated him."

Mathews gave him a long look across the table. "I want to forewarn you, Bryan. In my experience, people who have been missing for three weeks usually end up in a bad place. I've had no luck in tracking down Kanti Lyttle's Ford Expedition or anything about her movements over that time period. No activity on her credit cards. No calls or texts on her phone. She's a ghost in the wind. We have to face the possibility that she could be dead."

Hearing it expressed so bluntly deflated Bryan. "I understand.

But we still have to try."

"You bet we do. Let's go check out our pair of suspects."

* * *

They flew to Flathead National Forest. This was Bryan's first ride in the new copter and he was amazed at how quiet it was in the passenger cabin. They could carry on normal conversations and didn't have to wear the bulky headsets that were required in the chopper Peter Lacroix flew for the Forest Service last year. And this chopper was quite a few levels above the Huey gunships he rode in Afghanistan, when they flew with the doors wide open to the sand and wind, and the rotor blades that thundered and rumbled and an engine that roared, producing a racket that could wake the dead.

Yes, this aircraft is certainly primo, Bryan thought, silently congratulating Peter for securing such an excellent flying machine.

He peered out the window on his side, seeing the Flathead River winding through the lush forestland. The snowcapped mountains of Swan Range dominated the horizon with Holland Peak standing like a majestic granite pyramid. They flew over Flathead Lake, a shimmering mirror that reflected the surrounding landscape. Clumps of small islands dotted the lake's placid surface. A little farther on he saw alpine meadows where elk roamed.

During the 35-minute flight he thought about the call he and Loretta received this morning from Atlee Pinnaker. The Animal Emancipation Faction had agreed to a settlement of ten million dollars to avoid going to trial. Atlee had negotiated them up from the original seven million. They had an appointment tomorrow at Pinnaker's office in Missoula to sign the nondisclosure and promissory documents. Authorized representatives of the AEF had already put their signatures on the paperwork, the lawyers doing their best to prevent an awkward, possibly confrontational scene.

He and Loretta millionaires? *Multi*-millionaires even! It was an American Dream fantasy come true. The whole thing boggled his mind. But Bryan would give it all up in a heartbeat if he could erase the catastrophe of last August. He would pay out every penny of the settlement money to have Jimmy Enright back, alive and well. And he'd forfeit a small fortune to regain his strength to where he could return to his mechanic work, ride horses again and walk without the damned cane.

Mike Mathews spoke from across the aisle, rousing him from his millionaire musings. "Sure is a smooth ride."

"Yes it is," Bryan replied. "We've got one of the best pilots in all of Montana at the controls. Actually, *two* of the best."

Mathews turned to look out his window. "You can never fully appreciate the beauty of this part of the country until you see it from the air."

"So true, Mike. Beats hell out of where I grew up."

"Where's that?"

"Northwest Texas. Lubbock to be exact."

"What brought you here?"

"My Army buddy and his sister. You met her—my wife, Loretta. Where're you from, Mike?"

"I'm a native Montanan. Spent my entire life in the Billings area."

"I've never been to Billings. I hear it's nice."

"It is. Great place to raise a family."

They flew on, both of them immersed in their thoughts. Bryan could hear Loretta's nagging voice in his head, laying down the law, telling him she forbade him from flying on any of the meteorite retrieval outings. And she was especially against him going with Hayden and Nora on their dinosaur scouting jaunts. But when it came to finding Kanti Lyttle—one of Loretta's closest friends—she was all in for him going on this flight with the private investigator.

Peter's voice boomed over the loudspeakers. "Our GPS readout tells me we're close to our destination, gents. As you can see, the forest canopy is thick, and we're not seeing any openings for a safe landing."

Bryan pressed a button on his armrest, activating his mic. "Thanks, Peter. Don't worry about it. This is just an aerial surveillance trip."

"Good to hear, Bry," came Peter's reply. "We're seeing some

of the ranch structures straight ahead. I'm going to take us down low, give you guys an up close look."

Bryan felt the aircraft's sharp drop in his stomach, like the first big fall on a roller coaster. They came in low over a grouping of buildings. A sprawling, two-story stone-and-timber house was partially concealed by towering Douglas firs and western larch. Expansive windows dominated the lower level, looking out on the forest like dilated glass eyes. A row of white-trimmed dormers sat along the top ridge of the roof, the casement windows reflecting the afternoon sunlight. A pair of golf carts sat behind the house. Several footpaths branched off the main building like spokes on a wagon wheel, leading to a number of outbuildings. Three barns with gambrel roofs and wide doors. What looked like a caretaker's cottage with a wraparound porch that held a glider and wooden rocking chairs. A few low-slung storage sheds. A three-door garage with a group of vehicles parked on asphalt pavement: a Chevy Silverado, a Dodge Ram pickup, a Jeep Wrangler, a Yamaha ATV.

"You seein' anything peculiar, Mike?"

"Nope," Mathews answered, face to the window. "Nothing out of the ordinary. Lots of cars but no sign of Rendaya's green Toyota 4Runner."

Peter banked the chopper and they picked up the Flathead River, following it on its winding path as it went in and out of view, meandering through the thick woodland. Soon they were flying over open pastureland. Field grass waved gently in the breeze. Wildflowers splashed the meadows with prismatic colors. Three white-tailed deer scampered a hundred yards, then disappeared into the woods.

Bryan asked Mathews, "This guy Rendaya owns all this?"

"Yeah. He's loaded. Inherited a boatload from his family, but he also made a bundle selling his veterinary practice."

"Not really much to see out here is there, Mike?"

"No. Tell your pilot to take us back around the other side of the house. Let's check out what's on the other side of the river."

Bryan instructed Peter and they banked again, backtracking along the river as it played hide-and-seek under the thick vegetation.

They passed back over the ranch house and outbuildings, then picked up the river again on the opposite side. They followed the flow to where the river widened and the forest thinned out. The whitewater rushed over smooth boulders, glittering like sprays of diamond chips. They followed the rapids for a mile or two—the verdant forest closing back in—coming to what looked like bridge struts. The framework was well hidden under bushy cottonwood leaves, but Bryan could tell it was a bridge as they flew over. He looked out further, scanning the treetops, seeing what looked like a gap in the trees, maybe a half mile away. Saw a bright flash come from there, followed by a second.

He pressed the intercom button and said, "Peter, you see that clearing on our left at nine o'clock? About a half mile out?"

"Indeed I do. You want us to head for it?"

"Yes. I thought I picked up a reflection off something."

"You got it, Bryan."

Mathews got up from his seat and came to Bryan's side. "What are you seeing?" he asked, stumbling as the chopper leaned sharply.

"Don't know yet."

As they got closer, the clearing came into view and Bryan could see two vehicles parked next to a tall chain-link fence: a silver Ford F-150 and a larger freight truck. Three men unloaded Styrofoam containers off the back of the pickup. The men stopped their work, craned their necks and stared up at the chopper. Two of the men wore cowboy hats. The hatless man bore a striking resemblance to the man they had looked at in the photos.

"That look like Rendaya to you?" he asked Mathews.

"I didn't get a good look."

As they cleared the chain-link fence, Bryan saw the mesh netting covering a spacious enclosure.

His jaw dropped.

Four Dromaeosaurs ran in circles, alarmed by the helicopter that stirred up dust in their pen.

A bad déjà vu feeling collected in his gut.

Memories of his own ill-fated dinosaur zoo swept through him.

They flew over a network of other enclosures that stretched out behind it. Bryan caught a glimpse of a couple of larger dinosaurs that moved beneath the heavy canopy of cottonwoods.

Tyrannosaurs?

He looked at Mathews, wide-eyed, disbelieving. "Holy shit!"

"Yeah. *Holy shit* is right. Have your pilot take us back for another look. I'm gonna get my camera."

Bryan pressed the intercom button. "Hey, Peter, could you circle back for another flyover? We need second look."

Peter said, "Sure thing. That's quite a compound they have out here in the middle of nowhere. Some big beasts in those pens. Brings back memories of your ranch last summer."

"Please don't remind me," Bryan said. "Do me a solid, would you?"

"What's that?"

"When you bring us back around, hover in place so we can get some video."

"Okay, we can do that. But if those cowboys start shooting at us, we're outta here. That's a memory from last year I never want to relive."

"Understood. You and me both, my friend."

Mathews unpacked his camcorder and stood at the floor-to-ceiling window.

Peter rolled the chopper into a wide, looping U-turn and they came in low, hovered over the site.

They are T-Rexes, Bryan realized. *At least two of them. They dwarf the ones I had in my zoo.* He peered down at the mesh-screened adjoining enclosure, seeing the Dromaeosaurs all worked up, bringing back painful memories of when he was attacked by one a little over a month ago.

Mathews shot video, letting out an occasional "Wow!" and "Unbelievable!"

"Be sure to get some footage of the zookeepers," Bryan said.

The men seemed to be in as much of a frenzy as the dinos. They were pointing up at them, walking around aimlessly, one of them shaking his head. Finally, one of the men wearing a cowboy hat ducked into the cab of the pickup and emerged holding a rifle.

Bryan hit the button. "Uh, Peter, I think it's time to cut out. The natives are getting restless."

"Ten-four, good buddy."

The copter lifted swiftly, pulling away with no shots fired.

"Well *that* was special," Mike Mathews said, reviewing his video on the small display screen.

Peter's voice on the loudspeakers: "Where to next, gentlemen?"

Mathews responded. "Do you guys have internet connectivity in the cockpit?"

"Yes, we do. What do you need to know?"

"I know it's not in our flight plan, but we need to make a stop at the FBI field office in Missoula. I believe Missoula is on the way to Lolo, correct?"

A slight delay, then, "Yes it is, Mr. Mathews. We're forty-five minutes north of Missoula. From there it's a hop and a skip of maybe ten minutes to Lolo. Is that the route you want us to take?"

"Yes, please."

Bryan looked at Mathews. "FBI field office?"

"Yeah. We've got enough now for a search warrant. Keeping dinosaurs in captivity for use other than public exhibition is a felony in the state of Montana. That didn't look like a roadside zoo back there. And even if it was open to the public, they would need a permit to operate. Those dudes on the ground didn't look like the permit types, you ask me."

"No they most certainly did not," Bryan said. "But I didn't have a permit last summer either."

"You didn't need one. You allowed the government to use your zoo as a research facility. I'll wager good money on it the government doesn't know jack shit about this operation. The feds will be swarming this ranch when they see our video, especially when we present evidence that the ranch owner is a prime suspect in a kidnapping case."

Bryan sat back in his seat, feeling like they were finally on to something.

Is it possible that Kanti is here?

Wherever she was, he just hoped they weren't too late.

Kelton's Tribulations

July 21: Rendaya Ranch
Flathead National Forest, Montana

KELTON HAD BEEN LOOKING OVER HIS SHOULDER the past week, going through his days wondering if the law would show up. Anxiety rode his spine like a boogeyman spirit. His world had collapsed in the wee hours of the morning on that North Dakota highway eight days ago. Two cops killed by one of the two Tyrannosaurs they were transporting. He was still shocked at how fast the deadly deed had developed, how quick the Rex had slaughtered the two troopers and disappeared into the brush. Shocking as it was, he and Thorn had sucked it up and drove south of Bismarck, delivering the second Tyrannosaur to the customer, doing their best to keep their spooked emotions in check. When they arrived at the crack of dawn, Kelton had to endure a tongue lashing from his irate buyer—cattle baron Richard Nossett—for showing up with only half the promised goods.

"It's a clear breach of our contract, Rendaya!" Nossett screamed in his face. "You're nothing but a grifting con artist thief."

Exhausted and frustrated, still jittery from the cop killings and in no mood for a chewing out from a pompous, self-serving money-bags, Kelton had let Nossett have it right back. "Our contract was done over the dark web. It was illegal from the get-go. Why don't you try suing me, see how far you get with that."

Nossett took a step back, the truth of Kelton's words setting in. "I want half of my money back. And the deposit."

Kelton laughed, a mirthless chuckle. "The deposit is non-refundable. Plus you only transferred the down payment, which was fifty percent, so I'm considering us even."

Nossett spat in the dust. "I don't see my money in the next week, you'd best be watching your back. I'm warning you, Rendaya, you better sleep with one eye open."

They left in a hurry, the cattleman taunting them, yelling threats at their backs. He wasn't about to refund Richard Nossett a dime. Kelton had already suffered a substantial loss on two escaped T-Rexes. He couldn't afford to shell out more to a guy who probably wiped his ass with hundred-dollar bills. And he and Thorn only had enough cash to get back to Montana. The law would be looking for them—might already *be* searching for them—and credit cards would leave a trail.

Kelton had dropped Thorn off at a car rental place with enough cash for a one-day rental. Thorn leased one of their cheapest models, a Chevy Spark, then followed Kelton, who drove the truck to an isolated jetty on the Missouri River north of Fort Rice. They wiped the truck clean of prints and blood spatters, covered it with tree limbs and brush, and abandoned it there. Not great, but it bought them some time. They drove through the day and evening, nearly 800 miles, across most of Montana, taking turns at the wheel, arriving back at the Rendaya ranch at three AM the following morning. It had been a white-knuckle ride, with every police car they passed sending jolts of distress through Kelton. Once home, he crashed into a deep, dreamless sleep for twelve hours.

He'd spent the past week following the news reports about the North Dakota cop killers and their possible connection to the illegal animal trafficking trade. So far they had nothing that could identify him and Thorn. No witnesses. No new evidence from the recovered rental truck. If Richard Nossett knew about the cop deaths, he wasn't talking. But then, why would he? He had to keep his illegal animal refuge hidden from authorities.

They were in the clear.

Or so Kelton thought until three days ago.

He'd been out at the glen helping Hoops and Thorn feed the Rexes and Dromes when that mysterious candy apple red helicopter came buzzing in, flying over his dinosaur enclosures. The chopper made a couple of passes and hovered while some asshole shot video through the window. The aircraft had no markings other than an identification number on the tail section too small to read from where he stood. Unfortunately, the spy chopper got a look at the largest dinosaur inventory he'd had yet. All the animals in the pens—four Dromaeosaurs and a pair of Tyrannosaurs—had been bought and paid for by longtime customers and were awaiting shipment. Kelton had put a hold on deliveries until the heat died down. He'd nervously watched the skies the past three days, but the helicopter had not returned.

So who was interested in his operation? Law enforcement? Competitor animal traffickers? Civilian curiosity seekers? It was unsettling, coming so soon after the police officer fatalities.

Could this possibly be Tank Mahaffey's doing?

Gordon Tank Mahaffey had to be dealt with. Kelton remained convinced that Tank had messed with his tranquilizer chemicals. The two highway patrol officers would probably still be alive were it not for the tainted xylazine that allowed the one Rex to go on the killing spree.

Kelton paid a visit to his ex-employee at a rundown apartment complex north of Kalispell where Tank moved after his dismissal three weeks ago. Kelton found him catching a few rays at the apartment pool, getting into a shouting match with him after accusing him of carrying out his diabolical deed.

"You've got a hell of a nerve comin' here busting my balls about your stupid tranq juice!" Tank yelled, jumping up from his lounger.

"I *know* it was you, Gordon," Kelton shot back, angry, using Tank's birth name that he despised. "You're the one who knew the ingredients. You're the one who's filled the syringes in the past. You're the one who had access. It *had* to be you, Tank."

"Fuck you, Rendaya! I don't have a clue what you're goin' on about. You fired me. Isn't that enough? You took away my livelihood and kicked me out of your bunkhouse that was my home for thirty years. Your dad never would have done me like that. He had a lot more class than you. The old man always treated me with respect. From the first day you took over you've been on my ass about everything. Now you come here and accuse me of some vague offense? Get bent, you jerkoff!"

The arrogance of the man!

Kelton wanted to knock his fat head off his cinderblock shoulders, but thought better of it. Tank was twice his size and looked like he'd added even more beef since he'd been unemployed. Kelton glanced around the pool at the sunbathers who were taking an interest in their confrontation, a couple of oiled and bronzed teenage girls in string bikinis, and an older guy with a hairy back in a speedo, much too old and furry to be wearing a speedo. Kelton decided it best to proceed quietly. He leaned in and said just above a whisper, "Tell me the truth, Tank. You doctored the tranquilizer dosage on that first Rex that got away from us, didn't you?"

Tank stared at him, a look of wide-eyed surprise that quickly softened into pity. "You're talkin' nonsense, Kel. I think maybe you've finally lost your marbles."

"C'mon, Gordy," Kelton said, keeping his voice low, "we both know you have a history of screwing with me. But this is serious. You've cost me a lot of money with your shenanigans this time." He was about to say he'd caused a couple of deaths, too, but caught himself. "Just admit to it and I promise, I won't press charges."

"*Charges?*" he exploded. "You're batshit crazy! If you don't leave right now, I'm gonna phone the authorities and tell them all about the illegal operation you've got goin'. You don't seem to realize I could have done that many times in the past. I came real close when you fired me. But I didn't. You know why?"

"Yeah, I *do* know why, Gordy," Kelton said, the anger thick in his throat. "You haven't because it would implicate you as well. You've always been a sniveling coward. Not to mention incompetent. I should have fired your useless ass years ago. I would be much better off right now if I had."

Tank clenched his big fists, took a step toward Kelton. "I've had a lot of time to think about stuff since you canned me. I've come to the conclusion that you're a really shallow dude. The only thing you give a damn about is money. It's why you're alone. You're a loser,

Rendaya, and I'm glad to be through with you. And if you don't leave in the next minute or two I'm gonna make that call." He gave him a snide look. "Or maybe it'd be more fun to beat the everlovin' shit outta you."

Kelton backed up a step, held up his hands in surrender. "No need to get nasty. Just know that I still think you're behind it and you know damned well what I'm talking about. You've been a huge disappointment to me, Gordon."

With that, he turned and left.

So, was that helicopter Tank Mahaffey's doing?

Kelton pushed Tank out of his mind and steered his golf cart down the narrow path. He was on his way to the snake barn when his walkie-talkie squawked on the seat beside him. He picked up. It was Arlene, his part-time vet assistant. She helped him with his lawful trade, the small group of veterinary clients he retained to maintain the guise of running a legitimate business.

He pulled the cart off the path. "Hey, Arlene. What's cookin'?"

"You have some visitors, Dr. Rendaya."

Her voice alarmed him. Arlene sounded stressed. It wasn't like her. "Clients?"

"No. They're federal agents. FBI."

Kelton's felt a lurch in his stomach, a fist of fear that hammered its way down and squeezed his testicles. "They show you IDs?"

"Yes. I called their field office to confirm their employment. The lead agent advised me to do that. They're for real."

A storm of thoughts crashed through Kelton's mind, all banging against each other, competing for his attention.

What do they have me on? Harboring illegal animals? Transporting illicit goods across state lines? The highway patrolmen killings? Identity theft?

My first—and possibly last—mistake was getting involved in the dinosaur trade, he realized with regret.

Arlene's voice brought him back. "Look, Dr. Rendaya, I don't mean to be nosy, but—"

"Tell them I'll be there in a few minutes, Arlene. Make them comfortable. Give them coffee or soda pop."

He clicked the talkie off and turned the cart around. Headed back to the main house, his hands shaky on the wheel. He parked the cart behind the house, under the deck, walked up the steps and entered through the kitchen.

Special agents Drew Clevenger and Alan Morrissey greeted him in the foyer, both sipping from cans of Coca-Cola. They wore navy blue windbreakers with small gold **FBI** lettering embroidered on the front above the left breast, and duplicated in a larger font across the back. Clevenger was tall and rangy with sleepy eyes and a jaded seen-it-all expression. Morrissey, obviously the junior agent, was short and stocky with cauliflower ears and a hyperalert demeanor. Both were packing Glock 9mm semi-automatic pistols, their jackets opened to display the hardware strapped to their sides in leather shoulder holsters. They left no doubts about their seriousness. A third man, a Flathead County sheriff's deputy, stood quietly in the corner, eyeing Kelton suspiciously from under bushy gray eyebrows. Stuart J. Fenski was engraved on his nameplate.

Kelton did his best to hide his unease. "What can I do for you fellas?"

Special Agent Clevenger said, "You have quite a spread out here in the wilderness, Mr. Rendaya. We're here—"

"Um, it's *Doctor* Rendaya, if you please."

"Okay, Dr. Rendaya. I won't beat around the bush. My team has been authorized to search your premises. Things will go smoothly if you give us your complete cooperation."

"Search my property? On what grounds?"

The FBI agent pulled a file folder from under his arm and opened it. Pulled out an official looking document and handed it to him. "This is a search warrant authorized by the honorable Senior Judge Darrell L. Bickler of the United States District Court of Montana in Missoula. You can read through it, but I'll give you the bullet points. First, we have evidence that you are sheltering exotic, dangerous animals on your ranch. More specifically, mature dinosaurs, the custody of which is illegal under federal regulations and the state of Montana wildlife laws. This warrant explicitly cites recently added bylaws in the Endangered Species Act and the Lacey

Act, which prohibits the import, export, transport, sale or purchase of these prehistoric animals. To simplify that, it is illegal to indulge in trafficking these animals and profiting from the sale of them. It is also illegal to keep dinosaurs in captivity. The only way you can get around that is obtaining the proper permits or exemptions. Can you provide us with proof of those documents, Dr. Rendaya?"

Kelton kept his eyes on the search warrant, all the legalese making his head spin. Without looking up from the warrant, he said, "That's ridiculous. I'm an equine veterinarian. What would I want with dinosaurs?"

"Come on, *Doctor*. You know as well as anyone that dinosaur trafficking has become big business. Now, if you don't have proof of permission from the state to house such animals, my team will proceed with the search. I must also inform you that the search also includes seizing all computers and hardcopy files on the premises to track your business transactions."

Kelton felt his anger boiling over. "Now wait just a fucking minute. I know my rights, and—"

"If you are going to make this difficult, we'll have to use force," Special Agent Morrissey said. "We have a van full of agents outside. We don't want to have to bring them in, do we?"

Kelton went to the window, swept the drapes aside and saw a group of five feds standing around a gray Ford Econoline van, smoking, talking, a couple of them laughing. He came back to the issuing agents. "You guys brought a small army with you. Seems like overkill."

"There's more, Dr. Rendaya," Clevenger said, reading from his file folder, "Do you own a 2021 Toyota 4Runner with a Montana Centennial license plate, number ADU421?"

Kelton wondered where they were going with this. "I own a number of vehicles, Agent Clevenger. I don't know the plate numbers on them."

"But you *do* own a 4Runner, right? Army green?"

"Well, yeah. What does that have to do with anything?"

"A vehicle of that make, model, and plate number is registered in your name."

"Yeah, so what? All my vehicles are registered in my name. I pay my registration fees every year. What's the problem?"

Clevenger frowned. "The problem is, your 4Runner was filmed at the scene of a kidnapping. To be precise, June twenty-sixth at Running Crane Trading Post in Heart Butte."

Kelton thought a minute. Heart Butte is where that rancher—Gillman or something like that—had that dinosaur zoo last year. "Heart Butte?" he said, surprise in his voice. "That's gotta be a two- or three-hour drive from here. I wouldn't have any reason to go there."

Agent Clevenger gave him a knowing smile. "Actually your car followed your accomplice, who drove the abductee out of the parking lot in her car. Kanti Lyttle is her name. Blackfoot Indian woman. That ringing any bells for you?"

What the hell is going on here?

"I didn't have any goddamned accomplice because I wasn't there. This is absurd!"

Agent Morrissey ignored the retort. "I understand you have several employees here on your ranch, besides Ms. Arlene here. You employ ranch hands, do you not?"

"I do, yes," Kelton said, alternating between red-hot fury and an overwhelming confusion about the kidnapping charge. "Two longtime ranch hands and two new hires to replace a guy I fired."

"Do any of these employees have access to your 4Runner?" Morrissey asked.

Kelton was starting to see the big picture here. "Yeah. All my staff is permitted to use the 4Runner and one of my other vehicles. I've got them set up as company cars."

Would Tank Mahaffey actually do something this sociopathic? Would the bastard frame me for felony kidnapping? Of course he would. He doctored my tranquilizer chemicals, probably twice. In essence, Tank murdered two North Dakota policemen. He could have killed a bunch of us.

Clevenger handed him a pad of paper and a pen. "We'll need their names, contact information, and a brief bio of each. Same with the employee you fired."

Kelton took the pad and pen. "Before I write anything, I want to see your proof that I'm harboring dinosaurs."

"We aren't required to divulge our sources, Dr. Rendaya," Clevenger said. "Local law enforcement like Stu here and Judge Bickler who issued the warrant are the only ones who get that privilege."

"That's just wrong," Kelton said, becoming more incensed. "I'm calling my lawyer."

"Be my guest." Clevenger again. "You can bring in the most high-powered attorney in the country and it won't change anything. We'll still go through with our search and seizure. Our warrant gives us license to do that."

"What bullshit! So I don't have a leg to stand on?"

"That's about the size of it," Morrissey said.

Clevenger spoke up. "There is one way you can reduce your potential penalties on the dinosaur rap."

"How's that?"

"By you giving us detailed information about your suppliers and customers in the animal trafficking end of things."

Kelton gave the two agents a long glare. *Do they know about the North Dakota incident?*

He said, "I do not, nor have I ever, trafficked in illicit animals. Therefore, I don't have any information to give you. And even if I did, there's no way I'd ever be your whistleblower. I'm not a snitch."

Clevenger sighed. "You might want to rethink that, Doctor. We are going to find out everything. Your cooperation might keep you out of jail."

"*Jail?* The idea that I'm being accused of kidnapping is absolutely ludicrous. I'm completely innocent of that bogus charge."

Agent Morrissey said, "So does that mean you're copping to the dinosaur trafficking charge?"

Kelton swallowed back his outrage. "As I said before, I'm an equine veterinarian of many years. A professional handler of all kinds of animals, specializing in horses, but dinosaurs have never been on my patient list."

Deputy Sheriff Fenski spoke for the first time. "Well then, how about you tell us where your 4Runner is so we can see just how innocent you are on the kidnapping charge."

Agent Clevenger said, "So, where to first, Doctor? Dinosaurs or Toyota 4Runner?"

Kelton Rendaya felt the world closing in on him.

All because I started dealing dinosaurs!

Rainy Days and Mondays

July 22: Gilliam's Guidepost
Heart Butte, Montana

LORETTA SAT NESTLED IN THE SUNROOM LOVESEAT, feet propped up on the ottoman, immersed in *The Seven Husbands of Evelyn Hugo*, a novel based loosely on the life of Elizabeth Taylor. She started the book two nights ago and the story had hooked her. Outside, the storm that started last night, continued to rage on this Monday morning. The rain strafed the sliding windows and cascaded down the glass in wavy streaks. Raindrops pelted the concrete patio, plinking against the pavement, sounding like tiny bells. Jags of lightning cut the sky, the flashes strobing across the quad. Thunderboomers shook the house. It was dreary, gray, and turbulent outside, but Loretta was dry and happy in the cocoon of the sunroom reading a good book.

So nice to finally get some much needed alone time after a hectic week. She had spent much of last Monday with construction contractors who were working on the barn conversion. Under her guidance, the helicopter hangar was taking shape. Tuesday was taken up with visits from aerospace companies Loretta had been negotiating with for the iridium. Representatives from SpaceX spent the morning with her in the Cretaceous Cavern checking out the purity of the prized heavy metal, running a few tests to ensure its suitability for use in their rocket engine nozzles. Reps from Lockheed Martin came Tuesday afternoon, examining the platinum-like metal for use in their jet propulsion systems and communication satellites. Loretta felt confident that large-dollar orders would be forthcoming. Wednesday Peter Lacroix had flown her to

Missoula for her weekly therapy session with Dr. Krickstad. Then Friday it was back to Missoula with Larry Bing flying her and Bryan for their appointment with Atlee Pinnaker to sign the AEF settlement paperwork. She loved the new helicopter. Such a luxury. They could now get to Missoula in an hour and a half as opposed to the difficult 215-mile, three-and-a-half-hour drive they used to make.

And then Saturday, Atlee had called informing her that, in keeping with the court order, he had set up a trust to handle distribution and taxation of the funds from the AEF settlement money. She and Bryan thought it best to keep the news from the kids. Ethan and Paul might lose their motivation and youthful innocence if they learned the family had attained multimillionaire status, and Lianne was too young to understand the implications. That was their thinking. Of course, the Gilliam children would know of it eventually, but Loretta wanted to delay it as long as possible. So they had waited until both boys were out of the house and Lianne in her room asleep Saturday night before she and Bryan popped open a flute of champagne and celebrated their newfound wealth.

She turned a page in the book and read about Evelyn Hugo meeting her fourth celebrity husband-to-be when something on the small flatscreen TV in the corner caught her eye. A news report. A middle-aged man in handcuffs being escorted by FBI agents to a van. The sound was muted, but the caption running across the bottom read: **Prominent Montana veterinarian arrested in exotic animal trafficking probe …. suspected in kidnapping case.**

Kidnapping case? What the…?

The scene switched to several federal agents carrying aquarium tanks and wire mesh cages out of a corrugated steel barn.

She set her book aside and picked up the remote, boosted the volume. Listened to the stern male newscaster's voiceover report.

">. . . and during yesterday's search and seizure, investigators found that the doctor had in his possession more than eighty highly venomous animals, all invasive species not native to this part of the world. Snakes, scorpions, Gila monsters, lizards, spiders, poison dart frogs. It's like the animal kingdom's murderers row of reptiles and amphibians. But that's only the half of it . . ."

The screen refreshed with a new video clip, this one showing Tyrannosaurs and Dromaeosaurs in well-shaded enclosures. Federal agents peered in at them through the fence.

"Dr. Rendaya also kept these beasts locked away in this bizarre forest menagerie . . ."

Rendaya? Oh my god, this is the ranch Bryan and the private detective flew over on Thursday.
She called out for Bryan to come see this.
"What is it, Lor?" he said, entering the sunroom holding a mug of steaming hot coffee.
Loretta pointed at the TV. "This is your kidnapping suspect. The FBI has taken him into custody."
Bryan watched, sipping his coffee.

". . . it is believed that the equine veterinarian is a key player in a dinosaur trafficking ring covering six states. Trading in dangerous exotic animals is a state and federal crime that could cost the doctor up to two-hundred-thousand dollars in fines and bring a prison sentence of five years. But Dr. Kelton Rendaya's problems go much deeper than that. Here is where our story takes a morbid turn. Could a murder charge also be tacked on to the doctor's other offenses? We'll have to wait and see, but after sedating and removing the dinosaurs from the pens, officials found a set of human bones inside the back fence. Experts tell us they are female and are fresh within the past week. This ties in with Rendaya being suspected of kidnapping at least one Native American woman, possibly more. Law enforcement officials tell us they have solid evidence of the veterinarian's participation in the abduction of Kanti Lyttle, taken from the Blackfeet Indian Reservation on June twenty-sixth . . ."

The video of the dinosaur enclosures was replaced by a recent photo of Kanti's smiling round face.

"Jesus H. Christ!" Bryan mumbled.

Loretta nearly lost it.

Oh please, NO! You have taken so much from us already!

She didn't think she would ever get over the death of her brother Jimmy, and her Blackfoot friends who perished at their cookout last year. And now her good friend Kanti? Missing for almost a month? It was too much.

Dearest God in heaven above. Please don't let those be Kanti's bones in that habitat.

She looked at Bryan, who wore the same hopelessly lost expression she was sure she displayed.

The news report continued:

"The animals were euthanized yesterday and the human bones taken to the forensic anthropology lab at Montana State University for identification. With today's heavy rains, the search of the sprawling fifteen-hundred acre ranch has been delayed until better weather sets in. We will bring you updates as we receive more information . . ."

Loretta shut off the TV. She sighed deeply and sat back against the cushions, feeling her body vibrating, apprehension surging through her in tumultuous waves.

Bryan came to her, sat on the ottoman and caressed her bare feet. "The feds will find her, hon," he said. "She's alive. I can feel it. Kanti is strong. Blackfoot tough, just like Ap. She's a survivor."

Just then, Loretta's cell phone buzzed, startling them.

She checked the caller ID: Unknown Number

She picked up, thinking it could be one of the aerospace

companies. She answered in her business voice. "This is Loretta Gilliam. How can I help you?"

"You can help me in several million ways, Loretta Gilliam," came the raspy male voice. "I understand you have come into a great deal of money recently. How does it feel to win the lottery?"

"Who is this?" she said, giving Bryan a *this is strange* look and putting the phone on speaker.

"Since you just put your phone on speaker, I hope your murdering husband is listening. Are you there, Bryan Gilliam?"

Bryan climbed up on the loveseat next to Loretta. "I'm here. My wife asked you who you were. How about identifying yourself."

"Who I am ain't important. What *is* important is the man you murdered. Surely you remember. The shootout in your absurd Gilliam's Glade dinosaur zoo? His name was Wyatt Thurgood. My best friend for more than forty years. Friends since grade school. We played basketball together on several teams. He was a great American. As opposed to you, he loved animals. Wyatt hated seeing those dinosaurs cooped up like prisoners on your ranch. He did what he thought was right and you gunned him down, leaving three boys fatherless and his wife a widow who grieves to this day."

"What do you want, asshole?"

"I called you, Loretta because I understand you control the money in the Gilliam family, right?"

"Well, we both—"

"That settlement money you just got from the AEF should rightly go to Wyatt's family. His memory deserves it more than you Injun lovin' creeps do. Now I have a trio of your redskin squaw friends that I will gladly trade for five million dollars. I'm bein' kind here, only askin' for half of what you're stealing from the AEF."

Bryan said, "What are their names, these Indian women you say you have?"

"Kanti Lyttle, Ahwee Red Crow, and Aiyana Halfmoon. Really stupid Injun names. Dumb cows, all three."

Despite the ominous tone of the conversation, Loretta felt a spark of optimism. "Kanti is still alive? She's okay?"

"Yeah, I'm getting sick of lookin' at her fat face. It took forever for this settlement to go through and I've had to hold onto her way longer than I wanted to."

"And Ahwee and Aiyana are okay, too?" Bryan said.

"Of course. Those two Injun bitches are money in the bank."

Loretta said, "We just saw on the news that the man suspected of abducting Kanti Lyttle is the veterinarian who got busted for trafficking dinosaurs. Kelton Rendaya. That wouldn't be you would it?"

"No. Rendaya is behind bars awaiting arraignment. Good place for him. He abuses animals, too. Just like you creeps."

"You have a warped view of reality, whoever you are," Bryan said, his voice rising with his anger. "We don't mistreat animals and I've never killed anyone who didn't deserve it."

"So self-righteous, Gilliam. It's unbecoming. I'll be contacting you in the next couple of days for instructions on wiring the money to an offshore account. Until then—"

"Wait!" Loretta shouted, coming up off the loveseat. "We need proof that Kanti and Ahwee are alive and well. If you have them, put them on the phone."

"No can do. Talk with ya soon."

The line went dead.

Loretta wanted to punch something.

Bryan stood and embraced her, rubbing her back. "We'll get them back, Lor. I'll get with Mike Mathews and see if he can trace that call."

On the Edge of a Nightmare

Late July

Location Unknown

A THICK MIST HUNG OVER THE CHAIN-LINK PENS, veiling the beasts in a gauzy haze. The fading sun broke through in places, creating shimmering rainbows that arched over the mesh netting. Wisps of fog swirled around the big creatures, gyrating like small ghostly twisters. The scene had an ethereal, otherworldly quality about it, and Kanti wasn't sure if she was hallucinating, or actually out at the dinosaur habitats experiencing it. The line between dream and reality had blurred since she was imprisoned in the dank root cellar and drugged repeatedly.

The bellowing, tuba-like cry of the Tyrannosaurs resounded through the trees. The smaller animals—the ones Pennywise called Dromes—snorted and blustered, digging up turf as they sprinted around their environs. Kanti breathed in the pungent smell of animal dung and the earthen, musky scent of wild animals. She shivered in the cooling dusk. *This is all too real to be a dream.* She believed she was out at the steel cages near the river. Pennywise had brought her here a few times during her stay. How many times, she couldn't be sure.

She had seen terrible things here. Frightening things.

Movement at the side of the Drome enclosure drew her attention. The mist separated and she saw a young Indian woman with dark, olive-colored skin. A wave of black hair flowed across her shoulders and down her back. She wore a cream-colored dress with colorful patterns, repeating prints of a Thunderbird, the supernatural creature of Salish mythology. Her feet were bare. Two masked men stood behind her, berating her, their voices loud and harsh. Both wore masks. One of them slapped her, the woman's head whip-lashing from the blow. The woman cried out, and Kanti tried to move forward to help her, but someone or some*thing* restrained her. She turned to look behind her but there was nothing there. She tried to push forward again. Same thing. She felt strong hands gripping her waist, holding her in place.

She twisted around to look. No one there.

Does this mean I'm dreaming?

The man who hit the Salish woman yelled insults at her. He sounded a lot like Pennywise, but he wore a Batman mask. Kanti heard *"Dirty redskin! Worthless squaw! Diseased Injun whore!"* She watched the other man—wearing a Spider-Man mask—push the Salish woman into the enclosure and slam the gate behind her with a clank.

A look of disbelief and terror registered on the woman's shadowy face. On the far side of the pen, the four Dromes stopped their chaotic sprinting and sat together on their haunches, staring at her with their outsized neon-red eyes. They sniffed the air, their wide nostrils pulsating, picking up her scent, sizing up their prey.

The woman screamed. A desperate shriek. A terrifying, chilling sound.

The Dromes were on her in the blink of an eye.

Kanti couldn't watch. The sounds were bad enough.

She tried to turn her head away. Couldn't.

Tried to close her eyes. Couldn't.

She was paralyzed in place.

She heard the men laughing as the poor woman disappeared under the onslaught of slashing claws and shredding teeth.

"Fascinating isn't it, Sacajawea?" Pennywise whispered in her ear.

Kanti thought she would be sick.

She let out a deafening yell.

She awoke mid-scream, drenched in sweat. Trembling. She was in her root cellar prison, wrapped in her bedroll.

Just a dream, she thought, sitting up, trying to talk herself down, attempting to find a sense of calm. But was it a dream? It was so vivid, lacking the randomness of most dreams. More like something she had actually experienced recently.

Was that Salish woman real? Did my captors really feed her to the dinos and laugh about it?

She climbed out of her bedroll and put on her moccasins. Paced the small area, tears sliding down her cheeks. *Swish-swish-swish,* she walked across the dirt floor, back and forth, sobbing, chanting to the Great Spirit, asking for her rescue, praying for the Salish woman's soul. Kanti felt like a caged animal. How long had she been imprisoned in this claustrophobic root cellar? Weeks? Months? She was worn down and tattered. Exhausted. Her body ached all over. She was terrified and lonely, the forced solitude and drugs playing tricks on her head.

Am I next to be sacrificed? Is my time near?

Pennywise told her she was more valuable to them alive, and she tried to gain strength from that. Something about getting ransom money from the Gilliams' legal settlement. But Pennywise was a criminal. How could he be taken at his word? Was that him out there feeding the Salish woman to the predators? And who *was* the Salish woman? What was her story? What had she done to make herself expendable?

Was any of that real?

Or was it a figment of my troubled imagination?

What is taking so long? Is anybody looking for me?

The questions overwhelmed her. She felt shaky, panicky.

Kanti wanted to die. To crawl back into her bedroll shroud and fade away from this depressing place. Put an end to this prolonged misery.

She felt her sanity unravelling. Her crying jag intensified, her tears flowing freely now. Kanti went to the wood paneled wall and punched at it with her fists, yelling "Get me out of here! Get me out of here! Please, somebody help me!" screaming at the top of her lungs, slamming the wall with as much force as she could muster, until her hands were bloodied and bruised.

Her shouts turned to wordless, ear-splitting wails that rivaled those of the Tyrannosaurs in the enclosures.

Finally, wearing herself out, she slumped to the floor.

There was nobody who could see her crying. Nobody could hear her shouts.

No one knew she was a prisoner in this windowless dungeon.

Criminal Proceedings

July 24: Gilliam's Guidepost
Heart Butte, Montana

"HEY, BRYAN. I'M GETTING BACK TO YOU ABOUT that phone call you wanted traced."

Mike Mathews' jovial voice on the phone annoyed Bryan. "Better late than never, I guess," he said, miffed at being ignored for two days. "You would think a call demanding five million bucks for the return of a kidnapping victim would get a quick response. My wife and I have been sweating it out the past forty-eight hours, Mike. I left a message with The Flathead County Sheriff's Office and the FBI field office in Missoula, too. Haven't heard squat from them either."

"I apologize for the delay, Bryan. We've been busy but—"

"*We've* been busy? Who is we?"

"I'm with the FBI team at the Flathead County Detention Center in Kalispell. We've been interrogating Kelton Rendaya with the oversight of a sheriff's deputy. The lead FBI investigator, Special Agent Drew Clevenger, is most appreciative of the leads we gave him, so he's letting me sit in. Giving me looks at the evidence they've collected. Drew's a good guy. Wants to see justice done. You're going to like some of the stuff I'm uncovering, Bryan. I believe we're close to finding Kanti Lyttle."

"Really? So you were able to track down the phone number?"

"I couldn't. But the Fibbies did. This morning. Most people think a burner phone can't be traced. And for the most part, that's true. But the FBI can with their deep reach and techy tools. They were able to get the purchaser's name and call history from the cellular carrier. They show a call going to your wife's cell phone early Monday morning, at approximately the same time you said you received the ransom call."

"Awesome! Is it the veterinarian? Rendaya?"

"No. Rendaya copped to the dinosaur trafficking charge but he's still claiming his innocence on the kidnapping."

"So who's the asshole who called us on the burner phone?"

"We believe it's one of Rendaya's longtime ranch hands. Name of Thomas Terrell. Lives on the ranch property in the bunkhouse. I did some checking on him. He's a known Animal Emancipation Faction sympathizer. He's never been a dues-paying member, but he's made some hefty donations to the AEF over the years. I also scanned his social media accounts. I found one long, rambling post on Facebook—it's called Meta now—in which he defended last summer's AEF attack on your ranch and the atrocities that occurred there. He also has a history of posting racial slurs against Native Americans and women in general. Terrell was actually suspended from Twitter twice for his racist and sexist rants."

That surprised Bryan. "I didn't think Twitter—or I guess it's called X now—policed their site."

"They do. But it has to be really bad before they notice. I wasn't able to pull up the offending posts that got him thrown off, so I don't know the specifics of it. Anyway, Terrell's boss, Rendaya, acted surprised when we questioned him. Said the man he called Hoops was quiet, usually preferring to suck on a cigarette than make small talk. Apparently Terrell was a big basketball star in high school, where he earned the Hoops nickname. Rendaya said he was probably good enough to play college ball, but that he had no drive or interest in furthering his education. The vet also told us Terrell has an animal rights tattoo on his left forearm. The way he described it, the tat sounds like the one we saw on your store security video."

"That's really good work, Mike," Bryan said, feeling a bit of guilt over the way he'd laid into the PI. Thinking maybe they were indeed getting closer to finding Kanti.

"Thanks. The current search warrant gives us the right to comb through the bunkhouse. But we're waiting on Judge Bickler to issue a criminal arrest warrant for Terrell. We'll probably get it this afternoon, late. The feds have agents there making sure Terrell doesn't leave the property. This guy checks all the boxes for the kidnapping. Maybe the murder, too."

"Yeah, I heard about the bones they found. Any word on those?"

"Nothing yet from the forensics lab. That kind of thing takes time."

"Of course. Sounds like things are proceeding nicely. But I gotta tell you, Mike. I'm feelin' left out. I'm just sitting around waiting for that hemorrhoid—Hoops Terrell or whomever—to call again, demanding money."

"Well, that's a big reason for my call, Bryan. The arrest will most likely go down later today, and hopefully we'll get Terrell to take us to where he's hiding Kanti Lyttle. Maybe Ahwee Red Crow and the Halfmoon woman, too. The feds feel as though you've earned the right to be here. They actually *want* you here, to hopefully identify the ransom caller's voice."

Bryan smiled. Nice that they wanted to include him. But then he realized something. "Damn. The chopper is out all day today. Don't expect them back before sundown. I could drive—"

"Don't be ridiculous, Bryan. That's a long haul over some rough terrain. Special Agent Clevenger acknowledges that they wouldn't have a case if it hadn't been for your determined effort. He's arranged for a helicopter to pick you up and bring you here. After all, you've got a heliport right there in your back yard. VIP service all the way. You want to be here for that, right?"

"Yes. Absolutely."

"They'll be there in an hour. I'll see you soon."

Otherworldly Armadillos

July 24: Bitterroot Valley, Montana
West of the Continental Divide

THEY FLEW SOUTH, OVER LUSH GREEN meadows and barley fields laid out in checkerboard patterns. Rolling hills ascended to the rugged summits of the Bitterroot Mountains in the west, majestic Trapper Peak standing tall. Dense woodlands of pine and fir carpeted the foothills. The Sapphire Range underscored the eastern horizon in a blue-green slash. The Bitterroot River meandered through the valley, punctuated by small sandbars along its path.

Nora couldn't pull her eyes away from the striking beauty of this area sixty miles south of Missoula. She and Hayden were the lone passengers on this flight. Peter Lacroix manned the controls solo as today was Larry Bing's day off. They were responding to reports of multiple T-Rex sightings in the area, hoping to do more GPS tracking. They had yet to spot any Rexes, but Nora had seen other extraordinary wildlife—a huge bull moose sporting an impressive rack; a small herd of bighorn sheep tight-roping craggy cliffs; mule deer foraging in the fields.

This outing was much more pleasant than their last excursion ten days ago, when they'd tagged those aggressive Triceratops. She smiled thinking about the rampaging Triceratops that had run Jackson Lattimer down and gored him in his egotistical ass. She knew it was intentional on his part, all for show, but it still gave her pleasure. *Couldn't happen to a more deserving ass!* That video, like so many of the man's filmed wildlife misadventures, had gone super viral on social media.

Why all the fuss about Lattimer? Why does he have hundreds of thousands of followers? The man is an arrogant fool with an ego the size of Montana.

Nora had been around Jackson Lattimer way more than was good for her wellbeing. She was less tense now, without his braggadocio machismo throwing her off her stride. Things were so much more pleasant in his absence. Quieter. Less drama. Even Hayden appeared much calmer without the photographer around. Lattimer had flown to California yesterday to work on a mountain lion documentary. He'd be gone for a week.

Maybe longer if one of the cougars gets hold of him.

She laughed. *Dare to dream, girl!*

She and Hayden had just returned from Minneapolis after a week at home working on the book. The publisher was getting impatient for more material, and they had worked together, penning new chapters about their Triceratops tagging adventure, the baffling new craze of Triceratop horn poaching, and Hayden's dinosaur migration theories.

Spending time together back home and sleeping in their own bed had reheated their relationship, a connection that had gone from sizzling red-hot to frigid ice cold once Jackson Lattimer entered the scene. The gonzo photographer had come between them, and she despised him for intruding. Hayden had been seduced by the man's star power, but every time she tried to discuss it with him, he just laughed it off. He was too emotionally myopic to recognize his famous new friend's control over him. Last week, however, separated from Lattimer's reckless influence, Hayden returned to his old self. He once again wooed her with his silly French phrases. Made her laugh with his nerdy jokes. Impressed her with his scientific knowledge. Delighted her with his recovered sense of intimacy. Screwed her like she was the last woman on the planet. They were a team again. Friends. Partners. Lovers. Authors. And now they were once again dinosaur scientists out doing fieldwork together. *All without the distraction and chaos Jackson Lattimer brings. Hallelujah!*

Hayden looked up from his laptop. "You've been awfully quiet over there, *ma dame*. You seeing anything of interest?"

"Miles and miles of barley and alfalfa. The occasional moose, but no dinos yet."

"It might be too early in the day. Especially for Rexes. Plus we've had a lot of rain the past few days." He returned his attention to his computer. "You know, the more we track these animals, the more I believe in my theory of limited migration. Our dinos aren't moving much. They're remaining in these same geographic regions they inhabited back in the Cretaceous. It's amazing really. Kind of goes hand-in-hand with my natal homing model. It's as if they are comfortable here and fearful of venturing too far. Of the five Rexes we're tracking, only one has ventured more than twenty miles. One of the Dromes has traveled thirty-two miles, but the other three don't show much wanderlust. None of the seven Triceratops are on the move. There's enough wheat and barley and potatoes in these parts to keep 'em happy."

"So what do you make of it?" she asked.

"It tells me they're homebodies," he said with a laugh. "Seriously though, I think there's a lot of truth in the news reports about dinosaur trafficking. The Rex that killed those cops in North Dakota and the Dromes that were spotted in Utah scream of false migration. They're outliers. It's animal trafficking. No way those dinos traveled all that distance on their own."

"Yeah, it *is* interesting. I liked the chapter you wrote for the book."

Hayden looked at her. "Thanks. It would be more conclusive if we had a larger statistical sampling."

"Have some patience, Hayden. It takes time. Our helicopter makes the tagging a bit easier."

"Maybe so, but today isn't helping. We're burning a lot of fuel and coming up empty."

"We'll find them," Nora gave him an amused smile. "You're the world famous dinosaur diviner, remember? We're out here dowsing for dinosaurs. We'll find them. I have faith in your special gift."

"My gift, huh? Do you really believe that bullshit, Lady Lemoyne?"

"I do, yes. I've seen it at work many times." She winked at him and blew him a kiss.

"We're scientists, not witches," he said. "Divining is just witchy superstition, babe."

"C'mon, Hayden. Lighten up. Things are good for us right now."

He went back to scrutinizing his laptop screen, pulling at his beard, grumbling about the ridiculousness of dowsing for dinosaurs and his so-called gift.

Nora scanned the valley as they flew on in search of elusive Tyrannosaurs. She contemplated her own gift, paleontology, and how she arrived at it. She could clearly recall the day her scientific journey began. She was seven, digging in the dirt behind her mother's garden in Wisconsin, uncovering a handful of Indian arrowheads and several bone tools. Excited by her find, she rushed inside, breathlessly showing her mother her prizes. Nora later learned the arrowheads were from the Menominee tribe, as were the bone implements—an awl and scraper used on animal hides and a small harpoon for hunting aquatic animals. She was hooked. There were buried treasures to be found. The earth held precious secrets. The mystery of what lay beneath the soil fascinated her. She became obsessed with mining for artifacts of antiquity. Nora dug up Indian pottery shards, 18th century British coins, ceramic tableware, and military buttons. She found French missionary crucifixes, religious medallions, and tobacco pipes. Her gift, if she could be so bold to call it that, was knowing where to look. Where to dig in with her spade or shovel. It came naturally to her. She intuitively knew where the relics were buried. The same way Hayden knew where to find dinosaurs.

But it wasn't until she was a little older and began venturing further into the woods on the far side of her neighborhood that she became interested in paleontology. There she discovered a new treasure—animal bones. The bones of things that once lived and breathed captured her imagination much more than inanimate objects. She dug up raccoon and rabbit bones, the fragile skeletons of songbirds, beaver skulls and limbs, turtle shells, the withered remains of assorted small mammals and reptiles. She took her discoveries back to her room and learned as much as she could about the anatomy of each species from her well-worn copy of *The Audubon Field Guide to North American Animals*. At age ten she made two incredible finds that sealed the deal for her: a nearly intact skeleton of a white-tailed deer, and a black bear skull and ribcage. Nora knew then that she had found her calling.

Her two big sisters, Cate and Debra, called her weird, and told their friends that their younger sibling was a dirty little tomboy. Many of her classmates shunned Nora, branding her as "the oddball who enjoyed playing with dead things." Girls she thought were her friends called her names: *Nasty Nora, Gross Girl, Loony Lemoyne, Dirty Dog.* The boy bullies were worse, using harsher language. The barbs hurt, but it didn't deter her from pursuing what she loved.

At age eleven, she started reading up on dinosaurs, which led to her dreaming of becoming a paleontologist. Nora kept hoping to unearth dino fossils on her woodland explorations, but soon learned that Wisconsin was not the place for such finds. Undeterred, realizing an education would eventually get her to the places she wanted to go, she buckled down on her studies. In middle school she adopted a studious persona, and the taunts softened from Nasty Nora to Bookworm Nora. Better, but still demeaning. High school saw her become a straight-A honor roll student. There she blossomed into a quirky, bespectacled beauty, with shiny coal-black hair, flawless porcelain skin, and intelligent emerald green eyes. Boys who previously heckled her suddenly wanted to be with her. Nora went on a few dates, but found the boys at Woodbury High to be juvenile and semiliterate at best. She would much rather be spending her Friday and Saturday nights doing research or engrossed in an absorbing novel. She went on to graduate valedictorian of her senior class and was voted "Most Likely to Succeed."

Her high school achievements led to full-ride scholarship offers from half a dozen universities, which ended with her earning a graduate degree in Paleontology and Evolutionary Biology from the University of Michigan. She was well on her way to realizing her dream job.

In grad school she came across Hayden Fowler's bestselling book about the Late Cretaceous-Paleogene extinction, *Ancient Life, Final Strife*. She read it more than once, memorizing passages like they were biblical scripture. It felt like the paleontology boy wonder (the media's buzzy description of him at the time) who had just burst on the publishing scene spoke directly to her, and only her, communicating in her language, getting into her head with his words and concepts. She remembered mooning over Hayden's dust jacket author photo, like a teenage girl obsessing over a pop idol, never dreaming that twenty years later she would be working with him. Co-authoring books with him. Running an aviation company with him.

Living with him.

Sleeping with him.

Nora had long been intrigued with the concept of Fate. There seemed to be a predestined orderliness about it, the way it positioned people and things according to where they were *supposed* to be when the time was right. She thought of it as metaphysical sleight of hand. A magic act. Spiritual puppetry. *It has certainly worked that way for Hayden and me.*

"Oh my god, Nora! Quick, come take a look at this."

Hayden's jubilant shout made her jump, bringing her back to the present. She looked across the seats at him, standing now, peering out his window through high-powered binoculars.

"Ankylosaurs! Three of 'em! They're magnificent! Grab your binocs and get over here, *ma chérie*."

Nora snatched up her binoculars and joined him. Scanned the area he pointed to, at the edge of a wide barley field near a grove of ponderosa pine. Her heart soared as she observed the bulky, low-slung quadrupeds feasting on barley plants with their beaked mouths.

Hayden exclaimed, "They've gotta be fifteen feet long! Where have you beautiful boys been hiding?"

Nora took in the bony armor plates that shielded their backs, their long spiky tails ending with clubs of bone, looking like wrecking balls, which she knew was an effective defensive weapon against predators. She marveled at their low, wide heads with backward facing horns on either side. They looked like giant, otherworldly armadillos, beautiful in their oddness. Not the most scientific observation, but it was how she thought of them, seeing them here now.

"They *are* magnificent, Hayden," she said, scoping the strange looking creatures. "This proves that the pair we thought we saw last summer wasn't a figment of our imaginations."

"Yeah, I was pretty sure they were Ankylosaurs," Hayden said. "We just couldn't get close enough to confirm it. Goddamn, this is amazing, Nora. To know there actually is a fourth species that hatched out of those meteorites. To the best of my knowledge we're the first to discover them."

"I'm not aware of any other sightings," she said, continuing to glass the area. "These guys grew to be even larger than Triceratops. They weren't as prevalent as the Tri-horns, but they had big numbers around what is now Hell Creek State Park, a good ways east of here. Check out those osteoderms on them," she said, referring to their thick, knobby scales. "The sketches the paleo artists have produced over the years got them exactly right."

"Yeah. Incredible," Hayden said, laying his binoculars aside and buzzing Peter in the cockpit.

"You don't have to tell me," Peter responded over the intercom before Hayden could speak. "I see them. I'll take you guys down."

"Don't get too close, Pete. We don't want to scare them off."

"If we haven't spooked them by now, we never will. But don't worry about it, Hayden. I have no plans to get anywhere near those things."

Hayden laughed as he checked his tranquilizer rifle and darts, and sorted out his GPS tracking chips. "Where's your sense of adventure, Lacroix? Ankylosaurs aren't as fearsome as they look. They're plant eaters."

Nora heard Peter's chortle over the loudspeakers. "Well then, it'd be just my luck they'd mistake me for a plant."

Nora laughed at that one as she pulled her own tranq gun and the videocam from the overhead bin.

Hayden said, "Looks like there's some open flat space along our right side. We can hoof it from there, come at them through the field."

"Gotcha. I'll park the bird a quarter mile upwind of them."

"Good idea." "No sense letting 'em get a whiff of us."

Two minutes later, Peter brought them down gently, the chopper skids settling into the soft soil on the edge of the barley field. He shut down the engine. The rotor blades whirred to a stop. "Be safe out there, guys."

Nora followed Hayden out, breathing in the fruity, slightly nutty smell of the barley. She activated the videocam and started filming, wanting to capture every minute of what would hopefully be a remarkable encounter. If the creatures didn't scatter on their approach, the world would be seeing them for the first time.

For once, we're beating Jackson Lattimer to the video punch. That realization pleased her probably more than it should.

She spoke to Hayden's back as they hiked down the wide service path between the trees and the barley. "You think we'll be able to get close enough?"

"Yeah, I think so. But if they take off, we'll be able to stay with 'em. They're not real fleet of foot."

"I hope they don't come at us."

"I have every reason to believe they are docile herbivores. I don't think they'd turn on us."

"The Triceratops were supposedly docile, too. You see how *that* turned out."

"Granted, but they were protecting their young. That's not the case here."

She continued following him down the path, filming their surroundings, very much on the alert for hungry Rexes or Dromes.

She said, "So do you think our sedation syringes will work on these animals, what with their armored hides?"

"We'll see," he huffed. "Their necks are vulnerable. It's the only area other than their undersides not protected by thick plating. It doesn't offer a big target. It'll be a difficult shot. Our sixty millimeter needles are good for penetrating elephant and rhinoceros hides, but *Ankylosaurus Magniventris* is a different beast altogether. They aren't called 'the stiffened lizard' without good reason."

"I hear that."

They came around a bend and Hayden pulled up short. Nora could now see the trio of Ankylosaurs, oblivious of them as they tore into clusters of barley leaves and stems.

"No more talking from this point on," Hayden said in a whisper. "We'll come at them from the side."

He entered the barley and Nora followed close behind. The plants were only four feet tall, so they had to walk hunched over to stay hidden. They moved tentatively, quietly, trying not to rustle the plants, stepping over broken stems that cluttered the narrow row.

They got to within thirty feet of the Ankylosaurs, and stopped to take a knee behind a screen of barley. Their position offered them an unobstructed view, and the beasts looked even more formidable up close. Built low to the ground. Chunky, powerful legs. Like living, breathing army tanks, they were. As she filmed, Nora became fascinated with their parrot-like beaked mouths, the way they clamped onto the plants near the base and ripped them out of the ground, roots and all. Their large muscular tongues worked the barley around four rows of small teeth, where they ground the leaves and stems to a pulp before swallowing. Their feasting was noisy and rhythmic, with a *grip-snort-grunt-grind-slurp* intonation in three-part synchronization.

The Ankylosaurs continued to gorge, their armored heads lowered, unmindful of them. Nora filmed Hayden as he raised the rifle and took aim on the lead animal.

He fired. The tranq dart streaked through the barley and glanced off the animal's plated carapace. Hayden cursed as he watched the orange-feathered dart flutter to the ground.

The creature didn't flinch. Just kept its armored head down chomping at barley stems.

He reloaded quickly.

Fired again.

Hayden's second shot hit its mark, the tranq syringe finding the soft nape of neck in front of the creature's shoulder plating. The beast lifted its head and let out an unnerving yowl, and turned in their direction. Started waddling through the barley, coming for them, the other two Ankylosaurs falling in line behind, trampling plants with their wide bodies as they slowly shuffled forward.

Nora backtracked, trying not to get tangled up in the barley, her heart rumbling in her chest. Panic found her and she fought it. Managed to keep videoing and backing up.

Unbelievably, Hayden stood his ground and got off another shot with his DanInject, the dart sailing high.

That's Jackson Lattimer's reckless influence at work, Nora thought as she yelled, "Hayden, you goddamned fool! Run!"

Suddenly, something on the other side of the advancing creatures made the Ankylosaurs stop their pursuit and reverse direction. Nora couldn't see what had distracted them. She pushed through a couple of rows of plants to get a better view.

Tyrannosaurs.

Two of them coming out of the woods.

Charging, shrieking.

The pair of non-sedated Ankylosaurs stood their ground, and squared off against the approaching carnivores. The Ank bearing Hayden's tranq dart lingered behind, quickly losing energy, winding down.

One of the Tyrannosaurs attacked, lowering its head, snapping its powerful jaws, attempting to put the killing crush on the Ankylosaur. The Rex thrust downward for the snatch, strings of saliva spraying from its gaping maw. With an agility and quickness Nora didn't think possible, the Ankylosaur shifted, instinctively protecting its vulnerable head and neck. The Rex's fearsome teeth scraped across the Ank's armor plated back with a metallic screech. The Rex released a confused squawk, shook its big head, and dove in for a second attempt, but again was unsuccessful in clamping down on its quarry. The Ank quickly counterattacked, its clubbed tail whipping through the air with a resounding *whoosh*, catching the Rex in the throat. Surprise registered in the big carnivore's blood-red eyes as it doubled over, gagging, wheezing, trying desperately to pull in oxygen. The second Ank advanced on the other Rex and landed a vicious tail-club blow to its abdomen, opening up a large, bloody gash, then, quick as a lightning strike, whipped its tail a second time, clubbing the Rex in the head and knocking it sideways. The wounded Rex stumbled and let out a long, plaintive cry of pain.

Nora stood in the barley filming this heavyweight fight between predator and prey. *This is extraordinary,* she thought. *I couldn't have dreamed I would ever witness something like this. But then, who could? Good thing I'm recording this. Nobody would believe us otherwise.*

She looked for Hayden, found him standing twenty yards away, open-mouthed and equally transfixed by the spectacle of this battle between prehistoric giants.

Both Tyrannosaurs staggered around, obviously baffled by the difficulty of snagging these bizarre creatures that dared to fight back. The Rex with the belly wound blubbered and squawked, flapping at its bloody gut with its short forelimbs. The Rex with the damaged throat went for a second attack, lunging at the nearest Ankylosaur, coming in low with its shovel mouth wide open. With a quickness that went against all laws of physics, the Ank spun and delivered another crunching tail-club blow to the side of the Rex's head, knocking it off its feet. The Rex shrieked and hit the turf hard, quickly bouncing back up to avoid a second or third crack with that lethal tail. Dazed and stumbling, shaking its massive head, it eyed the two Ankylosaurs warily, backing away, faltering, then turning and running up the hill into the woods. The second Rex followed, leaving a bloody trail in its wake.

Soon, the two victorious Ankylosaurs wobbled off into the forest, leaving the sedated Ank behind.

"I sure hope you got all that."

Hayden's voice brought her out of her trance. She shut off the camcorder. "Yep. Got every sensational minute of it. That was magical, Hayden."

"It was a miracle, my sweetness. We just witnessed the Terrible Lizards getting their asses handed to them by herbivores. This is good for at least three chapters in our book."

"Yeah, and Jack Lattimer can eat his heart out," she said, grinning, holding up the camcorder.

Hayden laughed, then came to her and kissed her. "You just couldn't resist, could you?"

"Nope." She smiled and kissed him back.

"C'mon," he said. "Let's tag that Ankylosaur and get on back."

As they hiked back to the helicopter, Nora could hear the Tyrannosaurs bellowing in the woods. Cries of the defeated.

Kanti's Gallows

Late July

Location Unknown

SHE DECIDED TO HANG HERSELF.

She couldn't take it anymore. *Refused* to take it anymore.

And so it had come to this.

Kanti decided the only option left was to leave this plane of existence and surrender her soul to the Great Spirit.

The men hiding behind the disturbing masks had finally broken her. Her abductors, with their sharp words and sharper syringes full of drugs that made her see visions. *Appalling* visions. Pennywise The Clown and the shorter one, who usually showed up wearing a Darth Vader mask. They had done this to her. Imprisoned her in this claustrophobically cold, musty root cellar that smelled of overripe vegetables and aged cedar.

They had ripped gaping holes in Kanti's sanity. They had shredded her once stable sense of reasoning.

The trips out to the dinosaur enclosures where they forced her to watch horrific things. The night frights that rudely awakened her on the rare occasions she managed to find sleep.

They were responsible. Pennywise and Darth Vader.

She hated them.

They had killed that Salish woman out in the dinosaur pens, and now they were killing her.

They had led her to this.

She held the coil of rope in her lap, her fingers tracing the coarse fibers. She glanced up at the broad oak beam overhead, shuddering as she realized it was to be her hanging gallows. She looked back at the length of rope. She began to fashion a crude noose, her hands shaking badly. Her fingers felt uncoordinated and arthritic as she struggled to tie the knot.

Too bad those drugs they shot into me didn't kill me. It would have been so much easier.

After several tries, she managed to create a loop and tie it off tight. She looked back up at the oak beam, questioning whether this would be possible with the low ceiling. *Six feet, seven feet at the most.*

She exhaled a deep sigh. Tears of frustration filled her eyes. Maybe she should just use the paring knife she'd found. A hard, deep jab to her jugular and it would be over quickly.

No, she hated the sight of blood. Especially her own.

She started laughing at the absurdity of it all, her chuckles evolving into raucous laughter.

You're losing it, sister!

Who are you kidding? You lost it a long time ago, Kanti Lyttle.

After several long minutes of contemplation, she stood and tossed the rope up and over the beam. Tied the end opposite the loop to a support post. She looked up at the low-slung ceiling. Glanced at the simple noose she had made.

Can I actually do this? My noose looks iffy. There isn't much space to work with.

She realized that even though it was a low ceiling, she needed to jump off something to jerk the noose and pull it tight. She dragged a wooden apple crate underneath and stepped up on it, ducking her head beneath the ceiling. Slid the loop around her neck. The rope was scratchy and rubbed her skin. She was uncomfortable with her head twisted around, so she vowed to make this quick.

"I tried my best to wait for you, Ap," she said, addressing her husband. "*Ksilistsikomm Nistsi'kimowan kipimsooyahk,*"
(Blackfoot for "Please know that I love you with all my heart.").
She also expressed her undying love for her two daughters, Kippy and Nitanis. "I hope you can understand."

She was about to speak to the Great Spirit when she heard the deadbolt scrape across the entrance doors, muffled voices coming from outside.

NO! Oh no! Oh no no NO! The masked men are here to inject me with more of their evil drugs. They're here to take me back out to the dinosaur habitats.

I can't let them take me again! I can't, I can't . . .

I CAN'T!

She leaped off the apple crate.

The rope tightened.

The noose squeezed at her neck.

She choked, gasped for air, trying desperately to suck in air.

Her neck burned like hellfire.

Her mind was in chaos.

She saw a blinding bright light. The doors had opened, pouring daylight into the cellar.

She saw a pair of hiking boots stepping down the stairs.

Those aren't the cowboy boots Pennywise wears, she thought just before she lost consciousness.

* * *

A voice brought her back.

"Are you Kanti Lyttle, dear?"

Kanti blinked, confused,. Through her blurred vision she thought she saw two men wearing blue FBI jackets. It was hard for her to get words out through her ravaged throat. "Yes, I am," she croaked. "Am I dead?"

"No. You're still very much with us," the man nearest her said with a smile. "Your husband and daughters have been worried sick about you, Mrs. Lyttle. They're going to be very happy to have you home again." He turned to the other agent. "Get this woman some water and oxygen, Phil."

The agent named Phil gave her a cup of water, which she drank thirstily. She handed the cup back to him and thanked him. He then placed an oxygen mask over her mouth and nose. She breathed in the cool pure oxygen in great gulps while she watched the lead agent pull a walkie-talkie up to his mouth. "We found her, sir."

Static, then, "Excellent. Whereabouts?"

"In a root cellar, way out in the west horse pasture. Looks like it might have been one of those old moonshine stills at one time."

"Good work, Morrissey. What kind of shape is she in?"

The lead agent examined her damaged neck, took her pulse. "She's a little out of sorts and I suspect a bit dehydrated, sir."

"Bring her on in and we'll get her fixed up."

"Sure thing. We'll be there soon."

Kanti looked at the length of rope laid out beside her, then from one agent to the other. "What happened?"

The lead agent said, "Looks like you tried to hang yourself, Mrs. Lyttle. Good thing the ceiling is low here. Are you feeling strong enough to stand up?"

"I think so, yes."

The two FBI agents helped her to her feet and assisted her up the steps.

She walked out into the glorious sunshine.

She was finally free.

The Great Spirit had been looking out for her after all.

Playing Hoops

July 24: Flathead County Justice Center
Kalispell, Montana

BRYAN GILLIAM ARRIVED IN KALISPELL after an hour flight from Heart Butte in a loud, cramped helicopter. Mike Mathews picked him up at the Riverside Heliport and gave him the good news about Kanti Lyttle.

The news lifted Bryan up. Energized him. "Where'd they find her?" he asked as Mathews drove.

"In a root cellar on Kelton Rendaya's property. I'm told it was one of the old bootleg whiskey stills from the 1920s way out in the fields. And the news just keeps getting better. I got a call from Deputy Fenski while I was waiting for you. The FBI search team also just found Ahwee Red Crow and Aiyana Halfmoon together in another root cellar just a couple hundred yards away from where they found Mrs. Lyttle."

"That's great news, Mike! You guys have been kickin' ass the past few hours."

"Yeah, it's been a busy day. Probably would have found them earlier, but the heavy rains washed out the search effort for the better part of two days."

"How is Kanti?"

"Exhausted. Worn down. Her neck is torn up and—"

"Her neck? What's wrong with her neck?"

"Apparently the poor woman tried to hang herself. She's been through a lot, Bryan. Those animals kept her down in that hole for a month, and some of the things they did to her . . . Jesus!"

Bryan felt a powerful flash of anger. *How can anyone treat sweet and innocent Kanti like that?* "Was she raped?"

"No. There's no indication of physical abuse."

"Well, at least there's that."

"Kanti tells us it was mostly emotional torture. Says they drugged her and forced her to watch horrible acts out at the dinosaur pens. She thinks she witnessed another Indian woman being killed and eaten, but can't be sure because she was so drugged up."

"Damn, man," Bryan said, feeling his internal gears slipping a notch or two. *The things human beings do to each other.* "Has Apisi been notified?"

"Yeah. Her husband's on his way here."

"Is that Terrell dude you told me about the prime suspect? The one they call Hoops?"

"Yeah. He's an arrogant piece of work. NBA tall and thin as a snake. Mean as one, too. Like a friggin' giraffe with irritable bowel syndrome."

Bryan laughed. "You paint quite a picture, Mike. Where are we headed?"

"To the county sheriff's department. They're gonna interrogate Terrell, but they're waiting on you to hopefully lock down his voice as being the one you heard on the phone. They want your testimony."

Bryan was pleased they were including him. He hoped he could remember the guy's voice. "Wish I'd gotten a recording of it now," he said.

"You'll know right away if it was him or not," Mathews said. "The man has a distinctive voice."

"I hope so. Memories can be tricky."

Mathews kept his eyes on the road as he talked. "When I left, they were trying to get Kanti to go to the hospital, but she wasn't having any of it. She says she wants to identify the sons of bitches who took her from her family and tried to destroy her."

Bryan grinned. "Yeah, that sounds like her. Kanti is sweet and she can come across as naive, but she has a fighting spirit that runs deep. My Blackfoot friends are a tough people. They don't back down from anyone." He looked across the seat at Mathews. "How about the ranch owner? That Rendaya fella? Where is he in all of this?"

"Kelton Rendaya is being held in the Flathead County Detention Center without bail. The investigation is still ongoing, but they're holding him on illicit animal trafficking charges. He'll be questioned again about the three kidnappings. He's got a pretty solid alibi on the abductions, but all three kidnapping victims were found on his property. There will also be murder conspiracy charges once the lab comes back with an identification of those remains they found out in the dinosaur enclosures."

Bryan thought a minute, then said, "I guess I have to change my tune about the FBI. I've gotta give them credit for their work on this. I told you about my bad experience with the Fibbies last summer, didn't I?"

Mathews nodded. "Yeah, you did. And you're not alone. Lots of folks are down on the FBI now that everything has become so ridiculously political and divisive. I've always found them to be diligent and professional."

They arrived at the Flathead County Justice Center, a sprawling complex of white brick and smoked glass surrounded by well-manicured lawns and cottonwood trees. Entering, they were led to Interview Room #3 on the fourth floor. Bryan's leg was giving him some pain and he hobbled along next to Mathews, relying on his cane for support.

They were met by Deputy Sheriff Stuart Fenski, and FBI Special Agents Drew Clevenger and Alan Morrissey. Sheriff's Detective Tal Boone sat at a short table behind the one-way mirrored glass, going over his notes and waiting on Thomas "Hoops" Terrell to be brought in from booking.

Bryan heard a joyful shriek and was nearly bowled over by Kanti Lyttle as she rushed up to him, hugging him, exclaiming in an excited rush of words, "Thank you, thank you, thank you, Mr. Gilliam! Detective Mathews told me what you did. He says they never would have found me if it hadn't been for you. I love you so much, Mr. Gilliam."

Her voice was hoarse and raspy. Bryan hugged her close, feeling her tears soak into his shirt. "It's so good to see you, darlin'. You're okay now, Kanti. The right people will be brought to justice. And Ap is on his way here."

"I know. I talked with him a few minutes ago. I'll never be able to thank you enough, Mr. Gilliam."

He stepped back and scrutinized her. Her shoulder length, graying hair was lank and oily. She had lost weight, her round face showing deep lines and sharp angles. Her dark eyes were jittery, reflecting the emotional upheaval she had been through. A nasty red welt circled her neck, looking like a cherry choker. Kanti was frazzled and shattered. Skittish, as if waiting for the other shoe to drop. His heart wept for her.

"Kanti, I think you should let them take you to the hospital to be checked out."

"I will when Ap gets here. First I want to help the FBI identify these creeps."

"How many were there?"

"Two that communicated directly with me. But there were more men involved. Three or four in all. They hid behind weird Halloween masks, but I'll never forget their voices, their laughs, the things they said. The way they moved. I also memorized a couple of their vehicle plates."

An officer brought Hoops Terrell into the interview room through a back door. Kanti stepped back from the viewing window, her back against the wall, a look of terror on her face. There was no mistaking her reaction.

Bryan put a hand on her shoulder. "It's okay. There's a mirror on his side. He can't see you. He can't hurt you."

"Is that him?" Special Agent Clevenger asked.

Kanti nodded vigorously. "I think so. Same string bean body. Same bent-over posture and loping strut. I'll know once he opens his mouth."

Hoops Terrell was seated across from Sheriff's Detective Tal Boone, his cuffed hands up on the table in front of him. The escorting officer left the room through the same back door.

Tal Boone's resonant voice echoed over the intercom. "For the record, sir, please state your name and address."

Terrell sneered at him. "I don't have to tell you shit. When your pig friends arrested me, I was told I have the right to remain silent."

Detective Boone emitted an amused snicker. "That's very true, Thomas. But you see, in our line of work, silence conveys guilt. Those who have nothing to hide talk. Those who want to see justice done, cooperate."

"I want a lawyer. I'm entitled to one. I know my rights, goddamnit."

"Do you have a lawyer?"

"No. I ain't never had a need for one."

That's him! Bryan thought. It only took a few sentences to convince him this was the same man who called him for ransom money. Same gravelly tenor, like something was irritating his throat. Same rhythm of speech. Same way of emphasizing certain syllables. He heard Agent Clevenger ask Kanti if it was the voice of her captor, and she bobbed her head up and down like a jack-in-the-box.

Clevenger said to Bryan, "Is he the guy who called you demanding the ransom?"

Bryan nodded. "Without question."

In the interview room, Detective Boone looked at Terrell. "Okay, since you won't provide your name for the record, I will. Today I, Talbot W. Boone, Detective First Class with the Flathead County Sheriff's Department, am here interviewing Thomas Herndon Terrell, the prime suspect in the Kanti Lyttle, Ahwee Red Crow, and Aiyana Halfmoon kidnapping cases. As previously agreed to, this conversation is being recorded."

Agent Clevenger asked Kanti, "Do you want us to have him say anything that would seal the deal?"

"Yes. Have him say *good afternoon, Sacajawea.* Or *fat little squaw bitch.*"

Clevenger went to the wall, spoke through the intercom, relaying the message to Boone's earbud, letting the interrogator know that Bryan had identified Terrell and Kanti was pretty sure.

The detective made the request to Terrell, putting heavy emphasis on the words *Sacajawea* and *squaw.*

Terrell's entire demeanor changed. Boone had struck a nerve. *It's just now dawning on Terrell that they had found Kanti,* Bryan thought as he watched the suspect squirm in his seat.

"Why the hell would I say those things?"

Detective Boone said, "Oh, I don't know. Just playing with words here. Throwing a few around to see what sticks. I understand you're a big fan of wordplay."

Terrell looked at Boone like he was from another planet. "What the hell're you jabberin' about, man?"

"Say those words, Thomas. Say 'Good afternoon, Sacajawea' and 'Fat little squaw bitch.' It's not hard. You do that and we'll get a lawyer for you."

"No! Fuck you!"

"Ah, those aren't the words I asked for, Hoops. Mind if I call you Hoops?"

"Yeah, I *do* mind. That name is reserved for my friends and you certainly ain't my friend."

Boone checked out the tattoo on Terrell's left forearm. "Nice tat there, Hoops. Great artwork. Is that an animal rights thing?"

The suspect quickly pulled his cuffed hands under the table, embarrassed, as if his privates were showing.

"Whatsamatter, Thomas? Are you ashamed of that tat for some reason? Could that be because you're afraid to let us see the tattoo that showed up on the trading post surveillance video the day you kidnapped Kanti Lyttle?"

Terrell flashed a quick look of surprise, then tried to cover it. "I keep tellin' you. I didn't kidnap anybody."

"Oh, but you did, Hoops. You didn't work alone but you definitely kidnapped a woman on June twenty-sixth. We've got you and an accomplice on video abducting Mrs. Lyttle from the Running Crane Trading Post in Heart Butte that afternoon. You drove Mrs. Lyttle out in her car while your partner followed you in your boss's Toyota 4Runner. We spoke with Kelton Rendaya and he tells us that the 4Runner in question is a company car that you had use of that day, and—"

"He lies, goddamnit! How the hell can that sorry ass son of a bitch know who used that car on a specific day a month ago? Goddamn, man, he's just tryin' to cover his own ass. Rendaya's the one who did the kidnapping. He's the one who put those Indian chicks down in the root cellars out in the pasture. Not me. Last time I checked, it's Kelton's name on the Rendaya Ranch deed. His property. His crimes. I just work there."

Detective Boone smiled. "I never told you where we found the women, Thomas. How could you possibly know they were in outlying root cellars without being involved?"

Terrell looked stunned. He knew he had been tricked into a confession of sorts. Bryan watched him fidget, his rawboned face contorting, desperately trying to come up with a plausible out. Boone sat quietly and watched him going through his thought processes.

After all that, the best Terrell could come up with was, "I want a cigarette and a glass of water."

"There's no smoking in this building, Thomas, but we will get you some water." Boone signaled to the one-way mirrored window.

They waited for a deputy to bring in a Styrofoam cup of water and set it on the table. Terrell took a long gulp, then said, "How do you know Rendaya wasn't involved in the kidnappings?"

"Because he has an airtight alibi. We interviewed the other ranch hands, Mark Thornberry and Gordon Mahaffey, whom I believe you know as Thorn and Tank respectively. Both claim that Kelton Rendaya was home all day on June twenty-sixth. His veterinarian assistant, Arlene Mitchell, reports the same. She remembers that day very well. She and Dr. Rendaya worked together performing colic surgery on a horse. All the records we checked confirm that. There is no way Kelton Rendaya was in Heart Butte on that day, Thomas."

Terrell huffed. "Well of *course* they would cover for him. He signs their paychecks. Duh! That alibi ain't the least bit airtight."

"Oh, I don't know about that," Boone said evenly. "We spent a good amount of time with Tank Mahaffey and I get the impression he isn't a big fan of your boss either. He certainly wouldn't do the man any favors. It gives more weight to his testimony."

Terrell wriggled and writhed. Beads of sweat dotted his forehead. "I want a lawyer. NOW!"

"You still haven't said the magic words, Thomas."

The two men faced off across the table in a staring match. Bryan thought it was sheer brilliance the way Tal Boone had manipulated this guy into a corner. Finally, Terrell sighed deeply and hung his head.

"You know, Thomas, you could do yourself a big favor and cooperate with us. Let us know who helped you. Give us details about what has gone on the past month you've kept Kanti Lyttle in captivity. It'll go a long way in getting you a lighter sentence."

"No. Absolutely not."

"You don't care about protecting yourself?"

"It's not that. I just don't wanna be a snitch."

"Funny, that's what your boss told us, too. But then he thought about it, and now Rendaya's squealing like a stuck pig. How do you think you came under our radar, Thomas?"

"That prick! He's always had it out for me and Tank. He's always been about saving his own skin."

Boone smiled again. "It strikes me that you have a great deal of animosity toward your longtime employer, Thomas. Tell me, you wouldn't have pulled off these kidnappings as a means of framing him, would you? Was that your plan?"

Terrell flushed a deep red. "Get bent, man! I told you I didn't kidnap no one."

"Still sticking with that are you? Before you dig yourself any deeper, I'll tell you we have a mountain of evidence against you. Your tattoo. The video from the scene. I have it right here on my laptop if you want to see yourself in action." Boone started to turn his laptop around for Terrell.

"No, goddamnit, no!"

Boone pulled his computer back. "We also have three rock-solid witnesses behind that mirror watching this interview."

"Witnesses? Who?"

"Kanti Lyttle herself. Yes, we found her just a few hours ago.

She's told us a lot about the way you tortured her and—"

"*Tortured* her? No fucking way. You're just—"

"Shut up and listen. I'm talking now, Thomas. We also just found Ahwee Red Crow and Aiyana Halfmoon. We haven't had the chance to debrief them yet, but I'm sure they'll have plenty to add."

"*Those* are your witnesses? Three worthless, dirty Injun squaws?"

"You just keep on digging your own grave, don't you, Thomas?" Boone said, his voice calm and collected. "We've checked out your social media history. We're aware of your racist rants against Native Americans and your misogynist views of women. Social media makes our work so much easier."

"You ain't got nothin' on me. Those bitches couldn't identify me. We covered up with masks and wigs and hats and gloves."

Boone let out a hearty laugh. "Your boss told us you were a quiet man. He apparently doesn't know you very well. You don't know when to shut your yap."

"None of them bitches could identify me in a lineup if their lives depended on it," Terrell boasted.

"Strike two, Thomas. You just acknowledged that you abducted Ahwee Red Crow and Aiyana Halfmoon along with Mrs. Lyttle. And we have another surprise guest standing behind that mirror. Someone who has already identified you by your voice. The person you tried to extort ransom money from to the tune of five million dollars."

Terrell looked up at the one-way glass and Bryan could swear he was looking directly at him.

"Bryan Gilliam's here?" Terrell blurted out, his weathered face coloring when he realized his mistake.

"Strike three, my friend!" The detective narrowed his eyes at Terrell and said, "Considering that you approached Mr. Gilliam with a ransom demand raises the seriousness of the crime from simple kidnapping to aggravated kidnapping. You also didn't release the victim voluntarily when we asked her whereabouts, and there's the fact of the emotional stresses you placed on these women. You're in some deep shit here. You're looking at life in prison, Thomas."

Terrell drank from his cup of water, his hand noticeably shaking.

Detective Boone said, "What happened to you, Thomas? Why have you gone so far astray? You're a man with no prior criminal record. Not even a traffic ticket to your name. Just one court appearance to contest your divorce. A man with long-term employment on the Rendaya ranch and a decent paycheck. Why does someone with your clean record and stable employment history resort to aggravated kidnapping? I really want to know."

Terrell stared at the tabletop, mute.

Boone persisted. "Tell me the truth. Did you kill that woman out in the dinosaur pens? Did you and your buddies throw her out there to be torn apart by voracious carnivores?"

Thomas Hoops Terrell suddenly lost his moxie. For the first time in the interview he looked scared. Rattled. Defeated. "I want my fuckin' lawyer now, goddamnit!"

"Okay. We'll get you an attorney, Thomas. You're going to need a damned good one."

The Pilot and the Groundhog

July 27: The Cellar Suites, Gilliam's Guidepost
Heart Butte, Montana

"SO YOU'RE FLYING TO IDAHO MONDAY?" Brin asked.

Peter nodded. "Yeah. Taking a team out on another one of Hayden's migration tracking trips."

They were seated on the couch enjoying after-dinner coffee and catching up on each other's day. Little Kimi was on the floor, absorbed in playing with her dolls—Baby Alive, Julie the rag doll, and Kookamunga Kid. At two-and-a-half, their daughter loved to play mommy, talking to her dolls as if they were real babies and she, their mother. The two interactive dolls cried and giggled and cooed while Kimi consoled them, pretend-fed them, and rocked them to sleep. She picked up Julie, kissed her on the cheek, reassuring the rag doll that Mommy wasn't ignoring her.

So cute.

Nights like this warmed Peter, pumping him full of domestic bliss. He got a kick out of watching their daughter emulate Brin. He loved listening to Kimi paraphrase many of the same lines Brin had used on her in recent months. He enjoyed these early evenings on the sofa with his beautiful wife, his imaginative daughter playing on the floor, putting on a show for them, giving them hours of entertainment. This was the family he'd always wanted, the one he'd fantasized about when he was single and lonely, trying to make it as a professional hockey player.

Granny Kachina watched Kimi all day while he and Brin worked. These nights gave Kachina a break and promoted Lacroix family togetherness. And Peter knew that when Kimi played with her dolls, the adults could talk freely.

Brin set her coffee cup down on a saucer. "Nora told me you're flying Hayden to Idaho to find the biggest, baddest Tyrannosaurs."

"I am, yes."

"She told me Hayden says where you're going—the Frank Church River of No Return Wilderness—is like another planet and is rumored to be where the biggest Tyrannosaurs roam. I don't like the sound of that, Peter. The River of No Return Wilderness?"

"It's not what it sounds like, babe. It's actually the Salmon River. It was dubbed the River of No Return in the Lewis and Clark days, when boats could navigate down the river, but couldn't get back upstream due to the raging currents and whitewater rapids."

"That might be so, but isn't that the place where the Air Force helicopter crashed last year and killed your pilot friend, Blair Minsinger? And isn't that wilderness area where Rusty Cavanaugh survived on his own for a week before he was rescued?"

Strange how Brin has total recall when it comes to tragedies.

He couldn't lie to her. "Well, yes," he said, "but that helicopter was an old Army reject that had a defective tail rotor among other issues. Our chopper is newer and has been thoroughly checked out by our mechanic, Carl Lacey. Carl's one of the best in the business."

"I still don't like it, Petey. Can't you just let Larry pilot it solo?"

"No, I can't. We need two of us on a trip of that distance. Hayden wants both of us in the cockpit."

"Why? Because it's not safe?"

"It's completely safe. Hayden and Nora *always* want Bing and me flying together when possible. It has to do with insurance regulations. It's smart aviation, Brin. You should feel better that Bing and I are there to back each other up."

"You've been flying a lot lately, Peter. You're working too much and I worry about you piloting while exhausted."

"I'm working on hiring two more pilots, but I haven't had much time to finalize that now that we've taken on so much business. I've been talking to a couple of the Idaho Forestry pilots I flew with last year in the meteorite roundup. When I can get them on board, my workload will lessen."

Brin exhaled a deep breath. "I still don't like this Idaho trip."

"Hey, I'm only the delivery guy here. Hayden's team is going into the wilderness for four days, not me. Bing and I are just transporting them there, then flying back to pick them up Thursday. Two hours there, two hours back. I'll be back here by one o'clock. We have to be back by then. Larry and I have another job Monday afternoon."

Brin looked at him, skepticism wrinkling her brow. "Nora's not going with them. That tells me something."

"What does it tell you?"

"That it's not safe."

"Brin," he said with a reproving sigh, "I'm only flying in and out. Nora should maybe be worried about Hayden. But you shouldn't worry about me."

"Who all is going?"

"Well, Larry Bing, of course. In addition to Hayden there're two wildlife biologists—Bill Carlton from the Idaho Forest Service and Jenkins McCraw from Montana Fish Wildlife and Parks. And nature photographer, Jackson Lattimer. With all their camping gear and scientific equipment, it's a full capacity run."

"Lattimer? You mean the wildlife videographer? He's crazy. He takes foolish risks. He's a selfish narcissist. The fact that he'll be onboard isn't real reassuring to me, Peter. This only adds to my bad feeling about the trip. Now I know why Nora isn't joining them. She told me she can't stomach the guy."

Peter took a sip of coffee to hide his frustration. Her calling him Peter rather than Petey or some other term of endearment was a tell that her old anxieties were creeping back in.

"As I said, Brin. Larry and I are only dropping them off and picking them up. Jackson Lattimer causes problems on the ground, not in the air."

"I don't know. It all makes me uncomfortable."

Peter let out an exasperated sigh. "Whatever happened with you being okay with my job? Two weeks ago you told me that when you love someone, you let them *do* what they love, and trust they can manage it, no matter how dangerous. What happened to that trust,

Brin?"

"Yeah, I don't know," she said, playing with her spoon. "With a new baby on the way, I worry more, I guess." She looked at Kimi, who was whispering in Baby Alive's ear. "I don't want anything to wreck our family."

Peter reached over and rubbed Brin's baby bump, which, in the past week, had become evident. "We're gonna be fine, sweetie. We're both doing what we love. We have your mother safe and sound with us. We have Kimi. We have each other. Life is great right now. Embrace it. I hate to see you sliding back into your 'waiting for the hammer to fall' mode. It's not healthy, babe."

"Yeah, you're right. I'm sorry. I think part of my problem right now is this underground living. I mean, these suites are nice and everything, but there are no windows. My work is downstairs in Cretaceous Cavern. I never see the light of day and it starts to get depressing. Don't get me wrong. I love working for Bryan, and I *do* like living here rent free. But honestly, it's getting to me, honey. I feel like a groundhog most of the time."

Peter chuckled. "Well, you're the hottest looking groundhog I've ever laid eyes on."

She grinned and slapped him lightly on the arm. "Stop it, Petey, I'm being serious here. We've got money now. Can't we start looking for a house near here? An *above ground* house? It's not good for us to be cooped up in these windowless suites."

"I understand. We'll start looking soon. After I hire more pilots."

"Promise?"

"Scout's honor," he said, holding up his right hand.

"You were never a boy scout, Petey."

"No, but I do have honor. We'll start looking next week. You can count on it."

"Thanks."

"Speaking of Cretaceous Cavern, how are things in the world of intergalactic jewelry?"

Her face lit up the way it always did when she talked about her craft. "The girls and I are churning out some really nice pieces.

There's a lot more iridium streaked through this rock, so we're getting some beautiful layering and coloring. Those pieces are selling as fast as we can make them."

"Loretta told me an aerospace company put in a big order for pure iridium rock."

"Yeah. Chogan and Apisi are working that end of it along with Bryan. I suppose you've heard that Bryan and that private detective tracked down Kanti Lyttle's kidnapper."

"I did, yes. Really great news. Apisi is so much better now that his wife is back. He was starting to lose it there for a while."

"It's all anyone can talk about at work," Brin said. "The way Bryan Gilliam is a hero to his Blackfoot friends. I don't know Apisi or Kanti very well, but I consider them and Chogan and the Blackfoot girls I'm training to be my Native brothers and sisters."

Peter reached over and put his hand on her distended belly. "How's our little boy doing in there?"

"What makes you think it's a boy?"

He caressed her stomach. "Has to be a boy. I can tell by the way he bumps around in there. That's male movement. Our sweet daughter never moved like this."

"You're so full of it, Petey," she said, laughing and flinging his hand away. "You can't feel anything. You just want a little hockey player."

"Guilty as charged."

She bent over and kissed him on the mouth. "I love you so much, Petey Edward Lacroix."

Peter's heart thumped double time. She had always had that effect on him. He ran his hand through her luxurious wave of raven hair and leaned into her kiss. "I love you, too, Brinshou Taleka Lacroix, my sexy little groundhog."

That cracked Brin up and Peter laughed along with her. Kimi looked up from mothering her dolls and joined in the laughter, even though it was obvious she didn't have a clue what her parents found so funny.

Wanting to get in on the action, Kimi left her dolls on the floor and climbed up on the couch, moving next to Brin and rubbing her baby bump the way she'd seen Peter doing. "Fat Mommy! Fat Mommy!" she yelped with unabashed delight as she pulled her small hand across Brin's belly.

Peter reached for Kimi's hand. "Hey, it's not nice to call somebody fat, little girl."

"She's okay," Brin said, pulling Kimi's roving hand up to her mouth and kissing it. "Do you know why Mommy is fat, Kimi girl?"

The toddler responded without hesitation. "Too much ice cweam?"

That brought a snorting laugh from Brin. "No, cutie-pie. That's your new baby sister in there."

"Uh, baby *brother*," Peter uttered.

"Whatever," Brin said through more laughter. She looked down at Kimi who was pressed up against her, hugging her leg. "My fat belly means you'll have a new play friend in January."

Kimi glanced up at her mother, a blank and thoroughly confused look on her face. She yawned widely.

"Okay, it's past your bedtime, kiddo," Brin said, standing and peeling Kimi off her leg. "C'mon, pick your dolls up and I'll help you get ready for bed."

Twenty minutes later, Peter and Brin were in their bedroom, calling it a day. Brin started undressing to put on her nightgown.

"Here, let me help you with that," Peter said, stepping up to her, his fingers nimbly unbuttoning her blouse.

Her musky scent and warm breath drove him crazy. He planted kisses on her face as he slipped her blouse off her shoulders, let it fall to the floor. She unbuckled his belt and yanked his pants down to his ankles. He unzipped her jeans and pushed her back on the bed.

"I like where this is going, darling," she whimpered.

He said, "You're the most gorgeous woman on the planet, Brinny."

Soon they were both lost in each other.

The pilot and the sexy little groundhog got it on.

Subterranean sex.

Underground love.

A night to remember in The Cellar.

The Rock Star

July 29: Gilliam's Guidepost
Heart Butte, Montana

THE GILLIAMS SAT AT THE KITCHEN TABLE eating an earlier-than-usual breakfast. All, that is, except for Loretta's oldest, Paul, who had grown accustomed to sleeping in this summer. Loretta doubted even an earthquake would wake that boy these days.

Yawns around the table, with Bryan, Ethan, and Lianne all looking worn and bedraggled, groggily shoveling food into their mouths. The helicopter had woken them at five o'clock, and Loretta was trying to make the best of it by serving eggs and pancakes.

Paul entered the kitchen with an irritable greeting. "Where the hell does Pilot Pete get off flying out so early in the freakin' morning?" With a bleary-eyed sigh and a flip of his shoulder length hair, he went to the cupboard and pulled down a mug, moved to the coffee pot and poured.

"Well I don't believe my eyes," Loretta said to his back. "Pauley Gilliam up before noon? I believe we're witnessing a miracle."

Paul turned, blew on his coffee, said, "Don't call me Pauley anymore, Mom. That's little kid stuff."

"You *are* a little kid, Pauley Puke," younger brother Ethan muttered through a mouthful of pancakes. "Pauley's a little wanker."

"Stuff it, Ethan! You're younger than me. So that must make you a toddler."

The boys glared at each other before Paul took a seat at the table, and brushed his hair out of his face. "So, I'll ask again. Why did Pete Lacroix fly the chopper out of here before the roosters got around to crowing?"

Loretta said, "Today is Hayden Fowler's trip to Idaho. It's a long flight and they wanted to get an early jump on it."

"Well they certainly did that. Jesus, whose idea was it to build a heliport so close to the house? The racket interrupts my beauty sleep."

"There's not enough beauty sleep in the world that can save that face."

"You should talk, Ethan. Your face looks like the surface of the Moon!"

"All right, stop it, guys," Bryan grumbled. "You're giving me a headache. You *both* sound like toddlers."

Loretta looked at Paul, said, "It might do you good to get up early once in a while. Just because you're a rock star now doesn't mean you've earned the right to sleep until noon."

"Rock star?" Ethan quipped. "He's no rock star. He's just a lazy ass."

Lianne giggled, milk from her cereal dribbling down her chin. Ethan started laughing along with her.

"Laugh all you want. You all can say you knew me well when I was a nobody."

Ethan smirked. "You'll *always* be a nobody, Pukeboy."

"Don't be so quick to crucify, little bro. You're looking at the lead singer-guitarist of a band that's just been signed to do a tour of the Northwest U.S."

Loretta gave Bryan a questioning look. Bryan only shrugged.

"What are you talking about, Pauley?" she said.

"Ah," Paul said, holding up his forefinger. "I said no more Pauley, remember?"

"Old habits die hard, son. So what's this about a tour?"

"My band, Moonrise. We signed a deal with a manager after our gig yesterday. He's been to several of our shows and he thinks we're really dope. He's setting us up for a six week run starting in September, playing midsize clubs in Seattle, Portland, Spokane, and Boise to name just a few. We'll be playing on some really massive stages. This whole thing is epic."

"Starting in September?" Loretta said. "What about school?"

"No problem. I'm gonna drop out."

"Wait, *what?*" Bryan said.

"Yeah. I don't need to be wastin' my time in school. They don't teach anything useful there anyway. I get my education every night on stage. I'm gonna be a rocker, not a doctor or lawyer."

Loretta felt like she'd been stabbed in the stomach. Paul had a weighty chip on his shoulder concerning his band, a chip that had grown to cinderblock size the past month.

"Like hell!" she snapped. "You're staying in high school and then you're going to college. You can play your music on the side. Besides, you're only seventeen. You have to be eighteen before you can legally sign contracts."

She looked to Bryan for support, and he spoke up. "I told you before, son. You come to me first with any offers like this. The music business is full of snakes and grifters. I don't wanna see you get taken by some sleazy promoter. And your mother is right on two counts: You are absolutely staying in school, and anything you signed with this guy is nonbinding."

Paul leaned back in his chair, eyeing his parents, mouth hung open in disbelief.

He's actually surprised we're reacting this way, Loretta thought.

Paul sneered at his father. "You don't know a damned thing about the music business, Pops."

"Oh, I know more than you think I do, bucko," Bryan said calmly. "You've heard of Elvis Presley?"

"Well, duh, yeah. Who hasn't?"

"Colonel Tom Parker robbed Elvis Presley blind, keeping him on the road to the point of exhaustion, stealing much of his tour money and collecting more than fifty percent of his song royalties. And then there's John Fogerty of Creedence Clearwater Revival fame. He signed a deal from hell with Fantasy Records at age nineteen that gave the record company one hundred percent of all publishing rights to Fogerty's songs. In other words, they stole all his song royalties. Then to rub salt in the wound, when Fogerty left CCR for a solo career, Fantasy Records management brought forth a legal injunction against him that prohibited him from playing his own songs on tour. But it didn't stop there, Pauley. When Fogerty started writing new songs for his solo catalog, Fantasy sued him for plagiarizing himself, if you can believe it. Those are just two of the cautionary music business tales. There are many, many more. Elvis and Fogerty were in their teens when they signed up for that misery. The music business is rife with corporate sharks taking advantage of young, idealistic, naive musicians. Your mother and I are trying to prevent you from making a colossal mistake like that."

Paul took a long swallow of coffee and shook his head. "Are you jerkin' me, Dad? Those things happened fifty years ago. Back before even you and Mom were born. Get current, will ya. The music business has changed."

"No it hasn't, son. If anything it's much worse today. I would urge you to do a little more research on management-artist relations. Especially the history of it. History sets a precedence for what evolves later."

Paul bit at his lip, considering. Finally he said, "Well, our guy Wally isn't like that. He's lookin' out for us."

Ethan chimed in. "Sure he is, Pauley. I looked up this manager you've been raving about, this Wally Reinfeldt. Yesterday he posted on his Instagram feed that he had just signed a deal with you, going into great detail about how you're one of the famous Gilliams of dinosaur fame. He didn't say one word about your music and he didn't mention Moonrise, which, by the way, is a dumb band name. He just went on and on about Mom and Dad and the dinosaur zoo and the tragedy that happened here last year. It's obvious he doesn't give a shit about you or your guitar playin' and singin'. He doesn't care about the band. He's just usin' the Gilliam name to promote himself."

"You're wrong, Ethan. You read one post about Wally and you're jumping to conclusions. He's a good man. I can tell."

Bryan said, "You're young and impressionable, Paul. Your band has only been together for six months. Yes, you guys are good for your age, but you're also ripe for the picking by some of these silk-tongued agent types."

"You don't know Wally either, Dad. You've never met him so you—"

"I haven't met him because you did an end-around on me and signed an agreement with this man on the sly."

Paul sighed and looked away.

Ethan said, "Tough truth time, big bro. You guys aren't as good as you think you are. And those original songs of yours are really lame. Nobody would ever download them."

"Eat me, Ethan! You've always had a tin ear. You're just jealous cuz you didn't get any musical talent."

"I like your music, Pauley," Lianne said. "That song about roses is nice. I like the one about your girlfriend, too."

Paul smiled at Lianne. "Thank you, Lee." He gave Loretta and Bryan the stink eye. "At least someone in this family appreciates my talent."

Ethan snorted. "Talent? So you can strum a guitar. Big effin' deal. Your vocals sound like a tortured cat."

"What the hell do you know, Ethan? You're just a dumb jock-strap."

"Boys! Stop it right now," Loretta demanded.

Bryan said, "Look Pauley, you're seventeen and still living under our roof. Our house, our rules, and the rules say you will finish your senior year of high school and go to a four-year college to earn a degree in something more substantial than pop music. Something with a secure future. You can still play your music, but your studies come first."

"Listen to your father," Loretta said. "Neither of us had the opportunity to get a college education. You do. Don't throw that away. Make a plan for your future and follow it."

"I *do* have a plan for my future. I've got it all mapped out. Moonrise is spending August in a recording studio and then we're hitting the road in September. Wally Reinfeldt manages some famous rock bands and he says we have the potential to hit it big. He's booking us recording time at The Vault in Missoula. Wally wants us to record an EP of five of my songs, maybe a full album if we can squeeze it in before the tour. This is the chance of a lifetime. This is *my* opportunity and I'm taking it. You can't keep me from doing it."

"Wrong, son," Bryan quipped. "You're staying in school, and that's final. A year from now, you'll be of legal age and you can call your own shots. But right now, we're your legal guardians and what we say goes."

Loretta watched Paul literally deflate at the table. He took one last long slug of coffee and stood. "None of you know anything about me or the music business. Now if you'll excuse me, I need to get some sleep before our rehearsal this afternoon. Later."

Loretta heard Paul stomp back up the stairs to his room. "What just happened here?" she asked.

"Teenage arrogance fueled by runaway testosterone," Bryan said, "mixed with a severely bruised ego. He'll be all right."

"I sure hope so," Loretta remarked, wondering whatever had happened to her little boy Pauley.

Flying Into the
Heart of Darkness

July 29: En Route Over Idaho

THEY FLEW OVER THE CLEARWATER MOUNTAINS at 13,000 feet. Hayden peered out his window at the rugged terrain below, his ears popping with the change in pressure. The 3,700 square mile River of No Return Wilderness Area stretched out in a forbidding expanse of deep canyons, fast-running rivers, dense forests, and imposing mountains.

The view was spectacular, but the bleak and unforgiving landscape unsettled him.

Why the hell did I organize this trip? I could be back home in bed with Nora. Four days and three nights out here? I must be insane. Nora certainly thinks I'm well on my way.

Hayden booked the trip in an effort to increase his T-Rex migration sample base. To this point he had just five Tyrannosaurs chipped and monitored. A statistical sampling of five animals didn't offer enough credibility to support his non-migratory theory. He needed dozens of Rexes to prove his concept. And he knew this no-man's land was where they had to go to find large concentrations of Tyrannosaurs.

But he was also here because of Jackson Lattimer.

Jack had pushed him for more than a month to make this trip. Hayden didn't want to admit his gonzo photographer friend had influenced him, but he had. The man could be most persuasive. There was something inside Hayden that pushed him to please the famous wildlife videographer. Some inexplicable itch that he needed to scratch. On a deep level, he knew Nora was right about him. Yes, Jackson was reckless and self-absorbed. Even unhinged at times. But there was something about the man that pulled Hayden in like a powerful magnetic field. Charisma? Fame? Lone wolf adventurer? Thrill seeker supreme? Hayden had analyzed the relationship from many different angles, and couldn't come up with a plausible explanation. At times he hated himself for his weakness.

But Jackson wasn't the only force pressuring him for this trip. The folks at the Smithsonian wanted more fieldwork from him, and they were the ones signing his paycheck. The Smithsonian management loved the results of his and Nora's Triceratops and Ankylosaurus outings, but they wanted more Tyrannosaurus Rex news. The big meat eaters were what their audience clamored for. Hayden liked the working relationship he and Nora had with their employers. The museum conglomerate gave them the autonomy to pick their excursions and plenty of money to carry them out. But from the beginning, when the Cretaceous meteorites came down last summer, the Smithsonian curators had pushed them hard for more Tyrannosaur encounters.

And so Hayden found himself on their new Fowler-Lemoyne Aviation Bell 407 headed into Idaho bush country where the big predators roamed.

This is a necessary expedition.

He'd been trying hard to convince himself of that ever since they lifted off the Gilliam helipad two hours ago.

The further they flew into the wilderness preserve, the more uneasy he became.

Much of the topography looked inhospitable from this vantage point. And he knew their drop-off point was near where one of Jackson Lattimer's longtime associates lost his life to a T-Rex two months ago. He tried to control his runaway fears with positive thoughts. The weather forecast for the week was good. His three crew were experienced outdoorsmen, all proficient at dealing with big game animals. Bill Carlton and Jenkins McCraw were career wildlife biologists. And Jackson Lattimer probably had more closeup experience with dangerous game than all of them combined.

He had assembled the right team for this trip.

But still, the situation unnerved him. Sleeping under the stars where they would be fresh meat for carnivores? He didn't relish the idea. His previous encounters with Tyrannosaurs had all been quick in-and-outs with no overnight campouts. Relatively safe trips.

Maybe Nora is right. Perhaps I have gone around the bend.

Jackson Lattimer's voice pulled him from his thoughts. Hayden listened in as the photographer told Carlton and McCraw tales of his recent California trip to film mountain lions.

"We managed to find four of 'em during my week out there," Lattimer said. "They're splendid animals. Very stealthy creatures."

"You got lucky," Bill Carlton said. "Cougars are elusive and solitary. Almost impossible to locate. Especially since they're nocturnal."

"Yeah," McCraw said. "I've been on a couple of those outings. Only saw one lion in almost two weeks of tracking. They know how to stay clear of humans."

"I was with an excellent guide," Lattimer said. "Guy named Benny Orton. He's been tracking cougars since he was a teenager. Good man, but crazy as a cross-eyed loon with vertigo. He knows where they hide. I got some incredible footage thanks to his expertise. But he *is* certifiable. Got one of them to charge us. Damn near shit my britches, I gotta tell ya."

The two biologists laughed. Hayden smiled. Jackson Lattimer calling anyone else crazy was farcical.

"Must've been a large cat to make you, of all people, crap your pants, Jack," Jenkins McCraw said.

"Yeah, Jenks. Plenty big. And quick. Lucky for us, we had bear repellant. Got that big cat square in the eyes before it could sink its teeth in me. Sucker came right for my throat. Got some video here if you wanna see it. I must say it's not my usual high quality. I was filming using night vision and I'm not embarrassed to admit I was shakin' in my boots. It was quite the rush, my friends."

The two biologists sat on either side of Lattimer, focused on his laptop screen, watching his confrontation with the cougar. Hayden went back to gazing out his window.

Peter's voice came over the intercom. "This is Captain Lacroix and First Officer Bing. But then, you guys already know that," he said with a chuckle. "We just passed over the Salmon River Mountains and we're dropping to lower altitude. We'll follow the river to the drop-off point, and will be touching down on a wide sandbar peninsula. We're about thirty minutes away, gentlemen. It's not that Larry and I don't love you guys, but due to the need to refuel, I'll need you to offload quickly. Please be ready."

Hayden pushed the comm button. "The dino troopers are ready, Captain," he responded, trying for a light tone even though an uneasiness bubbled in his gut.

Why am I feeling so anxious? I've faced the Cretaceous titans many times the past year. I've slayed many dragons with my tranquilizer guns.

So why am I coming undone?

Hayden wasn't superstitious. He had never bought into shadowy omens or dark portents. He'd never harbored threatening premonitions. But something about this trip felt off. The day felt out of sync. A heavy foreboding sat in the pit of his stomach like a jagged rock.

Maybe Nora's getting to me, with all her negative sass about Jack Lattimer.

Hayden tried to calm his nerves by following the Salmon River winding its serpentine path through the steep gorge. Whitewater rushed around boulders and small islets, branching off into swirling eddies and whirlpools near the banks. A couple of fly fishermen were in knee-deep water, casting their lines as though they were whipping the water.

A little farther along he was treated to a bald eagle divebombing the river. The bird struck the water with finesse and precision, plucking a fish out of the river, then winged away with the prized fish wriggling in its talons. Hayden smiled. He had seen scant few bald eagles in his travels.

He started to call out to the others about what he'd seen when a shadow dimmed the sun for several long seconds. He looked up, above the ridgeline.

He couldn't believe his eyes.

Could those possibly be pterosaurs?

They *were* pterosaurs! Flying parallel to the chopper and keeping pace. Hayden blinked a couple of times, thinking his eyes might be playing tricks on him. He refocused, counting a dozen flying in a loose formation, their distinctive head crests, long tails, and broad wingspans cutting dark outlines against the sapphire sky.

"Hey, Jack," he yelled out to Lattimer while picking up his binoculars. "Get over here with that videocam. You've got to see this."

"What is it?"

"Hurry! You don't wanna miss this!"

Noting Hayden's urgency, the other three men scrambled to his side and peered out the window, up above the ridgeline where he pointed.

"Never seen birds like those before," Jenkins McCraw said.

"They're not birds," Hayden said, scoping them with his binocs. "Believe it or not, they're pterosaurs. Flying reptiles."

"You mean like Pterodactyls?" Lattimer said, zooming in on the formation with his camera.

"No," Hayden said, adjusting the binoculars. "These are either Pteranodons or Quetzalcoatlus. Judging by their anatomy, I'm going with Quetzalcoatlus. Look at their long, telescoping necks, their sharp beaks and bony head crests. They're all wings and head. Those wingspans have gotta be fifteen feet. Maybe twenty."

"Incredible," Bill Carlton said, "Their flight pattern reminds me of albatrosses. I saw a few in New Zealand years ago."

Hayden continued to track their flight. "The million dollar question is where the hell have they been hiding? We didn't see any all last summer. And here it is almost August and this is our first sighting of them. It's really strange. This is the second new dinosaur species I've seen in the past week. Nora and I ran into a few Ankylosaurus on a T-Rex tagging trip last Wednesday. These pterosaurs had to have hatched out of one of the far-flung meteorites, maybe somewhere in this preserve."

Bill Carlton grabbed his own field glasses and scoped the

pterosaurs' flight. "It looks like most of their weight is in their wings. Not much to their bodies."

"You're right," Hayden said. "They're lightweight and stream-lined for flight. Very aerodynamic anatomy. Just enough weight on their bones to carry those massive wings. They were capable of flying long distances back in the Late Cretaceous."

Jenks McCraw said, "So why do you think none have been spotted until now, Hayden?"

"My guess is it took them more than a year to develop their wings. They were known to be omnivores so they probably lived on terrestrial plants and small prey until they were able to take to the skies. The thing that really surprises me is that they are flying as a group in a tight formation. Current wisdom in the paleo-science community is that Quetzalcoatlus were solo hunters. Most of the pterosaurs were solitary."

Peter Lacroix's voice blared from the loudspeaker. "Are you guys seeing this on our left side? What the hell are those flying things, Hayden?"

Hayden pressed the comm button. "They're Quetzalcoatlus. They disappeared from this area sixty-six million years ago in the Cretaceous-Paleogene extinction event. Could you veer in their direction so we can get a closer look, Pete?"

"I don't want to get too close. They look pretty big."

"Come on, Captain Lacroix," Lattimer urged. "I'm having to go to full zoom from here, which is blurring the image. "Have some balls and take us in closer. I need cleaner video."

Hayden pulled himself away from his binoculars and glared at Jackson, who continued shooting video. *The arrogance of the man!* Angrily, he punched the comm button. "Do what you feel is right, Pete. We don't want to create trouble for ourselves out here."

"I can take us a little closer, but we're running tight on fuel and anything much off our course might cost us."

"It's not gonna burn *that* much extra fuel." Lattimer again. "Just one passthrough to shake those birds up a little."

Hayden started to issue Jackson a rebuke when he was cut off by an extraordinary sight. The pterosaurs suddenly turned as a unit, as if controlled by a single brain, changing their course, flying directly at the chopper. It looked like an enormous dark raincloud rolling their way.

"Look at that!" Carlton said, excited, "they're coming straight at us!"

They've noticed us, Hayden thought, his mind racing. *Do they think we're a prey bird or a maternal bird?*

The intercom speakers blared static, then Peter's concerned voice: "This isn't good, gentlemen. How fast can these things fly, Hayden?"

"Uh, I seem to recall Quetzalcoatlus could reach speeds of up to sixty miles an hour."

They heard Peter say, "Hang on. We're going to try and lose them."

The chopper made a sharp turn to the right, throwing Hayden against the seats. McCraw and Carlton tumbled to the floor. Somehow Lattimer kept his footing and continued to film.

From his position stretched across the seats, Hayden saw a Quetzalcoatlus come in like a winged torpedo, its long beak snapping, its vibrant yellow eyes bulging. It hit the window at top speed with a loud, cracking *SPLAT*. Its beak shattered. The glass spiderwebbed; a spray of blood painted the cracked window an opaque crimson. The tremendous force of the blow knocked Lattimer across the passenger section, where he banged against the far wall with an *ooommph*, his videocam thumping on the floor.

Lattimer slumped against the wall, dazed, a desperate look in his eyes as he struggled to find a breath.

Several more Quetzalcoatlus slammed into the fuselage in quick succession—*CRASH-BOOM-BAM-SLAM*—each explosive impact knocking the chopper awry. Hayden clung to his seat, thinking: *These pterosaurs might be lightweight but they pack a punch. They're like small antiaircraft rockets.*

Are we going down?

The helicopter veered wildly, spinning, gyrating, doing a barrel roll, the men hanging on for dear life through the tumbling bedlam. Laptops and drinks and papers and backpacks scattered across the passenger section. Hayden saw sky, then trees, then river, then back to sky, as miraculously, Lacroix and Bing finally were able to right the craft.

But then Hayden heard high-pitched shrieks overhead as more of the flying reptiles hit the main rotor, the blades shredding the pterosaurs into a bloody spray of muscle and intestines and shreds of leathery hide that coated the viewing windows.

The engine sputtered.

The overhead rotor stalled for a few beats, then started up again.

Hayden looked up in time to see another Quetzalcoatlus come at the main rotor, hearing the beast getting sliced and diced, watching one of its amputated wings drift down to the river.

The main rotor labored through a dozen more revolutions before slowing, then dying.

Hayden realized with horror that Quetzalcoatlus body parts had jammed up the blades.

The chopper was in free fall.

Panicked screams filled the passenger section.

Hayden saw the forest fast approaching and knew they were all going to die.

The chopper skimmed over the treetops as they plummeted down a steep slope. The craft continued on for a distance before the skids caught in thick branches, flipping the aircraft end-over-end.

The noise was deafening as they bounced and lurched across the forest canopy, tree branches cracking violently against the airframe like drum rimshots.

Bodies tumbled and bounced off each other.

More terrified shouts.

Hayden heard desperate prayers to God.

Glass shattered as a stout tree limb plowed through the window, impaling Jenkins McCraw.

One final monumental slam threw Hayden against the wall.

And then all was silent.

He lay stunned, pinned against the wall by one of the tables that had broken loose from its anchor. Dizzy and disoriented, he came to the realization the wall he was pinned against was now the floor, as the copter tilted precariously on its side. The far wall had been stripped away, and he could see they were balanced on the side of a steep incline, looking down into a wooded ravine. Nothing but trees as far as he could see.

Smoke and dust drifted through the wreckage and he coughed several times, shocked when he spit out blood. His eyes burned from the smoke and he tried to wave it away but it was too thick. Visibility in here was poor.

Soon the wrecked helicopter filled with an acrid odor.

Aviation fuel.

Hayden knew he had to get out quick. Mustering all the strength he could, he pushed the table aside and stood, the effort draining him. Dizziness dropped him to his knees and he crawled to the opening, passing the body of Jenks McCraw, seeing the heavy cottonwood branch that skewered him like a shish kebab. Hayden nearly lost it seeing the biologist's vacant stare. He reached out and pulled the man's eyelids down, said a quick prayer for him.

Hayden dropped down to the forest floor, the sweet scent of pine resin a nice change from the smoky hell inside.

He felt weak and jittery, and collapsed in the loamy soil.

He tried to call out but his voice failed him.

Hayden knew he had to get as far away from the wreckage as possible, so he started crawling through the mossy earth. But he didn't get far.

When he vomited, he was alarmed to see more blood.

Maybe Nora had been right. Maybe I shouldn't have made this trip.

Subterranean Anxiety

July 29: Gilliam's Guidepost Cellar Suites
Heart Butte, Montana

PANIC HAD BRIN LACROIX LOCKED in a viselike stranglehold. She couldn't breathe. Couldn't think straight. Her heart hammered in her chest with the intensity of a locomotive piston. Her frantic mind played out numerous dark scenarios, all of them ending with the violent death of her dear Petey. Something had gone wrong. Some tragic event had befallen her husband. His luck had finally run out, she just knew it.

She had left her jewelry work in Cretaceous Cavern one floor below to come up to their Cellar apartment suite to have lunch with Peter. He was supposed to be back from his Idaho trip by noon. He and Larry Bing were supposed to be home two hours ago.

They never showed.

At two o'clock, completely at loose ends, Brin called Peter's satellite phone. No connection. Dead air. The call failed immediately, without any ringing or connectivity tones. When she'd called her husband on his sat phone in the past, it would go to a voicemail system if he couldn't answer. She'd tried Hayden Fowler's sat phone, getting the same result. She tried Peter again. Again, dead air.

Unsettled by this development, she called the Fowler-Lemoyne Aviation dispatcher, Nancy Diehl, who gave her the news Brin hoped to never hear concerning Peter.

"I'm sorry, Mrs. Lacroix, but we lost radio contact with the aircraft at nine-thirteen this morning. Attempts to reach them through cellular and satellite have been unsuccessful. We put in a call to Idaho Mountain Search and Rescue, and they are deploying search teams as we speak. I would have called you, but unfortunately I didn't have your contact information. I'm sorry."

Feeling slighted, Brin exploded. "I'm living right here in The Cellar at Gilliam's Guidepost. How hard would it have been to send someone to inform me? I mean, you said you lost them at nine-thirteen this morning. That was five hours ago!"

"I know how you're feeling, Mrs. Lacroix, but—"

"My name is Brin," she said, thinking, *She doesn't have a clue how I feel!*

"Sorry, Brin. I wouldn't be overly concerned yet. Loss of radio and phone communication is common on flights in mountainous regions."

"That might be so, but you wouldn't be calling out for search and rescue if you thought it was just shut-down communications. Not five hours after the fact. I'm *extremely* concerned, Nancy. Please! I'm about to lose my mind here."

"I understand. Please know that we are doing everything we can to locate your husband and his passengers. We've also enlisted the help of the Idaho Wing Civil Air Patrol. And we're constantly pinging the helicopter's VHF comm system for a response. Both your husband and Larry Bing are experienced pilots, and they would have sent us an emergency transmission if they were in trouble. The fact we didn't receive one means that their comm system most likely failed suddenly. I'm sure they are okay and are trying to get their radio back online."

Brin realized the woman was trying to put her at ease, but it wasn't working. The odds of two satellite phones going down at the same time the VHF radio quit were slim and none. Brin knew a lot about helicopters. She had researched them wanting to learn all she could about the dangerous aircraft Peter flew for a living. She asked, "Is the transponder sending out squawk code signals?"

Nancy Diehl delayed a beat before answering. "No."

Brin felt a hard jab in her belly. She hoped it was the baby kicking. "I know a little more about helicopters than the average person, Nancy. A dead transponder means trouble. *Big* trouble."

"Well, I won't say you're wrong. It's been a very trying day, to say the least. If it makes you feel any better, Nora Lemoyne has been notified. She's flying in from Minneapolis tonight. She'll be staying in The Cellar suites with you. You'll have company."

"I already *have* company!" she said, her anger flaring. "My mother and daughter are in the suite across the hall. You mean to tell me you contacted Nora all the way in Minnesota but no one could come out to The Cellar to let me know what was happening?"

"Look, Brin. I'm truly sorry you were left out. I'll take the blame. But you have to understand, there's been a lot going on today. I've been doing a lot of juggling, trying to keep many balls up in the air—oh, damn, sorry, wrong choice of words. Bottom line is, this was my oversight and I apologize."

Nancy Diehl sounded genuinely distraught. Brin suddenly felt sorry for the woman. She was just trying to do her job and work through a difficult situation.

"Look," Brin said. "I'm sorry I jumped on you. It's just that this is tearing me apart. I have lived with this fear for years. Helicopters are death traps."

"Well, I wouldn't say—"

"They *are*, Nancy," she said forcefully. "I know my husband is one of the best pilots in Montana, but still, it's always been a matter of not *if*, but *when* there will be an accident."

"Listen, Brin. You're all worked up and I certainly understand that. But try to relax and get some rest. I have worked with your husband at the Forest Service for a few years, and he has pulled himself out of more than a few jams. I feel quite sure he is okay and will be reporting in soon. I have your number now and I'll call you just as soon as we hear something."

"Relax? How do you expect me to relax when the love of my life—the father of my unborn child—is missing and unaccounted for? Even if he survived the crash, he's out there in the wilderness with big flesh-eating dinosaurs. I'm climbing the walls here!" Brin started to cry, deep heaving sobs.

"We don't know that the chopper crashed, Brin. You're making this harder on yourself. I know it's difficult, but it would be best for you and your baby if you laid down and did some deep breathing exercises. You said your mother and daughter are across the hall?"

"Yes."

"Why not go be with them?"

"I can't go over there. It will upset my Kimi to see me like this. To know her daddy is in trouble."

"I see. Well, just try to relax, Brin. Things are going to work out. You'll see. I'll call you when we know something."

An hour later, after much crying and many unsuccessful attempts to reach Peter on his satellite phone, there was a knock at her door.

Loretta Gilliam greeted her with a sad smile. "Hi, Brin. I thought you could use some company. I'm here for you."

Brin pulled Loretta into a hug and clutched her with a tight desperation.

Post Trafficking Blues

July 31: Rendaya Ranch
Flathead National Forest, Montana

KELTON RENDAYA WAS RELEASED FROM JAIL after paying a $10,000 fine for his animal trafficking crimes. He was acquitted, however, on the three kidnapping charges and the murder that occurred on his property. Authorities had turned up ample evidence that Thomas Hoops Terrell and two friends had committed those felonies. One find that connected Hoops and friends to the offenses was a chest of Halloween masks that Kanti Lyttle identified as being worn by her abductors throughout her captivity.

According to Kelton's lawyer, he had gotten off easy for his transgressions. Just a relatively small fine and two years' probation. Considering the magnitude of his operation, he easily could have had his ranch seized. Montana has criminal forfeiture laws that enable the state to seize properties where illegal animal trafficking has taken place. But that's only if the suspect is convicted in a criminal trial. Lucky for Kelton, the prosecutors did not want to pursue a trial. They had a bigger fish on the line for much bigger crimes. Namely Thomas Hoops Terrell.

They had nailed Hoops for the kidnappings of the three Blackfoot women, and the kidnapping and murder of Suyay Stiyak, a Salish woman whose remains had been found in the dinosaur pens. And Hoops and his buddies remained prime suspects in the kidnappings of two other Indigenous women who had yet to be located.

Hoops, the guy who's worked for me for years. The guy living in my bunkhouse for decades. The quiet one who tried to frame me. You just never know about people.

Tommy Hoops Terrell had put Kelton in a bad place. It hadn't been Tank Mahaffey after all.

Kelton shook his head in befuddlement. *This life sure does throw some sharp-breaking curveballs.*

And so the Sheriff's office in Kalispell collected Kelton's fine—which he was easily able to pay off—assigned him a probation officer, and sent him on his way.

He returned home to find a much different ranch than the one he'd been yanked out of ten days ago. The place was strangely quiet. No animal sounds coming from the barns. No bellowing of the Tyrannosaurs from out in the pens. No screeching of the Dromaeosaurs. No hogs squealing and snorting during carnivore feeds. No roar of trucks delivering exotic species to the barns and the dinosaur glen. Even the birds and squirrels and chipmunks seemed to have vanished. And he'd had to let his two new hires go, keeping Thorn as his sole ranch hand. The Rendaya Ranch had lost its vibrant heartbeat. The place was now a desiccated corpse, a skin-and-bones façade with no internal organs.

Kelton Rendaya felt as if he'd been emasculated by the Montana legal system. They had stripped him of what gave him his vitality. They had taken away his zest for life. And yet, on the other hand, he did realize he'd been supremely lucky. If things had played out differently, he could still be locked up in that claustrophobic, piss-stained jail cell in Kalispell, waiting transport to Deer Lodge and a long-term lockup in Montana State Prison. God only knew how long his sentence would have been if his part in the deaths of those North Dakota state troopers came to light. He felt blessed to have gotten away with a slap-on-the-wrist fine and a probation officer who would be mucking around in his business for two years. He could deal with that. A PO couldn't monitor him 24/7.

He was happy to be free of legal entanglements, but he was finding his new reality depressing. He now had to walk the straight and narrow path. Thinking about what lay ahead exhausted him. It would take months of hard work as a legal equine veterinarian to maintain the high standard of living he'd enjoyed with his illicit operations. Straight vet work didn't rev his motor the way trafficking exotic animals did. Working with dangerous and endangered animals was his high. His drug. He'd known for a long time that he was an addict. Only ten days gone by, and already he was having withdrawal symptoms. He wondered just how long he could hold out before returning to the dark side.

The powers that be had put a lot of pressure on him to turn over information about his animal trafficking contacts. They were especially interested in his dinosaur trade. They wanted names and locations and sales specifics. Kelton refused to give them anything. He wasn't about to become a snitch. He had spent years building relationships with expert trackers like Mick and Claire Prescott, and a dozen or more animal trappers like them. He had a long list of repeat buyers he felt obligated to protect. The feds had gleaned some information from Kelton's computers they had seized during the arrest, but it hadn't gained them much. He had always been security conscious, listing only aliases and using difficult-to-decipher code when recording addresses and phone numbers and sales transaction details.

In his more delusional moments Kelton thought of himself as noble for not cooperating with the authorities. But he knew the truth. He wasn't an honorable man. His refusal to snitch was based on more selfish motives, plain and simple. Ratting out his contacts would only hurt himself over the long haul. He knew that had he been facing a lengthy prison sentence, he would have given up his contacts in a heartbeat to cut himself a better deal.

He contemplated this ignoble side of himself as he sat in the snake barn, feeding the handful of non-venomous species left behind after the raid. The snake barn had once been his sanctuary. Now its empty gloominess only added to his depression. The place was dark, too cavernous for what little it now held. He looked around at all the empty glass aquariums and wire cages. He felt a pinch of sadness while surveying the plastic tubs along the wall containing the tools of his trade: snake tubes and hooks, venom collection containers, hypodermic needles and capillary tubes, tongs and forceps, long-cuffed gloves made of Kevlar and leather. All of it pretty much useless now that every last one of the venomous snakes had been taken away. Fifteen species, a total of 56 deadly serpents by his count, along with a couple dozen scorpions, spiders, and Gilas.

The bastards!

More than any of the other animals carted off in the raid, Kelton missed his venomous snakes—handling them, feeding them, milking them. In some strange way, it had become a sexual thing, a herpetological fetish, a secret he would take to his grave.

He heard the side door squeak open. The barn brightened. He turned to see Mark Thornberry standing by the mobile clinic van, hand resting on the attached horse trailer.

"Hey, Thorn. What gives?"

Thorn moved closer, took a seat across from him. Removed his bush hat and rolled it around in his hands as he spoke. "I visited Hoops this afternoon. He was in a talkative mood. Thought you might want to know what he said."

"Do I really want to hear this?"

"Yeah, I think you do, Kel."

"He enjoying his new accommodations?"

"Didn't seem to bother him none."

"Did the asshole show any remorse?"

"Only that they didn't get away with it. That they weren't able to collect the ransom money."

"Jesus," Kelton said, shaking his head. He had done a lot of thinking about Tommy Terrell the past few days, all of it bitter and resentful. "Did he have any explanation as to why he pulled such an idiotic stunt?"

"It was more than an idiotic stunt, Kel. It was premeditated murder. They killed that poor woman. Just threw her in that Tyrannosaur pen like she was a fast food treat and laughed about it. And now there's a good possibility that Hoops and his buds kidnapped and murdered two other Indian women."

Kelton thought about that. "Unbelievable. Tommy was a bit on the weird side, and I knew a little about his racist leanings. But I never thought it would lead to kidnapping and murder. Sweet Jesus! I pegged Tank for being capable of something like that but not

Tommy. He's done solid work for me for many years. I've known Hoops since high school—at least I *thought* I knew him. Christ," he said with a toss of his head, "I guess we can never fully know people can we?"

Thorn nodded. "Folks are complicated. Some more than others."

"What gets into somebody that makes 'em turn criminal like that, Thorn?"

"Well, they say money's the root of all evil. It certainly was in Hoops' case. He was lookin' for a big payday. Instead he got the Big *House*."

"He say why he tried to frame me?"

Thorn looked at Kelton in earnest, as if sizing him up. "Yeah, he went into a little of that with me. Said he never liked the way you treated the animals. Keepin' 'em caged up and pumped fulla drugs, then turning around and profiting off them. Said none of God's creatures should be treated like that."

Kelton felt an angry fire building in his chest. "Oh, I see. But it's perfectly acceptable to imprison and murder human beings, right?"

"I'm with you. It's fucked up."

"I loved those animals, Thorn. I fed them well and found them good homes."

"I know you did, Kel. Hoops had a skewed perspective on things."

"What we were doing here paid his salary for years. He was a big part of it. He never said a word about his discontent. He went along like everything was copacetic."

"Until he didn't. You knew he had recently become enamored with that animal rights group, didn't you? That AEF bunch that's been in the news the past year for domestic terrorism?"

"I know about it now, after Hoops' arrest. I mean, I saw that tattoo he got back a year or so ago, but I didn't think much about it. But then it all started making sense when I heard why he kidnapped the Indian women and who he went after for the ransom."

Thorn nodded. "Yeah, that rancher in Heart Butte. Gilliam. The guy that had the government-sanctioned dinosaur facility. The one the Animal Emancipation Faction shot up and torched last summer. One of the guys arrested with Hoops is a longtime member."

"You think that's what turned him? His association with that bunch?"

"No tellin', Kel. But I will say this. I've gotten to know Tommy pretty well having worked with him for so long. He's changed a lot over the past year or two. He lost both his parents. His longtime girlfriend left him. He was always quiet, but the last six months or so he's seemed different somehow. More withdrawn and sullen. More like somebody with an ax to grind."

"I didn't know any of that. He never said a word to me and I've never been one to delve into my employees' personal lives. He say anything else about me?"

"Yeah, he told me you weren't paying him enough, and that if he was gonna partake in illegal work, he should be compensated appropriately for the risk. He called you a cheap prick several times. Said the worst thing that ever happened here was when your father passed away and you took over."

Kelton's angry fire burned deep. He stared daggers at Thorn.

"Hey, don't look at me like that," Thorn said, hands raised in surrender. "I'm just the messenger here. I thought you'd want an unvarnished version of what Hoops said, that you wouldn't want me to sugarcoat it."

"You're right. Sorry. It's been a rough couple of weeks."

"It sure has."

"I never knew you and Hoops were that close, that he would confide in you like this."

"Yeah, it is kind of strange. He's always felt comfortable telling me things. Some of them more intimate than I want to hear. Maybe it's because I never lived in the bunkhouse with him. I know he didn't care much for Tank, and they've been roommates forever. Familiarity breeds contempt as they say. He was happier than I've seen him in a while when you fired Tank."

"He say anything to you about messin' with my tranquilizer chemicals?"

"Yeah. Said it was the perfect chance to frame Tank. He knew you would go after Tank for it, which you did. You didn't suspect Hoops for a second. Hell, *I* didn't suspect Hoops either. It was the perfect frame job. Too bad for him his frameup of you didn't fly. It's gonna get him a long sentence in Montana State.

"Good place for him," Kelton said, marveling at the duplicitous cunning of Hoops Terrell's manipulations. His tone turned more somber. "You been hearing any more about our North Dakota escapade?"

"No, nothing new. I've been checking nightly newscasts and googling online. It's been more than two weeks now, which is an eternity in today's accelerated news cycles. I think we might be in the clear. I hope so. I would surely be sleeping better if I knew that to be true."

"I know what you mean. Listen, Thorn. I need your word on this. If anybody approaches either of us about that night, we lie. We have never been in North Dakota, right?"

Thorn scrunched his brow in mock bafflement. "Where the hell is North Dakota?"

Kelton smiled and held out his fist. "Excellent. Are we tight on this?"

Thorn gave him a fist bump. "Yep. We're tighter than a virgin's pussy, Kel."

The Cretaceous Sisters

August 1: Gilliam's Guidepost Cellar Suites
Heart Butte, Montana

NORA WAS DOING HER BEST TO CONSOLE BRIN while working through her own hurt. Her heart was heavy, plodding, punctured. Peter and Hayden and his team had been missing for three days and the emotional pain in the Lacroix's underground suite was palpable.

Dark thoughts ripped through Nora's mind. She indulged in deep breathing exercises to chase the panic attacks she knew were lurking. Brin joined her, the two women gasping and exhaling in unison, trying to keep the bad karma at bay.

Peter Lacroix and Larry Bing had flown Hayden and his GPS tagging team into Idaho dinosaur country early Monday morning. They had lost contact an hour and a half into the flight. Now, here it was Thursday afternoon and still no word from them. Search teams called in regularly with the same bleak report: No sighting of the Bell 407 chopper; no sign of survivors or bodies. It was as if the six men had vanished off the face of the Earth. Nora imagined the River of No Return Wilderness sucking them in by way of some Bermuda Triangle astrophysics trick. She knew all about that expanse of Idaho, having researched it as a possible dinosaur preserve last year. At two-and-a-half million acres, it was the largest contiguous wilderness spread in the lower 48 states. Searching for a downed helicopter in that rugged wasteland would be a nearly impossible task. Rescuers had a good idea of where they were when they lost radio contact, but the chopper could have flown many miles in any direction while incommunicado.

Hayden dominated her thoughts. *I tried to convince him not to go, but he wouldn't listen. A very stubborn, obsessive man, he is. I should have been more demanding.*

And then there was Brinshou. Brin had spent much of the three-plus days sobbing in dramatic emotional outbursts while Nora—holding back her own tears—maintained a stoic silence. Realizing she wasn't the nurturing type, Nora knew the best thing she could do for Brin was to display a quiet strength. She remained quiet on the outside, but was at odds internally. She cursed Hayden's decision to go through with the flight. She was irritated with him for going. But then, she felt enormous guilt over being upset with her lover and business partner. After all, he could be seriously injured. Or dead. But when it came to Jackson Lattimer, she had no mixed feelings. She cursed the wildlife videographer with a vengeance, knowing there was a good chance his irresponsibility had something to do with the missing helicopter.

The first day, Nora had believed (hoped and prayed) that it was a communications breakdown on the aircraft. Some electrical malfunction or satellite glitch. But panic started creeping in the second day, her thoughts taking a gloomy turn. And now today, a dark cloud had rolled in, overwhelming her with the realization that something dire had occurred.

Nora felt weak and shaky. She wondered if she would ever see Hayden again. Or if she did, what kind of shape he would be in. One thing was sure. This experience had clarified something she'd been wrestling with for the better part of a year. She knew now that she loved Hayden Fowler. She loved him perhaps more than she'd ever loved anyone.

It has to be love, she thought. *Only love can cut this deep.*

Nora was in a bad way, yes. But Brin was worse. Peter's wife had been in a frenzied state of anxiety since the first day. When Nora flew in from Minneapolis Monday evening, Brin was unhinged. She shouted strange things about her omens coming true, ranting about how the ghosts of Gilliam's Guidepost had jinxed the flight. How malevolent spirits had doomed it to crash. Fortunately Loretta Gilliam was with her, keeping Brin from going completely over the edge, constantly reassuring her that there was not yet any evidence of a crash and that everything was going to be okay. Her beloved Petey would be back at the Guidepost soon.

Loretta, being the kindhearted and empathetic woman she was, knew Nora was also hurting, and that she was needed to comfort both women. She had stayed with them in the Lacroix family suite the past three days and nights. She'd also spelled Brin's mother Kachina, babysitting little Kimi in Brin's mother's suite so Kachina could spend some time with Brin. Loretta rightly thought that Kimi should not see her mother in this condition, and so Kimi had been kept apart from Brin. Of course, this confused Kimi greatly as she was used to being with her parents every night. The toddler questioned what was going on, wanting to know why she couldn't see her mommy. Wondering why her Aunt Loretta—as Kimi had taken to calling her—was babysitting her. The confused child made the stressful situation that much more difficult.

Nora thought, *Loretta is actually babysitting us all. She's the strong one here.*

Loretta had been through this herself. She knew about the pain of having to wait on horrific news, and was intimately familiar with heartbreaking loss. Her brother Jimmy was killed and devoured last summer by a Tyrannosaurus Rex. The same day, her husband Bryan had been gunned down off the dinosaur observation tower by the AEF terrorists and left for dead. She had spent many dreadful hours fretting about Bryan's status before learning he'd survived, albeit barely clinging to life. Her experiences made her acutely aware of what Brin and Nora were going through.

Finally, this afternoon, Brin had cried herself dry and fell into an exhausted sleep on the sofa. Nora sat at the dining room table with Loretta, both with their laptops open, working, the only sounds the clacking of fingertips across keyboards. Nora was trying to finish a chapter in hers and Hayden's book. Loretta was working on Gilliam iridium rock and Cretaceous Stone jewelry business.

Nora couldn't concentrate. She was trying to wrap up the chapter about the encounter with the Ankylosaurs, but every time she saw Hayden's name on the screen she lost focus. Would she have to finish the book without him? Would she be able to?

Oh, dear God, please don't take him from me!

She glanced at Brin, who slept restlessly, twisting and turning every few minutes under a thin blanket, letting out a soft whimper with each movement. Peter's wife was gorgeous, with her dark features and lustrous ebony hair that draped her delicately sculpted shoulders. She had that beautiful tawny satin skin that set Native women apart. Brin was blessed with favorable Indigenous genes, but to Nora's thinking, she was still a *girl.* A beautiful Kootenai girl on the verge of womanhood, yes. But still a girl.

Nora had a good fifteen years on her, and those years meant everything emotionally. Nora's career had taken her to many different parts of the globe. She had been married twice and had serious relationships with several other men in addition to Hayden. To the best of Nora's knowledge, Brin had rarely been out of Montana, growing up as she had in the sheltered confines of the Flathead reservation, and had fallen for Peter when she was very young. Brin became a mother to Kimi when most girls were still trying to figure out who they were and where they fit into this world. She really didn't have much of a chance to experience life off the reservation before being swept into marriage and motherhood. It showed in her naiveté and her occasional histrionics. And Brin's damaged relationship with her abusive father didn't help. Nora knew about that. Anyone who'd spent time at Gilliam's Guidepost knew that sad story. Nora believed Brin's father's horrible treatment of her contributed mightily to her problems with anxiety. But Brin also had a sweet, innocent quality about her that made most people love her and want to protect her. Nora had been taken with her after their first meeting, and quickly became a stand-in big sister to her.

Brin turned and lay on her back, the swell in her belly producing a small mound under the blanket. Nora was concerned for her. Four months pregnant and going through this trauma? The girl was so fragile, so full of dread and anxiety. She was what Nora's mother used to call a worry wart. Brin worried about minor things until they grew to cataclysmic proportions in her head. The slightest spasm in her ordered life always knocked her off her axis. Not good for mother or baby on the way.

What they were going through now was a major tremor and Brin certainly couldn't be faulted for overreacting. Brin's husband and Nora's lover/business partner were missing in the badlands of Idaho. It had exacted a heavy emotional toll on Brin and her both, with Loretta picking up her share of collateral damage.

If Brin loses Peter, will she also lose the baby?

Stop thinking like that, Nora, she thought, chiding herself.

"How's your book coming along?"

Loretta's voice was loud in the tomblike silence, pulling Nora out of her dark place. "Not good," she responded. "It's a tough slog without my co-author."

And then, without warning, Nora broke down, the past three days of little sleep and worry catching up with her. She closed her laptop and brought her hands up to her face, hiding her eyes as she wept, her shoulders shaking with each sob. Embarrassment tugged at her as she cried, but she couldn't stop. She had managed to keep it together through all of Brin's crying dramatics. But now she couldn't help herself, and she gave in to the tears, letting them flow down her cheeks and drip off her chin. She pulled off her tear-streaked glasses and wiped her eyes, trying to gather herself, but failing. The waterworks and snuffles wouldn't let up.

Loretta stood and came around the table to her. She wrapped her arms around Nora from behind and hugged her. Loretta's breath was warm in her ear as she spoke in a comforting whisper, "It's going to be all right, Nora dear. They're going to be okay, I can feel it. Keep the faith."

"I can't lose him, Loretta," Nora moaned between sobs. "I can't live without Hayden. I can't imagine a life without him. I *won't* live without him."

"Hey now, sweetie," Loretta cooed, sweeping Nora's hair away from her face. "We don't know anything for sure yet. Let's not jump to conclusions. Hayden's a big rugged man. He's been in some precarious situations this past year. You both have. He and you made it through those ordeals. Hayden is a survivor. So is Peter. They will endure. They all will, you'll see."

Loretta's pacifying tone soothed Nora. Loretta's confidence in the face of adversity was exactly the pick-me-up Nora needed in that moment. She stopped her sobbing and stood, turned and threw her arms around Loretta.

"Thank you," Nora said, her head nestled in the crook of the taller woman's shoulder as they embraced.

"It's going to be okay, Nora dear."

Brin came awake on the sofa and tossed the blanket aside. "Hey, make room for me," she said, coming to them and latching on, making it a three-way embrace.

The three of them remained suspended in the group hug for long moments. No words were exchanged. They made no eye contact. There was no need. They gained strength from the intimacy.

They hung on to each other for some time, none of them wanting to be the first to break away.

Nora felt greatly calmed, knowing she was in the company of two very special ladies.

Strange how a meteorite packed with dinosaur eggs had brought them together.

Nora smiled. *We're the Cretaceous Sisters*, she thought, her smile erupting into a wholehearted laugh.

"What's so funny?" Brin asked, breaking out of the hug.

Nora told them, and then all three were laughing hysterically.

The Cretaceous Sisters would get through this.

Together.

We Gotta Get Outta This Place

August 2: River of No Return Wilderness
Central Idaho

JENKINS MCCRAW, THE WILDLIFE BIOLOGIST, WAS DEAD. Five days after the crash and Peter was still haunted by the sight— Dr. McCraw impaled by a jagged cottonwood branch that burst through a hi-view window and speared him. The man had been skewered, run clean through. A horrible way to die. It all seemed like a fractured delusion, something that couldn't possibly be real.

But it *was* real.

Peter finally accepted it.

It was entirely my fault. That disturbing thought kept running through his head. A taunting chant.

They'd kept McCraw's body rolled up in a canvas tarp for four days, trying to decide what to do with him. Day after day, they thought rescue would be imminent. Then finally, yesterday, the realization sunk in that they wouldn't be getting off the side of this mountain anytime soon. Something had to be done with the body. Peter, with help from Jackson Lattimer and Bill Carlton, buried McCraw in a shallow grave deep in the forest. They'd rolled a boulder over the top of the burial site to serve as a crude gravestone, and to keep predators from digging up the corpse. They knew the longer they kept a dead body around, the more likely carrion eaters would move in.

Examining the wreckage, Peter remained amazed that any of them survived. Hayden was in the worst shape with serious internal injuries. Five days in and he was still pissing blood. Thankfully, he'd stopped vomiting up bloody globs of mucous. Peter had flown enough medevac flights to know Hayden had busted ribs and damaged kidneys. The severe bruising in his chest and abdomen indicated internal bleeding. It was unsettling to see the big man so weak and infirm. Peter knew Hayden to be a tough hombre, but feared he couldn't hold on much longer without medical assistance. Larry Bing had suffered a broken arm and shattered collarbone and could be heard groaning in pain much of the time. Miraculously, Bill Carlton and Jackson Lattimer had escaped with minor bruises and cuts. Peter himself felt lucky to get away with a sprained wrist and dislocated shoulder.

The five scruffy survivors lounged around a blazing fire in the small clearing where they had set up camp. Night had dropped like a heavy curtain, the surrounding forest gloomy and forbidding. This marked their fifth night out here in this merciless outback.

Peter found the nights out here to be unsettling. Frightening, if he was being honest. The cold. The strange noises. The ghostly shadows. The nights only intensified his uncertainty about their rescue. The previous four nights had been seemingly without end, with eerie nocturnal animal calls coming from deep in the woods and brisk winds blowing through the tightly packed trees, creating spooky flutelike sounds. The days were bad enough, but getting through the nights was the worst. Sleep was elusive in these condi- tions; any shuteye they got was a luxury.

Peter drank bad instant coffee and leaned into the fire for warmth. Mountain breezes fanned the flames, casting flickering shadows across the exhausted faces of the other four men. Three of them huddled around the fire while Hayden lay bundled up in a sleeping bag nearby. The men were battered and bruised, their faces etched with fatigue and despair. To Peter they looked like soldiers coming off a bloody battlefield in a long war. He imagined he looked equally beat-up.

He looked beyond the men, at the two tents, the sealed food bags they'd strung up in the trees to prevent hungry animals from getting at them. They'd been lucky that the originally scheduled trip called for them to camp out for four nights, so they'd had the tents and food onboard. But now, in day five, the food was nearly gone.

He fretted over how they would survive once those food bags were empty. Their potable water was low, too, but they had a nearby source of clean drinking water—a mountain stream that fed the Salmon River far below. It was a difficult hike getting to the water, however, through thick forest growth and over uneven, rocky terrain. The return trek was particularly difficult, weighted down with heavy water flasks.

For the thousandth time, Peter replayed the crash in his mind. He held himself responsible for the downed helicopter, for McCraw's death and the injuries to Larry and Hayden. Yes, Jenkins' death was due to a freak accident. But Peter thought if he had done a better job of stabilizing the aircraft, McCraw would still be alive and they'd all be back home, safe and sound.

Damn those prehistoric birds!

Why didn't I radio out when I had the chance?

Why didn't we send out the emergency beacon before our electronics failed?

Why didn't I take us down closer to the river, where the terrain was flatter and there was an easily accessible fresh water source?

Why, why, why? He continued to torture himself, questioning his piloting skills. Questioning his decisions, his lack of poise under extreme stress.

The wreckage was fifty yards up a steep incline: a heap of crushed metal, shattered Plexiglas, and twisted fiberglass rods that once served as rotor blades. All onboard electronics had been destroyed, including the two satellite phones. Jackson Lattimer's photography equipment had been smashed, but by some miracle, his main videocam had been spared, and he had been documenting their survival efforts. Fortunately, Lattimer was able to retrieve several charged battery packs, giving him plenty of power for many hours of recording time.

Less fortunate was the loss of the satchel containing GPS tracking tags. Hayden used Argos System transmitters in his dinosaur tagging work, which communicated with Argos satellites. If they had those transmitters in their possession they could activate them and search teams would have been able to pinpoint their exact location on day one. However, the satchel was nowhere to be found. They had combed the wreckage and surrounding areas thoroughly, but there was no sign of the canvas bag or any of the tiny waterproof transmitters with their short whip antennas. Peter figured they were lost when the chopper went into its rough-and-tumble barrel rolls over the treetops before finally crashing.

A mere two hundred feet from the clearing the mountainside dropped off a thousand feet or more to the Salmon River below. It was a precipitous drop, a sheer granite face that would induce dizzying acrophobia in the most experienced mountain climber. The sharp descent effectively cut them off from the river, leaving them stranded in this low mountain morass of soaring cottonwoods, Douglas fir, and ponderosa pine. They were trapped under the thick awning of trees on the side of a cliff. And the forest was much too dense to hike very far in any other direction.

Initially Peter cursed the thick, junglelike woodlands that kept them concealed and stationary. But after examining the helicopter wreckage, Peter realized the trees had saved them. Even though the chopper took on extensive damage through their intense tumbling and rolling, the treetop canopy gave them a pliable impact surface. Had they hit the solid cliff face, they would all certainly have perished.

Maybe I'm being too hard on myself. Maybe my piloting was better than I thought. Perhaps I should think of it as having saved five of us rather than killing one.

They had been lucky in another respect, too. The chopper never caught fire or blew apart. The fuel system had held tight through the forceful collisions. If it had burned or detonated, there would have been multiple fatalities. Perhaps none of them would have gotten out of here alive. Peter thanked his lucky stars he'd insisted on a durable stainless steel fuel system with aerospace-grade hoses when shopping for the chopper. The sturdy fuel line and their low fuel level at the time of impact had saved their asses.

Jackson Lattimer's ragged voice intruded on his musing. "I still say we should just torch these woods. Create a huge bonfire that can be seen for miles. Maybe then those search and rescue morons might could find us."

Since the second day, Lattimer had been on this kick of igniting a big forest fire or doing something equally drastic to attract the rescuers. His constant lecturing on this idea had worn thin with all of them.

Peter spoke up. "And just where are we supposed to go while this fire of yours burns all around us, Jack? The way these trees are packed in here, we'd never escape a fire. We'd fry before search teams would even have knowledge of a burn site. Take it from one who knows. I spent eight years flying fire patrol with the Forest Service."

"I second that emotion," Larry Bing said. "I've seen the ghastly results of out-of-control fires in my time with the Forest Service, too. I don't relish seein' another one."

Bill Carlton, on night watch tonight with a rifle across his lap, said, "Listen to them, Jackson. They know what they're talking about."

"Do they?" Lattimer snapped. "It's their goddamned fault we're stuck out here in the middle of this not-so-enchanted forest. They couldn't even deal with a few dumb birds."

"They weren't birds, Jack." All heads turned to Hayden, where he lay cocooned in his sleeping bag away from the fire. It was the first words he'd uttered since this morning. His voice was weak and wheezy. His eyes reflected the campfire, glittering like two shiny yellow marbles set deep in his bushy beard. "They're flying reptiles. Big difference from birds. Much bigger and stronger. And they aren't dumb either. Quetzalcoatlus was known to have larger brains than other pterosaurs of the time. My feeling is they are highly intelligent, especially with regards to spatial awareness. Did you see how they soared and glided? How fast they gained ground on us? It was a thing of beauty."

"It was a thing of fucking *tragedy*, Fowler," Lattimer scoffed. "If they're so damned smart, why'd they attack the helicopter?"

"I can't answer that."

"You're lying on your deathbed over there saying the things that put you there are beautiful. What the hell's wrong with you, bro?"

Jackson Lattimer had been bending their ears every day with his barbed negativity, and Peter was tired of it. "That's enough! Hayden's in no condition to take your bullshit, so lay off!"

Lattimer stood and took a couple of steps toward Peter before stopping. "I don't think you're in any position to be telling me what to do, Lacroix. You're the reason we're stuck out here. You're the reason we're all gonna die."

Carlton let out a disgusted grumble. "What the hell are you goin' on about? I recall quite clearly you demanding Peter fly us closer to those pterosaurs so you could get clearer video. If anyone put us here, it's you."

Lattimer turned to Carlton. "Really? You're gonna go there? If you'll recall, Lacroix didn't take my suggestion. He flew *away* from those creatures, and couldn't outrun 'em. This is all on him. And Bing. They were the ones flyin' that damn eggbeater."

Carlton spat in the dust. "You know, Jackson, when I first heard you would be on this trip, I was excited. I've seen your work, and it's impressive. I'll give you that. But now that I've gotten to know you, I realize you're an egotistical, self-centered, hateful narcissist. You walk around like you're some kind of gift to humanity. You might be a famous world-class photographer with thousands of followers kissing your ass. But what most of your idolizing fans don't know is what a loudmouth idiot you are. And blaming Peter and Larry for this just proves it."

"Don't you dare talk to me that way, Carlton!" Lattimer made a move toward Carlton.

Carlton raised the rifle. "Another step and I'll pull this trigger."

"You wouldn't. You don't have the balls."

"Just try me," Carlton said, standing, aiming the rifle barrel at Lattimer's chest. "You've got it all wrong. Lacroix and Bing are the reason you're still alive. The two of them are the reason we're *all* still breathing. Now sit down and zip your big mouth. I'm tired of listening to you whine."

Lattimer laughed a sarcastic laugh. His stare brimmed with animosity. "You're a fucking bozo, Carlton."

Peter spoke up, "Let's put a stop to this, guys. Put the gun down, Bill. The last thing we need is another dead body up here."

Carlton slowly lowered the rifle.

Lattimer turned to Peter. "Thanks, Lacroix."

"Not for your benefit, Jack. I just don't want to waste what little ammunition we have on your ass."

"Ooh, the vaunted helicopter pilot with the witty quip," Lattimer said to Peter with a look of annoyed amusement. He returned to his seat by the fire. "So I'm asking nicely here. What are we supposed to do? Just sit around on this godforsaken mountain waiting to die? I say we do something—*anything*—to save ourselves. I say we make an attempt to get down to the river. We're likely to run into some people on the water. We saw those fly fishermen just before we crashed. And I know there are guided whitewater rafting tours and kayakers that come through here."

Peter shook his head. "That's an impossible drop. Hayden and Larry are in no condition to even think about it. And I'm certainly not about to pull such a crazy stunt with my bum shoulder. Just have some patience, Jack. I know from experience how difficult it is to locate survivors in a wilderness this vast. But I have confidence that the search teams will find us. They'll never give up on us."

Lattimer laughed and waved an arm at Peter, as if what he just said was meaningless. "We're waiting for nothing, Lacroix. We shot off the last of our flares a couple days ago when we saw those jet planes. We've strung up mirrors and pieces of Plexiglas in the treetops as reflectors. We've yelled and screamed until we're hoarse. Shot off our guns. Nothing's worked. The searchers haven't picked up on any of it. Let's face it. They aren't gonna find us. We've gotta make a move on our own. Just saying."

"Bitch, bitch, bitch, Lattimer," Bill Carlton said. "You wanna try negotiating that cliffside down to the river, be my guest, fool. It's a death wish if you ask me. You might even win the Darwin Award. Of course, you wouldn't be alive to accept it, but—"

"*Darwin Award?*" Lattimer sneered at Carlton. "You gotta be fuckin' kidding me, Carlton." He looked from Peter to Larry Bing, then back at Carlton. "Christ, you guys are all pantywaists. You'd rather sit up here waiting for the Grim Reaper than take action."

"No one's stopping you," Larry Bing said. "Go right ahead. I just hope your life insurance premiums are paid up."

Lattimer let out a frustrated sigh. Rubbed his hands together close to the fire to warm them while he stewed and mumbled.

The five of them lapsed back into silent reflection. The sounds of nature intensified. The river murmured and hissed. Crickets chirped their scratchy melodies. Cicadas buzzed in a constant drone. A pair of owls hooted in call-and-response communication. Coyotes howled in the distance, their cries mournful and alien.

Peter's thoughts drifted to Brin. His wife had dominated his thinking since he'd climbed out of the wreckage. He worried about his emotionally delicate wife and her health, four months pregnant with their unborn child. He could only imagine what she must be going through. She had never handled adversity well. He recalled her mental breakdown last summer when he was gone for three weeks flying meteorite roundup missions for the Air Force. And she *knew* where he was then. She had no clue what had happened to him on this trip, and Peter knew she would immediately think the worst. This would indeed be a profound challenge for Brin, a draining, emotionally crippling ordeal. Knowing this made him sad.

He also fretted about his young daughter, Kimi, who was too young to comprehend the situation. How could Brin possibly explain this to their two-and-a-half year old?

Peter wasn't sure he believed in God, but he prayed for Brin and Kimi several times a day. Prayed for some higher power to keep them safe and in a positive mindset, to convince them that he would be back home with them soon.

He also prayed to the search and rescue gods to please hurry up and locate the five of them, get them off this windblown, desolate mountain.

Peter looked across the fire and locked eyes with Larry Bing. Larry's boyish, ruddy face took him back to last summer, when they were paired up flying that ancient bucket of bolts Sikorsky S-70 chopper, searching for Cretaceous meteorites for the U.S. Air Force. Peter remembered the horror of being informed that one of the other

Sikorskys had crashed out here in this same Idaho wilderness. A fellow pilot, Blair Minsinger, had been killed when their chopper slammed up against a rock facing. The co-pilot on that flight, Rusty Cavanaugh, survived the accident and spent a week out here in this uninhabited wasteland, alone, running from hungry Tyrannosaurs. Through sheer determination he managed to evade the beasts and was picked up twelve miles from the crash site seven days later. Cavanaugh had a lengthy hospital stay, but he eventually got back home to his wife and newborn son. Peter thought it would take Herculean strength, enormous courage, and an iron will to survive out here alone with prehistoric carnivores chasing you.

He looked around at the other four faces illuminated by the fire. He was pretty sure he'd never be able to survive out here alone. There was comfort in going through this hellish experience with others, even if one of them was Jackson Lattimer.

Brin had never been comfortable with Peter's profession. She had made that abundantly clear early in their relationship. And when she heard about the crash that killed three men and sent Rusty Cavanaugh running for his life, she stepped up her efforts to persuade him to find a new career. She fed him articles about the dangers of rotary wing aircraft, the statistics of helicopters going down in flight, thinking that type of raw data would sway him. But it didn't. It only angered him. He knew she was only looking out for him and trying to protect their family. But Brin's stern determination in influencing him away from the piloting life he loved drove a wedge between them, and marked one of the few difficult stretches in their marriage.

And now, *this*.

His chopper taken down by a dozen pterosaurs. Quetzalcoatlus is how Hayden identified them. Life had become weird and hugely unpredictable since those Cretaceous meteorites had come down.

Maybe Brin has been right all along.

Maybe I've just been extremely lucky to this point.

Maybe she was right with her *It's not if, but when* philosophy.

He realized it was Brin's way of loving him.

Oh, darling, I'm so sorry I was ever angry at you.

A warming rush of love for his wife overwhelmed him.

Hang on, my darling Brinny. I'm coming home to you and Kimi soon.

They had a house to buy and a baby on the way. He vowed to keep himself alive to see that through.

Suddenly, a muffled chorus of warbling chirps punctuated by sharp clicks resonated deep in the forest. Peter shivered.

"They're back," Jackson Lattimer said.

"Who's back?" Peter said, listening for a few long seconds. "Tyrannosaurs?"

"No," Peter heard Hayden say. "Those chirps and clicks are Dromes . . . Dromaeosaurs."

"They're closer than they were last night," Carlton said, aiming his rifle at the woods.

"Last night?" Peter said. "You heard them last night?"

Lattimer nodded. "Yeah. You were in dreamland, Lacroix. You missed out on all the fun."

The men listened attentively for several long minutes, the shrill chirp-clicks seeming to be closing in.

Jesus, will this nightmare never end? Peter thought.

Jittery, he got up and went inside one of the tents, grabbed the other rifle and checked to ensure it was loaded.

He came back out into the firelight, the Ruger feeling strange in his hands, a foreign object.

He hated guns, but this was survival.

Continuing Education

August 3: Gilliam's Guidepost
Heart Butte, Montana

SUNDAY EVENING. BRYAN AND LORETTA were in the den, enjoying their first night together in nearly a week. Bryan stretched out on the sofa, drinking a beer, watching the national news, with Loretta nestled in her easy chair, reading a novel, *Hello Beautiful* by Ann Napolitano. Muffled clips of music—thumping bass and drums and soaring guitar riffs—drifted in from the rehearsal barn. Paul and his Moonrise bandmates were really into it tonight.

Loretta had spent much of the week out in The Cellar suites with Nora and Brinshou, trying to comfort the two distraught women whose men had been missing in the Idaho wilderness since last Monday. Bryan knew his wife was doing a good thing, especially for Brin Lacroix. He knew Brin to be a good person with a sweet disposition, a talented jeweler, caring mother, and amazing cook of delicious Kootenai dishes. But she had a brittle, sensitive side, a neediness that required much tender loving care. Loretta had been providing that for her this week.

Bryan loved Loretta for her kindhearted compassion. He appreciated what she had been doing for Brin and Nora, but he was overjoyed to have her back in the house with him. He'd missed her, particularly during the long nights, finding it hard to fall asleep without her lying next to him, cuddling with him, engaging in pillow talk, making love to him. Loretta's presence calmed him, made him feel in the moment and whole. She had that effect on him.

Exhaustion seeped through every bone and muscle in his body. He (and Loretta) had been on an emotional roller coaster the past

ten days. The ride started with Kanti Lyttle's rescue and the jailing
of her abductors. Then came eldest son Paul's news that he planned
to skip his senior year of high school to go on the road with his band.
And finally, Monday, they had learned of the strange disappearance
of the new company helicopter. The status of Peter Lacroix and
Hayden Fowler remained unknown. Two good people representing
half the executive board of Fowler-Lemoyne Aviation gone in a
flash. Two people who had become their close friends were missing.
It was a kick in the teeth that had fully depleted Bryan. Loretta,
strong as she was, wasn't faring much better. And to further pierce
their tenuous emotional state, son Paul had been giving them the
cold shoulder the past few days. The stress over the past week and
a half had worn them both to a frazzle.

NBC news anchor Lester Holt drew their attention to the
flatscreen TV. The newscaster switched from coverage of the presi-
dential election to a story hitting closer to home.

"More alarming news about the latest craze that has become
the rave out west—snorting Triceratops horn powder, known
in drug circles as tri-horn huffing. Three more deaths attributed to this dangerous practice have been reported, two in
Montana and one in Wyoming. This brings the total to seven
people who have lost their lives to horn-powder huffing the
past month.

"The deadly trend started in early June when an internet
influencer proclaimed that the horns of the Cretaceous Triceratops, when crushed into powder form, provides a powerful aphrodisiac and hallucinogenic high that, and I quote here,
'will lift your libido to new heights and send you on a beautiful
psychedelic trip—kind of like taking Viagra and Ecstasy
together,' end quote. This drug is being sold online by
unscrupulous dealers for big money. But buyer beware.
Chemists with the Food and Drug Administration have
identified dangerous levels of dioxin and microbial toxins in

the horns, the toxicity of which rivals fentanyl. The FDA, in conjunction with the Department of Health and Human Services, has issued a stern public service warning, stating that tri-horn huffing is known to cause serious illness and death. And as a side note, we here at NBC News must inform you that it is illegal to kill Triceratops as they have recently become a federally protected species. Doing so can bring heavy fines and possible jail time . . ."

"Jesus, kids these days. Am I right?" Bryan said. "They'll take anything to get high. In our day we just had to worry about crystal meth and cocaine. There was no fentanyl back then."

Loretta's mouth curled in a halfhearted smile. "You're forgetting heroin, but I get your point. They're *all* bad drugs. We need to talk to the kids about this tri-horn huffing business."

"Yeah, for sure."

"When are we going to talk with number one son about his poor decision? About dropping out of school?"

"When he comes in from rehearsal. We're still in agreement about what we're willing to do, right, Lor?"

"Absolutely. It's a win-win for all of us. It's an offer Pauley won't be able to refuse."

"Uh, it's Paul now, remember?"

"Oh that's right." Loretta grinned. "He's a grownup now. How quickly I forget."

Bryan chuckled. "Yes indeed. A legend in his own mind."

That got both of them laughing.

He looked back at the TV. Lester Holt had switched to coverage of the missing helicopter:

". . . Idaho search and rescue teams are still hunting for the Fowler-Lemoyne Aviation helicopter that disappeared July 29th. Today marks day six of the search for survivors in the desolate outback of the Frank Church River of No Return Wilderness. Onboard were two celebrities: bestselling author, paleontologist and dinosaur tracker, Hayden Fowler, and Jackson Lattimer, known worldwide as America's Gonzo Shutterbug, the risk-taking videographer celebrated for his daring wildlife films. The team of six men were headed into the central Idaho badlands to track and tag Tyrannosaurs when their helicopter lost communications and went missing. We go now to Vaughn Hillyard, who interviewed Idaho Mountain Search and Rescue Incident Commander Chris Wilmer in Boise earlier this morning.

Field correspondent Vaughn Hillyard stood in front of a large yellow helicopter holding a microphone. Next to him was a tall wiry man with a broad chest and a sweeping handlebar moustache.

Vaughn Hillyard: I'm standing here with Incident Commander Chris Wilmer, the man heading up the search for the missing Bell 407 helicopter and its two pilots and four passengers. The vanished helicopter left Heart Butte Montana last Monday morning and lost communications in the skies over central Idaho a couple of hours into the flight. Commander Wilmer, could you please give us an update on your search?

Christopher Wilmer: Certainly. It's been a difficult task to say the least. The forestlands are extremely thick this time of year and it's tough to get a good view of what's underneath the canopy. The woodlands out here have a long history of swallowing up downed aircraft. Quite a few miles of the Salmon River is under cover as well. Add to that the rugged terrain and lack of safe landing zones, and you've got a hugely challenging mission. We also have only a vague idea of where they went down, which means we have had to cover hundreds of square miles. We've brought in the Idaho Wing Civil Air Patrol and their blackwater dive and salvage-dragger teams to search lakes in the area, most specifically Moose Lake, which is eighty to a hundred feet deep. We've also been utilizing the Idaho Air National Guard with their fixed wing aircraft fleet.

They have been very helpful. So far no success. But we'll find 'em. We always do. We have the experienced personnel and proper aircraft, like this specially equipped UH-60 Black Hawk chopper behind us, which is designed for mountainous terrain search and rescue. We have three of these out on daily search. The Black Hawk is the best SAR helicopter in the business.

Vaughn Hillyard: SAR helicopter?

Christopher Wilmer: Yes. Search and rescue helicopter.

Vaughn Hillyard: Thank you for that clarification. This is the sixth day the men have been missing. In your experienced opinion, what are the chances that any of them are still alive?

Christopher Wilmer: That's a difficult question to answer. It really depends on what happened to the chopper. Whether it crashed or just lost power and ended up buried under the forest overstory. We're told their excursion into the Idaho backcountry was to tag Tyrannosaurs as part of Doctor Fowler's dinosaur migration study. Their planned stay was four days, so their food and water supply would last them at least that long. I say their chances of survival are quite good, depending on the severity of the aircraft's malfunction. Of course, there is always the possibility they'd have to tangle with dinosaurs. But seeing that Hayden Fowler and his team of wildlife biologists have experience with those creatures, I'd say their chances are still quite good. We do need to find them soon, however, as I'm sure their food and water are severely depleted.

Vaughn Hillyard: Yes, it has to be a most challenging effort. Can you tell us a little about your air search procedures?

Christopher Wilmer: Sure. The helicopter is a bright candy apple red. Glittery metallic paint. Very unusual color scheme for a corporate copter. Should be easy to spot in all that greenery, like looking for a ripe tomato in a bed of lettuce. But so far it's been elusive. It tells us they went deep into the underbrush. We have the best technology available for this type of backcountry search. We use sophisticated infrared cameras to pick up heat signatures. We also employ GMTI radar—Ground-Moving Target Indicator radar—to detect moving targets on the ground. Additionally we fly at various altitudes looking for reflections, and we've picked up a few, but they turned out to be the sun playing tricks on us . . ."

Bryan shut off the TV with a flourish. "I can't take any more. It's only adding to my concern."

"Thank you, honey," Loretta said. "I've had enough myself."

"So, do you think they're still alive, Lor?"

She took a deep breath. "I'll tell you what I've been telling Nora and Brin. We have to keep the faith."

"How is Brin holding up?"

"She's doing better. She got back with her daughter this afternoon. Kimi seems to be a good pick-me-up for Brin, but the child is confused as hell about what's going on."

"Understandable."

Loretta started to say something more, but stopped, a troubled look flashing in her eyes.

"What? What's wrong, dear?"

She hesitated, looking away from him, as if contemplating how much she should say. "I wasn't going to bring this up, but it's been eating at me. Brin has been saying some strange things, Bryan."

"Yeah? Like what?"

"Saying the Guidepost is haunted, that the ghosts of last summer are inflicting their negative karma on us. That these ghosts caused the helicopter crash."

"We don't know that the chopper crashed, Lor."

"I know that and you know that, but there's no convincing Brin. I have to say, it hurts me the way she's dredging up our tragedy last August as an explanation to why her husband is missing and presumed dead."

"We don't know that anybody's dead yet, either."

"Brin has jumped to that conclusion. I don't know, Bryan, but it feels like she's blaming us for whatever's happened to Peter. It makes me angry. I know she's not in her right mind with what's happened. She's not herself. I don't think she understands how she's coming across. But as much as her comments rankle me, I can't let my anger show. It would destroy her right now if I lost control of my emotions, and that's the last thing I want to do to the poor girl. She's going through a serious trauma and I want to support her in her time of need, but all of this is really weighing on me, Bry."

"You're doing a good thing, Loretta. You can be proud of that. And I'm sure deep down, Brin appreciates you being there for her. We're all hurting over this. I know it's hard, but we have to remain solid for Brin's sake. How is Nora taking this?"

"She's had her weepy moments. It's obvious how much she loves Hayden. Nora's not her usual confident self, but she's hanging in there. She's a strong woman. Very independent."

"Yes she is. You never answered my earlier question, Lor."

"What's that?"

"Do you believe they're still alive?"

She gave him a long, penetrating look. "Yes, I do. We *have* to believe, don't we?"

Bryan started to respond, but stopped when he saw Lianne enter the room with a long yawn. She looked tired and irritable in her horse print pajamas. Her bare feet swished across the hardwood floor.

"I can't sleep, Mama," she said, going to Loretta and standing beside her chair.

"What's the problem, sweetie?" Loretta said, fluffing her hair.

Lianne leaned into her mother. "I'm worried about Uncle Peter."

Lianne had started referring to Peter as her uncle shortly after the Lacroix family moved to the Guidepost. Their relationship had bloomed quickly, with Lianne teaching Peter how to ride a horse, and he taking her for helicopter rides, answering her many questions about piloting a chopper. Bryan thought his daughter might be seeing Peter as a replacement for Lianne's late Uncle Jimmy. He was happy that Lianne had picked a good role model in Peter. But he knew Lianne calling anybody uncle other than Loretta's late brother made Loretta sad.

"Uncle Peter is fine, Lee-lee," Loretta said, pulling her up in the chair and onto her lap. She kissed the side of Lianne's head, brushed back a wisp of her hair. "He'll be back soon, darling."

"He promised me he'd go riding with me, Mama. I even got Blackie ready for him. Combed him real good and gave him a bath. And my Beau really needs to get out of the barn."

"I know, sweetness. I promise, Peter will be back home soon. I'm sure he hasn't forgotten about riding with you."

"How do you know that? It's been a week and you said he hasn't called."

Loretta stole a glance at Bryan, then said, "How about I go riding with you tomorrow, Lee? I'll ride Blackie and you can take Beauregard out for a good run."

"No! Blackie is Uncle Peter's horse! *Clancy* is your horse."

"All right then. I'll take Clancy. No worries, Lee-lee. We haven't ridden together in a long time. It'll be nice."

"Yes it will. But I still miss Uncle Peter."

"I know you do, baby." Loretta stroked Lianne's shoulder and pulled her close. "I'm sure he misses you, too, and he'll be in a hurry to get back here to see you. He told me before he left that you're his favorite niece."

Lianne pulled back, looked at her mother doubtfully. "Did he really say that, Mama?"

Loretta nodded and winked at her.

Lianne grinned.

Bryan noticed the Cretaceous necklace around Lianne's neck, the black stone pendant flopping against her pajama top as she moved. He said, "Hey, Lee, I see you're wearing the necklace I gave you. First time I've seen it on you this summer. What gives, baby?"

Lianne glanced at the pendant dangling from the silver chain as if she had just discovered it. She fondled the black stone as she said, "This is to keep Uncle Peter safe. Since Aunt Brinny made it and she is married to him, I think it will give him special powers."

"Yes it does have special powers, Lee. I told you that when I gave it to you."

"I'm sorry it didn't work for you, Daddy. But it'll work for Uncle Peter. I just know it will."

The innocent apologetic look on his daughter's face made Bryan want to cry sentimental tears. *Too bad she can't remain eight years old forever.*

"Are you okay, Daddy? You look funny."

"Yes, I'm fine, sweetcakes," he said with a sniffle and a wipe of his eyes. "Why don't you come give me a goodnight hug. You're gonna need a lot of sleep if you're going horseback riding with your mother tomorrow. You'll need your energy to keep up with her. She's a hard riding cowgirl once she hits that saddle," he said with an impish grin directed at Loretta.

Loretta rolled her eyes as Lianne got down out of the chair and went to him, threw her thin arms around him and hugged him tight. He breathed in her pleasing scent: lavender and baby powder from her nightly bubble bath.

"Goodnight, Daddy. See you in the morning, Mama," she said, then scampered up the stairs to her bedroom.

"Did Peter really say that, Lor?"

"Say what?"

"That Lee-lee is his favorite niece?"

Loretta shook her head. "Peter is quite taken with Lee but he never said anything specific like that, no. But it's a moot point because I don't believe Peter has any real nieces."

Bryan drank his beer, thinking, then said, "You know you're setting Lee up for a heavy fall, don't you? I mean, what if the worst has happened and Peter never comes back? That will crush our girl. Especially after what happened to Jimmy last year."

Loretta grimaced at the mention of her brother. It had slipped his mind that he was not supposed to bring up Jimmy Enright's name in her presence. It was part of her (their) yearlong therapy.

She ignored Bryan's misstep, saying, "You sound like you've given up on Peter and Hayden."

"No, it's not that. I just don't want to see Lianne hurt again. Lee went through more last summer than any child her age should have to go through. What happened to me, and especially to Jimmy, was enough for a lifetime of therapy for her. I don't want to pile on top of that in case we learn the worst has happened."

"You're overreacting, hon. I was just trying to comfort her, to get her to go back to bed."

"I know. But you were telling her things that aren't true, or *might* not be true. You were getting her hopes up, and that has a way of backfiring."

"Lianne will be fine, honey. She's a lot more resilient than you give her credit for."

"She's at a very impressionable age, Lor. We have to be careful how we handle her."

Loretta let out a flustered sigh. "How is what I said to her any different than you telling her that necklace has special powers that will protect her and the people she loves?"

"That's different."

"Is it? My point is that we both tell the kids half-truths and lies to get them through. We've done that since Pauley was a little tyke. We did it for Ethan and now we're doing it for Lianne. We deceive them to build their confidence, to protect them and give them a sense of security in this uncertain world. I'm not saying it's right but I think most good parents do it. Don't you?"

A long guzzle of Coors, then, "Yeah, I guess you're right. We parents are the great deceivers, aren't we? Santa Claus, the Easter Bunny, the Tooth Fairy? Damn we're such good liars!"

Paul entered the room, halting further conversation. He carried his guitar case and walked briskly, avoiding eye contact.

Bryan said, "You guys were sounding good out there tonight."

"Thanks," the boy said, walking through the den.

He had reached the hallway when Bryan said, "Your mother and I have stayed up late because we want to talk with you."

Paul stopped and hunched his shoulders, his back to his parents. "Jesus. Again?" He turned to face them. "What about this time?"

"About your plans to quit school."

"We already discussed that. I told you what I'm gonna do, so it's a waste of time if you think you can change my mind." He spun and moved into the hallway.

Loretta said, "I think you're going to want to hear what your father has to say, Paul. I believe it's something you will like."

Bryan watched as Paul shrugged in an agitated gesture. Heard him take a deep breath, then come back into the den and set his guitar case on the floor. "Okay, talk to me, Pops. I'm all ears."

Bryan sat up, patted the place beside him. "Come, have a seat."

Paul hesitated, then reluctantly flopped down on the far end of the sofa. He flipped his long brown hair out of his eyes and crossed his arms, waiting with a bored, put-upon expression.

"How's the band doing these days?"

He looked at Bryan. "Moonrise is cookin'."

"How're things with your girlfriend, Sinopa?"

"Sin and me are fine."

"Is she part of the band now? You told me she wanted to be."

"She's our backup singer—singing the high harmony parts. Banging the tambourine, shakin' the maracas. The guys are cool with that because it makes us sound better. Look, Dad, we both know this isn't what you wanted to talk to me about. I'm like, really exhausted, so why don't you get to the point."

"Okay, fair enough. I'm gonna lay it on the line, Paul. I know how much your music means to you, but you need to finish out your education—"

"No way! I'm not—"

"Wait. Just hear me out, please," Bryan said, holding up his hand. "You have a real gift, and we want to nurture that gift. We want you to succeed in a big way. Your mother and I have agreed to fund your music exploits if you stay in school and earn your high school diploma."

That got the boy's attention. "Fund my music how?" he asked.

"We'll pay for all the studio time you need to record your first album. We'll hire a top-notch publicity agency to get your name out to the world. We'll buy you guys newer and better equipment."

Bryan could tell Paul was gobsmacked, though his son was trying hard not to show it. "That sounds like, way too good to be true. What's the catch?"

"You've got to stay in school and focus on your studies, maintaining a B or better grade average. You fall below a B average, we cut off your funding."

Paul considered that. "What about touring?"

"No touring. Just local gigs and occasional weekend travel. You've got to be home to attend classes and concentrate on getting your homework done."

"That won't work, Dad. My manager has got us booked into those bigtime venues I told you about."

"Well, you're gonna have to say adios to your manager if you want our deal, Paul."

"What? We need management to oversee all the shit we don't have time to handle. Who's gonna manage our bookings?"

"We are. Your mother and me."

Paul let out an derisive laugh. "You two?" he said, looking at Loretta. "No offense, but what do you guys know about managing a rock band?"

"It'll mostly be me managing you," Bryan said. "Your mother will handle the band's accounting and paperwork."

Paul shook his head, exasperated. "You're delusional, old man. You're a broken down old rancher mechanic who doesn't know a damned thing about the rock n' roll world. How in the hell are you gonna take Moonrise to the top? How are you gonna make us famous?"

Loretta spoke up, fire in her eyes. "Don't you *dare* talk to your father that way, young man! We're offering you a deal I'm sure any young band would kill for, so how about showing some respect."

"It's okay, Loretta," Bryan said, maintaining his cool on the outside even though he was seething inside. Paul had certainly learned how to push his buttons. "You might know all about rock music and how to play it, but you know nothing about business. That's where I come in. That's where I can be the most help. I've succeeded at many business endeavors over the years, and I guarantee you I'll make Moonrise a success."

"How? What're you gonna do for us, Pops?"

Christ, the arrogance of my first born!

He began the monologue he'd been rehearsing the past couple

of days. "One thing I plan to do is capitalize on our family name. In case you forgot, we Gilliams are already famous. You overlooked that little nugget, my friend. You missed that opportunity. Every week I turn down maybe a half dozen interview requests from major news outlets. People are interested in us because we discovered the first dinosaur meteorite. We were the first humans to encounter Dromaeosaur hatchlings and had the first officially sanctioned dinosaur zoo. We hosted world famous paleontologists and geologists and paleobiologists. There still remains a national curiosity about us Gilliams, and I plan to put you and Moonrise front and center in our story. Because you see, son, everything in the business world—hell, everything in *any* world—is a story. The more intriguing we make our story, the more interest it generates. Subsequently interest generates sales. Sales mean success in our capitalistic culture. And success builds upon itself. Entertainers like Taylor Swift and Beyoncé and Oprah Winfrey and the Kardashians have it down to a science, and so do I. You've seen the heights your mother and I have taken our Cretaceous Stones jewelry line to, right? You can't do better than your mother and I for your management needs, Paul." He stopped when he noticed Paul snickering. "What's so funny?"

"You had me until the Kardashians. *Really,* Dad?"

Bryan cracked a smile. "Hey, they make tons of money with literally no talent other than being accomplished storytellers. This is one great country, isn't it?"

That elicited a laugh from Loretta.

Paul said, "What about after high school?"

"What about it?"

"Do I have to go through four years of college to keep your deal?"

"How about we just take this one year at a time."

Paul looked around the den, thinking. Finally he said, "How are you gonna pay for all this? It's gonna cost like, eons of dollars."

Bryan saw no upside to informing their children about the millions they had won in their civil lawsuit. The kids were already spoiled enough. Knowing about the wealth they were sitting on wouldn't help them.

"You just study hard and continue playing good music and let us handle the money. So what do you say, Pauley, er, I mean Paul? Are you ready to start using the Gilliam name to take Moonrise to the top of the Billboard charts?"

Paul stood, grabbed his guitar. "I'll have to think it over."

"*What?* What the hell, son!"

"I'm too exhausted to make a decision tonight. And it's not just me. I've gotta talk it over with Sin and the guys. You and Mom should get some sleep. You're like way too old to be up this late."

They watched Paul leave the den.

Bryan was furious. "Of all the ungrateful—"

"Easy, Bry," Loretta said, coming to him, pulling him up from the sofa and wrapping her arms around him. "He'll come around. You'll see."

"We give the boy Fort Knox on a silver platter festooned with a golden bow and he says he'll have to think about it? What the hell, Loretta!"

"C'mon, love," she said, caressing his back. "It's late, but not too late for some things we're still young enough to do, if you catch my vibe."

He pulled back and looked at her, seeing the hunger and desire there, the excitement dilating her dark brown eyes.

"I do believe you're singing my song, Loretta."

Stalked By Dromes

August 4: River of No Return Wilderness
Central Idaho

HUNGER IS A RAVENOUS BEAST. IT GNAWS at your gut like a tenacious rodent, stripping away your strength and resolve as it consumes your being.

Jackson Lattimer felt that bloated hunger rat going to work on his insides. His stomach rumbled and grumbled in a grinding ache. He sat by the fire, waiting out another long, cold night. He couldn't recall ever being this hungry, not even on that trip to Botswana's Okavango Delta, filming giraffes and cheetahs, when their caravan had been stranded on the savannah for three days due to an early summer flash flood.

That was bad, but this was worse.

They'd consumed the last of their food two days ago. Their water was getting low, too, here on day seven of this hellish ordeal. Someone would have to make the arduous trek to the stream soon to fill up the nearly empty flasks. There were no volunteers. None of Jackson's fellow survivors wanted to leave the relative safety of the campsite. Fowler and Bing got a pass as they had been laid low by serious injuries. But Lacroix and Carlton were another story. They'd been hearing dinosaur calls from across the ridge and deep in the woods, and they were scared like the frightened girly-girls he knew them to be. They were both in good enough shape to make it to the stream and back, but both claimed their wounds and lack of sleep had sapped them of the strength needed to make the hike through the dense brush. Lacroix argued he couldn't carry heavy containers of water with his shoulder banged up the way it was.

How fucking lame is that?

Jackson had made the last water run the day before yesterday, getting severely raked by thimbleberry thorns and stinging nettles. His arms and legs still itched from those damned nettles. Reminded him of when he'd suffered through shingles in his thirties. He had done his part. Now it was somebody else's turn to be the water boy.

Lacroix and Carlton are pussies. Cowards. Afraid of their own shadows. I've survived in much worse places than this—some of the most inhospitable places on the planet.

Their need for water was crucial. Add to that they were going to have to find another food source soon. Starvation would bring all five of them down if they had to depend solely on the blackberries and mountain huckleberries that grew wild near the camp.

It pissed him off that the others left it up to him to make the trips to the stream. They were probably waiting for him to do something about their food shortage, too. Yes, he was in far better physical condition than Lacroix and Carlton. He was much better acclimated to the rugged wilderness. But that didn't give them the right to dump everything on him. They needed to start pulling their weight.

Jackson's mouth was parched, his throat dry and scratchy. The cold stung his hands and feet. He guessed it was around fifty degrees, but the brisk mountain breezes chilled him to the bone. What he wouldn't give for a bottle of premium scotch right now.

He observed the others sitting around the fire. There was no conversing; talking would only deplete what little energy they had left. Carlton, Lacroix, and Bing stared into the fire, mesmerized by the dancing flames. Dull, empty expressions marked their grimy, scarred faces. Carlton, leaned into the fire, cradling his rifle like it was a severed appendage. The son of a bitch had dared to call him out two nights ago. Fuck him! Who the hell was he, anyway? A wildlife biologist. What the hell was that? Probably spent all his time in an air-conditioned lab. And self-righteous ex-jock, Lacroix, regarding the Ruger in his hands as if it was an alien object. How could anyone who was afraid of guns call themselves a man? Jackson hadn't changed his mind about Lacroix being the reason they were stuck in this hellhole thicket of woods on the side of a cliff. The others defended Lacroix but Jackson knew the truth. A skilled pilot would have been able to avoid this shitstorm. Larry Bing was just as much to blame. He was propped up, back against a cooler, his arm and shoulder heavily taped in a temporary sling/cast. Jackson was sick of them. Entitled elitists, all three of them. Quitters ill equipped to handle the rugged challenges of outdoor survival. Sorry excuses for the male of the species.

The only real men here are me and Fowler, he thought, looking beyond the fire at Hayden, cocooned in a sleeping bag near the tents.

Why couldn't it have been one of these other clowns who suffered the brunt of the crash? Why did it have to be Fowler?

Jackson would have left these losers days ago had it not been for Hayden. He couldn't leave his brother from another mother out here to die. It wouldn't be brotherly. Wouldn't be *manly.* Jackson vowed to see this thing through, whatever that brought.

He worried constantly about his paleontologist friend. Hayden was in a bad way and needed a doctor. Jackson got up and went to check on him, the night air chilling his fire-warmed face.

"How're you doin', bro?" he said, blowing into his hands and taking a knee next to Hayden's bedroll.

"Really . . . sick," Hayden spluttered, his voice weak. "Putrid. Feel like I have to, um . . . die to feel better."

Hayden's face was contorted into a pale gray mask of pain. He had worsened from this afternoon. His eyes were glazed. His cheeks and forehead had a ghostly pallor to them. Even his beard looked stringy and dead, like a tumbleweed had blown in and landed on his face. It alarmed Jackson to see this usually cocksure, self-confident man laid so low.

"You're not gonna croak, Fowler. You hear me? I won't let that happen. We've got a lot more tyrant lizards to track down in our future, you and me."

"Yeah, whatever you say, Jack." Hayden grabbed Jackson by the arm in a desperate, palsied clench. "Promise me, Jack. If you get off this mountain without me, please tell Nora I'll love her always."

"You can tell her yourself, dude. You and me, we're getting out of here together. Our fans would be lost without us."

"Our *fans* . . . yeah," Hayden replied with a weak snicker.

Jackson looked around the clearing. "You know, I'm kicking myself for not bringing my Godfather OG along. Havin' a weed stash out here would sure make this place more tolerable."

Hayden offered up a strained smile. "I dunno. Probably just make me more paranoid."

"Yeah. I remember how wonky you were the night we indulged in some Godfather fun at my house. You'd think you were doin' acid the way you acted, seein' happy trails and things melting and other strange hallucinations. You don't drink and you can't handle weed, but I love ya anyway, bro. You've got character." Jackson pointed his elbow at the fire. "And you've got more balls than all three of those fools combined. You've got class, man. You ain't heavy, but you're my brother. Just like in that old Hollies song."

He looked down at Hayden, expecting some wiseass comment about his dorky pop music reference, but Hayden had fallen asleep. At least he hoped he was asleep and not dead. He reached down and felt for a pulse in his neck. His heartbeat was strong. Still alive.

Hang in there, Fowler. Don't leave me alone with these three losers.

Jackson returned to the fire. Sat thinking. Wondered what his millions of followers were saying about his disappearance. Social media must be burning up with all kinds of outrageous conspiracy theories about what had happened to him. Many of them would certainly believe he died in the helicopter crash. But then, surely, many others were exchanging much more creative and inventive ideas of what had happened to America's Gonzo Shutterbug, also known as the Digital Cowboy, a.k.a., the Wildlife Wild Man. Thinking of his nicknames and his fans brought a smile to his face. His smile grew wider as the quote from the great 19th century circus impresario Phineas T. Barnum ran through his head: *"There's no such thing as bad publicity, as long as they spell your name right."*

He suddenly became aware of the preternatural silence that had closed in around them—a suffocating, claustrophobic thing. Very noticeable. A quite different feel from past nights out here.

No frogs peeping and croaking.

No crickets chirping or katydids scratching.

No trilling calls of screech owls. No coyote howls.

The usual haunting hoots of barred owls and the melodious song of the whippoorwill were conspicuously missing. The only sounds were the crackling of the fire and the burbling whisper of the river far below.

His experiences in the world's jungles told him silence this resolute usually meant a feared predator was in the vicinity.

Jackson looked at the others to see if they had picked up on it. *Of course not. The three blind mice are lost in their pathetic little worlds.*

He glanced in Hayden's direction and saw his paleontologist friend propped up on an elbow, pointing at the woods to Jackson's left, behind Larry Bing. *Of course Fowler notices something strange in the air. The overwhelming silence woke him up. He's in tune with the natural world.*

Jackson looked to where he pointed, surveying the wall of ponderosa pine lining the clearing. At first he didn't see anything peculiar. Just the heavy drape of foliage and broad tree trunks.

And then he *did* see it.

Eyes.

Four of them. Peering through the greenery.

Gleaming like garnet gemstones. Illuminated by the campfire.

Four deep scarlet elliptical orbs.

Unblinking. Dark round pupils watching.

Observing.

Alert. Patient.

An electric current of adrenaline raced up Jackson's spine.

As his eyes adjusted to the camouflaged foliage cover, he saw the outlines of two Dromaeosaurs standing motionless, like side-by-side taxidermy mounts in a natural history museum.

How did they sneak up on us so quietly? He knew Dromes to be thrash and crash, not stealthy and restrained.

Very odd.

Slowly, careful not to make any sudden movements, he picked

up his night vision videocam, which, of course, was always close by. He could feel his heartbeat in his hands as he brought the camera up and pressed the record button.

He tried to control his breathing and steady his hands as he filmed.

They're sizing us up. Very intelligent predators.

My fans are going to love this!

He thought about warning the others but then discarded the notion. Those dweebs would only shit their pants—the helicopter pilot who was afraid of the rifle he carried and the biologist who'd probably never fired a gun in his life. Certainly Bing and Fowler wouldn't be able to do anything with their injuries.

Best to remain quiet and keep videoing.

This footage is priceless, he thought, but wished the creatures would move a little to give the shot some motion, some needed perspective.

His heart thumped triple-time under his ribs as he filmed. He *loved* this shit! Made him feel hyper alive.

Larry Bing looked up from the fire and noticed Jackson working the videocam. "What the hell are you—?"

It was all Bing could get out before the clearing erupted in a raucous screeching and clicking, a rapid-fire machinegun staccato burst of low-pitched guttural chittering and clacking.

The Dromes burst through the trees and into the clearing, wailing like a couple of banshees breaking out of a coffin. They stood only five feet tall and weighed less than a hundred pounds, but their aggressiveness and thickset bodies made them a fearful foe. They bounded across the campsite, salivating, hop-skipping on their two heavily muscled legs, big heads bobbing, mouths open displaying their razor-edged teeth.

Jackson leaped to his feet and retreated to the tents, near where Hayden lay. He never stopped recording.

The lead Dromaeosaur caught Bing from behind before Bing knew what hit him. The beast snatched him up in its wide maw, taking the plastic cooler with him, clamping Bing in its mouth and locking him in with those deadly jaws. Bing's panicked screams echoed across the campsite. The beast bellowed and shook the co-pilot's body violently in what Jackson thought was a show of hunting prowess: the creature showing off its prize. Strips of medical tape fell to the ground as Bing's makeshift sling came apart, reduced to shreds of blood-soaked confetti. Sprays of blood and drool and pieces of the cooler flew like shrapnel. Bing's head whipped from side to side with each vicious swing of the Drome's head, his screams for help snuffed out by the creature's wild snorting and huffing.

Lacroix and Carlton scrambled away from the fire, frantically taking potshots at the second Dromaeosaur as they backpedaled.

Gunshots reverberated like howitzer blasts.

BOOM! BOOM! BOOM! BOOM!

Their shots went high and wide into the trees.

Chaos.

Confusion.

Larry Bing's hoarse screams faded out then died as the Drome dragged his body off into the woods, leaving a wide trail of blood and a severed arm in its wake.

The second Drome went after the shooters, making a straight line for Lacroix. He and Carlton continued firing. Several shots sailed wide. Two slugs tore into the dirt at the Drome's feet, bringing the creature to a halt for a few valuable seconds. But then it surged forward and was almost on Lacroix when a bullet caught it in the chest. A second shot blew off its shoulder in an explosion of cartilage and tendon.

The creature collapsed in a heap close to Lacroix, snapping its frightening jaws and emitting weak squeals as it convulsed and spasmed in its death throes.

Jackson moved in on the dead Drome, keeping the videocam rolling. It all happened so fast he couldn't tell if it was Carlton or Lacroix who had delivered the fatal shots.

The metallic scent of blood lingered along with the acrid stench of spent gunpowder and a pungent wild animal odor. Jackson heard loud slurping noises coming out of the woods, the contented moans and yaps of a carnivore enjoying its meal.

Then he heard Peter Lacroix sobbing.

The helicopter pilot had surprised him. Carlton, too.

Jackson directed the camera at the two novice gunslingers. Both were on their knees, vomiting into the dirt.

He got it all on film.

Jackson had to admit, he was a bit shaken, too. The way that Dromaeosaur took Larry Bing. The suddenness of it. The brutality. It brought back painful memories of his assistant Milton Haynes being devoured by a large Tyrannosaur two months ago in a cave near here. Jackson had cried that night.

He had wept heartfelt tears, just like Lacroix.

And then the thought hit him: *Could I have done something to prevent it? Should I have shouted a warning?*

Jackson shut off the videocam. He would delete the crying part of that footage.

Some things just do not belong in the public domain, he thought as he went to check on Hayden.

The Lotus Position

August 5: Gilliam's Guidepost Cellar Suites
Heart Butte, Montana

ONE FOOT IN FRONT OF THE OTHER. One day at a time. Live in the moment, not in your head. Breathe in the positive, exhale the negative.

These were the things Brin told herself each day. To keep on keeping on. To maintain some semblance of sanity in the face of this monumental adversity.

I'm enduring, Petey. Please come home to us.

One week ago today she had kissed her husband goodbye and watched him fly off to the Idaho backcountry with five other men. That kiss was the last contact she'd had with Peter.

Seven days was an eternity when somebody you loved went missing.

Brin had been locked in a delirious state the first few days, She lost count of how many times she had called Peter's cell and the two satellite phones they had onboard the helicopter. Every call ended with the same silent disconnect. No ringtone. No going to voice-mail. Just an abrupt cutoff and a muted void. Like a soundless slap in the face.

She couldn't cry anymore. She was all cried out. Crying seemed to be a wasted emotion anyway. No amount of tears would bring Peter back. Prayer probably wouldn't either, but she prayed any-way. The act made her feel like she was doing something to help the cause, even if it was all in her head.

Nora and Loretta—bless their beautiful souls—had helped her get through the early part of the week when she was her most stressed. They eventually convinced her that negative thinking wouldn't rescue her husband. Excessive worry would only bring harm to Brin and her unborn baby, they'd told her. She believed them, and tried valiantly to follow their advice. Brin would always be a worrier. Anxiety flowed through every strain of her DNA. It was her curse and had been since she was a child. She hated this corroded part of herself, and often wished she could take a sharp knife and carve it out of her being. Excise it like the malignancy it was.

Her sadness and fear lingered one week into this vigil, but the weight of her moods had lightened thanks to Loretta and Nora's help. She felt blessed that she had two strong female friends to calm her. She especially appreciated Nora, who remained dedicated to lifting Brin up despite her own suffering. It was obvious Nora missed Hayden Fowler, but she controlled her emotions well.

Perhaps it's her scientist mindset?

Brin smiled thinking of Nora's name for them: *The Cretaceous Sisters*. It was comforting. Fitting.

Today Brin felt the best she had all week. She sat on her cushioned exercise mat, situated in a modified prenatal lotus position (unable to cross her legs all the way due to her bloated belly), doing the meditation and stretching exercises Nora had taught her. The exercises were a mixture of yoga, tai chi, and breath awareness that did wonders for her.

Earlier in the week, Nora introduced Brin to the benefits of mindfulness and breath awareness meditation, confessing to her that Nora herself had been plagued with panic disorders throughout her life. The meditation and stretching had helped Nora gain control over her problem, and she felt it could do the same for Brin. The revelation brought Brin closer to her, Brin feeling honored that Nora would confide in her with something so intimate and personal. Nora told her about the crippling panic attack she'd suffered last summer here at the Guidepost out by the dinosaur enclosures. A pair of T-Rexes in Gilliam's Glade had triggered her, bringing back her horrific memories of the Fourth of July Livingston Roundup Rodeo tragedy. She was so bad off Hayden and paleozoologist Franz

Krause had to escort her back to her Cellar suite. Nora's anxiety became so devastating she couldn't leave their suite for a couple of weeks. She was plagued by horrible nightmares that robbed her of sleep and suffered a series of panic attacks while writing about her dinosaur encounters.

Nora's revelation helped Brin immeasurably. It was reassuring for Brin to know she wasn't alone, floundering in her anxiety abyss. Nora Lemoyne—a respected scientist, successful author, and astute businesswoman—suffering similar afflictions? Who could have imagined that? To know that someone as together and high functioning as Nora could be plagued with the high anxiety demon made Brin realize there was no shame in the brokenness she often felt.

Loretta suggested scheduling an appointment with the Gilliam's family therapist in Missoula, telling her that Dr. Helen Krickstad had worked miracles with all five family members. Brin was receptive to the idea. She preferred it over Peter's long-running advice that she get a prescription for antidepressants. Brin was against most forms of prescription drugs, even more so now that she was pregnant. But Loretta's idea had merit. Therapy was a healthful and holistic remedy. The Gilliams had been through unimaginable trauma and seemed to have come through it okay. At least from what Brin could tell. So maybe a few sessions with the psychologist would help. Plus, it would give her a good excuse to return to Missoula, the city she loved.

Brin stretched out on the mat, breathing deeply with each change in position. She was feeling better than she had all week. Part of her elevated mood was due to her walk with Bryan Gilliam this morning. He had knocked on her door and insisted she go topside with him to get some sunshine and fresh air. She was reluctant at first, preferring to stay cocooned in the safety of her suite where she had been holed up the entire week (shades of Nora's agoraphobic two weeks?). But Bryan could be most persuasive, and he coaxed her out under the big sky.

They walked along the barbed wire fence that ran along the rear of the Guidepost, Bryan poking his way along with his cane, a rifle strapped over his shoulder due to recent Dromaeosaur sightings.

Despite the potential danger of running into flesh-eating beasts, Brin felt good getting out of her windowless suite and stretching her legs, getting some sun on her face and fresh air in her lungs. And she felt safe with Bryan Gilliam by her side.

"We've really missed you in the Cavern this week, Brin" he said. "The girls are kinda lost without you there to lead them."

"Oh, hey, Bryan, I'm sorry for laying out, but—"

"No need to apologize, hon. Everybody's pulling for you—the girls, Apisi, Chogan . . . me. There's absolutely no need for you to hurry back. You've got a lot on your mind with the baby and Peter. It's quite a heavy burden, I'm sure."

"It's hard, yes. But sometimes I think it would be better off if I got back to work. Focus my attention on jewelry making."

"Well, you take all the time you need, darling. We've got plenty of meteorite rock to keep the assembly line going. Your job will still be there when you return. You trained the girls well. They've been churning out premium, high-priced iridium pieces that we'll start selling next week. The silvery-blond striations in the rock are dazzling." He stopped and pulled something out of his pocket. "Speaking of which, here," he said, handing her a pair of glittery silver-white teardrop earrings. "The girls made these for you, Brin."

She held the earrings in the palm of her hand, admiring the stylish craftsmanship. "They're absolutely beautiful," she said. "You're right, they *are* dazzling."

"They're pure iridium. The girls know you have pierced ears and that you love earrings. They wanted the best for you."

"Thank you, Bryan. It's a very generous gift. Please thank Koko and the girls for me."

"I will." They started walking again. "Loretta tells me you're doing better."

"I am. Your wife and Nora have helped me quite a bit. They're an inspiration to me. They're both so accomplished and have good hearts."

"Yeah," Bryan said, squinting into a shadowy thicket of hemlock trees. "Loretta has helped me through some tough times, especially when I came home from Afghanistan. She's good at taking care of people. That's her thing, her magic. But she's going through a tough stretch of her own dealing with her brother's death. I try to be there for her, but truth be told, it's tough for me, too. Jimmy Enright was my best buddy. He introduced me to Loretta."

"Yeah, she told me about some of that. Your wife is a strong woman. I wish I had some of her strength."

"You do, Brin. You just don't allow yourself to see it."

She liked the sound of that. Thought maybe there could even be a small sliver of truth to it. "Do you really think so?"

"Absolutely, young lady. You're a natural born leader. The Cavern girls look up to you. You've gained their utmost respect. You're also a mother with another child on the way. And you have a successful jewelry shop in Missoula. How is Brinshou's Baubles and Jewelry doing these days?"

"It's doing pretty well, thanks for asking. I have two really great women running the store and they're doing a fantastic job. You remember Luana and Nuna, right?"

"Sure do. Both are really hard workers. Dedicated."

"Yes they are. I miss working with them. I miss talking with the regular customers. I miss Missoula and our friends there." She pulled up short, realizing she might be sounding ungrateful of the Gilliam's hospitality. "Oh, I'm so sorry, Bryan. I like it here at the Guidepost. I really do."

Bryan laughed. "It's okay. I understand. Life on a ranch out in the sticks isn't everyone's idea of nirvana. You've always struck me as a cosmopolitan type. Nothing wrong with that."

"But I just want you to know how much I appreciate all you've done for me and Petey, er … I mean *Peter*. And my mother and Kimi. The Cellar suite apartments are really nice and I do enjoy working for you. I promise I'll be back in a few days."

Bryan chuckled again. "You worry too much, Brin." He leaned on his cane and touched her swollen belly. "It's not good for the little guy in there."

Brin smiled, looking down at Bryan's hand on her stomach. "Peter wants a boy. He has ideas about teaching him to skate and play hockey."

"Girls can play hockey, too."

"I know. But try to tell that to Peter." She felt the weight of tears in her eyes. She didn't want Bryan to see her cry and quickly changed the subject. "How is your cane holding up?"

He leaned against a fence post and lifted the walking stick, peered down the length of it. "It's a solid cut of oak, holding up under the strain of my lard ass." He jammed the staff in the ground, admiring the knob of Cretaceous stone on top that Brin had fashioned into dinosaur claws poking out of a meteorite crevice. The pair of inset garnet stones representing a pair of scarlet eyes sparkled, the intended effect being a hatchling breaking out of its meteorite tomb. "You did a masterful job on this, Brin. It makes being handicapped classy."

"Stop it, Bryan. You are *not* handicapped."

"My bum leg says otherwise." He pulled the cane out of the dirt and studied it for a long moment. "We've got enough rock to make another line of limited edition dino-canes like this one. You remember what a hit they were."

"I do, yes."

"Maybe when you come back to work."

"I'd like that, yes. Let's plan on it."

Brin admired Bryan Gilliam's enthusiasm for selling ideas and products. Peter had called him a marketing genius. Told her he thought with Bryan as acting general manager of Fowler-Lemoyne Aviation, the company would be extraordinarily successful. And in the first month of operation, Bryan had proved him right, signing up a diverse group of clients—mining officials, real estate developers, politicians, tourists. The helicopter was booked solid for weeks to come. Of course now the chopper was missing (crashed?), and that depressing thought brought her down again.

They walked on in silence, following a horse path down into a shallow bowl of a valley, a heaviness bearing down on her. She blinked back tears.

"You okay, Brin?" she heard Bryan say.

She turned away from him and wiped her eyes. "I'll be fine. Just curious, though. What do you think happened to the helicopter?"

He looked at her and touched her arm. "Are you sure you want to talk about this?"

She nodded uncertainly, still looking away.

"Look at me, Brin."

She turned to him, embarrassed by the tears wetting her cheeks.

His sad expression showed empathy and concern. "I'll say this. I've gotten to know Hayden Fowler and your husband quite well. They've both been through some very risky, dangerous situations. They're smart and they can handle a lot. They're survivors. You can tell just by talking with them. Larry Bing is wired the same way. If you remember back to last summer, it took more than a week to find that helicopter pilot who vanished in that same area. My guess is that Peter and Hayden and the others are alive, but concealed in a remote area. I have to believe they'll be found soon."

"Really?"

He tilted his head forward in a half-nod. "Keep your chin up, Brin. Things will get better."

"You think so?"

"I do."

"Well, thanks for the walk and talk, Bryan. It did me good to get out."

"Glad I could be of help."

Bryan was only a dozen years older than her, but Brin had always seen him as a father figure. A kind and compassionate man with the patriarchal qualities that came from raising a family. As they stood there looking at each other, Brin was hit with a twinge of affection for him. *These Gilliams are such good people,* she thought as she impulsively reached out and wrapped her arms around him in a loose-limbed, awkward hug. "Thank you for being who you are, Bryan."

"Uh, yeah," he said, giving her an uncomfortable, weak hug, then stepping back from her, embarrassment coloring his face. "We'd better be getting back. This is the furthest I've walked in a week."

They returned to The Cellar in silence, Brin wondering if the hug had been too much.

That had been this morning. And now she finished her meditation program with a couple of yoga stretches, then went to the kitchenette for a glass of lemonade. She returned to the living room and settled in on the couch. Picked up the remote and clicked on the TV. The local news came on, a young female news anchor reporting on the latest dinosaur attack:

"... a tragic scene late Saturday night at the outdoor Big Sky Amphitheater in Missoula where three twelve-foot-tall Tyrannosaurs invaded the Big Sky Brewing Company concert grounds during a performance by indie rock band favorites Manchester Orchestra. Seven people were killed and ten others were rushed to Providence Saint Patrick Hospital. The creatures entered from the north end of the park creating pandemonium as they trampled two vendor tents and chased down screaming concertgoers. Two of the animals were shot and killed with the bodies of victims hanging like broken dolls from their mouths. The other T-Rex escaped. We have cellphone footage taken by guests, and we warn you it is very graphic ..."

Brin shielded her eyes while the clips played. The audio was bad enough.

She knew it wasn't healthy for her to watch the news. Peter had drummed that into her, constantly reminding her that it spiked her anxieties. But she was a diehard news junkie, and like any self-respecting addict, Brin craved her fix. She had an irrepressible need to know what was happening in the world. *Maybe I'm a hardcore masochist,* she had often thought. But she felt strong today, buoyed by her morning walk with Bryan and feeling a sense of calm following her meditation and yoga. She felt she could take anything the newscasters threw at her. And maybe, just maybe, she might hear breaking news about what happened to her dear Petey.

The newscast returned to the anchorwoman in the studio:

"It is not clear how the creatures got into the concert grounds undetected as the amphitheater is bordered by two major highways. To reiterate from one of our earlier reports, dinosaur attacks on humans are down significantly from last summer's count. Saturday's attack is only the second in a major metropolitan area this year. Experts we contacted at the Montana Wildlife Fish and Parks Department—the MWFP—tell us they think the lower death toll is due to the prehistoric creatures having learned to fear humans and their guns, and subsequently have moved into vast wilderness areas in Idaho, Montana, and Wyoming, finding plenty of big prey to sustain them, such as moose, elk, cattle, and bears.

"In a related story, the search for the helicopter that went missing a week ago while on a dinosaur scouting mission in the wilds of Idaho is looking bleak. Idaho Mountain Search and Rescue reports that they have combed more than a thousand square miles looking for the missing aircraft, and have found nothing. There were six men aboard the aircraft, including well-known celebrities such as the famous wildlife videographer Jackson Lattimer, and paleontologist and bestselling author Hayden Fowler. It is believed that if there are any survivors, they might be out of food and water and in serious trouble . . ."

Suddenly Brin felt very ill. A lightning bolt of intense pain sliced through her abdomen. Waves of nausea rolled through her, followed by cramping so forceful it made her double over on the couch. She held her stomach, knowing what it was but hoping she was wrong.

And then she felt wetness in her crotch. She looked there but couldn't tell much with her yoga pants being dark brown. It was painful getting in a position where she could yank the pants down over her hips.

Her white panties were soaked with blood. Lots of blood that was now staining the couch cushions.

She picked up a pillow from the end of the couch, brought it to her mouth, and muffled her screams with it. She didn't want her mother and Kimi across the hall hearing her distress.

Feeling faint, she picked up her cellphone and called Nora, who Brin knew was next door working on her book.

"Hi, Nora," she said, her voice shaky and raw. "Please help me. I need to get to the hospital. I think I just lost my baby."

Dino Shish Kebab

August 6: River of No Return Wilderness
Central Idaho

THE DROMAEOSAUR MEAT WAS TOUGH and sinewy. Gristly, unappetizing. Oily with a bitter, acidic aftertaste. Not your usual breakfast fare. But it was solid food. Protein. A replenishment of precious vitamins and minerals that had been sapped from their bodies through eternal days and nights of throbbing hunger.

Greasy sustenance that kept them alive.

Yesterday Bill Carlton had butchered and fileted the Drome they killed the night before, carving out a dozen thin steaks from the animal's compact muscular carcass. The yield produced just a few pounds of edible dino steaks, and they had consumed most of it while it was still fresh. This morning they were finishing it off.

There were only four of them now—four tattered souls clinging desperately to the fading hope of rescue.

Hayden roasted his Dromaeosaur steak on the end of a kebab skewer, the meat sizzling and popping over the campfire flames. The reptilian fare hadn't agreed with him last night; he'd spent the early part of the evening in upchuck hell spewing undigested chunks of Drome meat in a bloody gruel. But his insatiable hunger this morning drove him to have another go at it. The meat also made Peter sick last night, but he recovered quickly. Bill Carlton and Jackson Lattimer seemed unaffected by the intake of the gamy dino steaks. *Those two must have cast-iron stomachs,* Hayden thought with a touch of envy.

He felt like he had been at death's door last night, but he was greatly improved this morning. He'd finally managed to get a few hours of sleep, and despite the sickness he'd experienced from the alien meat, he figured the small amount of steak he was able to keep down had strengthened him and fueled him with new energy.

However, he wasn't deluding himself about his overall condition. The bruising had lightened—from the original dark purple to a sickly yellow—but he remained weak, and his body continued dishing out the pain. His abdomen felt like he'd been pierced by a hundred knives, and he was still occasionally passing blood in his urine. His ribs zapped electric jolts of pain through his entire body every time he moved. But this morning he fought back the pain to escape the imprisonment of the sleeping bag, with its cloying mothball odor and scratchy lining. It was liberating to join the others around the fire.

Today marked the ninth day of survival on this claustrophobic mountainside. Hayden thought it strange to view a wide open wilderness area as claustrophobic, but it was. The only way down was a thousand-foot drop over a sheer cliff to the Salmon River, a sure death plunge. Not even Jackson Lattimer—crazy as he was— would attempt scaling down that rock wall. And getting out any other way required cutting through hundreds of acres of dense forest on a steep incline. Hence, this small clearing where they set up camp had become an open-air prison cell.

They thought their stay here would be short; none of them ever imagined they'd be here nine days.

Throughout the vigil they had seen and heard search planes and helicopters buzzing in the distance, always too far away to make contact. Earlier this morning, as the sun crested the mountain peaks in the east, they heard the *thwop-thwop-thwop* thump of helicopter blades. It had sounded like more than one chopper, and much closer than previous search aircraft had come. Lacroix and Lattimer rushed out to the edge of the drop-off and spotted two choppers maybe a mile to the west, circling, dipping, searching. Peter and Jackson had waved their arms frantically and yelled until their vocal cords gave out. All to no avail. Still too far away. They could only watch miserably as the two aircraft disappeared behind the mountaintops.

The two of them returned to the campsite bearing expressions of crushing disappointment.

"Not happening," Peter said, his voice raw. "We could have set off explosives and they wouldn't have picked up on it."

Jackson croaked, "Those incompetent clowns couldn't find their assholes with a colonoscope and a tour guide for Christ's sake! Why don't they follow the river?"

Carlton said, "It's a big river. They probably *are* following the river. Just not our section of it."

"They're morons!" Jackson said, shaking his head in disgust. "The F-Troop of rescue squads!"

Peter said, "Searching wilderness areas like this one isn't easy, Jack. I'm sure they're doing their best."

"If you say so, Lacroix."

Now, an hour later, the brief excitement over and his hopes dashed, Hayden went back to pondering Larry Bing's death. The sights and sounds of the Dromaeosaur crushing Bing in its powerful jaws would forever be burned into his memory, playing like a scene from a disturbing horror flick.

Only it was no movie. It had been real.

Too real.

And he'd watched Jackson sit there quietly and film the Dromes in their hiding place just minutes before the attack. Lattimer could have shouted a warning, but apparently capturing video footage was more important to him than Larry Bing's life.

But Hayden knew he couldn't blame his videographer friend when he had spotted the creatures the same time Jackson did. *I could have called out, too, but I failed to. Why didn't you, Hayden?* He'd asked himself that question repeatedly the past two days. The only answer he came up with was that everything happened at warp speed.

A cool wind swept through the campsite with a whispery sigh. Silence prevailed, much as it had since the Drome dragged Bing's body into the woods two nights ago. Conversation was sporadic as the four of them grappled with the pilot's violent demise. It had all happened so fast—a lightning strike by swift otherworldly creatures. Hayden scanned the faces of his fellow survivors. Their stunned expressions, slumped bearings, and brooding silence said it all. Would they *ever* get off this fucking mountain? Were they safe from marauding carnivores?

He pulled his roasting skewer from the fire and bit off a strip of the steamy, leathery meat. Chewed. Swallowed. Felt the greasy burn as it went down. Grimaced. Groaned as it hit his devastated stomach.

"You okay over there, Hayden?" Peter called out.

"Yeah," he said with a cough, feeling bitter bile rise into his throat. He turned his head and spat a glob of bloody saliva in the dirt.

"You don't look okay, Fowler," Jackson said.

Hayden held up his skewer, the chunk of Drome meat bobbing on the end. "No shit," he squawked, spitting again. "This crap isn't exactly a gourmet meal."

Carlton said, "It's not even Kentucky Fried Chicken good, which I know isn't saying much. But it's food. Something to keep us going." He gave Hayden a thoughtful stare. "Didn't think you were going to make it last night, partner. You either, Peter."

Peter was more overwhelmed by Larry Bing's death than the rest of them. It only made sense. Lacroix had flown the meteorite roundup missions with him last summer and hired Bing as a Fowler-Lemoyne Aviation pilot. They had obviously developed a close friendship. Peter buried Larry Bing's severed arm yesterday, near the big boulder where they had buried Jenkins McCraw. The arm was all that was left of Peter's friend.

Hayden was suddenly hit by a stream of stomach acid flooding his throat. He choked, trying to clear his windpipe. Dropped his skewer in the dirt and fell over on his side. Threw up bloody morsels of partially digested Dromaeosaur meat.

Jackson was at his side immediately, lifting him, arms around his chest, squeezing, trying to clear his airway. After long moments of intense struggle, Hayden recaptured his breath.

"Hang tight, good buddy," Jackson said. "I'll get you some water."

Hayden was dizzy, his stomach doing flip-flops, his mouth tasting of bile and blood and regurgitated reptile meat. It took all his energy to stay propped up. Jackson returned with a tin cup of cold water (Carlton had made another run to the stream yesterday to fill up the flasks), and he held Hayden steady, helping him tilt his head back and drink. Hayden couldn't coordinate his mouth properly, and he felt the water wetting his beard, dripping down his neck.

Jackson Lattimer had done an about-face with his attitude the past few days. He had ceased provoking Lacroix and Carlton. No more bullying them or blaming them for their predicament, realizing they were all in this horrible mess together and they had to get along to survive. Yesterday he even thanked Carlton for making the difficult hike to the stream to fill up the water canisters. It was as if Larry Bing's shocking death had flipped a switch in Lattimer, changing him from acerbic asshole to empathetic soul.

Last night, sitting around the campfire, in what was the longest monologue of the day, Jackson had reflected on how Bing's violent end had brought excruciating memories rushing back of his late assistant's death. Milton Haynes had not only been a longtime assistant photographer to Lattimer, but also a friend. Hayden, Peter, and Bill Carlton listened to Jackson's graphic telling of Haynes being taken apart by two big Tyrannosaurs in an Idaho cave in early June:

". . . so we found the nest and six huge eggs. Next thing we know three enormous Rexes are on us. They had to be six-hundred pounds. We're trapped in the back of that cave, no way out except going right at them. Milty starts shooting even though I said to hold fire. He winged one of them. The other two were on him in a flash, ripping him limb from limb while me and Sam Beeson made a run for it. Milty never had a chance, same as Bing. When the beasts want you, they get you."

They all had seen the iconic video of the attack in the dim cave, but hearing Jackson tell the tale brought a whole new gruesome perspective. Hayden, for one, wished his friend hadn't gone into such detail. Especially with them being out here where the dinos roamed. He knew just how vulnerable to attack they were.

"I was rough on Bing, and I regret it now," Jackson confessed.

"Jesus, nobody should have to die the way Bing did. Milty either. If there is a god, He damned well better be giving them the royal red carpet treatment in the afterlife, or He'll have me to deal with!"

Lacroix and Carlton were surprised at Jackson's turnaround, but Hayden knew his gruff and outspoken videographer friend had a softer, more sympathetic side to him. Since the crash, Jackson had tended to Hayden like he was his personal physician, fetching him water, doling out Tylenol and anti-nausea medication (ondansetron) from the chopper medical kit, assisting Hayden into the woods to take care of his biological needs, if not a bit reluctantly.

"Let's set expectations, Fowler," Jackson had told him the day after the crash. "I'm not going to hold your pecker while you take a leak, and I'm certainly not going to wipe your ass for you, but I will escort you to and from nature's bathroom," It got Hayden laughing to the point where it hurt so bad he had to take a seat until the pain passed.

And now Jackson was at his side again. "C'mon, bro, let's get you stretched out in your sleeping bag. I think you'll feel better lying down."

Hayden didn't want to return to the straitjacket confinement of that smelly sleeping bag, but knew Jackson was right. He *would* feel better stretched out on the ground.

Jackson helped him get situated in the sleeping bag.

Back into my cloth coffin, Hayden thought with a weary sigh.

Reclining calmed his turbulent gut and soon the nausea was gone. But the pain persisted, sometimes stabbing and sharp. So he did what he'd been doing since the crash to take his mind off the agony: he thought about his lovely, sexy Nora. Fantasized that he was in bed with her, making love to her, pleasuring her. She pleasuring him. Pictured every delicious nook and cranny of her petite body and could feel the soft silkiness of her creamy pale skin as his hands explored those contours. Could smell her musky perfumed scent, a jasmine and rose fragrance that sent his libido soaring. Her eyes—like two emerald gemstones magnified behind the lenses of her designer frames—expressing a heady blend of carnal desire and intellectual curiosity. Her lilting voice and warm breath against his cheek as she whispered sweet vulgarities in his ear, spurring him on. Her emotional vocalizations as she climaxed. Yes indeed, Nora was his hot librarian fantasy, and thinking of her in this objectified manner served to tamp down his pain.

But Nora was more than just a sex object to him. Much more. She was his best friend and trusted confidant. Extremely intelligent, with a deep, orderly scientific mind. She was an engaging conversationalist. He missed her sweet laugh when he told one of his nerdy jokes. He missed her dry wit and equally nerdy sense of humor. He missed doing fieldwork with her at his side. He missed discussing paleozoological discoveries with her. He missed co-authoring books with her.

Oh hell, face it, old man. You miss everything about Nora Lemoyne. She's changed your life for the better in every which way.

He pondered what might be going through her mind right now. Did she believe he was dead? Was she keeping the faith? She hadn't wanted him to fly off to Idaho with Jackson Lattimer, thinking Jackson might cause problems. Nora had been right, but Jackson wasn't the cause. It had been one of those *wrong place at the wrong time* scenarios that had brought them down in these mountains. A freakish accident brought on by aggressive flying reptiles.

He thought about those pterosaurs, the Quetzalcoatlus that had caused the copter crash. The way they soared so free and easy, expertly using thermal wind currents to increase their speed and change altitude. Their extraordinary wingspan he estimated to be fifteen feet across. Their long ostrich-like necks and pointed beaks. The prominent ridged keel on their breastbones that gave them a proud bearing. Their sharp, three-clawed talons. Birds of prey. *Raptors.* But then, they weren't really raptors. They were flying reptiles, not mammals, which made the experience even more interesting to him. It had been an impressive sight, the way they dipped and turned in a loose formation, darkening Idaho's big sky with their shadowy presence.

But ultimately they'd turned into a threat. A menace that caused a catastrophe.

He still was puzzled as to what drew them to their chopper.

They were attracted to the candy apple red Bell 407 for some reason. The bright luminescent color? The sound of the rotors whipping the air? Maybe mistaking it for a kindred flying ally? Or was it that they saw the helicopter as an aerial threat and went into attack mode? Whatever it was, their curiosity or fear brought them too close to the rotors and they had paid the price. A few of them escaped harm, but Hayden hated to see any of them die. They were an impressive animal, even at this young age. At full maturity Quetzalcoatlus would reach the size of a giraffe, weighing up to five-hundred pounds with thirty-five foot wingspans. They would fly at speeds up to eighty miles per hour and were the most aggressive of all the flying carnivores. A fascinating species refined to perfection through millions of years of evolution. While Tyrannosaurus Rex was king of the land during the Late Cretaceous, Quetzalcoatlus ruled the skies.

Crazy.

Surreal.

The misadventure with the flock of Quetzalcoatlus would make an intriguing chapter in his and Nora's book. He wished he'd had the chance to study the flyers, but all that was left of them were two shredded wings wrapped around a section of rotor blade and a beak embedded into the rubber seal around a window.

Will I ever get to write that chapter?

Will I ever work with Nora again?

Will I ever see Nora again?

Larry Bing's family would never get to see him again. It took Hayden to a sad place every time he recalled the savage Dromaeo-saur attack. If Hayden survived (*and that's the big question right now, isn't it?*) he would have to tell the story of Bing's tragic death. It wouldn't be easy, but as horrible as it had been emotionally, his paleozoological side knew it would make another fascinating chapter in his and Nora's book. The scientist in him marveled at the way the Dromes stalked them for long, drawn-out minutes, remaining still, observant, gazing at them from the interior of the woods with their predatory crimson eyes before launching the attack. The patient way they waited and watched, sizing up their prey. Their persevering stalking showed a hunting intelligence never before attributed to Dromaeosaurs. They were close cousins to the Velociraptors, and therefore classified as impulsive, highly aggressive creatures. Paleontologists and paleozoologists had long been in agreement about Dromes, labeling them as impatient predators ruled by their hyperactive metabolisms. However, the pair that attacked their campsite clearly refuted that finding.

Another interesting zoological fact: these Dromaeosaurs were larger than what was in the scientific records based on skeletal finds. Hayden estimated the two that invaded their campsite weighed more than a hundred pounds each while paleontological journals were consistent in reporting Dromaeosaurus weight at forty to fifty pounds. This made him believe that the Dromaeosaurs hatching out of the meteorites probably had lineage going back to Deinonychus in the Early Cretaceous. Deinonychus was a much larger theropod of the dromaeosaurid family that shared a few characteristics with the Dromes Hayden had run across—the extended sharp claws on their hind feet; the blocky, oversized head; the grasping hands; the lack of feathers usually found in other dromaeosaurid raptors.

Hayden and the scientific community had learned so much about these Cretaceous creatures that arrived via the meteorites last summer. He and his colleagues were getting an education, learning things that could never be gleaned from studying bones and fossils, much of it contradictory to original findings and theories. Now that he had spent the better part of a year studying these living creatures up close, Hayden doubted he would be able to return to basic paleontology with the same joy and passion he'd once had. Old bones just didn't juice him up anymore. They were too stagnant. Dull. Often they produced erroneous conclusions. The living breathing animals revealed biological and zoological truths about these species, and he felt honored and extraordinarily lucky to be on the leading edge of it.

But first things first. He had to survive this horror and get off this mountain.

That reminder hit him hard. An electric zap of pain stabbed him in the gut. He moaned quietly and rolled over on his side, turning away from the others gathered around the fire. He faced the woods, trying to ease the pain by repositioning himself in the sleeping bag.

After several minutes of squirming agony, the pain eased and exhaustion overcame him. Drowsy and on the edge of sleep, he heard a sound that was all too familiar. Like a donkey braying in a deep baritone. From deep in the forest.

No mistaking that sound.

Tyrannosaurus Rex!

A second Rex bellowed behind him, from the woods on the opposite side of the campsite.

He heard the pounding and crashing of the predators slamming through the dense woodlands. The muffled thrash of Tyrannosaur feet crushing the undergrowth. Loud pops and cracks as they splintered small trees and knocked them to the ground in their forceful approach.

The unnerving braying became louder, mixed with snorts and clicks.

An icy chill zipped down Hayden's spine and froze his testicles.

This can't be happening again!

And then he saw the beast coming straight at him through the thicket, a lumbering ten-foot tall wide load of prehistoric fury knocking back brush and bouncing off tree trunks in its clumsy haste to get at him.

The scene unfolded like one of those nasty bad dreams where everything is washed over in a hazy, slowed-down unreality.

He couldn't move.

Oh shit! This is the end! I'm a dead man, his mind screamed at him as the creature broke into the clearing, lowering its massive head, training its beady eyes on him.

Hayden tried to scramble out of the sleeping bag, but found it impossible to move his limbs.

Gunshots erupted behind him followed by the distressed cries of a wounded Rex.

More gunshots. The Rex bearing down on Hayden stopped its advance, raised its head and peered across the way at its wounded counterpart.

Hayden tried to move again, but he was paralyzed with fear at the huge creature looming over him, the revolting smell of decayed meat wafting off it with each heavy breath.

The Rex returned its attention to him, the beast opening its wide maw and displaying those lethal rows of teeth.

The creature lowered its head to snatch up its prize. Hayden closed his eyes, knowing for sure that this was his dying day, hoping his death would come quickly.

But then he heard Jackson Lattimer scream, "*NOOOOOOH YOU'RE NOT GONNA DO THAT, YOU STEAMING PILE OF PREHISTORIC SHIT!*"

Hayden dared to open his eyes, saw Jackson distracting the beast, provoking it, his eye fastened to the viewfinder of his camcorder, recording the challenge. The Rex shifted its clawed feet, snapped its goliath head around quick as a flash, and snatched Jackson up in its powerful jaws.

Jackson screamed. His videocam dropped to the ground, the red recording light still illuminated. His shrieks were quickly stifled as the creature closed its immense jaws in a forceful chomp, sending a spray of blood across Hayden's sleeping bag.

From his prone position, Hayden watched Bill Carlton plug the Rex with two shots to the chest. The injured creature ran in confused, anguished circles, Jackson's legs flopping out of the side of its mouth. Then, instead of running back into the woods, it ran from the clearing to the cliff's edge and straight over, plummeting a thousand feet into the Salmon River.

The River of No Return.

Pharmaceutical Dysfunction

August 6: Gilliam's Guidepost
Heart Butte, Montana

LORETTA SAT IN HER SUNROOM RECLINER engrossed in her latest read: *The World According to Garp,* the John Irving classic. She had seen the movie starring Robin Williams as T.S. Garp with Glenn Close as his uber-feminist mother, Jenny Fields, but she had never read the novel on which the film was based. The dramedy was the perfect winding-down book, an entertaining story to get lost in following a hectic twenty-four hours.

She and Nora spent last night at Blackfeet Community Hospital in Browning, where they had taken Brin after her emergency. Doctors had kept her under 24-hour observation due to her extensive bleeding and the fact that she was well into her second trimester.

Brin's anguish had been through the roof on the 30-minute drive to Browning. Loretta had driven her old Pontiac Torrent SUV, with Nora in back attempting to calm an out-of-control Brin with quiet reassurances. Loretta had a difficult time keeping her eyes on the road as she repeatedly glanced in the rearview mirror, seeing the blood-saturated bath towels Nora kept changing out and Brin's sickly, washed-out complexion. It had been an unsettling, tense drive.

But ultimately it had all worked out.

Thankfully Brin had not suffered a miscarriage.

She had not lost her baby.

Last night, following a physical exam, and transabdominal and transvaginal ultrasounds, OB/GYN Dr. Sandra Atwater presented Brin with her diagnosis.

"You experienced a chorionic hemorrhage, Mrs. Lacroix. That's where blood builds up between the embryo membrane—the chorion—and the uterine wall. Hemorrhages of this type can be very frightening, especially with as much blood as you lost. They mimic miscarriages precisely, so you were smart to come in and get checked out. Let me assure you that you did *not* have a miscarriage and your baby is fine. The imaging we did indicates your child is very healthy and growing according to schedule."

Brin had looked up at the doctor from her hospital bed, an exhausted smile on her drawn face. "Thank you, oh thank you so much, Doctor."

Dr. Atwater gave Brin a compassionate look and touched her wrist. "We're going to keep you overnight just as a precaution. We're going to replace the iron you lost, but you have nothing to worry about. You and your baby are fine."

Shortly after they arrived, Loretta had taken Dr. Atwater aside and briefed her about Brin's missing husband, telling the doctor that Brin had been under a lot of duress and was very anxious. The staff responded accordingly, treating Brin with kid gloves. And unbeknownst to Brin, Dr. Atwater had ordered a minimal dose of Valium to be included in her IV solution, which kept Brin serene and steady through the night.

Early this afternoon, Dr. Atwater examined Brin and pronounced her fit for release. The bleeding had stopped and Brin was feeling stronger.

Just before checkout, the doctor gave her some last minute instructions. "You can expect a bit of spotting over the next day or two. Nothing to be worried about. But I want you to lay low for the next four days. That means bed rest with no physical activity and no heavy lifting."

"What about yoga and meditation?" Brin inquired.

"Meditation would be very beneficial for you, but I'd stay away from yoga for a while. At least until we're sure the hematoma has stabilized. I would like to see you back here in a week for a follow-up. If you have any problems—" Dr. Atwater noticed Brin's uneasy reaction to the word *problems*, so she added, "—which I'm sure you won't have, you can call me." She handed Brin her business card with a comforting smile and touched her wrist again.

Loretta had complete confidence in the medical professionals at Blackfeet Community. They had saved Bryan's life last summer performing emergency surgery after he suffered near fatal gunshot wounds. They had also treated Loretta for her wrenched shoulder and twisted neck, and son Paul's broken arm after an aggressive Dromaeosaur caused Loretta to flip the Gilliam pickup truck in the east meadow. Upon leaving the hospital, she personally thanked Dr. Atwater and her nursing staff, thanking them for their expert care, and for the considerate and professional way they handled an emotionally fragile Brin.

Brin called her mother from the road, giving Kachina the good news. The conversation took place on speaker phone and Loretta could hear little Kimi in the background, urging (harassing?) her *gwanny* to play tea party with her and her dolls. Loretta smiled, reminded of how her Lianne behaved not too many years ago.

After the call, Loretta turned to Brin, who sat across from her in the front seat, "How are you feeling?"

"Much better, thanks. You Cretaceous Sisters are my guardian angels. I couldn't have done it without you and Nora."

Or a few drips of Valium, Loretta thought. She said, "Why are you so against modern medicine, Brin?"

"What do you mean?"

"Well, I've heard you say a number of times you won't let prescription drugs poison your body. When Nora and I suggested anti-anxiety medication, you shut us down. I'm just trying to understand why."

"I don't know. I guess I just believe in healthy healing. Something that doesn't affect my chemical makeup," she said, shifting in her seat to look at Nora in the back. "Like your yoga/tai chi meditation exercises, Nora."

"Yes, I get that," Nora said. "But sometimes a woman needs more than that. Sometimes our brains play tricks on us and we need something to straighten it out. I've been on Zoloft for a couple of years now, and it's really helped me."

"What, *you?*" Brin said with a tenor of astonishment.

"Yes, there's no shame in it, Brin. Sometimes our brains shift frequencies on us. Medication helps tune us back in to the right channels, so to speak."

Loretta felt it was a good time to reveal more of herself in the quest to help their friend. "Yeah, Nora's not alone. I've been taking fluoxetine—better known as Prozac—for almost six months now."

"*What?* You ladies are blowing my mind!" Brin's head swiveled between Nora and Loretta, her eyes wide with skepticism.

Loretta said, "I've been pretty down since my brother Jimmy died last year. It's like a light was extinguished in me and I needed something to switch the lights back on."

"But I thought you said that therapist you recommended to me helped you with that."

"Doctor Krickstad *has* been wonderful. She has helped me and my entire family. As I told you, she would be good for you, too. But I've needed an additional boost. Nora's right, Brin, there isn't any stigma anymore in taking pharmaceuticals to improve your mental health. I believe there would be a lot less trouble in this world if more people tried it. Think about it."

Loretta decided not to disclose that Bryan had also been on antidepressants as part of his therapy and recovery from last summer's tragedy.

Brin looked to be in a quandary. "I don't know," she said, gazing out her window at the expansive flat grasslands rolling out to the Rockies. "Peter has been after me to see a doctor about my, um—my *problem.* He's wanted me to get medicated for a long time, but it scares me. Especially now that I'm pregnant."

Loretta didn't have the nerve to tell her about the diazepam (Valium) that flowed through Brin's veins last night, keeping her calm and restful during her hospital stay.

"My dear Petey has always been my best medicine," Brin said, her voice cracking. "And now he's *gone.* I really don't know how I'll go on without him."

Brin wept and snuffled the rest of the drive back to Heart Butte. Loretta and Nora tried to soothe her but nothing seemed to settle her.

Where is that Valium when you need it?

They got Brin back to her apartment suite at three o'clock. Nora stayed with her while Loretta returned to the house to chill and get into *The World According to Garp.*

Loretta finished the first chapter, where Garp's mother—no-nonsense feminist nurse Jenny Fields—is arrested in 1942 for stabbing a soldier in a movie theater with a scalpel after the man attempted to rape her. In describing her actions to the police, Jenny says, *"If I'd wanted to kill him, I'd have slit his wrist. I'm a nurse and I know how people bleed."* Learning of this incident years later, Garp writes in his journal: *My mother was a lone wolf. She went through her life on the lookout for purse-snatchers and snatch-snatchers."*

Stimulating beginning, Loretta thought, turning the page for the second chapter.

Just then, Paul walked in, toting his guitar and a small Marshall amplifier. "Hey, Mom," he said, setting his equipment down. He plopped on the loveseat next to her and gave her a crooked grin. "Whatchya reading?"

His hair is getting so long now, she thought. *Long and stringy and raggedy.*

She closed the book and eyed the cover. "I just started it, but it's a crazy tragicomic tale of a very dysfunctional family."

"Oh, kinda like us, huh?" he said with a snort.

She frowned at him. "Is that what you think of us? That we're dysfunctional?"

"No. It's what other people think of us. When I'm out playin' gigs people come up to me between sets wanting to know all about us—about our dinosaur zoo, about last summer's tragedy, about Dad being gunned down, about our meteorite jewelry business. They wanna know about our relationship with the two famous dinosaur trackers . . . about our heliport and aviation company. All that and more, but the main interest is always the dinosaurs. Most of 'em look at me like I'm a circus freak. You can tell the way they ask questions they think we're aliens fresh off the mothership. You've gotta admit, Mom, we ain't exactly normal."

"*Aren't* exactly normal."

"Yeah, whatever."

Loretta emitted a quiet sigh. "True, we're not normal, but that doesn't make us dysfunctional. Eccentric perhaps. Colorful maybe. But never dysfunctional. We've had a highly unusual, very public journey the past year, so of *course* some people are going to look at us as being different and offbeat. So what? You're a budding rock star. You should embrace that Gilliam mysteriousness. As your father said, use it to your advantage."

Paul thought it through for a long beat. "You know, you're right, Mom. We *should* be proud of being different. Of being mysterious." He reached down and fiddled with the handle of his guitar case, and she thought maybe the conversation was at an end. But then he said, "How was your night in the hospital?"

"Well, I've got a crick in my neck from sleeping in a chair. And I hate the way hospitals smell. Other than that, it was fine."

"How is Mrs. Lacroix doing?"

The question threw Loretta. Paul had never cared much about other adults at the Guidepost, except for maybe Hayden Fowler, who had taken an interest in his music.

"She's better. It wasn't as serious as we initially feared."

"That's good. Still no word on the missing helicopter?"

"No." She glanced at the guitar case and amplifier sitting on the floor. "I take it you were on your way to rehearsal?"

"Yeah. But I wanted to talk to you first. Where's Dad?"

"He's out in The Cellar Cavern working with Apisi and Chogan, chipping away at meteorite rock. Why?"

"Well, I know he's pissed off at me and—"

"He's not mad at you, Paul. A little disappointed maybe. A little frustrated by the situation, but he loves you and wants what's best for you."

"Look, I know an education is important, Mom. I'm not an idiot."

"I know you're not, hon. You're a very smart, creative, talented young man. But you're only seventeen and your father just wants you to understand the realities of the career path you want to head down."

"That's why I wanted to talk with you alone."

"Okay. About what exactly?"

"I've been thinking about your and Dad's offer, and I have to ask—do you really think Pops can handle managing the band? I mean, he's a lot more frail these days. I don't think he has the stamina it's gonna take to keep up with us. And I'm sure he's not gonna be able to book us into the places where we need to be seen if Moonrise is gonna get anywhere. He doesn't have the connections that Wally has."

"Wally?"

"Yeah, our current manager, Wally Reinfeldt."

"Oh yeah, *that* Wally." She cast a stern look. "Let me tell you a few things about your father, Paul. I learned a long time ago to never underestimate him. He has a will that won't quit and a fertile imagination that would do Disney proud. There isn't anything he can't do when he puts his mind to it. He's a natural born salesman. He could sell ice to the Eskimos and TVs to the blind. And as far as him being frail? I witnessed him take on that Dromaeosaur in the quad early this summer. It takes a pretty tough hombre to come out on top in that battle, don't you think?"

"Yeah." Paul nodded slowly, showing his admiration. "That *was* impressive. I'll give him that."

"And not many people would have survived taking three bullets the way he did. Your father is one of the strongest, most courageous and heroic men I have ever known. He wants this very much for you and so he will be successful. He'll do great things for Moonrise. *We* will do great things for your band. But we want you to have a backup plan, just in case. Staying in school is the smart thing to do, Paul."

"I know that, Mom. It's just hard giving up a manager like Reinfeldt. He knows all the right people in the industry. Kit and Ox aren't onboard with replacing him with Dad. Not at all. And Sin is only lukewarm to the idea, and she's crazy about Dad."

"It's *your* band, son. You're the leader. It's your decision. Sometimes leaders have to make tough decisions. They have to make unpopular choices. But I will say this. A lot of musicians would kill to get a deal like the one your father and I are offering you."

"I know. You're right. But it's a really hard thing. Kit and Ox are my friends. Sinopa's my girlfriend."

"Welcome to the adult world, kiddo."

Eleven Days of Hell

August 8: River of No Return Wilderness
Central Idaho

ONLY THREE OF THEM REMAINED. The camp felt deserted.
Abandoned.

Ghostly.

Day eleven on this merciless mountain.

Peter and Bill sat on stumps in the center of the clearing, gnawing on roasted Tyrannosaurus Rex. Hayden slept in one of the tents,
in critical condition, continuing his downward spiral.

The afternoon sun peeked through gaps in the forest canopy,
dappling the dirt floor with stipples of light. A spectral stillness
enveloped the campsite, an almost supernatural hush that spooked
Peter. Even the birds had halted their usual chirpy chatter, as if
paying their respects to the dead. Peter hoped it wasn't another
woodland silence like the one that preceded the Dromaeosaur attack
earlier in the week.

Peter's back hurt more than it had since the crash. On that first
day, realizing he dislocated his shoulder, he had popped it back into
place. It was a painful maneuver he'd been forced to do a couple of
times during his hockey playing career. For three or four days after,
his shoulder had felt almost normal. But then, after sleeping on the
ground in the cold mountain air, colossal pain set in and had now
extended down his back. It seemed to be worsening daily. When he
moved too quickly or in a certain way, scorching strikes of pain
traveled down his back and nausea would take him down.

Eating dinosaur meat the last few days was not helping his
cause either.

He sat by the fire chomping on Tyrannosaur flank steak. The meat was tough and his jaws ached from the heavy chewing. He had eaten leathery beef jerky sticks that were more tender than this. But it was tastier, albeit saltier, than the Drome meat they'd feasted on. Carlton had once again put his butcher skills to work, carving several filets out of the flanks of the Rex they had killed two days ago. It had been a day of unforgettable horror—the day Jackson Lattimer was crushed in the powerful jaws of the second Tyrannosaur and taken over the edge of the cliff.

As he had done repeatedly the past two days, Peter replayed Jackson Lattimer's last moments. He still couldn't get over how Lattimer had saved Hayden's life. Jumped right in there when the beast was going after his defenseless and vulnerable friend, recording the event right up to the final instant. Neither he nor Bill had the stomach to watch the footage Jackson had captured before his demise. But one thing was for sure—Jackson Lattimer would be seen as a courageous and selfless hero when (and if) his millions of followers saw the video clip.

Peter couldn't wrap his head around the fact that three of the six team members he had flown out of Heart Butte eleven long days ago were now gone. Dead! All three killed in shocking violent ways. And Hayden was so bad off he and Bill had to check on him regularly to see if he was still breathing. Peter feared the paleontologist didn't have much longer. Hayden Fowler's survival to this point was a testament of the big man's physical strength and intestinal fortitude. A lesser man would have died days ago.

A putrid odor drifted through the clearing, mixing with the ashy wood-smoke smell of the fire. It came from the Tyrannosaur carcass lying in the corner of the clearing. The immense corpse was beginning to bloat up and stink. A cloud of black flies swarmed over the bullet wounds and bloodied sections along the animal's side where Carlton had gone to work with his buck knife. Peter and Bill had been able to drag the beast to an area farthest from the tents, but the body was too heavy and cumbersome to move into the woods where they'd been able to dispose of the much smaller Drome remains. Peter worried the repulsive scent might possibly attract more big predators.

"Do you think Lattimer was suicidal?" Bill Carlton mumbled between bites of Rex meat.

Peter shook his head. "No, not really. Someone with an astronomical ego like he had wouldn't want to kill himself."

"Then what made him do it? He certainly had a massive ego. I've known a few similarly narcissistic and egotistical men in my line of work, and none of them would ever think about sacrificing themselves for someone else. Lattimer might not have been suicidal, but he certainly had a death wish. Don't you think?"

"Well, I will say this. Jack was crazy. Crazy for fame and attention. He chased celebrity. It was his addiction, his drug of choice. His final act will cement his legacy, his legend. He'll live on forever in the minds of his fans as a hero. I think that's what he wanted ultimately. That's my take on it anyway."

"Seems like a high price to pay for hero worship status."

"Yeah, it was. But Jack always pushed the envelope. He loved to tempt the Grim Reaper. He died the way he lived. On the edge."

"Maybe," Bill said, getting up and going to the tent where Hayden was holed up. "He was a sad case. I don't think he liked himself much. If he wasn't suicidal, he certainly was an extreme masochist." He pulled the tent flap back to check that Hayden was still asleep, then returned to his seat on the stump. "That sure was a strange bond Lattimer had with Fowler. The way he nurtured him and played concerned nursemaid to him. You think they had a homosexual relationship?"

Peter had to laugh. "You're talking about two of the most macho dudes I've ever known, Bill."

"That doesn't always mean anything."

"I've gotten to know Hayden pretty well over the past year. Even had him and his lady friend Nora visit us in Missoula a couple of times. He's madly in love with Nora Lemoyne. There's no way he's gay. You're letting your inner homophobe show, Bill."

"I'm *not* homophobic," he said, indignant. "Damn you for even thinking that! I'm just trying to make sense of what happened."

"Understood," Peter said. "I really think Hayden and Jack had a powerful friendship. They were close like brothers. On the same wavelength. Maybe like a fraternal twin connection or something."

"You're probably right. But what Lattimer did seemed so out of character for him."

"I don't disagree. To say that people are complex is a huge understatement."

Bill stared into the fire, resignation lowering his voice to a husky whisper. "I was so excited about this outing with Hayden. We worked together on a short jaunt in June. Tracked a couple of big Rexes. Hayden is a walking-talking encyclopedia of Cretaceous dinosaur zoology and behavior. I've learned so much from him and I was looking forward to a further education on this trip. But for whatever reason, it just wasn't meant to be."

The two men returned to their silent eating. Peter bit off a chunk of Rex meat and struggled to chew. Washed the greasy fare down with a slug of water.

He thought back to the first few days after the crash, when they all had been filled with hope for a quick rescue. The way he had prayed so fervently. But now, after eleven long days and three deaths, the hope and prayers seemed naive to him. Sitting here with a scruffy beard and overpowering body odor, munching on tough dinosaur meat, he was pretty much resigned to the idea they might never be found. The ever increasing possibility that he could die on this heavily forested highland was a sobering thought. He had long since given up praying. What was the use? God wasn't listening.

Maybe if I dragged my ass into church once in a while, I would have God's ear.

He still talked to Brin and Kimi, even though he realized the absurdity of it.

Nobody can hear you, dummy, he reprimanded himself.

"Do you believe in God?" he asked Bill.

"I did until we ended up here. How about you?"

Peter nodded. "Same. For me, the jury is still out. This place is so far removed from civilization, I don't think God even knows it exists."

"Lattimer might have been right. If we just keep sitting up here expecting a miracle, we'll die. We should think about making a move, Pete."

"No can do. I wouldn't get far with my bum shoulder and bad back. And we can't leave Hayden behind."

Bill Carlton emitted an exasperated sigh. "I just feel so helpless sitting here day after day."

"Well, we need more firewood, Bill. Water, too."

Carlton mumbled something unintelligible. Peter figured it wasn't complimentary.

He checked his aviator watch that he'd been using as his calendar. With a start he realized the significance of this day—August 8—the one-year anniversary of the AEF attack on Gilliam's Guidepost ranch. It all came back to him in a rush: the bulldozers storming the east meadow as he flew over in the Forest Service chopper; the gunshots popping like firecrackers; terrorists taking potshots at his helicopter; the freed dinosaurs running helter-skelter through the fields; the partygoers running for their lives; the Gilliam home and barns blazing; touching down to pick up Brin, Kimi, and Kachina with Dromaeosaurs in hot pursuit. That afternoon had been a warped unreality, a bleak dystopian vision, and he started to tell Carlton about it.

"Hayden gave me some of the background of that day. I understand he was in the helicopter with you when it all went down."

"Yeah. I just happened to be flying Hayden and Nora around on a sightseeing flight when the shit hit the fan. A lot of good people lost their lives that day."

Conversation ceased as they finished their lunch and stared vacantly into the fire. A gust of wind howled through the cottonwoods. The songbirds started up again. Peter recognized the *chik-a-burr chik-a-burr* chirrup of the western tanager and the melodious rise-and-fall cheep of the yellow warbler, among others. The birds soothed his ravaged, exhausted psyche with their sweet music. He closed his eyes and took in the chorus of avian song, a pensive smile on his face.

Sometime later he heard a sound that made his heart soar—the faint sound of chopper blades cutting the air in the distance.

Becoming more distinct.

Getting closer quickly.

"You hear that, Bill?"

"I do indeed."

Peter struggled to get up, pain shooting down his spine. "Let's go," he croaked, grimacing, standing hunched over to ease the discomfort. "Let's get out to the ledge. See what's up. Give me a hand, will you?"

Carlton came to Peter's side and propped him up, helping him walk out to the cliff ledge where they could be seen from the air. The wind whipped at them as they stood on the narrow swath of granite, overlooking the Salmon River a dizzying distance below. Carlton held on to Peter as they gazed at a fast-approaching helicopter flying over the river, coming straight at them. As the aircraft came closer, Peter saw it was a Sikorsky S-92 SAR helicopter, and could make out the markings on the fuselage: **IDAHO MOUNTAIN SEARCH AND RESCUE**.

Could it be?

Are we finally going to be plucked off this nightmarish mountain?

They waved their arms frantically, the motion sending torturous bolts of pain through Peter's shoulder and back. He fought back tears. Tears of physical agony mixed with tears of emotional joy.

The chopper flashed a bright white spotlight on and off repeatedly, the beam strong enough to be seen in daylight.

They see us! They're coming for us!

The aircraft flew in over the ledge and hovered, the downdraft whipping the trees behind them into a frenzy. The thump of the rotors pounded in Peter's ears like gunshots.

A side door opened and a man wearing a helmet and vest was lowered in a padded longline basket. Peter had overseen this hoist rescue procedure many times during his eight years with the Forest Service.

An overwhelming swell of wellbeing and gratitude coursed through him as the basket settled on the rocky ledge. The rescue technician unbuckled his harnesses and jumped out. He was a young guy with a strong cleft chin, alert eyes, and a compact muscular frame.

"I'm Eddie Franklin of the Idaho Mountain SAR unit," he yelled over the roar of the engine and whirling rotors.

Carlton leaned in close to Franklin's ear. "I'm Bill Carlton, Idaho wildlife biologist, and this is Peter Lacroix, pilot of the missing helicopter. Man, are we ever glad to see you folks!"

Franklin shouted, "We're happy to have finally found you."

"How'd you locate us?"

"We found a dead Tyrannosaurus Rex and the remains of a man downriver a couple of miles," he barked. "They were washed up on a small midstream island. So we backtracked, concentrated our search effort along this section of the river. Was the body we found with the dinosaur in your group?"

"Yeah. Jackson Lattimer," Peter hollered. "He went over the cliff with the T-Rex two days ago."

"I'm so sorry to hear that. How many of you are there."

"One more besides us. He's in rough shape up at our campsite," Peter said, pointing up the incline to where the tree line began.

"Okay, we'll get him first. Lead me up there."

As they walked—Carlton and Franklin supporting Peter on either side—Peter leaned into Bill and shouted, "I guess maybe God exists after all."

"You just might be on to something there, Pete."

And so ended eleven days of hell.

Nora's Soliloquy

August 9: St. Luke's Medical Center
Boise, Idaho

NORA SAT AT THE EDGE OF THE BED in an uncomfortable chair, squeezing Hayden's limp hand, wishing for all the world that he would squeeze back. She had been squeezing and talking for an hour now, hoping and praying he would open his eyes and give her some kind of response.

A young doctor—Dr. Adam Hodges—had informed her that Hayden arrived at the hospital in a comatose state. She had been existing in a stunned stupor ever since.

She scanned the wires and tubes that bound Hayden to the bed like medical shackles—the tube running from an IV bag of caramel-colored liquid, EKG leads, a pulse oximeter, blood pressure cuff, urinary catheter, feeding tube, EEG brain monitoring electrodes, along with a few other hookups she couldn't readily identify. Computerized diagnostic equipment hissed and hummed above his head. Colorful LED graphs displayed health data she could not decipher.

The usually indomitable Hayden Fowler looked vulnerable, smaller somehow. His typically ruddy complexion was a pallid gray touched with a jaundiced yellow that lent him the appearance of a sickly bearded alien. His arms were covered in ugly blood-filled lesions. Dr. Hodges explained they were coma blisters that would heal within a week or two (leaving out the implied *if he pulls through*). Seeing Hayden reduced to this undignified state and trapped in a sterile hospital bed was almost too much for her.

She looked at the soapy melodrama playing on the TV bracketed to the far wall. A young woman dressed to the nines and adorned in expensive jewelry gave a man the third degree for sleeping with her sister. The volume was low but the actress's vitriol came through loud and clear.

Why in the hell do they have a television on in a room with an unresponsive patient? Coma therapy? This annoying crap isn't therapy, it's torture!

She found the remote and turned off the offensive blather. Returned to her bedside watch. Plopped down in her chair with a tired exhale.

Nora and Brin had received word of the rescue late last night. They left early this morning, driving two hours to Great Falls in Nora's rental car, then taking a Delta flight to Boise (four hours with a stopover).

Nora's fame preceded her; the hospital had rolled out the red carpet for them. Ordinarily, because she wasn't immediate family, doctors and staff would not have briefed her or allowed her into Hayden's room. They would have waited for Hayden's mother, Miranda, who was on her way from Indianapolis. But Nora was well known as Hayden's co-author of their huge bestseller, *Cretaceous Stones: The Return of Prehistoric Life to Earth*—the book everyone was reading these days. She was one-half of the famous dinosaur tracking couple, and so usual hospital protocol had been abandoned in favor of her celebrity status. Several nurses had gushed in her presence, telling her how much they enjoyed reading her book and eagerly pressing her for information about the sequel. Dr. Hodges even asked her to sign his copy. Nora was appreciative of the interest but embarrassed by the superstar treatment, finding it inappropriate considering the situation.

But her fame *had* gained her entrance into Hayden's room, and for that she was thankful.

Upon their arrival, Brin was told that Peter was doing well, though he would be held a few days—possibly as long as a week— to regain his strength and mobility. Ecstatic, she had let out a joyful shriek and hugged the hospital administrator who had given her the news. When she finally got to see Peter, she nearly bowled him over with her enthusiasm, clutching him tight as she cried out, "Petey,

Petey, oh my sweet Petey! I thought I'd lost you! I love you so much!" her voice resounding through the hallway, so loud a hospital official had to tell her to tone it down. Peter did his best to hold on and kiss her while grimacing through the pain. Nora thought he looked thin and alarmingly frail. He was hunched over, his movement restricted by his medical accoutrements: a neck brace, a tight sling binding his damaged left shoulder, and a body-hugging back brace to keep his spine in place. An unkempt beard and a disquieting weariness added years to his age.

Unfortunately the news about Hayden wasn't as positive as Peter's diagnosis. When Dr. Hodges approached Nora in the visitor waiting area, his defeated posture and severe frown told her the news would be bad. The doctor had taken her to a consultation room to drop the bomb.

"Mr. Fowler has suffered massive internal blood loss," he said directly. Nora wanted to tell him it was *Doctor* Fowler but she didn't interrupt. "The decrease in blood volume has cut the oxygen and nutrients going to his vital organs and brain. I'm sorry to have to inform you of this, but Mr. Fowler is in a reduced state of consciousness."

Nora remembered gasping. "But he's still alive, right?"

"Yes, but he's not responding to external stimuli. He's in a coma, Ms. Lemoyne. I'm sorry."

Nora felt her entire being plummet, a rush of vertigo making her dizzy. "Does that mean brain damage?"

"I'm afraid it's too early to tell. We'll know more after seventy-two hours. Typically coma patients come out of it after a few days, but we'll have to see. A good sign is that he's breathing on his own so we didn't have to resort to an endotracheal tube." He gave her a stern look. "You have to understand that comas are highly unpredictable. Each case is unique. Mr. Fowler seems to have been in pretty good shape before the accident. That works in his favor, but he's been through a lot. On top of the blood loss, he's severely dehydrated and malnourished. One of his kidneys is dead and the other is working at only fifty percent capacity. His liver function has been severely compromised. We're doing our best to bring him back around physically, and I think we'll be able to do that, but regaining consciousness is entirely up to him."

"Can I see him?"

"Of course. Please talk to him as if he was awake and aware. It's been my experience that loved ones talking to coma patients is very helpful for the patient in regaining their cognitive abilities. I will inform Mr. Fowler's mother of this as well when she arrives. It might seem strange at first, talking to someone who is unresponsive, but studies indicate comatose patients can hear and process information. They just can't respond. No guarantees, but talking to Mr. Fowler will surely help revive him."

Nora felt odd initially, going on and on while Hayden lay there in a deep sleep, expressionless, lost in his silent internal landscape. But after a while she got into a rhythm and it became effective therapy for her, allowing her to minimize her grief and keep her panic monster at bay.

She thought his family would be a good place to start. Nora knew Hayden was an only child who had lost his father Max to a heart attack nine years ago. His mother, Miranda, was the only family he'd ever discussed with her. With that in mind, Nora thought Miranda would be an effective connection point.

"Your mother is on her way here, Hayden. You've told me how much you admire her and I know her presence here will be good for you. Miranda is such a beautiful name. Very lyrical the way it rolls off the tongue. So lyrical in fact that Shakespeare used it in *The Tempest*. Shakespeare's Miranda is compassionate and kind and loving. You can't get much more artistic street cred than Shakespeare. I looked it up and the name Miranda is from the Latin meaning 'worthy of admiration' or 'to be wondered at.' From what you've told me about her, that sounds pretty right on. You told me she has become less social and more reclusive in the years since your father passed—no more garden club or Tupperware parties or volunteer work—so I'm glad she's getting out to make this trip. I'm looking forward to meeting her, Hayden. I'm sure she will be glad to fill me in on all the secrets you've been keeping from me." She reached out and touched his hand. "Oh don't get so upset. It's just a joke, honey, just a joke."

His complete obliviousness made her want to cry, but she carried on.

"I've been doing the best I can on our book, but it's just not the same without you. Molly liked my chapters on the Triceratops tagging and our encounter with the Ankylosaurs. She loved the title of the Ankylosaur chapter: *Otherworldly Armadillos*. You came up with that one and I gave you full credit for it, dearest. You are so clever when you want to be. Everyone at the publisher and our Smithsonian friends have been keeping you in their prayers. I haven't had a chance to speak with any of them since I learned of your rescue last night, but I'm sure, like me, they are overjoyed that you made it through alive. Bryan and Loretta are coming to see you tomorrow. They've been concerned about you, too. You are loved by so many people, Hayden. I think you sometimes lose sight of that fact, with your nihilistic misanthropic view of the world, a view, by the way, that turned me off at first, but I now find quite charming seeing as how I believe you espouse it in a satirical way.

"I came here with Brinshou Lacroix. I don't know if you are aware, but Peter made it. He's here on another floor of the hospital, wrapped up like a mummy in a neck brace and a back brace. A shoulder sling completes the ensemble. I hardly recognized him at first with how much weight he's lost and his shabby beard. Except for his shoulder, he's okay. Well, his back isn't so great either. They're keeping him a few days to replenish his fluids and get him started on a physical therapy program to get him mobile again. You can imagine how Brin reacted. She went wild. It's a beautiful thing to watch, a young married couple like them, so much in love. And, oh yeah, we all had a big scare a few days ago when Brin thought she had lost her baby. She was so distraught and out of sorts through all this and suffered what she thought was a miscarriage. It ended up being a chorionic hematoma—a false miscarriage. It was a scary twenty-four hours, let me tell you. But she's fine now, especially since she has her cherished Petey back. That's what she calls him— *Petey*. It's so cute as to be nauseating, but I'd never tell her that.

"They tell me your wildlife biologist friend, Bill Carlton, is doing well and is scheduled for release tomorrow. I so wish you could tell me what happened out there, Hayden. You lost three of your team? It had to have been hell. I wasn't able to spend much time with Peter and I don't know Bill Carlton, so I'm in the dark about what transpired. All Peter would tell me was that some pre-historic birds caused the helicopter to go down. I didn't want to bother him too much seeing that he was in pain, but when I pushed him about the prehistoric birds he told me they were some kind of large pterosaurs with a name he couldn't remember and couldn't pronounce even if he could. He also told me Jackson Lattimer saved your life by sacrificing his own. I'd really love to hear how that came about. I really can't picture him saving anybody's life but his own, but I am sorry he died. I'm sorry you lost your good friend, Hayden. I know you saw him as someone special. I remember you telling me he seemed like the brother you never had. It's hard to lose a brotherly friend. I'm sorry for your loss, honey. And Larry Bing? He was Peter's good friend and fellow pilot. Such a nice guy. Christ, what happened out there in the wilderness, Hayden?

"Oh, listen to me. Going on about death and destruction and hellfire when I'm supposed to be filling your head with positive vibes. Let's see. What can I talk about that's positive in all this? Oh yeah, you'll be happy to know that I didn't suffer one panic attack in your absence. Oh, I came close a couple of times, especially when trying to deal with Brin's craziness. But I held those nasty suckers off and I'm proud of myself. But nothing gives me strength against the panic attack boogey monster like the way you hold me and comfort me when I feel one coming on. You are *so* good for me, Hayden. In every which way.

"Damn how I miss you, big guy! I've missed your corny jokes and awkward French expressions. I miss your boisterous laugh that warms my heart so. I miss being out in the field with you. I miss your childlike wonder about the mysteries of the natural world. I miss discussing scientific theories with you. I miss writing books with you. I know you didn't enjoy our book tour much, but I miss going on the road with you to promote our book and meeting our fans. You're one hell of a great travel companion. I know it sounds funny coming from my mouth, but you have restored my faith in the male of the species. You're the first man in my life I've wanted to spend all my time with. When we first met I thought you would be trouble, and you were. You're half-crazy but you're my kind of crazy, so there is that. You've taught me that a little bit of trouble can be a good thing. Fun even. You've loosened me up, pointed me in directions I never thought I'd go."

She looked at him. Hayden hadn't so much as twitched a muscle. The only proof that he was still alive was the rise and fall of his chest as he breathed free and easy.

Maybe he'll show some kind of response if I liven things up a bit.

She got up and shut the door, returned to the bed, deciding a carnal approach might get a rise out of him. Literally.

"I love the way you whisper sweet nasties in my ear when we're fucking. I miss those big hands of yours on me, caressing me, exciting me, urging me on. I miss the magic of your mouth and tongue when you go down on me and the delicious way your beard tickles my thighs. I love the way you fuck me the way you do, like you really mean it. I love the feel of you in my mouth, so hard and slick, the taste of you."

She pulled the sheets off of him and peeled back his gown to see if her lascivious ramblings had any effect on him.

No response. No erection. Limp as a wet noodle.

She felt a stab of guilt for violating his personal space.

What the hell were you thinking, girlfriend?

Nora voiced a quick burst of a laugh, thinking how ridiculous she'd sounded. She pulled his gown down over his legs and tucked the sheets up under his chin. Brought the one-sided conversation back to safe ground.

"I guess what I really want to tell you is that I love you, Hayden. I know I don't tell you that often enough. It's never been easy for me to say those words. But while you were missing, I realized just how much you mean to me. I love you so goddamned much, Hayden Fowler," she said, tears welling up, her face feverish. "Please come back to me, big guy. Please don't leave me in this screwed-up world by myself. I need you. I love you. I *want* you! I wish I could jump into that bed with you right now."

She leaned in and kissed him, startled by the cool lifelessness of his lips.

She heard someone clear their throat behind her. She turned away from Hayden and saw a woman in her late-seventies standing in the doorway. Snowy white hair in an elegant layered cut, stylish designer outfit of pale blue silk blouse under a matching cardigan, navy blue pants, dressy suede flats, a small cream-colored clutch in her grasp. She matched the photos Hayden had shown her.

Miranda Fowler.

Nora blushed, embarrassed, wondering how much the woman had heard of her monologue. "Mrs. Fowler?"

"Please, dear, call me Miranda. And I take it you are Hayden's Nora?"

"Yes, um . . . yes, I am. It's so nice to finally meet you." Nora stood. "I didn't hear you come in. How long have you been standing there?"

"Oh, a few minutes."

"How much of that did you hear?"

Miranda smiled fiendishly. "Most of it."

Oh, dear god!" Nora's blush deepened. "You must think I'm terrible, saying those um—those *perverted* things."

"Nonsense. I'm an old woman, Nora. There isn't much I haven't seen or heard in my years. I think the things you told my son are sweet. Shows how much you care about him. How much you love him. I've never seen Hayden happier than he's been since you came into his life."

"Oh, thank you, Mrs.—er, I mean Miranda," Nora said with a relieved exhale. She moved to Hayden's mother and held out her hand. "Very nice to meet you in person. Hayden has told me so many good things about you."

Miranda looked at Nora's proffered hand and said, "This isn't a business transaction, dear. Come here and give me a big hug. We're family now."

Nora embraced the older woman, taking in the citrusy floral

scent of her perfume. They maintained the clinch for long moments, their shared grief passing between them.

When they broke apart, Miranda looked at Hayden and asked, "How's our boy doing, Nora?"

"Well, I worry when he doesn't respond to my erotic advances. That's not like him at all."

Miranda smiled weakly, as though appreciative of Nora's attempt to keep things light. She said, "That young doctor told me it's a good sign that Hayden's breathing on his own."

Nora nodded. "He told me that as well. He also said the best thing we can do for him is talk to him like he's aware and present. That's why I've been in here blabbering my fool head off the past couple of hours. I'm running out of things to say."

"Well, you've got a reinforcement now," Miranda said, laying her purse on a bedside table and pulling up a chair. "I've got plenty to say to my son."

"Will any of it be juicy family secrets that Hayden has been reluctant to divulge about himself?"

"Probably. As you can imagine, Hayden was a hyperactive, inquisitive child. He got into all kinds of mischief. And then there were those three ex-wives of his and his troubles with the law. Lordy I'm surprised I'm still above ground with all the stress he brought down on me and my dearly departed Max." She looked at Hayden and said, "But you've redeemed yourself, my dear sweet son. Especially by being smart enough to hang on to this lovely woman beside me."

Nora's heart swelled. She liked Hayden's mother more than she thought she would.

Miranda said, "The good doctor says talking is the best medicine so let's throw a few words at him, shall we, Nora?"

They worked as a tag team over the next two hours, talking to the lifeless body in the bed, with Nora learning so many intriguing things that shed new light on her lover and business partner.

All the while, Hayden slept on.

The Big Pinch

August 10: Rendaya Ranch
Flathead National Forest, Montana

KELTON RENDAYA SAT AT HIS KITCHEN TABLE drinking coffee, waiting for an expected delivery of venomous snakes. A morning newscast played quietly on his portable TV as he mentally reviewed his purchase—three western taipans, a pair of banded kraits, two saw-scaled vipers, four black mambas, a fer-de-lance, and a very rare Mozambique spitting cobra—an order he'd placed with his biggest reptile supplier before his arrest. He'd considered canceling it due to his recent run-in with the feds, but old habits die hard. Serpent trafficking was in his blood. He wanted to restock his snake barn and bring it back to life. He had several eager buyers lined up who were willing to pay top dollar. Kelton figured if he got caught, the authorities would only slap him with another fine, so he deemed it worth the risk.

He had two more snake orders coming next week and he saw no reason to cancel them either.

He felt the buzz returning.

He was back in the game!

No government officials with their ridiculous laws would keep him from doing what he loved.

He had to do something. He was losing equine veterinary clients due to his very public arrest. Three horse owners had canceled their appointments last week, and he felt sure more client cancelations would follow. He had to make up for the lost revenue somehow. At least that's how he justified getting back into snake peddling.

Movement on the TV screen caught his eye—a video clip of a

candy apple red helicopter flying through a canyon, the aircraft a crisp metallic cutout against a craggy mountain backdrop. He listened in as the female newscaster explained.

"The nation and the world are in mourning today over the death of iconic nature videographer, Jackson Lattimer. The celebrated video documentarian, known as America's Gonzo Shutterbug, was one of six people aboard this Fowler-Lemoyne Aviation helicopter you see here, which crashed in the central Idaho mountains while on a dinosaur tagging operation. Three survivors were found after an intensive eleven-day search headed by Idaho Mountain Search and Rescue units. A second onboard celebrity—paleontologist Dr. Hayden Fowler, famed dinosaur tracker and author of the bestselling book, *Cretaceous Stones: The Return of Prehistoric Life to Earth*—survived, as did the pilot, Peter Lacroix, and Idaho wildlife biologist William Carlton . . ."

Kelton couldn't believe his eyes.

That's the same chopper that buzzed my dinosaur pens!

He hadn't been keeping up with the news since his arrest so he had no clue about the helicopter crash and lengthy search for survivors.

There's no mistaking it! They're the ones who dropped a dime on me! It's Fowler's helicopter. Was this Lacroix guy the one who piloted it that day, when they snapped photos of my compound?

"Social media has been lighting up with tributes to Jackson Lattimer, who was forty-five years old. The general consensus is that he was one of the greatest and most courageous nature photojournalists of all time. His daring videos of charging hippos in Africa and deadly saltwater crocodiles in Australia are being mastered for an *Animal Planet* cable special, and video clips of his audaciously bold encounters with Tyrannosaurus Rex, Dromaeosaurus, and Triceratops are in the process of being packaged for a *National Geographic* broadcast . . ."

Kelton seethed as he watched the shiny red copter fly along the ridgeline. *If it hadn't been for them, I'd still be wheeling and dealing dinosaurs, raking in substantial profits. Assholes!*

"Biologist William Carlton was released from Boise St. Luke's Medical Center yesterday, but has declined to speak with the press. So we got what information we could from the rescue team. The lead on the rescue effort—Eddie Franklin of the Idaho Mountain SAR unit—released an official statement to the press this morning confirming the cause of Jackson Lattimer's death."

The scene switched from the stock footage of the helicopter to a short stout man with chiseled cheekbones and a broad chin holding a mic. A gusty wind blew his long brown hair in his face. The banner at the bottom of the screen identified him as Edward Franklin of the Montana Mountain Search and Rescue team.

"It appears that Jackson Lattimer survived the helicopter crash only to be killed by a rampaging Tyrannosaur. The famous videographer finally met his end doing what he loved. We found his remains in the jaws of a twelve-foot-tall Tyrannosaur that had plunged off a cliff and into the Salmon River. From the air we spotted the battered beast and what was left of Lattimer's body washed up on a small island a quarter mile from where we eventually found the three crash survivors. Finding Lattimer's remains was the key that led us to them. Without that find, we probably would still be looking."

The picture returned to the studio and the female anchor.

"One of the deceased died in the crash: Jenkins McCraw, zoologist from Salt Lake City, Utah, age thirty-nine. Co-pilot Lawrence Bing of Bozeman, Montana, age thirty-three, survived the crash but like Jackson Lattimer, was attacked and killed by a dinosaur. We're told it was a Dromaeosaur. Jenkins McCraw is survived by his wife and two young children while Lawrence Bing, a bachelor, is survived by his parents. James and Trudy Bing of Billings, Montana. Pilot Peter Lacroix is in stable condition at St. Luke's and is expected to be released within the week. He also is refusing to speak with reporters at this time. Dr. Hayden Fowler, we're sorry to report, has been comatose since his arrival at the Boise hospital due to injuries suffered in the crash. His recovery is uncertain . . ."

Kelton watched the newscast for a few more minutes, then shut it off. He wondered what caused the crash. He also pondered how they had discovered his dinosaur enclave when he'd taken great pains to conceal it. Of course he knew the plate on his Toyota 4Runner that Hoops Terrell had used in the Kanti Lyttle kidnapping led federal authorities to his front door. But why did a privately owned helicopter search his property from the air? What was their role in all of this?

He retrieved his laptop and googled Fowler-Lemoyne Aviation. Discovered it was a recent startup company (inaugural flight, July 9) that operated out of Heart Butte on Gilliam's Guidepost Ranch. Kelton thought it more than a little coincidental. People involved with the renowned ranch that housed dinosaurs for government study last year discovering the Rendaya Ranch dino habitats? He checked the list of company officers—Dr. Hayden Fowler, Dr. Nora Lemoyne, Peter Lacroix, Bryan Gilliam.

He googled Bryan Gilliam and found a new report published in the *Missoulian* Sunday edition just last week, stating that Gilliam had been instrumental in locating three missing Blackfoot women: Kanti Lyttle, Ahwee Red Crow, and Aiyana Halfmoon.

It was all starting to make a bit of twisted sense to him now. It was Gilliam who had spearheaded the search for the abducted Native women. Bryan Gilliam and this helicopter pilot were definitely in on it. They hadn't found the kidnapped women the day they flew over his property, but they did stumble on his dinosaur habitats, gleaning enough criminal animal trafficking evidence to take to the feds.

Visions of revenge danced through his head when he heard a vehicle pulling up out front.

The squeak of brakes.

Voices.

He checked the time. 8:35.

Excellent, he thought, getting up and walking down the hallway into the front room. *My snake delivery is twenty-five minutes early.*

He pulled up short. Through the bay window, he saw a familiar police car, its beacon strobing blue light. The dark gray sedan with the blue mountain peaks emblem and the words *Sheriff—Flathead County* emblazoned on the side. A black Ford Explorer parked behind it. Three law enforcement officers walked toward the front porch, conversing. Kelton recognized the sheriff's deputy, Stuart Fenski. He also recognized FBI Special Agents Clevenger and Morrissey, decked out in their familiar navy blue jackets with gold lettering. All three men were heavily armed.

The Three Musketeers are back!

The presence of the feds told him it had to be serious.

He felt a squeeze in his testicles.

What the hell do they want now? Didn't they get enough of my skin three weeks ago?

Kelton opened the front door and stepped out on the porch. Tried to keep his voice cordial, though fear and anger swept through him.

"Good morning, gentlemen. I would have brewed more coffee if I knew you were coming. What brings you all the way out here again?"

Agent Clevenger spoke. "We didn't completely finish our investigation the last time we were here, Mr. Rendaya."

"How quickly you forget. It's *Doctor* Rendaya if you please."

Deputy Fenski stepped up on the porch and pulled a set of handcuffs from his belt. Kelton felt his hands on him, roughly jostling him, trying to turn him around.

The deputy said, "Doctor Kelton Rendaya you are under arrest for—"

"Get your fucking hands off me!" Kelton yelled, slapping the cop's hands away and backing up. "This is getting old. What the hell am I under arrest for this time?"

Agent Clevenger again. "You're under arrest for identity theft, illegal interstate animal trafficking, and murder."

"*Murder?*" Kelton said, feeling the cuffs pinch his wrists. "You're out of your goddamned mind!"

Deputy Fenski recited, "You have the right to remain silent. Everything you say can, and will be, held against you in a court of law. You have the right to an attorney. If you cannot afford one, one will be provided for you."

Kelton stood his ground, though he knew he was in deep shit. "Who did I allegedly murder?"

Clevenger stared at him with a steely gaze. "Two North Dakota state troopers on the morning of July thirteenth. West of Bismarck on I-94. Highway patrol officers Edward Irving and Francis Darby to be exact."

"That's bullshit!" he responded, trying to guess at how they had finally connected him to that awful night.

"No it's not. We have two witnesses who tell us you were out of town making a dinosaur delivery in North Dakota on that date. They even specified that your cargo consisted of two Tyrannosaurus Rexes, which, not coincidentally were what killed the officers. Our wits said you were gone from the ranch from July twelfth through the fourteenth, which aligns precisely with their murders."

"What witnesses?"

Agent Clevenger shook his head. "You know we're not at liberty to give you that information. But I'm guessing you can figure it out without taxing your brain too much."

Had to be Tank Mahaffey and Hoops Terrell.

Agent Morrissey said, "Does the name Bradley Anderson mean anything to you, Dr. Rendaya?"

Hearing that name hit Kelton like a thunderbolt. *I'm screwed,* he thought. He struggled to hide his recognition but managed to get out a convincing "No, should it?"

"Yes, you should be *very* familiar with Bradley Anderson. He's your alter ego, the identity you used to rent the Penske truck in which you hauled the murder weapons—the pair of Tyrannosaurs. Brad Anderson is the identity you gave the North Dakota patrolmen when they pulled you over. We know that because we found Officer Irving's clipboard in the woods along that highway where the Tyrannosaurs dragged off his body. It had all of Brad Anderson's personal information written down. His address in Helena. His driver's license number. Also attached was the original rental agreement showing the credit card number of his Visa account you used to rent the truck."

"That doesn't prove a thing. It certainly doesn't prove it was me."

"Oh, but it does," Agent Clevenger chimed in. "You see when we swept your property to execute our search warrant a few weeks back, our agents found two complete sets of picture IDs in your office desk. Your photos were on them but the name Kelton Rendaya was nowhere to be seen. One of those sets was in the name of Bradley Anderson—driver's license, passport, birth certificate, Social Security card, credit cards . . . the full monte."

Kelton stood there staring blankly at the three officers of the law, his shackled hands cramping up behind his back.

Agent Morrissey said, "And to put the icing on your cake, we also found a hypodermic needle and two vials of animal tranquilizer—xylazine—in the recovered rental truck with your real name on the labels as the prescriber. You well know that xylazine is a specialized drug that can only be prescribed by licensed veterinarians and certified wildlife biologists. You had to use your vet credentials to obtain xylazine."

Kelton felt desperation squeezing at his throat. "You're lying! If any xylazine was found in the truck it was planted."

"Give it up, Rendaya," Agent Clevenger snarled. "That's a weak argument. We went to the veterinary compounding pharmacy in Kalispell where you purchased it. They're quite familiar with you. They told us you're one of their better customers, that you buy all your equine drugs there, including large amounts of xylazine. So you see, all of this ties together in a nice neat package. We've got you on so many counts you might never get out of prison: negligent homicide of two police officers; illegal interstate transport of illicit and highly dangerous wildlife; a double count of identity theft; grand theft auto for ditching the rental truck. And let us not forget about the remains of the Salish woman found in your dinosaur pens. That'll bring another count of accessory to murder. You disappoint me, Doctor. You have been very sloppy. I'm surprised a man like you with your elite education and high standing in the community has been so careless." He looked at Fenski. "Take him in, Deputy. I'm sick of looking at him."

Kelton sat in the back seat of the cruiser on the trip to the Flathead County Jail, embarrassed, shamed by Clevenger's words.

How is it that I've managed to screw up my life like this?

He realized he might never see his ranch again, and that realization brought on a wave of sadness.

Attempting to elevate his low mood, he began plotting a viable defense for his crimes. He knew it would be a tough road considering the goods they had on him.

As he reasoned through his actions, he thought: *How in the hell did we miss the needle and vials of xylazine in the rental truck? We scrubbed that vehicle top to bottom before we dumped it.*

He wondered whether they had picked up Thorn for the North Dakota fiasco. Kelton didn't want to think so, but he realized with a growing sense of alarm that Mark Thornberry possibly could have planted the syringe and vials.

Just goes to show, you can't trust anybody.

Especially his employees.

The Dreamy Tour Guide

August 12: St. Luke's Medical Center
Boise, Idaho

NORA'S BACK ACHED. THE CRIMP IN HER NECK throbbed. These institutional chairs weren't designed for sleeping, or even sitting for long periods. The nurses had brought her a blanket and extra pillows, but it didn't help much. She had spent the better part of four days in this ultra-uncomfortable chair watching over a still comatose Hayden. He hadn't so much as fluttered an eyelid during that time. He breathed easily, which was a blessing, but his other systems remained shut down.

Bryan and Loretta had visited the second day, and Nora could tell they were uneasy, circling the bed cautiously, casting uncomfortable glances at Hayden as if he was a sideshow attraction. Nora understood the Gilliams' reaction. It *was* a shocking sight, seeing the usually vigorous and virile Hayden Fowler laid up and silenced. Miranda had finally given up yesterday and gone home to Indianapolis after Dr. Hodges told them it could be a long wait. But Nora had stayed on, committed, determined to stick it out. She wanted to be there for him when he woke up.

But four days in this claustrophobic hospital room with its antiseptic smell and the constant *click-whoosh-beep* of medical machines had taken its toll. She eyed Hayden, looking like an inanimate figure in Madame Tussaud's wax museum, and she questioned her decision to stay.

The trauma doctors and nursing staff continued to encourage Nora to keep talking to him, but she was all talked out. Trying to communicate with him had become an exercise in futility. She was out of topics she thought might engage him. She had lost count of how many times she had expressed her love for him. The more she talked without a response the more frustrated and depressed she became. She now sat in her uncomfortable chair with her laptop open, working on the new book, dismayed by the thought she might have to finish it alone.

He will come out of it, she told herself repeatedly.

Stay on a positive track, Nora.

Word had leaked to the media that she and Hayden were here, which only complicated matters. Nora had worn a path to and from the hospital cafeteria during her stay, and on three different occasions, she had been blindsided by reporters lying in wait. Each time she'd brushed them off with a brusque "No comment" and a hurried pace to the elevator. But then yesterday morning, just after Hayden's mother left, a TV reporter had sneaked past security and barged into the room, a cameraman trailing.

"Ms. Lemoyne, we're with KTVB Channel 7 here in Boise. I'm Murray Brinkley of the News At Five team. Our viewers want to know how you're holding up since your business partner Dr. Fowler is in a coma."

"How'd you get in here?" Nora asked, perturbed by the intrusion.

"We have our ways," the newsman said haughtily. "Would you mind if we shot a video of Dr. Fowler?"

Where the hell is security?

The audacity of these people knew no bounds. Nora, her Styrofoam cup of coffee in hand, stood and walked toward Brinkley. Raised her voice while poking him in the chest with her free hand. "If you don't leave within five seconds, your viewers will see your death on the five o'clock news. Please leave now!"

"Okay then, no video of your lover. Would you mind telling our viewers what you know about the helicopter crash?"

Nora was furious. "I'm warning you. If you don't leave this instant I'll throw this scalding hot coffee in your face! You'll never work in TV again."

"Okay, okay, we're leaving," Brinkley said, backing away from her. He turned to the camera and said, "You saw it here first. Bestselling author and noted dinosaur tracker, Nora Lemoyne, is devastated by the loss of her famous paleontologist lover, Dr. Hayden Fowler."

Nora flexed her arm to launch the coffee, then thought better of it. She went to the nurse call button beside the bed and pressed it, calling for security. To Brinkley she said, "I haven't lost anybody yet, asshole! Get out before I kill you and feed pieces of you to your precious viewers!"

They were gone when the security guard arrived—a young male in uniform, a shiny black baton bouncing against his hip. He apologized profusely for missing the TV news crew and promised they would keep a guard posted outside Hayden's door from now on.

She left the room and paced the hallway in a rage. Nora couldn't believe the disrespect and utter rudeness displayed by this Murray Brinkley buffoon. She would definitely be calling KTVB Channel 7 to register her complaint and threaten a huge lawsuit if they dared to air the footage they shot.

Hayden deserves so much better than those two bad actors.

She decided to head down to the cafeteria for another cup of coffee. Her frazzled nerves and raw stomach told her she should probably lay off the caffeine, but the deep rich roast specialty coffee they served here was so addictive. Besides, it was the only thing keeping her awake at this point.

Returning to Hayden's room, she was greeted by an older female security guard who told her she would be posted outside until eleven o'clock. At that point she would be replaced by the graveyard shift guard. Nora cringed at the guard's use of the word *graveyard,* but thanked her for being there. She went inside and closed the door behind her.

At first she thought she had entered a dreamscape.

Hayden's eyes were open. She thought she detected a gleam in them as she approached the bed.

"Hayden?"

"Where . . . where am I?" he said, his voice scratching out in a parched whisper.

"Oh, my god!" She nearly dropped her coffee. Nora thought her heart would burst right through her blouse. "I can't believe it! You're awake!"

Hayden opened his mouth to speak but nothing came out. He gazed at the medical equipment surrounding him, confusion clouding his expression.

She went to him and kissed him on the cheek, his beard tickling her nose. "You're in a hospital in Boise Idaho," she said, caressing his arm. "Welcome back. I'm here for you, Hayden. I've been waiting for you."

"*Mon amour,*" he said with a thin smile. "I . . . I missed you."

"I've missed you, too, big guy."

"Lots of strange dreams," he croaked. "You were . . . um . . . you were my tour guide."

"Tour guide?"

"Yep . . . in my dreams. Kept talkin'. My dreamy tour guide."

"You heard me talking to you?"

He nodded weakly. "The best part was . . . uh . . . when you kept sayin' how much you loved me," he rasped. "Like a song to me."

She felt a lurch in her chest. "That's really sweet. And I really *do* love you, Hayden. I realized while you were gone how little I've said those words to you."

"How, um . . . how long . . . away?"

"Four days here, plus the eleven you were lost in the wilderness. Do you remember flying to Idaho?"

Hayden shook his head, then stared at the ceiling with a reflective expression.

Nora pressed the call button, informed the nurse station that Hayden was awake and talking. "Please bring a pitcher of water," she told them. "His throat is dry as a desert." She noticed his face contorting in agony as he shifted in the bed. "I think he's going to need some painkiller, too."

Hayden reached for her arm, struggling to say something. "Saved my life . . . died . . . just for me, Nora."

"Are you talking about Jackson Lattimer?"

He nodded vigorously, pain showing with each bob of his head.

"Jack, yeah."

"I know. Peter told me. He's here in this hospital, too."

"How is Pete?"

"Banged up but he's going home soon."

"Tha's good. Not—" he stopped, cringing as a wave of pain struck him. "—not his fault."

"What? You mean the crash?"

"Yeah, yeah, yeah . . . Good pilot."

"Yes, he is. We're lucky to have him flying for our company."

"But Jack . . . reason I'm still alive . . . good man."

She could see his desire to talk was causing him great pain. She patted him on the hand and said, "Best to keep quiet and rest, my love. You can tell me everything later."

The nurse entered with a large metal pitcher of water while Nora was on the phone with Hayden's mother.

"Hi, Miranda. Great news. Your son is awake and talking. Hop back on that plane and get to Boise."

"That's wonderful! I'll be there as soon as I can. May I talk to him?"

"Absolutely."

She handed the phone to Hayden, and listened as mother and son expressed their love for each other.

Nora smiled, thinking this might well be the happiest day of her life.

Home of the Dromes

August 20: Gilliam's Guidepost
Heart Butte, Montana

"I HAVE NO INTEREST IN DISCUSSING the kidnappings," Bryan said. He was on the phone with MSNBC executive producer Scott Freeholt.

"But you tracked down three of the missing Indian women," Freeholt replied. "With all that's wrong in the world today, people need stories of heroism more than ever. Especially when it comes to aiding minorities."

"First off, they are *not* Indians. They are Native Americans. A little history lesson for you, Mr. Freeholt. That greedy, mass-murdering dolt Christopher Columbus thought he landed in India and so he called the Indigenous people Indians. My Blackfoot friends consider it a racial slur."

"Sorry to ruffle your feathers, Mr. Gilliam."

"I don't mean to get up on my high horse, but it just chaps my ass when people disrespect my Native friends."

"I respect that," Freeholt said. "You led authorities to the fourth abducted woman—the murdered Salish woman, Suyay Stiyak. You also exposed a dinosaur and illicit reptile trafficking ring. That makes you a hero in the eyes of many. The world deserves to know about your heroic exploits, Mr. Gilliam."

"I'm no hero. I was merely helping my friends who were being ignored by the authorities. I just happened to stumble on some really bad shit in the process."

Bryan rolled his eyes at Loretta, who sat across from him in the den, wearing her reading glasses and thumbing through a magazine.

She returned a knowing smile.

He said to Freeholt, "I'm familiar with your interview tactics, your ways of getting me to talk. I'm telling you, it won't work on me. I've already done all the talking I'm gonna do about those kidnappings. I've told the Flathead County Sheriff's Office and the FBI all they needed to know to make the arrests and I have nothing more to say about it. However, I'm more than willing to talk about a really great up-and-coming young rock band I'm managing. They're starting to make a name for themselves locally."

"Is that right?" Freeholt sounded like he couldn't care less.

"Yeah. They call themselves Moonrise."

"Interesting name, but I don't think—"

"I believe you'll find an intriguing feature story in it," Bryan said, cutting him off. "They're quite a talented power trio. My son Paul is the lead singer and guitarist. The other two players are pure Native Blackfoot blood, as is the female backup vocalist. Gives the story a colorful multiracial angle, don't you think? But it's much more than that. Last summer my son was right in the middle of the dinosaur madness here on our ranch. He helped geologists chisel down the Cretaceous meteorite that hit our property. He assisted with the Dromaeosaurus hatchout. He fed and cared for the Tyrannosaurs, Dromaeosaurs, and Triceratops we housed here at our ranch. He's on a first-name basis with all the famous scientists who came through here studying the creatures. He's mentioned several times in Hayden Fowler and Nora Lemoyne's bestselling book."

Freeholt said, "Yes, I have read that book. I'm familiar with what went on at your ranch last summer and I'm very sorry for all of your losses. It was a tragically fascinating story that captured the hearts and souls of a nation. But that's old news. The media has covered what happened every which way and squeezed all the life out of it. We're interested in breaking this new story. Your victory in spite of overwhelming odds. The way you jumped in and took action to find these women when everyone else in authority turned their backs on you. The way you hunted down these kidnapper-killers. We want your thoughts on the plight of your downtrodden

Indigenous friends and how the U.S. government treats them like indentured slaves. I've watched a couple of your local TV interviews from last year. You are very compelling in front of a camera, Mr. Gilliam. Your speaking out could make a difference. Your story could shine a light on police negligence when dealing with crimes against minorities. And your, um . . . *troubles* from last year make you a sympathetic character. You're definitely a hero. Why not take your bows?"

Bryan thought: *This guy has flattery down to a science.*

"Well, thank you for that," he said. "I do feel very strongly about my Blackfoot friends. But I must tell you I have no interest in putting myself out there—no desire to put a target on my back again. My wife and I learned our lesson the hard way last summer. And I must respectfully disagree with your point that there is nothing new or marketable about what went on at our ranch last year. The huge popularity of the Fowler-Lemoyne book shows that the public has an insatiable craving for knowing more about the return of the dinosaurs and the Gilliam family's role in it. Interviewing my son, who is seventeen, would give the story a fresh angle, a Gen Z perspective, if you will."

"You make an enticing pitch, Mr. Gilliam, but I think an interview with you about the abductions is more timely. It's the hot story, a cultural touchstone. It's breaking news."

Bryan wouldn't be deterred. "We would guarantee MSNBC an exclusive," he said, winking at Loretta. She had heard him make the same promise to CNN earlier in the week. "Think about it. A feature story that would give your viewers the inside scoop on our experience with the dinosaurs, tying it in with my son's music. It would make a stimulating human interest story. You could call it something like *The Dinosaur Drumbeat* or maybe *Reptile Rock*."

Freeholt chuckled. "Very clever. But again, our interest is in your involvement with the kidnapping cases."

They were two stubborn salesmen, both trying to close a sale when the other side wasn't buying.

Bryan knew he wasn't getting anywhere with the producer. He said, "Very well. In that case, I can steer you to the private investigator who worked with me on the abductions—Mike Mathews from Billings. He might give you some details about how we went about finding the women. If nothing else, he'll certainly be a colorful interview."

"Sure. I'll take you up on that, Mr. Gilliam. But if you change your mind about talking with us, you've got my number."

Bryan ended the call, disappointed he hadn't done better for Paul.

The call from MSNBC was the sixth from media outlets the past two weeks, wanting to interview Bryan about the Blackfoot kidnapping cases. Each time he redirected them to Paul and Moonrise. It had worked once so far, with a televised western Montana variety podcast site doing a show with Paul, which led to a pair of upcoming high profile weekend gigs for the band.

"Reptile Rock?" Loretta said, laughing. "*Really*, Bry?"

"Hey, what can I say? MSNBC is one of the big boys."

"You're a piece of work, dear hubby of mine," she said with an amused grin.

"Paul wanted aggressive representation. I'm providing that."

As if on cue, Paul entered the den with a drowsy yawn. His Foo Fighters t-shirt was rumpled, his jeans dirty, his bed-head hair spiking out in all directions. It was almost noon and Bryan's oldest was just now greeting the day. It would be his last day of sleeping in as the new school year started bright and early tomorrow morning.

"Just caught the end of that," Paul said, stretching his arms over his head and yawning again. "What are you providing, Pops?"

"Band support. I just got off the phone with an MSNBC producer."

"MSNBC? That's lit! How'd it go?"

"We'll see. I told him how great Moonrise is and gave him your contact information. I'll text you his info if you want to be proactive and follow up with him."

"Cool." He yawned a third time. "Damn, I need me some coffee. Rehearsal went late last night."

"So I guess Ox is back on board and happy again?" Bryan said, referring to the drummer, Hass Oxendine, who quit in a huff when

Paul informed the band that Bryan would be assuming management duties, and that the planned fall mini-tour was off. The boy had a change of heart, however, when Bryan and Loretta bought him a new Yamaha Stage Custom birch-shelled five-piece drum set with top of the line hardware and premium Zildjian cymbals.

"Oh yeah, Ox is in heaven sittin' behind that new kit you got him. Sounds bitchin' too. You guys saved the day," Paul said, head swiveling between his parents. "I didn't want to have to audition drummers. Would've set us back a few weeks. And let me tell ya, drummers are a pain in the ass to deal with."

Loretta spoke up. "Are you ready for school tomorrow?"

"As ready as I'll ever be," he said over his shoulder, on his way to the kitchen.

Bryan watched his son leave the room. "I still don't think he appreciates what we're doing for him, Lor."

"Oh, I think he does. But he's a teenager. He's not going to be real demonstrative with his thanks."

"Ethan is. He thanks me every day for that new baseball glove I bought him."

"Our boys are as different as night and day, Bry. Ethan's always been more openly affectionate and appreciative. Paul is more in his own head. They're both good boys. Just different. At least Paul's finishing high school. That's something. But I wonder. Do you think we're doing the right thing, pushing him out under the spotlight. Lots of crazies out there, as we've seen."

Bryan nodded. "You're not wrong. But the boy wants to be a rock star. To do that he has to get out there and show off his stuff. Sure, he'll attract some unsavory types along the way. He'll have to deal with the hangers-on who want to get close to him. He'll be tempted to go down some dangerous paths—drugs, alcohol, girls. He'll have to learn how to handle the extreme ups and downs of the business. But I think our oldest has a good head on his shoulders. And I believe he learned a lot about the pitfalls of fame from what we all went through last summer. That said, the rock-n-roll world is hugely competitive. Odds are he won't be one of the Chosen Ones singled out by the rock gods for superstardom. But we can't keep him bottled up here on the Guidepost forever, Lor. We've got to let him go out and make his own way at some point."

"I know," she said, a reflective sadness in her eyes. "I just worry about him is all. In a lot of ways, he's still my little boy Pauley. It's hard watching him grow into a man. I don't wanna lose him."

"I'm with you on that. But look on the bright side. He's staying in school so we'll have him around the homestead for at least another year. Us buying the band new equipment is a small price to pay for that."

Suddenly, chilling screams from out in the quad ripped through the quiet.

Bryan heard the slap of shoes hitting pavement, the sliding glass door of the sunroom being yanked open aggressively.

Lianne and Ethan's shrieks stabbed him in the heart.

The horses neighed wildly out in the stables, their cries high-pitched and strained, spooked by something.

What the hell—?

A thunderous slam as the sliding door banged shut.

More indecipherable shouts.

He and Loretta exchanged wide-eyed looks of alarm. Both sat motionless for a surprised half beat, stunned by the racket. Then, as if governed by a single brain, they jumped into action.

Lianne's half-sobbing *No, No, Noooh!* calls frayed Bryan's nerves as he and Loretta rushed down the hallway, his leg hurting as he limped along, trying to keep up with her.

Entering the sunroom, Bryan halted, panting heavily as he took in the bizarre scene. A mature, five-foot-tall Dromaeosaur stood on the patio outside, punching at the door with a forelimb, its three clawed fingers scratching against the glass. Slobber dripped from its jagged, blade-like teeth and pooled on the concrete at its feet. The creature peered down on a trembling Lianne, who shakily stood her ground and thrust the pendant of her Cretaceous Stone necklace out in front of her like a priest brandishing a crucifix to ward off evil.

"Go away! Get lost, you bad lizard!" his daughter commanded, her voice thin and tenuous.

The beast let out a muffled growl, shaking its oversized head as though denying her.

Bryan looked at Ethan—just back from morning baseball practice and dressed in his uniform—pressed up against the far wall, huffing and puffing, blinking rapidly, looking on in fear.

Paul came crashing into the bright room behind them. "What's with all the—" Further comment caught in his throat as he spied the monster on the patio. "Jesus! Those things creep me out! I'm so outta here," he yelled, disappearing as quickly as he'd appeared.

Loretta went to Lianne and pulled her back from the glass, gathered her in protectively. Lianne shook and wept profusely in her mother's embrace.

"It's okay, Lee," Bryan said, shuddering as he recalled his fight with a Drome in the quadrangle back in June. "He can't hurt us. That glass is strong," he said hoping he was right. He knew firsthand how deceivingly powerful these Dromaeosaurs were.

As if hearing Bryan, the creature slammed its immense head against the glass, inducing terrified gasps from Lianne and Ethan. The door wobbled, juddering in its track, but held firm.

A second headbutt, the creature showing its determination to get at them. The door shook precariously but didn't break. A line of slimy saliva dribbled down the glass.

Bryan knew that the four of them standing here was only enticing the beast. He thought about going to get his rifle, but knew that would take precious minutes. Instead he opted for getting everyone to safety.

"Okay," he said, "let's all of us slowly back out of here and I'll barricade the door behind us. No quick movements."

The animal thrust its snout at the door a third time, a heavy hit that made Bryan jump. The blast cracked the glass, spiderwebbing the panel down to the floor. It was a miracle that the door held.

Another long, drawn-out growl.

Frustration or something else?

Bryan kept his eyes trained on the creature as the others cautiously cleared the room.

Just before he left the sunroom, he saw the Drome's attention being diverted by something behind it. He couldn't see what it was at first with the creature blocking his view. But then the animal turned and Bryan saw a pair of juvenile Dromaeosaurs hop up on the patio. Miniature versions of the adult, no bigger than two feet tall. Their movement and interaction with the mature Drome told him there was a bond between them.

Did these juveniles hatch out of the nest Hayden and I found in June? The one in the east meadow meteorite strike site?

He watched the mother Dromaeosaur (if that's what she was) give a long final stare into the sunroom—its unnerving blood-red eyes boring into him like twin fires from hell—then turn and leave the patio, the two juveniles hop-skipping behind. He watched them amble across the heliport pad and disappear behind the utility barn, presumably into the woods.

"What're you doing in there, Bryan?" he heard Loretta call from the hallway. "C'mon, get out of there! Hurry!"

"I believe we're okay now," he said, stepping out, seeing Lianne wrapped in her mother's shielding arms, tearful and sniffling, Loretta whispering reassurances in her daughter's ear.

"Is it gone?" Ethan asked.

Bryan gave him an exhausted nod. "What happened out there, Eeth?"

The boy was breathless and obviously traumatized. His speech was hurried, his voice tight and strained. "Mr. Dover dropped me off down by the road after practice and as I was walkin' up the drive I saw Lee in the quadrangle t-t-taking out the trash. From my view I could also see the Drome stalking her. She couldn't see it but I could. It was crouched behind the retaining wall near the stables, lickin' its chops. I—I ran like the wind and grabbed her, p-pulled her with me to the patio, that . . . that *thing* wheezing and sounding like a locomotive behind us. I thought we were gonna d-d-die, Dad."

"You saved your sister with your quick thinking, Ethan," Bryan said. "I'm proud of you, son."

"I thought my necklace would protect me, Daddy," Lianne said from within the cocoon of Loretta's arms. "It brought Uncle Peter back. I thought it would chase away that nasty dinosaur, too."

Bryan leaned on his cane and smiled at his daughter's youthful naivete. "Yes, it did bring Peter back, sweetie. But these dinosaurs are very unpredictable. Sometimes your magic necklace doesn't work on them." He looked up from Lianne, addressing Loretta. "This has been a wakeup call for us. We've become too lax with the Drome problem. We need to be more vigilant when we're outside."

"Are we ever gonna be rid of these things, Bry?" Loretta said.

"Don't know," he said, glancing at Ethan and Lianne, trying to determine how much he should say. "Hayden and Nora both think they're here to stay. After what I just saw, I believe they're right. There's definitely something to Hayden's natal homing theory."

"Whaddaya mean?"

Bryan rubbed at his chin. "I just saw two Dromaeosaur juveniles that I think hatched out of those eggs Hayden and I found at the east meadow meteorite site a couple months back."

"What makes you think that?"

"Their size, for one. They were about two feet tall and weighed thirty to forty pounds if my guesstimate is right. That's how big they would be after two months based on our experience with the Dromaeosaurs we hatched out last summer. And Hayden's migration study says these Cretaceous animals stay close to the nest area after hatching out, and return there to propagate. I think our meteorite strike crater has become a Drome breeding ground."

Loretta looked crestfallen. "You mean Gilliam's Guidepost has become a home for the Dromes?"

"It looks that way, yes," he said. He tried to lessen the severity of the news. "But it could be worse. At least we're not seeing any Tyrannosaurs."

"Knock on wood really hard when you say that, Bry," Loretta said, pulling Lianne closer.

"I'm scared, Daddy," Lianne whimpered.

He swallowed hard. *We all are, sweet pea. We are all scared.*

Seeing the look of abject fear on his young daughter's face, he wished he had kept his mouth shut.

Six months later . . .

A Cretaceous Homecoming

February 23: Lacroix Housewarming Party
Florence, Montana

IN DECEMBER, THE WEEK AFTER CHRISTMAS, with a very pregnant Brinshou about to pop, Peter and Brin closed on a four-bedroom home situated on a picturesque six-acre wooded lot in Florence, twenty miles south of downtown Missoula. They were back home again after a summer and fall with the Gilliams in Heart Butte. Peter loved the bucolic setting and the house's Mountain Modern stone-and-timber architecture, with its wide front porch, sunny upstairs loft, large bedrooms, and spacious finished basement boasting a bar area constructed of beautiful reclaimed barnwood.

Plenty of elbow room for the family, including their new addition, Jacob Mato Lacroix, a healthy seven-pound-ten-ounce boy born January 14. Brin had a far easier delivery than she'd had with Kimi. Baby Jake entered the world bawling and kicking, as though eager to start his new life. Peter swore his son's cries sounded like laughter. He was convinced it was a sign that Jacob would be a happy child.

Peter had taken the swaddled boy in his arms. "There's my little hockey player," he'd said, looking down at the squirming newborn.

To which Brin, sweaty and exhausted, replied, "He looks more like a soccer player to me, Petey, the way he's kicking those chubby little legs. I guess you're going to have to get into a new sport, my love."

Peter couldn't remember the last time he had seen Brin this happy. There had been no postpartum depression or baby blues like what she experienced after giving birth to Kimi. A month after delivering Jacob, bright-eyed and cheerful, Brin returned to work, making the daily commute into Missoula to manage Brinshou's Baubles & Jewelry while Kachina and he took care of Kimi and baby Jacob.

While Brin's happiness and Jake's birth gave Peter some peace of mind and much joy, he wrestled with his demons. Those weird flying reptiles that brought the chopper down haunted his dreams, reminding him of when, as a young boy, he'd had nightmares after watching *The Wizard of Oz*. Those grotesque flying monkeys had invaded his sleep for months. His current night frights featured a strange hybrid of the menacing winged monkeys from the land of Oz and the large pterosaurs that had crashed the helicopter. As if the visual wasn't bad enough, his night terrors were accompanied by the spooky soundtrack music from the film. The spiraling "Flight of the Winged Monkeys" score taunted him, bringing him awake with a gasp and drenched in a cold sweat time and again.

And those eleven harrowing days and nights he'd spent on the side of that Idaho cliff continued to mess with his head, too. Memories of the violent deaths of Jenkins McCraw, Larry Bing, and Jackson Lattimer still rattled him. Worse, he couldn't escape the feeling that the entire lethal experience was his fault. Peter had replayed the morning of the crash many times, and no matter how many times he went over it, still thought he could have prevented it. He was trained for such emergencies but had not reacted properly. He had lost his shit when he saw those pterosaurs coming at the chopper. Peter knew he could have done better.

And then there was the physical pain. His left shoulder injury had been misdiagnosed as a separation and had not set right. He'd had to undergo surgery in early October to repair a displaced clavicle fracture. The bone had broken in three places near where it attached to the shoulder blade. The recovery had been difficult, with three months of physical therapy supplemented by a drug regimen. He'd finished physical therapy sessions just before Jake was born, and was able to escape the arm sling last month, but he still relied on the oxycodone to combat the lingering pain. He knew he should get off the oxy. He'd given it a valiant effort several times, but he just couldn't ween himself off of those soothing little pills.

But perhaps worse than the psychological and physical pain was his sense of worthlessness. He couldn't fly in his condition. He was grounded, a bird with a broken wing. Piloting a helicopter was physically demanding. A chopper pilot needed a good bit of arm and shoulder strength to work the cyclic and collective sticks. He also needed a strong back to operate the yaw foot pedals, and his damaged shoulder still affected his spine. His doctors told him it would be probably May or June before he could even remotely think about piloting again. That news devastated him, sending him into a spiraling depression. As did Brin's constant declarations that his flying days were over, full stop. She was adamant about it; she wasn't having it any other way. And so he spent his days doing the best he could to help Brin's mother with the baby and entertaining Kimi while Brin worked at her shop in Missoula. As much as he enjoyed spending time with his family, Peter felt utterly inadequate. Useless. He'd become restless and irritable. Moody.

But his determination to fly again just wouldn't quit.

Regardless of what Brin dictated, he *would* fly again. That determination is what kept him going most days. He was born to be in the cockpit of a helicopter. He would make his wife understand and accept that fact. Just not now. He didn't want to burst her happiness bubble.

Fortunately Nora and Hayden (who had his own health issues) had kept Peter on the Fowler-Lemoyne Aviation payroll. Peter was a business partner after all, but Hayden and Nora controlled the company purse strings. It was really *their* company. But last week, after nearly a half year of collecting a paycheck for doing nothing and feeling guilty about it, Peter surprisingly received a pay raise and a promotion. With Hayden trying to get healthy enough to go on a May book tour, and he and Nora focused on final edits to their book, they had little time and energy to devote to the company, and so they had made Peter Chief Operations Officer. He remained grounded, but at least his new position gave him a sense of purpose. His first tasks were to purchase two more helicopters and hire four pilots. Fowler-Lemoyne Aviation hadn't crashed and burned along with their Bell 407 in Idaho backcountry as Peter feared it would. Instead, there were big plans to expand the company operations, one of which was to build a second heliport in Missoula.

Some good news at a time he needed it most.

Things were finally starting to turn around for him.

But today was dedicated to his and Brin's first-ever house-warming party. He felt festive and high (no, it wasn't the oxycodone, thank you very much, though he *had* downed a couple of tabs this morning). Today he wanted to celebrate the family's good fortune: their newborn baby, their new house, their circle of good friends.

Their new *lives*.

He and Brin had invited a long list of people and most had accepted. Some had flown in—Peter's parents (Pierre and Janine from Phoenix); his older sister Celeste from Quebec City; Hayden and Nora from Minneapolis; fellow crash survivor Bill Carlton from Boise. Many of their friends drove the three-and-a-half hours from Heart Butte—Bryan and Loretta Gilliam with their two youngest, Lianne and Ethan (oldest son Paul was playing a gig with his band and couldn't make it); Apisi and Kanti Lyttle; Chogan Stimson with his girlfriend Mika; Nancy Diehl and Carl Lacey, two Fowler-Lemoyne employees who Peter knew from his Montana Forest Service days. A few lived in Missoula and made the short drive south—Peter's young friend George Dantley who now worked for the Forest Service, his fiancée Emma, and George's parents (Sam and Elizabeth Dantley); Luana Percival and Nuna Whitehorse, Brin's Blackfoot friends who worked with her in her shop.

Most of them were gathered in the basement around the bar, sipping drinks served by the bartender Peter had hired. The catering service was scheduled to arrive at six.

Peter made the rounds downstairs while Brin entertained upstairs. As he walked around chatting with folks, it struck him as to how fortunate he was to have these people in his life. He had never been good at making friends or maintaining friendships. But this group was special. There were some genuine connections here. Brin had taken to calling Loretta Gilliam and Nora Lemoyne her Cretaceous sisters. Peter had scoffed at that initially, but he now realized there was a lot of truth to her claim as he saw the closeness his wife shared with the two women. And he now felt that same close attachment to most everyone gathered in their new home today. A meteorite loaded with dinosaur eggs striking an outlying field on the Gilliam ranch had brought them together. The notion was absurd, really. But looking past the ludicrousness of it, he realized it was providence. Destiny. It was as if some far-off divine event had manipulated the people gathered here today, like a cosmic grandmaster chess player strategically moving pieces on a celestial chessboard. Whatever it was, Peter was thankful for it. So much so that he and Brin now referred to the group as the Cretaceous Crew. He knew it was goofy and unsophisticated, but he liked it.

The Cretaceous Crew.

Lifelong bonds hatched from a stray meteorite.

Peculiar . . . uncanny.

Kismet.

A fateful circle of friendship.

Easy listening pop music played softly on the stereo as he gravitated to a small group surrounding Bryan and Loretta. Bryan drank from a bottle of Coors and leaned against the bar, going on about the Gilliams' problems with Dromaeosaurs on their property.

"We haven't seen any near the house since late October, with the cold weather settin' in and all. But we have spotted them along the horse trails this winter. The cold makes 'em lethargic, but it still makes for some daunting horseback rides. We've tried everything to get rid of 'em: exterminators, pest removal companies, baited bear traps. Nothing's worked. Dromes are shrewd. They're smart. Hayden says they're a determined breed and very territorial. His natal homing instinct theory certainly applies. He thinks that once they've established their nests, they're tough to eradicate. Just our luck their nesting site is in our east meadow where the meteorite hit." He drank from his beer, noticing Peter standing nearby. He acknowledged him. "There he is. We were just talking about you, Pete. Were your ears burning?"

Peter gave off a short chuff of a laugh. His ears were literally burning. He suspected it was the oxy tabs working on him. "Good things, I hope," he said.

"Only the best," Bryan said. "I was just telling Sam and Liz here about how you let me keep a lot of that meteorite rock during the Air Force's Operation Roundup. You could have taken it all but you didn't. I was telling them about how you also found a second meteorite this summer, enough space rock to restart our jewelry operation. If it hadn't been for Peter, that business would have dried up last fall. Peter and his wife, I should say. Brinshou Lacroix has been my genius visionary jeweler. She gave the business legs." Bryan lifted his oak cane, displaying the knob formed from meteorite stone, with the miniature claws and garnet gemstone eyes of a hatchling. "Brin made this beauty for me. It led to a limited edition run of twenty dino-canes that sold out in three days."

"It's gorgeous artistry," Liz Dantley said, running a finger over the stone knob.

Peter nodded. "Yes, my Brinny is very artistic. Have you visited her shop on Madison Street?"

"Not yet. I've been meaning to get down there."

"Brin does quality work," Loretta said. "Unfortunately her pieces have generated a lot of counterfeiters. Many unsuspecting buyers are being duped on eBay and Amazon for fake Cretaceous Stone jewelry, allegedly authentic Gilliam pieces designed by Brin."

"I've wondered about that," Liz said. "I've seen some of those pieces online. Some of the prices are outrageous."

"The fraudsters love big-money scams," Loretta said. "It's easy to pass off obsidian or black quartz as genuine Cretaceous meteorite rock, and many are getting away with it. But last September a few of them got caught selling magnetite jewelry, claiming it was authentic meteorite stone. It was an easy catch—magnetite has strong magnetic properties while Cretaceous meteorite rock does not."

"Did you sue them?" Sam Dantley asked.

Loretta smiled at him. "No. It's not worth the hassle or the expense. Lawsuits only feed the lawyers' portfolios. But one thing the fraudsters can't fake is our iridium rare earth metal business. We've had a great deal of success selling to technology companies."

Bryan said to Peter, "You got any ideas where another of those missing meteorites might be?"

"I have a few solid clues, but it'll be a while before I can fly again. Right now I'm tasked with buying a couple of helicopters and interviewing pilots to replace Larry and me. But I'll be back in the cockpit soon enough."

"Oh yeah, congrats on your promotion by the way" Bryan said.

"Thanks. I hope you're not upset."

"Why would I be upset?"

"Well, you *are* the general manager and I'm just—"

"Nonsense, Peter." Bryan waved his cane, dismissing it. He pulled Loretta in close. "Lor and I are doin' just fine, my friend. We're rolling in the clover, as they say. We're just glad you survived your ordeal."

"Thanks. You and me both."

Bryan took a pull from his beer, then said, "Damn shame what happened to Larry Bing."

"Bryan, dear," Loretta said in a chastising tone, "I'm sure Peter doesn't want to discuss that."

Peter smiled weakly. "It's okay, Loretta. Really. I didn't know him long, but Larry was a skilled pilot. I admired him and I miss him every day."

Bryan said, "Sorry for your loss, Peter. For *our* loss. I liked him a lot. Enjoyed working with him."

"No worries," Peter said, though it *did* bother him. This was supposed to be a party, a celebration. Not a memorial service.

"Oh, hey, I almost forgot," Bryan said, pulling a jewel cased

CD out of his jacket pocket and handing it to him. "Would you mind playing this?"

Confused, Peter glanced at the cover—four young people standing atop a large dark boulder, a crescent moon hanging in the darkening sky behind them. "Sure . . . um, what is it?"

"It's my son Paul's band. Moonrise. Their first recording. An EP of four original songs. Two of the tunes are getting heavy airplay on college radio stations. "Reptile Rock" was number five last week on the University of Montana's Spinitron Top Forty." Bryan dropped into a silky smooth quasi DJ voice. "Coming to you from KGBA Missoula, 89.9 on your FM dial. Great hits of the college scene."

"Reptile Rock?"

"Yeah, that's my hubby's idea," Loretta said, rolling her eyes. "Cute, isn't it? Bryan's quite proud of himself."

"I just gave them the title. The music is all theirs."

Peter looked at the cover again, now recognizing Paul Gilliam flanked by two Indigenous boys and a Native girl. Long hair and petulant stares. They had the rock 'n roll image nailed. The words **MOONRISE AT REPTILE ROCK** flowed across the top in a bold blue font.

"Awesome, Bryan," Peter said, going to the stereo setup behind the bar. "I'd be honored to have a listen."

Moonrise music filled the room: raucous, shrieking, up-tempo rock—a jarring switch from the soft music that had been playing. Screeching guitar riffs, thrashing drums and crashing cymbals, thumping bass that shook the cedar plank walls. Conversations came to a halt, the guests looking around, bewildered. Peter wondered if it wasn't too much. Too loud. After an extended instrumental intro, the vocals came in, a gruff, growly voice that seemed to struggle to keep up with the frenetic pace of the song. But then it slowed into the first chorus and two more voices blended with the lead vocal. The three-part harmony was a thing of beauty.

He heard Hayden Fowler shout over the music," Is that your kid, Gilliam?" and Peter saw Bryan give Hayden a proud thumbs-up. Hayden yelled again, "I always knew your boy had the *It* factor.

That there is great kick-ass rock-n-roll! Really catchy stuff."

The guests started tapping their toes and bouncing their heads in time to the beat. "Reptile Rock" ended with a bang and the second song, a melodic ballad played: "You Can't Take the Heart Out of Heart Butte." George Dantley and his fiancée Emma started slow dancing, which drew Apisi and Kanti Lyttle into the cleared-out dance space. Soon Lianne Gilliam pulled Peter's daughter Kimi into the circle, the two kids laughing and emulating the dance steps of the adults. *So cute*, Peter thought, looking on. By the fourth song, there were several couples dancing. And when that song ended, there were calls to play the Moonrise CD again.

Peter made his way over to Hayden and Nora, where Hayden was describing his coma experience to a rapt audience.

". . . so many weird dreams, some of them with me riding a Triceratops bareback, holding onto its bony frill as it loped across an alien landscape sprinkled with glowing psychedelic cactuses and pulsating meteorites. Sometimes the Tri-horn would morph into one of those winged Quetzalcoatlus beasts that took down our helicopter, and up we would soar, the pterosaur flapping its huge wings effortlessly as we flew far out into deep dark interstellar space. I remember fiery comets whizzing past, satellites booming out travel instructions. It was like I was a dragon rider in one of those special effects high fantasy movies . . . like an amusement park thrill ride on steroids. So bizarre. You'll read more about it in our book when it's published. I wrote two chapters about my experiences in Neverland."

"Did you see God?" Carl Lacey asked with a chuckle.

"No, but I saw plenty of my *goddess*, my lovely better half here," Hayden said, grabbing Nora's hand and giving it a gentle squeeze. He smiled at her. "*Mon amour* was there with me and got me through it, brought me back. I heard her honey throated voice constantly, mostly coming from the satellites. Many of her instructions were triple-X rated, like a dominatrix urging me on. Being the gentleman I am, I'll keep the specifics to myself."

"TMI, Hayden!" Nora slapped his arm playfully, a mischievous grin on her face. To the group she said, "Hayden has a perverted imagination."

That brought several laughs.

Nancy Diehl said, "How have you been feeling, Hayden?"

"Good, actually. I'm down to one kidney, and knock on wood," he said, tapping his cane against the bar, "it's working at a hundred-percent capacity. Some days I have zero energy and severe back pain. Water retention causes me to bloat up at times. I'm on a kidney transplant waitlist, but so are ninety-thousand other people, so I'm not holding out much hope for that. However, my docs reassure me that I can live a normal lifespan provided my one kidney continues to function. But to answer your question, Nancy, overall I'm good. Thanks for asking. Looks like I'll be fit enough to make the book tour in late May. Too bad. I was hoping to miss this tour, if I'm being honest. But our publisher has been good to us so I'll comply with their wishes."

"You don't like promoting your books?" Peter's mother, Janine, inquired. "You don't enjoy meeting your fans?"

"Oh, I love the promotional part. Far more fun than the writing. I just don't like bein' on the road and answering the same dumb questions over and over. Nora likes all of that, don't you, honey?"

"Only if we're doing it together."

Hayden blushed like a virginal schoolboy. He leaned over and kissed her on the cheek.

"Aw, that is so sweet," Janine remarked.

Peter's father Pierre brought the mood down a notch, saying, "That must've been hell up there on that mountain. How did you guys ever survive?"

Peter said, "Dad, I don't think Hayden wants to revisit—"

"It's all right, Pete," Hayden said. "I did want to say a few things about my late friend, Jackson."

Peter wished Hayden wouldn't go there.

Nora excused herself to get another drink and mingle before Hayden got going with his tribute. It was obvious by her reaction that she had heard what was coming more times than she cared to. Peter knew well of Nora's disdain for Jackson Lattimer, and six months after his death, she still made no attempt to hide her feelings.

Hayden launched into it. "The media has already covered Jack's legacy in depth, but it can't be stated often enough. To me, Jackson Lattimer was much more than a media superstar. He was my brother. Not in blood or DNA, but in soul and spirit. I would not be standing here today if it wasn't for him. He saved my life, without question. He sacrificed himself for me, threw himself in front of that charging Tyrannosaur to spare me. That was bravery and courage the likes of which I've never before experienced. Without Jack's intervention I would certainly be dead. The thing that's most difficult about this is I will never be able to thank him or repay him for what he did. It leaves me feeling unfulfilled. It's like there's something that will always remain undone in my life. It makes me feel incomplete." Hayden paused, taking a deep breath, his eyes misting with tears. He took a sip of Coca-Cola, then continued.

"Bill was there," he said, nodding at Bill Carlton. "He saw it all go down. In fact he helped save my life, too. He wounded the Rex with a well-placed rifle shot. Made the beast go over the cliff. Unfortunately the creature took Jack with it."

"You've always given me too much credit for that," Carlton said. "I was just defending our campsite. And you well know my opinion of Lattimer differs greatly from yours. You say it was his bravery that saved you. With all due respect, I believe the man was a lunatic with suicidal tendencies. He was looking for a way to die."

Hayden smirked in a half-smile. "I respect your opinion, Bill, I really do. I've heard that same sentiment from several folks who knew him. And perhaps there is a kernel of truth to what you say. But there is no denying Jack saved my life in a selfless act. Courageous or suicidal, either way I loved the man. He was my brother from another mother. Brothers aren't perfect, but they're there for you. I just wish I could be there for him now . . ."

The conversation continued on about their time on the mountain and their eventual rescue. Peter couldn't take any more. Too much talk about things he was trying to put behind him. He felt the walls closing in on him. The air was warm and stuffy. The voices were warping into discordant sounds. He felt beads of perspiration spotting his face, sweat trickling down his back. The oxy was making him feel wonky. He excused himself before he got dragged into the talk, saying as host, he needed to circulate.

He needed some fresh air and headed for the stairs, only to be intercepted by George Dantley and his fiancée Emma.

"Howdy, Pete," George said to him at the foot of the stairs. "Great party. You've got a lot of interesting friends. And we love your new home."

"Thanks. Glad you're having fun. I saw you two cutting the rug out there on the dance floor. You both showed some slick moves."

"Thank you," George and Emma said in unison.

Emma said, "Your baby, Jacob, is such a darling."

"Yeah, he's a little fighter, that one," Peter said, feeling faint.

George said, "And your Kimi can say my name now. It's Uncle George now. No more *Unca Jaw*. She's growing up fast."

"Yes she is. Hard to believe she turned three last week."

George said, "So happy to see you doing well again, Pete. We were worried about you last summer."

"I appreciate your concern. How's your job going?" he said, wanting this conversation to end but feeling the need to be sociable.

"Good. I'm finally off deskwork. Now I'm going out each day with veteran rangers for my field training. I'll be taking my field test in May. If I pass I'll be a certified forest ranger."

"You mean *when* you pass," Emma said.

"Yes, *when* I pass." To Peter he said, "Being in the office all day I hear a lot of talk. I've heard a couple of the new helicopter pilots talking about your time there. It seems you're a bit of a legend at the Forest Service."

"Well, legend is such an overused term, George. But I did have some good years there, yeah."

"And now you're famous."

"Perhaps for the wrong reasons," Peter said, his mind drifting back to the crash. He was hit with a dizzy spell and he gripped the stair banister, trying to make it look like a natural move. "Hey, good chatting with you guys, but I need to get upstairs to get some more snacks."

"Oh sure," George said, moving aside. "One last thing. Emma

is graduating in June and we plan to have a June twenty-first wedding. You and Brin will be getting an invite."

"Hey, congratulations! Brin and I will look forward to it."

He made his way up the stairs, short of breath, his shoulder aching, sharp pains in his lower back. He couldn't escape the basement fast enough. Too much talk about death, suicide, coma dreams, and survival tactics. Peter hurried through the living room, hustling past guests who were engaged in conversations, giving a hasty wave to those who greeted him. He didn't see Brin anywhere.

He grabbed his coat from the foyer closet and walked out on the front porch, a chilly wind slapping him in the face. He breathed in a deep lungful of cold, alpine air, the action settling him somewhat. A gentle snow had begun to fall, covering the guest vehicles parked in the U-shaped driveway. He moved to the railing and peered out over his property, taking in the grove of western larch off to the left. Winter-blasted branches reached high into the sky, the trees looking skeletal and gaunt in the falling snow. He took in the sprawling Bitterroot Valley beyond his yard, with its snow-dusted sagebrush and bitterbrush blowing in the wind. The Bitterroot Mountains rose in the distance, monolithic in their grandeur. Trapper's Peak cut a stark silhouette against the tawny sky. This was glorious country out here. Wild and untamed. Beautiful in its rustic simplicity. The perfect place to raise a family.

Beats the hell out of living underground at Gilliam's Guidepost, he thought.

And then he spotted something that made his breath catch in his throat.

Along the ridge.

A flock of birds flying in a tight formation.

But wait. Are they birds?

Long telescoping necks. Wide wingspans. Long pointy beaks.

Herons?

But herons don't have wings like that, do they? No, they're too large to be herons.

Aren't they?

Too distant to get an accurate read. Peter wished he had

binoculars. Even if he did, the curtain of snow blurred his view.

Their size and flying movements reminded him of the pterosaurs that had crashed his helicopter. The way they flapped those long wings. Their easy gliding on the thermals. They appeared to be the airborne reptiles Hayden called Quetzalcoatlus.

Were they Quetzalcoatlus?

An intense wave of nausea hit him. *The Wizard of Oz* "Flight of the Winged Monkeys" soundtrack music swirled in his ears. Memories of Quetzalcoatlus attacking his chopper ran through his head in a satanic vision. He began to hyperventilate, gasping, struggling to catch his breath.

Is this an oxycodone hallucination?

Peter sank to his knees, watching the flock of maybe-Quetzalcoatlus disappear behind the mountains. He inhaled deep breaths of cold mountain air, trying to regain his equilibrium.

What did I just see here?

Was it real?

Or was it a pharmaceutical daydream?

Gradually he was able to pull himself together and take a seat in one of the Adirondack chairs.

What the hell just happened here? Get a grip, Lacroix old boy.

A few minutes later, he heard the front door open, the music from downstairs drifting out. Brin approached, a worried smile on her face.

"There you are," she said, coming to him. "I've been looking all over for you, Petey. What are you doing out here alone?"

"Just catching some fresh air, babe."

She took a seat on his chair's armrest and caressed his hand. "Are you okay? You look tired."

"I'm fine."

She looked at him, her dark eyes questioning.

Brin knows me too well, he thought. "Really, I'm fine," he said, gathering his strength to stand and offer her his hand.

She took his hand. He pulled her up from the chair and kissed her. A long, deep kiss. She leaned into him with a soft moan.

"I love you so much, Brinny," he said, holding her close.

"I love you, too, Petey."

"We have it good here in our new home, don't we?"

"Yes we do. So many dear friends, too. We're so lucky."

"That's the truth. Long live the Cretaceous Crew," he said with a grin. "C'mon, our friends await. We're supposed to be hosting this bash." He took her hand and led her the length of the porch to the front door.

Hand in hand, they entered the house. Brin's touch energized him, filled him with a feeling he couldn't adequately define.

It transcended mere love. It was mystical. Magical. *Spiritual*.

She smiled at him and gave his hand an affectionate squeeze.

Peter never wanted to let go.

About the Author

Jeff Dennis is the former editor-in-chief/publisher of the award-winning speculative fiction magazine, *Random Realities.* He is the author of six novels and a short story collection, and is currently working on the third, and final, book of the Cretaceous Chronicles trilogy.

jeffdennisauthor.com

jeff@jeffdennisauthor.com

Printed in the USA
CPSIA information can be obtained
at www.ICGtesting.com
CBHW022101270124
3677CB00001B/2